Once More into the Fire

A SHERIFF BEN STILLMAN WESTERN

ONCE MORE INTO THE FIRE

PETER BRANDVOLD

FIVE STAR
A part of Gale, a Cengage Company

GALE
A Cengage Company

Farmington Hills, Mich • San Francisco • New York • Waterville, Maine
Meriden, Conn • Mason, Ohio • Chicago

LIBRARY OF CONGRESS CATALOGING-IN-PUBLICATION DATA

Names: Brandvold, Peter, author.
Title: Once more into the fire / Peter Brandvold.
Description: First edition. | Waterville, Maine : Five Star, a part of Gale, Cengage Learning, 2018. | Series: A Sheriff Ben Stillman Western | Identifiers: LCCN 2017053607 (print) | LCCN 2017057581 (ebook) | ISBN 9781432842994 (ebook) | ISBN 9781432842987 (ebook) | ISBN 9781432842963 (hardcover)
Subjects: LCSH: Sheriffs—Fiction. | BISAC: FICTION / Action & Adventure. | FICTION / Westerns. | GSAFD: Western stories.
Classification: LCC PS3552.R3236 (ebook) | LCC PS3552.R3236 A6 2018 (print) | DDC 813/.54—dc23
LC record available at https://lccn.loc.gov/2017053607

First Edition. First Printing: May 2018
Find us on Facebook–https://www.facebook.com/FiveStarCengage
Visit our website–http://www.gale.cengage.com/fivestar/
Contact Five Star™ Publishing at FiveStar@cengage.com

Printed in the United States of America
1 2 3 4 5 6 7 22 21 20 19 18

For Buddy

CONTENTS

★ ★ ★ ★ ★

ONCE MORE WITH A
VENGEANCE

★ ★ ★ ★ ★

CHAPTER ONE

The silky afternoon quiet of this humid, late-summer day along the Milk River was shattered by the crack of a pistol.

The horse hitched to Sheriff Ben Stillman's rented buggy gave a start, as though it had spied a rattlesnake slithering onto its trail. The buggy lurched, the singletree squawking.

The claybank whickered anxiously.

Stillman drew back on the reins. The horse stopped, snorted, and lifted another dubious whicker.

Stillman automatically lowered his right hand to the long-barreled, walnut-gripped Colt .44 holstered for the cross-draw on his left hip as he stared ahead and off the left side of the trail he'd been following out from Clantick. He studied a thick copse of cottonwoods and box elders sparkling gold and silver in the summer sunshine.

The revolver cracked again sharply, the echo caroming off the surrounding bluffs.

Crows rose from the trees Stillman was staring at, cawing angrily. They winged out over the milky green water of the slow-running river to the north, on Stillman's hard left. The birds rose up over the buttes looming over the river like lumpy mounds of white chalk, or like the ruined Norman castles Stillman had read about during the previous, long, northern Montana winter, when bad men had been holed up like everyone else out of the blistering cold and hip-deep snow, huddling from the chill winds howling down from Canada only forty miles away.

Stillman had had plenty of time to read—especially after the back surgery that had laid him up for four months.

There was another crackling pistol report. Another. And another.

Stillman had been a lawman for a lot of years. First a deputy U.S. marshal before a drunk whore had put a bullet in his back and the injury had forced him to retire for a time before he pinned another badge to his chest only a few years ago—this one the badge of Hill County Sheriff, based in the county seat of Clantick in northern Montana Territory. All those years of hazardous badge-toting had taught Stillman the difference between threatening gunfire and benign gunfire.

These shots were regular enough, thus benign-sounding enough, that they were likely those of someone taking target practice in the trees yonder. Probably the young man Stillman was on his way to see. Not only to see, but to arrest.

The sheriff patted the warrant written out by Judge Vernon Hoagland in the Hill County Courthouse in Clantick. The official document was still where he'd tucked it, in the breast pocket of his chambray work shirt, secured by the suspender that trailed up over the pocket.

Part of him wished he'd lost it.

Muttering a curse, voicing his reluctance to fulfill the judge's order, Stillman shook the reins over the clay's back, and the horse lurched forward, breaking into a trot. The shots continued as Stillman drove the rented buggy along the curving trail and into the trees where a small, gray log cabin sat, flanked by a gray log barn and adjoining corral. The river curved around behind the barn and corral, hidden by the trees, and that's where the pistol reports continued from, six at a time before a minute or so pause while the young man who called himself

Johnny Nevada reloaded.

Johnny Nevada.

That was the fanciful youngster's made-up name. His official name, inked in proper form on the arrest warrant, was Jonathan Hulbert Fenton, formerly of Carson City, Nevada, but recently of Clantick in the Montana Territory. He now lived here with his grandfather, Hector Fenton, who ran a few cattle now and then, and bought and sold horses, but who mostly survived by hook and by crook, like so many former independent frontiersmen and cattlemen forced into retirement by mortality as well as the economic reality of changing times.

There simply weren't any buffalo to hunt anymore, and the fur companies were long out of business, fur no longer being the lucrative enterprise it had been for so long. Hector had once punched cows for area ranchers, as well, but those days were over for him, too, as arthritis had made climbing in and out of the hurricane deck of a brush-tailed range pony much too painful. A fall from a horse would likely snap his brittle spine.

As Stillman halted the clay in front of the shack, the shooting started again after another pause, the shots spaced roughly two seconds apart. Stillman was close enough to the shooter now that he could hear the clinks of the airtight tins and the shattering of the glass bottles Johnny Nevada was shooting at.

The shack's plank door opened and a grizzled head peered cautiously out, one eye narrowed.

"Hello, Hec," Stillman said.

The grimace on the older man's face was unmistakable when he recognized the Hill County sheriff, and the milky brown eyes found the five-pointed star pinned to his visitor's shirt. The grimace wasn't personal. Stillman considered himself a friend of Hector Fenton, and he knew Fenton felt the same about him.

It was just that the old man was well aware of why Stillman

was here, and he didn't like it. Just as Stillman himself didn't like it.

Fenton stepped out onto the little boardwalk that served as his stoop, near a clay olla hanging from the roof's overhang to his left, a gourd dipper resting in the pot. The old man turned to the pot and grabbed the dipper. "What's wrong, Ben? Rustlers out this way again? If so, I ain't see none."

Stillman climbed gingerly out of the buggy. His back felt fine, though Doc Evans, keeping council with the Denver surgeon who had dug the bullet from Stillman's back late last fall, had forbidden him from straddling a horse for another month. Stillman considered it an over precaution, but the numbness he still felt in his feet on occasion compelled him to follow the doctor's orders, which were Stillman's wife's orders, as well. The lovely Fay's orders were even harder to ignore than the doctor's.

Stillman walked up alongside the claybank, running a soothing gloved hand over the horse's back. The clay was a fine mount, but Stillman was looking forward to saddling his buckskin, Sweets, again and running the stable green out of the beast. "What makes you think anything's wrong, Hec?"

Fenton sipped from the dipper, working his mustached lips. He dropped the dipper back into the bucket, wiped the sleeve of his grimy buckskin shirt across his mouth, and said, "Ben, you and I have known each other a lotta years. When was the last time you rode out to my place when somethin' *wasn't* wrong?"

It was true. Stillman saw Hec Fenton mainly in town. The sheriff often bought the firewood Fenton cut to keep the courthouse stoves burning, and he and Hec occasionally played poker or checkers in the Longhorn Saloon. Fenton had known Stillman's best friend, "Milk River" Bill Harmon, who'd lived on a ranch near here before he was murdered some years ago.

It was the urge to track down Bill's killer that had plucked Stillman out of an early retirement and, ironically, had given him a new lease on life, which included marriage to a beautiful woman, and, more recently, a beautiful little son in Benjamin William, Jr.

Stillman turned his mouth corners down and thumbed the pocket in which the warrant nestled. "He's been implicated in a killing, Hec."

If Fenton was at all surprised, which he probably wasn't given his grandson's storied past, he didn't show it. "Who?"

"You know who. Dave Bliss."

"Goddamnit!"

"I know."

Fenton turned his grizzled head to stare off toward where the gunshots were resounding again, one after another, faster now. Judging by the pings and the screeches of shattering glass, Johnny Nevada's aim was true.

Turning back to Stillman, Fenton said, "What makes you think he did it?"

"I don't have an opinion on the matter. Not yet. All I know is that three of Vince Patten's men said they saw him bushwhack Bliss from a tree on Bliss's range, and then mount his horse and ride away. They described the kid's speckled strawberry roan to a T."

"Vince Patten, huh?" Fenton said in disgust.

"Yep." The same disgust was plain in Stillman's voice, as well.

"You know you can't believe a goddamn word Patten says. He's had it out for Johnny ever since he accused him of stealin' beef from him. He's had it out for Dave Bliss, too, ever since he decided Bliss was crowdin' him."

"I know that," Stillman said. "But I also know Patten and his men came in and testified in front of a coroner's jury, then signed affidavits. That's why Judge Hoagland wrote out an arrest warrant. It don't matter what I think, Hec. I have to take Johnny in for trial. We have a good public defender in Ed Nobel."

The old man stared at Stillman in astonishment. "Do you hear what you're sayin', Ben? You know as well as I do that both Patten and the judge have their own reasons to lie about Johnny, and you know what the judge's reason is as well as anybody. Hell, the whole county knows about what the judge and Johnny have in common!"

"I know that, Hec. I do. But what you and I also know is that Johnny was heard threatening Dave Bliss in the Drovers Saloon only two weeks ago. And you know what that trouble was all about, too."

"Yeah. That makes it real convenient, don't it? Makes it real convenient for Patten to accuse Johnny of Bliss's murder, now, *don't it?*"

"Yes, it does," Stillman had to agree. "Be that what it may, I have to take him in."

"He hasn't left here, Ben. He couldn't have killed Bliss. He hasn't left my place in days."

"Bliss was killed last Friday night."

"Yeah, well, Johnny was right here last Friday night. We shot a bear up on the Little Clara, and we roasted a haunch over a big fire and washed it down with my chokecherry wine. I played my fiddle a little, and we was both in bed by eleven."

"Glad to hear it," Stillman said. "You can testify to that at the trial. If it's true, it'll likely be enough to get Johnny off."

Fenton narrowed an eye and bunched up his face, not just skeptical, but deeply cynical. He knew the kind of men he and his grandson were up against. Shaking his head with barely bridled emotion, he said, "You know that ain't true, Ben."

Yes, Stillman did know.

"Just the same, Hec . . ."

The sheriff turned and walked back to the buggy. He pulled his sheathed Henry repeater out from where he'd laid it under the leather seat. He slid the sixteen-shot rifle from its sheath. It was a pretty piece of shooting iron outfitted in glistening walnut, and it sported an inlaid pearl bull's head in the stock. The rifle had been a gift from the late Johnny Dawson, a famed deputy U.S. marshal of Dakota Territory. He'd sent it to Stillman to celebrate Stillman's tenth year as a deputy U.S. marshal out of Montana.

Stillman had hauled down many a bad man with the trusty repeater, as well as with the Colt he wore on his hip. He hoped he would need neither weapon today. He hoped he'd earned Johnny's trust when he'd convinced Vince Patten to forego pressing charges for the missing beef, since there'd really been no way that Patten or anyone else could have proven that Johnny and the two young ne'er-do-wells he'd taken up with had long-looped those cows.

Stillman had also had a long heart-to-heart with Johnny after that trouble, and he thought he'd convinced him to walk the straight and narrow. To live with and work for his grandfather, a good man, and learn from Hec Fenton just what a good man really was. After all, it had been Johnny himself who'd come back here from Nevada, after a bout of law trouble out there, to get to know his grandfather and settle down, or so he'd told Stillman.

Johnny had had damned few good examples so far in his eighteen years. The boy's father, Fenton's son, had run astray when he was only fourteen years old and ended up dead in a pauper's cemetery in Virginia City, shot by a card sharp he'd tried to fleece, but not before he'd spilled his seed into a pretty young whore who'd died of typhoid three years after Johnny was born. Johnny had been raised, if you could call it raised, by another alcoholic prostitute in Virginia City, where he'd had the run of the streets, quickly taking up a life of crime including, as the rumors went, killing for hire.

Stillman tossed the sheath back onto the buggy floor and jacked a cartridge into the rifle's action. He turned to Fenton watching him narrowly.

"You stay here, Hec."

"He's good with that hogleg, Ben," Fenton warned. "He wasn't just braggin' about that. I've seen him use it."

"Like I said, Hec," Stillman said, "stay here."

He started walking in the direction of the river from where Johnny's pistol was speaking again. Angrily, this time. Or so it seemed to Stillman's discerning ears.

CHAPTER TWO

Stillman walked around behind Fenton's barn and corral.

He followed a path through the trees and stopped when he came to a clearing, around the edges of which the Milk slid through its low, chalky banks. The kid was just then triggering off another round of .44 shells. Johnny Nevada stood to Stillman's left. He was firing at cans and bottles that were propped up on several rocks, a couple of upended packing crates, a wheelbarrow, and two narrow tree stumps to Stillman's right, about twenty yards from the curving river.

The kid's head turned slightly toward Stillman. His eyes widened in recognition, and he stopped firing. Stillman thought he'd snapped off only five rounds.

Which meant Johnny Nevada still had one in the wheel . . .

Johnny lowered his smoking, silver-chased Colt Lightning .44 and smiled beneath the brim of his bullet-crowned black hat banded with bright Indian beads, the chin thong dangling against his chest. "Well, hello, Ben." A brief pause. A tightening of the kid's smile. "What're you doing here?"

Stillman approached him and stopped. Johnny looked at him curiously. The boy, who was in that uncertain territory between raw youth and manhood, was about five inches shorter than Stillman's six-two, and a good bit slighter of frame. He had a splash of fading red pimples across his forehead. Despite the blemishes, he was a good-looking young man. Boy-faced, but with a man's ironic humor in his soft gray eyes.

He wore a thin blond mustache and a somewhat scraggly spade beard that drooped about a half an inch off his chin. His straight, sandy-blond hair was long, tumbling over his shoulders, and almost as thick as a girl's. He wore a black vest trimmed in small silver conchos over a faded red shirt, a brown cartridge belt and holster, and black whipcord trousers stuffed into hand-tooled Justin boots.

A fine-looking young man with a sensitive gaze. Stillman could see why the girls—and, in one case, a young woman five years older than Johnny—were attracted to him. There was a guileless vulnerability in the boy who called himself Johnny Nevada. And a poetic sensitivity tempered by a boyish reckless-ness and danger. Johnny was like a young dog that hadn't been treated right—yearning to be patted and cared for, but quick to strike at the first sign of threat.

Stillman had approached such pups before, both the human and animal kind. He smiled. "Afternoon, Johnny."

"Afternoon, Sheriff. You come out to see Granddad? He's in the cabin. Didn't he answer your knock?"

"I rode out here to see you, Johnny."

"That so?" The kid frowned, cocking one boot in front of the other. "What about?"

Stillman tilted his chin toward a deadfall tree lying back a ways from where Johnny had been shooting, in the shade of a sprawling cottonwood. "Let's have a seat, shall we?"

Casting Stillman a skeptical glance, Johnny shrugged and said, "All right," and walked over to the deadfall. He kept the pistol in his right hand, holding it barrel down against his right leg. Stillman wasn't sure that it had been a conscious decision to keep the gun in his hand or one born of instinct, Johnny somehow sensing danger was near.

Had that been why he hadn't fired off that last shot in the cylinder, as well?

The air around the clearing reeked of the rotten-egg odor of powder smoke.

Stillman took a seat to Johnny's left and rested the Henry across his knees.

Johnny looked at him searchingly, that skeptical cast growing in his cautious gaze. "There's been trouble, hasn't there?"

"Yes."

Johnny sighed. "Let's have it." He held the Lightning in both hands on his right thigh, his right index finger still curved through the trigger guard.

"Dave Bliss was murdered last Friday night."

Johnny looked shock. "Bliss? Oh, no! What about Sarah? She wasn't—"

"Sarah's fine, Johnny."

"Well, that's a relief! Who killed Bli—" Johnny cut himself off, and recognition broke across his young face. "Wait. That's what you're here for, ain't it?"

Johnny rose from the log and walked several feet away from Stillman. He didn't say anything for a time. He just stared off through the cottonwoods toward the river.

Then he turned, and a bitter smile twisted his lips. "You think I killed Bliss."

"I don't think anything at this point," Stillman said, plucking the folded paper from his shirt pocket and holding it up by one corner. "But I am sorry to tell you, Johnny, that the judge filled out this arrest warrant and ordered me to deliver it."

"Why me?"

"Three of Vince Patten's men said they saw you pull the trigger."

"Patten's men are bald-faced liars."

"You didn't do it?"

"I sure as hell did not!"

"Settle down, Johnny. I'm just tryin' to get to the bottom of the matter."

Johnny strode quickly to Stillman, leaning forward at the waist. He still held the Lightning low in his right hand. "You have to believe me, Ben. I didn't kill Dave Bliss. Why, I'd have to be seven kinds of a fool for ambushin' Bliss after that threat I made in the Drovers!"

Stillman narrowed an eye at the young man standing before him. "How did you know he was ambushed?"

"What?"

"How did you know Bliss was ambushed?"

Johnny hesitated. "I . . . I just assumed. You said Patten's men saw me—"

"Pull the trigger. I didn't say from ambush. How do you know I didn't think you'd faced him straight on?"

Johnny stared as though in shock at the lawman. The bitter smile again took hold of his mouth, and he shook his head slowly. "I didn't do it, Ben. I didn't ambush Bliss or shoot him straight on. Patten's men probably shot him themselves. But it's just so damn easy to blame me, isn't it? Sure, sure. You got Patten blamin' me, an' the judge writin' out the warrant. You and I both know why both Patten and the judge—especially the judge!—would want to see me hang . . . even for a killin' I didn't do . . ."

"Look, Johnny—I'll get to the bottom of it. But I gotta take you in. You have to stand before a jury of your peers. They'll hear Patten's men's side of it and your side of it. Why don't you begin by telling me where you were last Friday afternoon, early evening?"

"I was right here, Sheriff. All day and all night long."

"That's a good start. Your grandfather said the same thing, and he'll tell it to the jury."

Stillman could tell the young man had stopped listening as soon as the words "a jury of your peers" had left the sheriff's mouth. The angry, ironic smile had made a mask of the kid's face, and he was shaking his head slowly, darkly, from side to side.

"You know I can't get a fair trial around here, Ben. And who's gonna be presidin' over it? Judge Hoagland? Now, that's a kangaroo court if I ever heard of one!"

"I'm sure he'll recuse himself, Johnny, considering your relationship with his daughter an' all. In fact, I'll insist he does. He'll have to bring another judge in from another county. In the meantime, I'll do everything I can to find out who killed Bliss." Stillman leaned his Henry against the log, rose, and stood looking down at the kid. The sheriff extended his left hand. "Give me the gun."

Johnny looked at his Colt as though seeing it in his hand for the first time. Keeping the gun by his right leg, he looked again at Stillman. "If you take me in, Ben, I'll be dead in two weeks. Three at the most. Depends on how long it takes the judge to call in a hangman and get a gallows built."

Stillman drew a deep breath and scowled down at the younger man. "If you think you're gonna shoot me and run, you got another think comin', Johnny. If you run, you'll hang for sure. This is a matter for the law. Let the law work."

"The law don't work for folks like me."

"It can if you'd give it a chance, Johnny."

"Not after I threatened Bliss in the Drovers a couple weeks back."

"That was a fool move. It dug you in, makes you look bad. But I guarantee you the truth will come out. I'll see to it. If you're innocent, you'll walk." Stillman flexed his hand. "Now, the gun . . ."

Johnny stared at Stillman, his eyes darkly pensive. A nostril flared and his mouth quirked a taut smile as he said, "What if I don't?"

23

"I'll take it from you."

"How are you gonna do that? You got a bad back, Ben. Besides, you're old. Why, you must be pushin' fifty. Shit, I can move like a cat. I'm mighty fast at bringin' up a hogleg." His lips quirked another challenging grin, and he shook his head. "I'm thinkin' maybe I should just shoot you and light out and spare myself a stretched ne—"

Stillman didn't let him finish. He stepped forward and, catching Johnny off guard, slapped the kid hard across the face with the back of his right hand. Stillman was a big man, powerful through the chest and shoulders. His back twitched only a little at the sudden, violent movement. Johnny screamed as the blow sent him flying backward, twisting around and hitting the ground with a thud, rolling.

Johnny scrambled onto his left shoulder and, bunching his lips with fury, began to raise the Lightning, which he'd held on to. Stillman kicked the underside of the kid's right wrist. He heard the bone snap just before the gun barked, the bullet sailing skyward. The kid screamed again as the Lightning arced backward into the brush.

"Ow! You broke my wrist, you son of a bitch!"

Stillman stood over him, balling his fists tightly at his sides as he glared at the young man, who'd lost his hat in the tumble. Johnny's hair hung messily to his shoulders, flecked with dead leaves and seeds. "You must've misunderstood me, kid," he grated out through clenched teeth. "I wasn't askin'."

"You broke my wrist, Ben!"

"Consider yourself lucky. Most men I would have shot if they'd pulled a stunt like that. Now, get to your feet and stop caterwauling. I'm taking you in and locking you up, and you're gonna stand trial for the murder of Dave Bliss."

Johnny held his right wrist in his left hand. The right hand shook. It hung at an odd angle. Broken, all right. Stillman felt no regrets. The kid had been about to shoot him. That disappointed him deeply, and he felt a little foolish for having believed the kid wouldn't pull such a stunt. Not on him, someone who'd tried hard in the past to earn Johnny's trust.

He felt like a man who'd been bit by a dog he was trying to feed.

But he had to remember that plenty of folks in the past had beaten this poor, miserable dog moaning before him. He couldn't take it personally. The kid had felt cornered, boxed in. Stillman wondered if it was because he'd shot Dave Bliss or if he was just accustomed to running.

He'd withhold judgment for now.

He picked up the Henry and wagged it. "Let's go." He kept a hard, commanding tone in his voice. The time for gentleness had passed the minute the kid had refused to hand over his gun. "My buggy's in front of the cabin."

"They're gonna kill me, Ben," the kid said, his tone wheedling now as, clutching his injured wrist, he pushed up off his knees. "They're gonna blame Bliss's killin' on me cause I'm an easy mark. They'll hang me, an' the real killer—probably Vince Patten himself—is gonna walk free!"

"Maybe," Stillman said. "We'll see what the jury says. Now, frankly, Johnny Nevada, I'm a little tired of listening to you. You either start walking toward the cabin or I'm gonna brain you and carry you!"

"I'm goin'! I'm goin'!"

The kid strode to the trail that cut through the trees. Stillman followed him. Hec Fenton stood by Stillman's rented buggy, a double-barreled shotgun in his arms. He looked grimly at his grandson stumbling toward him, clutching his broken wrist to his chest.

Johnny stopped before him. "He's takin' me in, Granddad. He thinks I killed Dave Bliss."

Fenton scowled. "Did you, Johnny?"

"No!"

"Do you know who did?"

"Christ, no!"

Fenton nodded. "That's good enough for me. I'll back you."
He stepped aside. Johnny climbed into the buggy.

Stillman walked forward, turned to the old man, and glanced at the shotgun in his arms. "Which one of us was that for?"

A sheepish flush crept into Fenton's weathered face marked here and there with warts and liver spots. He glanced at the ground, deeply troubled. "I'm not sure."

CHAPTER THREE

Sleep was a deep well of soothing warm water.

Doctor Clyde Evans, M.D., was trying desperately to remain at the bottom of that well, though someone or some thing seemed bent on pulling him up out of the comforting depths.

"Damn you to hell," he muttered, though he couldn't quite get the words out. To his own ears, the rebuke sounded like some foreign tongue spoken from behind a deep feather pillow. "Go away! Go away!" he tried to yell in that same garbled tongue. Anyone else in the room—there were only a few flies buzzing around the two empty bottles, empty glasses, and a plate with last night's supper leavings on the table by the bed—would have heard the doctor's words as something akin to: "Guh-ayy! Guh-ayy!"

They would have seen the stocky man lying belly down, clothed in only his longhandles, on top of the rumpled sheets and quilts, face buried in his pillow, arms closed over his head, as though he thought his old house on a bluff overlooking the Milk River at the western edge of Clantick were about to cave in on him.

Then there was someone else in the room. Evans was rudely made aware of this fact when that someone tugged brusquely on his arm. "Doc! Doc! Wake up, Doc! You have to wake up!"

The words sounded only a little clearer than had his own. While he could make them out, they seemed to be shouted from the top of the deep well and had to careen through several feet of water to reach his ears. The hand travéléd well through that water. It tugged his arm hard until suddenly he lifted his head to stare into the face of a young woman with blue eyes and sandy-blond hair and a generous swell of breasts beneath a fetching pink gown.

She stood crouched beside the bed, pulling on his arm and yelling, "Doc! You have to wake up!"

Evans blinked, trying to get his eyes to focus. When they did, he looked at the high, pale plains of the girl's breasts above the gown's corset. "Evelyn," he said in his sleep-gravelly voice. "Oh, Evelyn . . . thank god it's you, you heavenly child!"

Evans grabbed her arm, drew her toward him, and slid his face up against her chest, sinking his nose into her cleavage and drawing a deep breath scented with oatmeal soap and lilac water and the musk of ripe, young womanhood.

"Doc, no!" the girl cried, and pushed him away with a grunt.

He rolled onto his back, gasping for air, feeling raw desire hammering in his loins.

"Doc, you're about to be married, you fool! Why aren't you up?"

A two-by-four slammed across the doctor's cheek couldn't have stirred him any more than the words she'd fairly screamed. They penetrated his brain, further plucking him up out of the seductive water-slumber that wanted to cling to him most desperately.

But the water was gone now.

Now he was ensconced in the horror of hard reality. And inside that regrettable, uncompromising lack of illusion he was realizing, as well as he could realize anything with a brain throbbing from way too much drink, that the reason Evelyn Vincent, his young friend and one-time lover and the waitress at Sam Wa's Café in downtown Clantick, was dressed so brightly and fetchingly, her lips painted, cheeks rouged, and a feathered hat pinned to her upswept hair, was because Evans was getting married today!

The shock of that improbable knowledge must have shone in his eyes. Or the beginnings of that knowledge must have shone there, anyway. As though to send it all the way home, Evelyn got down to eye level with the doctor, placed both her hands on Evans's shoulders, and shook him as she enunciated very clearly and forcefully, "Doc, it is four o'clock on August twenty-fourth. You are going to be married in one hour. I brought your wedding suit over from Lu Chang's Laundry, just like you asked. I knocked on your door for nearly ten minutes. Didn't you hear me? I finally went around back and found the rear door open, thank god."

Evelyn stared at him, no doubt discerning the red in his eyes, the pallor in his cheeks, and smelling the whiskey and brandy on his sour breath. Then she looked at the night table with its additional evidence of his debauch before shuttling her gaze back to the medico himself. Lines dug into the smooth skin of her forehead as she shook her head in disbelief. "Have you been sleeping all day, Doc?"

"Huh?" Evans said, raking a hand down his face, scrubbing sleep from his eyes. "All day? No . . . I . . . I, uh . . . woke up around noon. Felt so damn miserable, I"—he snorted ironically—"had another drink . . . an' then another . . . and . . ."

"Oh, my gosh, Doc," Evelyn said in astonishment. "Why would you do that? You're getting married today!"

She'd hesitated on the last word, almost not finishing it.

Evans felt a deep flush rise in his cheeks. He also felt a sheepish quarter-smile twitch across one half of his mouth. Evelyn stared back at him, the girl's expression betraying her realization that the very fact of the wedding was the reason he'd drunk himself comatose.

Evans opened his mouth to speak, but she wouldn't let him

get a single word out.

"No," Evelyn said, shaking her head vigorously. "No, no, no. Don't speak. You're going to get to that wedding, Doc. And you're gonna walk down that aisle, and you're gonna get hitched to the Widow Kemmett. I don't care if I have to kill us both getting you there on time, but *you will be there on time!*"

Evans was still semi-drunk. The lingering inebriation coupled with his massive hangover made not only his head feel twice its normal size, with a twice-the-normal-sized heart banging away at every nerve in his tender skull, but it made his tongue feel twice its normal size, as well.

Still, he managed to say with some degree of tenderness, he thought, "Evelyn . . . sweet Evelyn . . . don't you remember the night we shared . . . the night we made such sweet love . . . right here, in this . . ."

"No, Doc!" the girl said, her pale blue eyes crossing sternly as she rose to her feet. "I don't remember a thing about that night. Because it didn't happen." She stomped her foot in bitter frustration. "Oh, all right—maybe it did. But it shouldn't have. You love Katherine Kemmett. I gotta admit you'll always have a place in my heart, and there might never be another man in this world I'll admire as much as you, and I'll probably size up every man I meet *against* you, but you and I both know it would never work for us.

"I was bein' a foolish girl, lettin' what happened happen that night. I'm just a lowly waitress at a greasy-spoon café. I come from low people. Dirt farmers an' outlaws. Grovelers an' scratchers. Illiterate folks. You—why, you're a doctor! You read Mister Shakespeare and Mister Byron. The widow—why, she's the Widow Kemmett! A preacher's widow. And she helps you mend folks. All by herself, she's delivered half the babies in this county. She's the one who truly loves you. And it's a woman's love. Not a girl's love."

Evelyn paused to quickly, furtively swipe a tear from her lightly freckled right cheek. "And you love her back." Her voice had grown thick. She sniffed.

"Ah, hell," Evans said, lying back down heavily, feeling the entire world swirling around inside his half-drunk, half-hungover brain, also feeling that seductive tug from the well of sleep once more. "I just don't know if I'm ready for the widow to move in here and—"

"Well, she is moving in here, and that's that! You just got cold feet. You've been a bachelor so long, married to your stethoscope, your books, an' your thunder juice, that it's only natural you'd be reluctant when the chips are down. Like I said, Doc, I'm gonna get you to the church on time if I have to kill us both doin' it. Now, since you stink like a plow horse, I'm gonna go down and rustle up some water for a bath. The water's gonna be cold because I don't have time to heat it, but that'll sober you up. In the meantime, I'll build a fire in the range so we can get some coffee down you before you pull out of here. You're gonna be at least halfway sober when you marry the widow!"

Evelyn had retreated to the bedroom door. Now she stopped to glance at the miserable Evans over her shoulder. "Up, up, now, Doc! Look alive! You skin out of them longhandles, and I'll be up with a tub and water pronto!" She left the room, but stomping down the hall toward the stairs, she yelled, "In the meantime, you can clean your teeth. Your breath smells like the inside of a wolf den!"

"Ah, Jesus," Evans complained, pushing himself up onto his elbows. He dropped his heavy legs over the side of the bed. His heart hiccupped, thudded slowly, heavily, then hiccupped again. He picked one of the empty bottles up off the table, tipped it back. A drop managed to roll onto his tongue. He set the bottle down quietly, so Evelyn wouldn't hear downstairs, and picked up the other one. There was still about a quarter inch of amber liquid on the bottom of that one.

"There is a god in heaven, after all." Evans tipped the bottle back, encouraged when his tongue was bathed in the sweet burn of Spanish brandy.

He swallowed and almost felt compelled to smile as the liquor hit his belly and spread a thin but soothing hand against the prickly edged misery pervading him from the far reaches of his soul to the thick, dark red hair standing up in spikes around his handsome head, which bore the crooked nose of a former pugilist.

Evans had done some bare-knuckle fighting to help put himself through medical school back east, though he'd spent most of the extra money on firewater and *doves du pave.*

The sporting girls were still his addiction.

Had been his addiction until the widow had entered his life with her persnickety ways and chaste views on personal relations.

He'd managed to sack her twice, catching her in two fleeting, unguarded, and uncustomary amatory moments. But those had happened under the covers and under the cover of darkness, to boot. He'd still never seen her naked. Oh, he knew from exploring her with his hands and other sundry extremities that she had a good body for a woman in her early forties, around Evans's own age. But he remembered distinctly—couldn't forget it, in fact—that she'd been far less responsive than the younger, more sensual and adventurous Evelyn.

He rose from the bed and slowly, thoughtfully skinned out of his smelly longhandles.

The problem was, he thought as he splashed water into a cup and fumbled with a tin of tooth powder, he didn't love Evelyn. He *wanted* Evelyn. He adored the girl, but he didn't love her. What he loved was her body. He couldn't imagine sharing his house with young Evelyn Vincent any more than he could imagine sharing it with the widow.

Maybe the whole problem was that he wasn't ready to share his house and his life with anyone just yet. But if not now, when?

Would he be doomed to live out his life here in this old, cluttered, rambling house alone—reading his Mister Shakespeare and his Mister Byron and Mister Plato and Horace and Sir Walter Scott and Thoreau and Emerson while drinking himself into the welcome oblivion of sleep?

Day after day, night after night?

With nothing, no one else here except the wildcats and the half-wild collie he fed, and the northern Montana wind blowing over the river buttes to strum beneath his eaves . . . and the ghosts of long-dead authors, his only friends, scuttling like draft-driven dust about these old rooms and dingy halls . . . ?

Three hard knocks on the door.

Evelyn's voice: "Doc, cover yourself—I'm comin' in with that bath!"

Evans grabbed a sheet off the bed, and steeled himself against the onrushing tide of his future.

"Okay," he said, clearing his throat. "I'm ready, Evelyn. I guess."

CHAPTER FOUR

Shakily, feeling more than a little queasy, Evans followed Evelyn Vincent out onto the front porch of his sprawling house. He drew the door closed behind him.

He stood staring at the door while he fumbled with his four-in-hand tie, his concentration on the tie waning. His gaze went to the door itself and on the reflection of the bowler-hatted, mustached, bespectacled gent in the window. The one with the lumpy nose more befitting a saloon bouncer than a man of medicine.

But then there was so much about the doctor that broke the mold.

He stared back at himself, and it seemed as though another man resembling him was staring through the window at him, silently asking him, "What in the hell are you about to do, you simple fool? Do you have any idea?"

Oh, shut the hell up. I've made my decision. I'm going through with it, by god . . . and let the devil take the hindmost.

Fresh out of the cold-water tub, Evans wore his best three-piece suit with celluloid collar and four-in-hand burgundy tie. Katherine had bought the tie for him when, inspecting his wardrobe, she couldn't find a single tie without food or drink stains on it. Of course, the Widow Kemmett was not going to marry a man with a stained tie.

Evans stared at the door through which his incredulous second self stared back at him. The next time he stepped through that door, he would be with Katherine Kemmett.

The next time he stepped through that door, he would be married.

"What's the matter, Doc?" Evelyn asked.

"Huh . . . what?" He turned to her, still fumbling ineptly with the tie. "Oh, it's just this damn . . . my hands are shaking."

"That nervous, huh? Here, let me help."

She reached up and worked the tie. "I can't say as I'm much of a hand with a man's tie. What man ever decided to wear such a frilly, complicated thing, anyway? Why, a man's tie almost has a woman's corset beat for being needlessly hard to tangle with!"

"A woman likely came up with it, to get even with us about the corset." Evans added snidely, "One much like the one who bought me this one."

"Oh, hush. Here, I think I'm getting it." As she continued to adjust the tie, Evelyn glanced up at the doctor and smiled proudly. "I set a broken wrist today, Doc."

"What's that?"

"Ben brought that handsome young firebrand—the one who calls himself Johnny Nevada?—into the jail. I guess some folks think he's the one who killed Dave Bliss."

"Oh? Well, I can believe it. Never mind he's going to be a father," Evans grumbled.

"Yeah," Evelyn said. "Kind of hard to believe it about the judge's daughter, ain't it? I mean, *isn't* it?" She quickly corrected herself before the sawbones had a chance to.

Evans chuckled.

Evelyn said, "Anyways, Johnny had a broken wrist. Ben knew that I'd worked with you a time or two, helping you out when you needed it, so rather than bother you on your wedding day, he asked me to have a look."

"How'd you do?"

"Set it like nothin'!" Again, she smiled proudly. "Even made a plaster cast just like you showed me." She lowered her hands from his neck and stepped back to inspect her handiwork. "And I don't think the widow . . . er, Mrs. Kemmett . . . could have done a better job with that tie, neither!"

"Don't you go competing with me, young lady," Evans playfully chided her. "You might be able to do *my* work, but if I have to go to work over to Sam Wa's and try slinging hash, my goose is cooked!"

Evelyn laughed, then frowned. "Come on, Doc. We don't have time to horse around." She turned and, holding the skirts of her gown above her ankles, hurried down the porch's rotting steps. "No time to hitch old Faustus to your chaise, Doc. I hope it doesn't look too unseemly, you ridin' to your wedding with a waitress in Sam's old farm wagon!"

The wagon sat just off the porch; Evelyn's young sorrel, May, was in the traces and tugging at a thick tuft of weeds growing in the doctor's untended yard. Evans had gifted the young woman with the horse a year ago. A rancher had turned the sorrel over to him in exchange for medical work, but the sawbones already had a horse—his beefy, mule-stubborn, but still trusty Faustus, now milling in the shade of the small corral off the stable and buggy shed flanking the house, probably kicking his empty oat pail around.

"I'm not a Du Pont or a Vanderbilt," Evans said, climbing up into the driver's seat beside Evelyn and wincing against the enlarged heart still hammering away against his brain plate. "Just a lowly country sawbones. Nothing one bit unseemly about hitching a ride in such a contraption . . . or with you, dear girl," he added with emphasis.

As Evelyn released the brake, she glanced at him, a sheepish blush and stiff half-smile showing in her heart-shaped face. Instantly, Evans wished he hadn't said that last. Evelyn probably thought he was referring to their former dalliance . . .

which hadn't been a mere dalliance at all, but an out-and-out night together—one that Katherine Kemmett had discovered them at, nonetheless!

One she'd also forgiven them both for, thank god . . .

Evans hadn't been referring to that night. It was too embarrassing now, as his inebriation wore off, to talk about. Best to shove it in the cellar and not discuss it further. But he realized now as Evelyn flipped the reins over May's back and they set off upon the rough trail down the bluffs toward Clantick, it was not a night that would ever/could ever totally leave his mind, either.

He cast a furtive glance at the comely, earthy, open young lady steering the horse beside him, and felt a warmth in his loins as he remembered her love cries . . .

Oh, Christ . . . you simple fool, the sawbones scolded himself.

Here you are, on your way to be married, and you're sitting here getting a stiff one fantasizing about the girl, young enough to be your daughter, driving you to the church!

"I don't care. I'm going through with it. She's a good woman, and she'll make me a better man."

"I couldn't agree more, Doc," Evelyn said.

Evans looked at her, blushing. He hadn't realized he'd voiced that last bit aloud.

"It's true," he said, nodding with resolve.

"It is true," Evelyn said, winking, then nodding with a similar determination.

The steepled white-clapboard church lay ahead, atop a low hill on the town's southwest corner, one mile from the doctor's house. Behind it lay another rise of buttes. At the base of those buttes ran a narrow creek sheathed in cottonwoods and box elders. A small cemetery lay between the church and the creek, and between the cemetery and the creek, under the sprawling trees, was where Sunday afternoon church picnics were often held.

There would be a picnic today, as well, though it wasn't Sunday. The picnic today would follow the wedding ceremony. The Clantick Lutheran Church Ladies' League, of which Katherine herself was the director, had two long tables set up out there, draped in oilcloth and mounded with food baskets covered in white cloth. There was a buckboard wagon, as well, with a couple of barrels in its bed.

Three young boys of various ages, decked out in suit jackets, knickers, and wool watch caps, milled around the wagons. Two were playing with sticks, while the smallest sat on the wagon seat. They'd probably been picketed out there by their mothers to keep dogs and other freeloaders away from the food.

The barrels likely held sarsaparilla and ginger beer for the children. There was doubtless a punch bowl on one of the tables for the grownups, though almost certainly untainted by anything of the "spirituous" variety. Damned shame. When this was over, Evans was going to be dying for a drink. Possibly, quite literally dying, he thought, as he skidded his gaze back from the creek to the church and the dizzying sprawl of saddled horses and buggies and crude wooden wagons parked in the gravel lot fronting it.

A good two-dozen people milled in front of the church, the men and ladies dressed to the nines, parasols of all colors of the rainbow twirling in the deep-summer sunshine. Children ran about. A baby cried against a young mother's shoulder. All heads turned toward the doctor and Evelyn as a man whom Evans recognized as the mayor, Roy Taylor, pointed and moved his mouth.

"Here we go, Doc," Evelyn said, joyously. "Too late to back out now. Even the mayor's here!"

Oh, boy . . . Evans grabbed the iron sides of the wooden seat as the wagon made the last lunge up the hill and then rocked to a stop near an old buckboard and a hefty coyote dun whose saddle straps hung free.

Evans felt the eyes of the crowd on him. He wasn't used to that—being the center of attention like this. Oh, why couldn't Katherine have agreed to a private ceremony in the courthouse? No, that hadn't been enough for her. The wedding had to be a public display. Of course she'd invited the entire county and likely a good half of the two surrounding ones. Evans wouldn't be surprised if stringers for a couple of eastern newspapers were in attendance, as well!

Automatically, he brushed his hand against the suit coat pocket in which he usually carried a flask.

The flask wasn't there.

Damn.

I'm going to have a heart stroke . . .

While the gray-headed preacher called the crowd into the church from the doorstep, beckoning broadly and just as broadly smiling, Sheriff Ben Stillman and his wife, Fay, walked over toward where Evans sat stiffly in Evelyn's wagon, taking deep, slow breaths. Stillman was dressed in a black suit, white shirt, and string tie, his pearl Stetson set back on his handsome head. The lawman's longish, wavy, salt-and-pepper hair hung down nearly to his shoulders, and his thick mustache of the same color rose with a wry grin.

"We were beginning to wonder if you got cold feet and lit out for Canada, Doc," Stillman said. He was cradling his and Fay's toddler, Little Ben, high against his chest.

Evans climbed down from the wagon and turned to Stillman, frowning. "You shouldn't be carrying that lug, Ben," the doctor reprimanded the lawman. "Why, he weighs as much as a yearling calf! Fay, would you please take your son from your husband before I take a switch to his backside—your husband's, I mean!"

"Of course, I will, Doc," said the former Fay Beaumont, the brown-haired, brown-eyed daughter of a French rancher from down along the Powder River and easily the most beautiful woman in Montana if not all of the frontier West—at least, to Evans's lusty, discerning mind. He knew Stillman and more than a few other males in these parts were of the same opinion. No woman could attract a lusty, hang-jawed stare the way Fay Stillman could.

As Fay reached for her boy, who was tugging on an end of his father's mustache, she added cajolingly to Stillman, "I said you were going to get into trouble, didn't I?"

As Stillman handed the knickered, curly-headed toddler off to his mother, he said, "Back feels fine, Doc. I'm staying off my horse, just like you and Doc Willoughby said, but I'm ready to start lugging this lug around again."

Willoughby was the surgeon who'd taken the train here from Denver to perform the delicate, risky, four-hour surgery on Stillman. Evans had assisted. H. Edgar Willoughby, a youngish man, was one of the few doctors in the country, educated in New York and Europe, who knew how to cut close to the spinal cord without paralyzing the patient. Similar procedures had been done successfully only a half-dozen other times, three of those times by Willoughby himself.

"Be that as it may . . ."

"Be that as it may, Doc," Stillman said, canting his head to scrutinize the medico, "you look a little yellow around the gills. You feelin' all right?"

"I'm sure the doc's just a little nervous," Fay said.

"Yeah, just nervous," Evelyn said, coming up to stand beside the edgy groom and greeting the Stillmans. "Well, we'd better get you in there, Doc."

"Yes, yes," Evans said, as he started following the girl toward the church into which most of the folks who'd been waiting around outside had gathered.

Stillman stepped up beside him, Fay and Little Ben flanking

them. "You really all right, Doc?" Stillman asked under his breath. He was Evans's closest male friend here in Clantick—in fact, he would be standing as the doctor's best man today—and he knew very well Evans's ambivalence on the subject of marriage.

"You wouldn't have a bottle on you, would you?"

Stillman smiled. "Sorry, Doc."

"I heard you had an interesting day."

"Evelyn tell you about Johnny Nevada?"

Evans nodded. "Did he really kill Bliss?"

"That's what I aim to find out."

They were approaching the church now, and Evans's heart was racing, sweat popping out on his forehead. "You have the ring—don't you, Ben?"

"Sure do, Doc."

Evans stopped and looked beseechingly at Stillman. "You sure you don't have a little flask? Just a little one hidden away in your boot?"

Stillman grabbed the doctor's left elbow and pulled him up the church steps. "Come on, Doc. Mrs. Kemmett . . . the soon-to-be Mrs. Clyde Evans . . . is waitin'. If we don't get in there soon, the parson's wife is going to run out of organ tunes, and the parson is gonna get nervous and start swillin' communion wine."

"Communion wine," Evans said, smacking his lips. "Don't tease me, Ben!"

And then he and Stillman parted and stumbled into the men's cloak room for some final throat clearings and curses while Katherine and her bevy of attendees were no doubt straightening and pinning or altering this or that and powdering the widow's . . . uh, *Katherine's* . . . cheeks. He wasn't sure if bells were tolling in his head or in the church's bell tower, because time speeded up right along with his heart, and he found himself taking a deep, deep breath and striding through the church's sanctuary, along the red-carpeted aisle toward the altar and the sacristy.

Why had the damned church suddenly become the deck of a clipper ship on extraordinarily choppy seas?

And all at once the three-man and three-woman choir fairly leapt to its feet and, hymn books raised, began belting out a jarringly raucous wedding anthem. The hammering of the organ and the roar of the choir nearly knocked Evans backward. He wasn't sure if he stumbled. If he did, no one in the congregation let on. They all gazed at him, smiling as though at a real twit who was making a big, big mistake, and this was going to be hilarious; just you wait and see!

He made out many faces he recognized, of course, since he knew and had administered to virtually everyone in Clantick and even most folks from the surrounding counties. He saw quite a few children he himself or Katherine had delivered over the years.

Evelyn sat near the aisle, beside Stillman's deputy, Leon McMannigle, who'd donned a three-piece suit trimmed with a silver watch chain. Evans had never known the deputy, a former Buffalo Soldier, ever to wear a suit before, and he hoped Leon hadn't bought it just for this occasion. It had to have cost him a pretty penny.

And there was Jody and Crystal Harmon, the young couple he counted as an adopted niece and nephew—who ranched south of town in the Two-Bear Mountains. Little Bill, named after Jody's father and Stillman's best friend from the old days— Milk River Bill—sat between them in his little-boy's wool suit with waistcoat, short breeches, buckle shoes, and sailor's hat. Jody looked uncomfortable but otherwise happy to be here in his own suit jacket and string tie. The blond-headed Crystal, tanned from the range she worked right along with Jody, was the picture of wholesome young motherhood in her lacy yellow frock Evans was sure she'd sewn herself, probably with the help of her older sister, Marie, who lived with them.

Crystal caught the doctor's eye and blew him a kiss.

Evans felt another blush burn his ears, and he quickly looked away.

The young family had ridden all the way to town from their ranch for the occasion. Evans hoped he wouldn't pass out or otherwise let them down.

And then time skipped ahead again, and he was standing with Stillman and the preacher near the altar. The choir took their seats, and the parson's wife calmed the organ down and began playing the "Bridal Chorus."

The quieter notes with their slow, regular beat caused Evans to hear the war-drumming of his heart in his ears. Sweat oozed from his every pore. Was it his imagination, or did his perspiration reek of Spanish brandy?

God, he could use a drink!

The vestibule door opened at the front of the sanctuary. All heads turned with a whisper of collectively displaced air and the soft creaks of the varnished pews. Katherine strode very slowly and elegantly down the aisle, beaming at her betrothed. Her neighbor, fellow widow, and maid of honor, Irma Bentley, tagged along behind, holding a bouquet of flowers and smiling so that her plump cheeks looked about to burst into flower.

"My god," Evans muttered under his breath, staring at Katherine fairly floating toward him, dragging the short train of her gown.

She rarely wore her long, chestnut hair in anything but a fist-tight bun or even two buns atop her persnickety head. Today, however, she wore it down. Streaked with fine strands of silver, it glistened as it tumbled across her shoulders, lovingly caressed by the white silk wedding veil. Just over her right ear she'd pinned a red rose. It gave her the visage of a handsome, alluring, time-seasoned bride in a classical painting fashioned by a master.

Katherine was a slender, full-busted woman, and the somewhat tight, white silk and taffeta wedding dress, an heirloom passed down from her great-grandmother, did nothing to hide this fact. She was not what anyone would call ravishing, and her face was not what anyone would call beautiful, for her features were somewhat raw, her mouth pertly narrow, nose judgmentally upturned, lips chastely thin, and eyes a rather insipid brown when she wasn't smiling. Evans often reflected that they were the eyes of a disapproving schoolmarm.

But today she was smiling, and that changed everything. Her eyes, honing in on Clyde Evans as though they were trying to mesmerize him, appeared as though tiny suns burned deep inside them. They lit up her face. Why, a bright star seemed to be exploding at the core of her very being!

Evans's heart slowed as the woman . . . his woman . . . approached.

He felt a genuine smile etch itself across his own crudely featured face. A sense of well-being fluttered through him. It was like an ungainly bird rising out of him, easing the tension straining his shoulders and making his stomach roll. Meeting Katherine's gaze with his own, he lifted his elbow. Katherine, coming up beside him, hooked her arm through his with an intimate little nod of acknowledgment that this was their day.

Their day together. Just the two of them.

The first of many.

They turned to the preacher, who opened his mouth to speak but then closed it again suddenly. Evans had been only vaguely aware of a rumbling at the front of the church, out in the vestibule. Now the rumbling became thunder as the sanctuary's double doors burst open and a man stumbled several yards down the aisle, dragging his boot toes. His blond head wobbled on his shoulders.

A collective gasp echoed throughout the church.

The man was Logan Wright, the tall and ungainly loan officer from the bank. His butternut suit was stained red, and his gold watch swung by its chain. He wore no hat, and his hair hung in his eyes.

"Sheriff Stillman!" the man bellowed as he lurched forward, knees buckling, holding both hands to his upper belly. "The bank's been robbed!"

He fell facedown in a large, quivering lump on the red-carpeted aisle.

CHAPTER FIVE

Stillman bit out a curse as he ran to where Logan Wright lay unmoving in the church aisle, about ten yards from the open double doors. Several men from the wedding audience had bounded out of their pews to hover over Wright.

"Get back!" Stillman ordered, shoving one man aside and dropping to a knee beside the loan officer. Wright, who lay belly down on the red carpet, wasn't moving. He didn't appear to be breathing, either. Stillman pressed two fingers to the man's neck.

No pulse.

He looked up to see his deputy's wide-eyed face in the field of his vision. Leon McMannigle was on one knee on the other side of Wright's unmoving body. His polished-silver deputy sheriff's star was pinned to his crisp black leather vest, behind his natty claw-hammer frock coat.

"I think he's dead," Stillman said.

"Let me take a look, Ben," Doc Evans said behind him, and he dropped to a knee beside him. The doctor turned the man over. A woman screamed when she saw the blood oozing out of what appeared to be two holes in Wright's upper chest.

Evans turned an ear to the man's chest, then looked at Stillman and shook his head.

Rising, Stillman glanced at McMannigle and said, "We have to get over to the bank."

"I'll meet you there, Ben!" Donning his black bowler, Leon

leaped to his feet and ran out the open double doors.

The audience was on its feet now, and women gasped while men talked in hushed, incredulous tones, shifting and craning their necks to get a look at the dead man. Evans had turned to Katherine Kemmett, who'd walked up behind him. They were conversing quietly, with grave expressions, Katherine nodding dully as she stared down at the dead man who had preempted their wedding.

Stillman hurried over to where Fay stood by Little Ben, who'd climbed onto the pew, looking around bewilderedly, a wet finger in his mouth.

Stillman squeezed Fay's arm. "I have to get over to the bank. You and Ben stay here until I know it's safe to go outside."

Staring back in brown-eyed shock at her husband, Fay nodded quickly. "Ben, be careful!"

Stillman planted a quick kiss on the boy's head, then swung around and negotiated the crowd spilling into the aisle as he tried to reach the doors. He paused to ask a couple of men he knew to cover Wright's body and take him over to the undertaking parlor, then hurried out of the church, removed the lead weight from the bit of his rented horse, and climbed gingerly but quickly into the buggy.

Thumps rose on the church steps behind him, and Evans called, "Ben, I'm comin' with you!"

"Good idea, Doc!"

Evans jogged out to Stillman's buggy parked in the middle of the crowd of other buggies, wagons, and saddled horses parked on the church's grassy lot. Evelyn hurried down the church steps behind him, holding the hem of her gown above her leather shoes. "I'll get your bag and meet you in town, Doc!" the girl yelled as she headed for Sam Wa's wagon.

Evans climbed into Stillman's buggy. The sheriff gave him an incredulous glance. Taking a seat to the sheriff's right, Evans flushed a little and said, "I would have sent Katherine for the bag, but I think she's a little shaken. Evelyn's always game for a challenge."

Stillman turned the horse and shook the ribbons over its back, letting the gelding make its way through the lot toward the trail snaking down the bluff toward the main road into Clantick. "Understandable—Katherine bein' shaken," Stillman said. "Poor woman wanted this in the worst way . . . and it got rather rudely interrupted."

"Yes, but interrupted only," Evans said, adjusting his bowler on his head and glancing over his shoulder toward the church. "We'll pick it up again where we left off."

As the claybank raced off down the hill, with Stillman holding the reins loosely in his hands, the sheriff leaned toward the medico and said loudly enough to be heard above the buggy's clattering and the horse's clomping hooves, "You were really gonna go through with it. I have to admit, Doc, I wasn't sure you would."

"Of course, I was," Evans said a little defensively, holding his hat on his head, rocking to the coach's sway. "I'll go through with the whole thing if we ever get the chance!"

Stillman stared straight ahead now as the horse pulled the buggy onto the main trail, heading east. Under the circumstances, he felt a little naked without his guns. As a lawman, he usually wore the Colt everywhere except to church, and he certainly hadn't wanted to wear it while standing up for the doc.

Now he wished he'd placed the pistol in the buggy, but both his prized weapons were locked in the gun cabinet at his and Fay's little chicken farm perched on a butte north of Clantick. He'd thought the odds of his needing them today were slim. Clantick had become relatively quiet of late, far from the rollicking outlaw haven it had been when he'd first come here nearly three years ago after accepting the county's offer to make him sheriff by a special vote of county supervisors, given that their last sheriff had been killed by owlhoots, and those killers had still been running off their leashes.

Judging by the odds, he shouldn't have needed his weapons today. But now, as he and the doc pitched, jostled, and bounced onto the main street, First Street, of Clantick, he saw the grim evidence that trouble had erupted. Two men lay unmoving in the street out front of Clantick's Stockmen's Territorial Bank, a long, low, sandstone building with barred windows sitting on the south side of the east-to-west stretching street.

No, there were three men. Stillman saw the third now as he halted the buggy in the center of the street. Several men had been standing or kneeling around the third man lying slumped against one of the bank's awning support posts, his chin tipped toward his left shoulder.

Yet a fourth man—one whom Stillman recognized—sat back against the bank's front wall, left of the open door. This man was alive, his blue eyes open, lips stretched back from his white teeth in agony. His long, thin legs, clad in faded denim and brown leather chaps, were extended straight out before him. A red bandanna was tied around his right leg, just above the knee.

Stillman recognized this regal-looking, red-faced, gray-headed, middle-aged gent as one of the largest ranchers in the county—Carlton Kane.

The president of the bank himself, George Garth, was down on one knee beside the injured Kane, waving his derby hat before the rancher's craggy, sunburned face, trying to cool him off. Standing beside her father was Clarissa Kane, a blond young woman in men's rough trail garb complete with undershot boots and chaps.

She turned a hard-edged gaze toward Stillman and Evans as they both clambered down from the buggy. "Sheriff Stillman!

Doctor Evans!" She threw up an arm, beckoning. "Over here!"

Stillman and Evans shared a glance. The sheriff jerked his chin in the rancher's direction, then walked over to check the other three men lying in the street. All three were dead. Stillman recognized the one lying slumped again the bank's awning support post as Grant Fitzgerald, a burly Coloradoan who'd been Kane's foreman.

Stillman walked over to where the doctor was examining Kane's bullet-pierced right leg. The rancher was snapping out curses and snarling like an injured beast, kicking his good leg, writhing. The boardwalk was littered with glass from the building's front windows, both of which had been shot out during the attack.

"Sheriff Stillman," Clarissa Kane said, glaring up at him. "Is there anyone at the helm here *at all?* Where is your badge . . . your gun? Where were you when my father was *shot?*"

"We were at my wedding, Miss Kane," Evans said. "Ben was standing up for me."

"Well, isn't that nice?" The young woman kept her fiery gaze on the sheriff. "Meanwhile, you left no one in charge?"

Stillman looked at George Garth, who returned the look with a constipated one of his own. "What happened here, George?"

"Robbers hit us when we were transferring Mister Kane's strongbox to his wagon."

"Payroll transfer?" asked Stillman.

Garth shook his head. "Mister Kane sold his interest in a mine. The money came by train two days ago. They shot Mister Kane and three of his men, including his foreman, and made off with the wagon. Wright was overseeing the transfer. He took a bullet, as well."

"Wright took more than one bullet, and he's dead," Stillman said. "He never should have made that ride to the church."

"Oh, no!" Garth looked horrified. "I don't think he realized how bad he was hit. I left the responsibility of the transfer up to him. You know what a conscientious man he is. As soon as the smoke cleared, he mounted the first horse he could find, and galloped off to the church to fetch you and McMannigle."

Stillman looked around. "Where is Leon, anyway?"

"He headed after them," said Kane. "Four of my men rode after those killers as soon as they shot their way out of town, so he's not alone."

"At least one lawman is doing his job around here," said the less-than-charming Miss Kane, sneering.

Stillman tried his best to ignore the girl, whom he considered a spoiled, uppity brat who spent her winters attending a private academy for young women back east. Around Clantick, she carried herself like a queen in rough range garb. She liked the contrast between the gear she wore summers and her natural beauty, which indeed was significant. Stillman would give her that.

He looked inside the bank, at the frightened tellers and several townsfolk who'd apparently been in the bank during the attack. They all stood around, talking quietly and comforting each other.

Not finding who he was looking for, Stillman turned back to Garth. "Where's Riley Hedges, my night deputy? I had him on duty while Leon and I were at the wedding."

"I haven't seen him, Ben."

"Neither have I," chimed in Miss Kane tautly. "How bad is my father's leg, Doctor?"

"I think the bullet went all the way through the flesh," Evans said, lowering his head for a close inspection. "There appears to be an exit wound. No telling how much damage it did on the way out, however. Someone help me get this man over to the Boston. No point in rough-riding him over to my house, when he'd be more comfortable in the hotel. You'll pay for a room in the Boston, won't you, Mister Kane?"

"Of course, of course!" Kane grunted. "Just get me over there, and someone for godsakes fetch me some whiskey!"

The rancher's daughter stepped in front of Stillman, crossing her arms on the impressive bosoms pushing out from behind her collarless cream blouse with fancily stitched red piping. Her suspenders bowed up around the edges of the saucy orbs, emphasizing the comeliness of her womanly physique. Her face was narrow, delicate, and liberally splashed with freckles. She was jade-eyed and beautiful, and she was well aware of it. She wielded her beauty around here during summers like a Sioux war lance.

"Sheriff Stillman, those outlaws got away with over a hundred thousand dollars in scrip and specie," she said. "I want you to promise me you will get every cent of it back!"

Stillman was incredulous. "A hundred thousand dollars!" Most businessmen let him know when a transfer of that size was about to occur, so he could be on the lookout for possible trouble. He'd received no such notification concerning this current transfer.

"Oh, for chrissakes, Clarissa!" her father yelled as several townsmen helped the rancher to his feet. "Will you do us all the favor of shutting your lovely trap? Our men and McMannigle are after them now, and if they don't run them down, they'll at least get a good handle on where they're headed. I'm sure Ben will send a posse out after them. We'll get the money back!"

The rancher looked at Stillman. "I'm sorry, Ben. We should have let you know." He cut another admonishing gaze at his daughter.

Flushing with the embarrassment, Clarissa flared a nostril at Stillman. "We'd better. That money didn't grow on a tree, Sheriff!"

"Never heard of any that did," Stillman grunted, stepping off the boardwalk fronting the bank and heading for his buggy.

"Where are you going?" Miss Kane called after him.

Stillman stopped and turned back to her, unable to keep a peeved grimace from twisting his lips. "Tell me, Miss Kane—did you get a good look at the robbers?"

"I had a passing glance at a few of them. Everything happened rather quickly, as you might imagine. Why?"

"Write out as complete a description of each man as you can. Might be helpful later. Describe them right down to their horses. Stick close to the Boston. I'll be over to check your work."

Stillman pinched his hat brim to the young woman—who gave him a hard, insinuating, sidelong look of open defiance—and walked toward his buggy.

CHAPTER SIX

Stillman climbed into the buggy and was swinging the clay around when Evelyn rattled toward him in Sam Wa's buckboard. She had Evans's black medical kit on the seat beside her.

The waitress asked for the doctor, and Stillman pointed toward the Boston Hotel a half block to the west. The Boston was nearly as fancy a sleeping and eating establishment as you'd find in Denver or Fort Worth, and now that the railroad had come to town, bringing commerce along with it, the Boston did a healthy business all week long, not just on weekends.

As the girl clucked her horse toward the hotel, Stillman swung south along Second Avenue. The new courthouse building still smelled of raw lumber there on the west side of the dusty, hay-littered street, behind Auld's Livery Barn.

The Hill County Courthouse, consisting of two rambling stories, wasn't much by city standards, but aside from a few warehouses along the Great Northern tracks, it was so far the largest building in Clantick. Both the Stars and Stripes and the territorial flag flapped from tall wooden poles in the front yard, in the middle of the cinder-paved, rock-lined circular drive leading to the broad wooden veranda and the front door.

Stillman's office was on the first floor, along with the offices of sundry other county officials, including the county treasurer, the public defender, and the county clerk. The courtroom, judge's chambers, and bailiff's office were on the second floor. It was all very official and organized, a far cry from his former sheriff's office and jailhouse on First Street. The jail was in the stone-block basement with barred windows just above ground level. That's where Johnny Nevada was being housed.

Stillman wasn't here about Nevada, however.

He looped the horse's reins over one of the three hitch racks fronting the courthouse, then mounted the veranda and pushed through the heavy oak front door. His own office was beyond the first door on the right, his name stenciled in gold leaf on the door's upper, frosted glass panel:

BEN STILLMAN, HILL COUNTY SHERIFF

His name written on glass was a first for Stillman, who still considered himself a simple country lawman. He supposed the changes were for the good, however. They meant things were getting more civilized around here, though he secretly hoped they wouldn't become overly so. Too many laws and regulations, too much official business and names being written on glass could get too complicated in a hurry, choking the color out of the day-to-day.

Stillman threw the door open, and stepped inside.

His heart turned cold. "Riley!"

He rushed over to where his night deputy, Riley Hedges, slumped back against Stillman's swivel Windsor chair, behind the desk on the far side of the room. Hedges was a potbellied, sixty-one-year-old ex-cowboy who'd worked on several of the area ranches, including Carlton Kane's, before age and arthritis had forced him into retirement.

Hedges was a lifelong bachelor who lived alone in a local boarding house, and was a reliable part-time deputy when he wasn't over at the Drovers, drinking beer and playing cards and checkers. At least, he *had been* a reliable deputy. The blood oozing from the bullet wound in the dead center of his chest attested to the undeniable fact that Hedges was dead.

Murdered.

"Goddamnit, Riley!" Stillman took the old man's gray-whiskered chin in his right hand and turned the gray head toward him. The half-open eyes were glazed in death. Hedge's lower jaw hung slack, tongue peeking out one corner, beneath a soup-strainer mustache. *"Shit!"*

Stillman looked down at the old man's right hip. Hedges's old Remington was still in its holster. He hadn't even unsnapped the keeper thong from over the hammer. A *Policeman's Gazette* lay open atop the desk blotter, near a stone mug of coffee and an ashtray with a half-smoked quirley resting on its edge, an inch of cold gray ashes slumping worm-like into the tray beneath it.

Riley had been reading when someone had come in and shot him from maybe three or four feet away. He'd likely been dead before he'd hit the chair.

Immediately, Stillman thought of Johnny Nevada. Had a friend of the kid shot Hedges and broken Johnny out of the basement cellblock? He whipped his enraged, befuddled gaze at the cellblock door in the wall left of Stillman's desk, beside the chained wooden gun cabinet. The heavy, steel-banded oak door to the cellblock was closed, but that didn't mean the kid or his murderous accomplice hadn't closed it after they'd left.

Stillman grabbed the key ring from the top of a filing cabinet flanking his desk and hurried to the cellblock door, glancing through the small barred window near the top. He couldn't see anything in the murk of the cellblock below.

A little surprised to find the door locked, he quickly unlocked it and, unsheathing his Colt, dropped down the two dozen stone steps into the bowels of the cellblock lit by only daylight, pushing through the six, small, rectangular windows up high in the stone walls.

"Hold on, hold on, there, Sheriff!" Johnny Nevada's voice

echoed, giving a disembodied voice to the murky dankness. His shadow moved in the first cell on the corridor's right side, near the bottom of the steps. "I didn't have nothin' to do with what happened up in your office. I was just sittin' here, lickin' my wounds and bidin' my time, is all."

Nevada was the only prisoner in the cellblock, which contained twelve ten-by-twelve-foot cages, six on each side of the stone-floored corridor, at the center of which stood a wood-stove, cold this time of the year. The kid stood at his cell door, holding his broken, cast-ensconced right wrist in his left hand. His hat was off and his hair was rumpled.

"You heard the shot?" Stillman asked.

"Sure did. What the hell happened, anyway? That old man get shot?"

"Riley's dead."

The statement sent a fresh wave of anger and sorrow careening through Stillman. He'd liked Riley Hedges, a contrary old drunkard who could hold an entire saloon rapt by one of his stories of the olden days. One of the last of a dying breed. Someone had gunned him down in cold blood. Executed him. Hedges hadn't even had time to get his old Remington out of its holster.

Likely no one else had heard the shot. At the time, Riley had very likely been the only one in the courthouse—aside from Johnny, that was. Like Stillman, everyone who worked in the courthouse had been at the church for Evans's wedding.

"What else did you hear?" Stillman asked the kid. "Any voices?"

"Yeah, I heard Hedges's voice and some woman's voice. At least, I think it was a woman's voice. Kind of hard to tell from way down here."

"A woman's voice?" Stillman was skeptical.

"I think it was a woman's voice."

"How long did they talk?"

"Not even a minute. The woman said a few words and then the old man yelled, 'No, no, no!' real loud-like. Man, I jumped a good foot when I heard the shot!" Johnny smiled, sheepish. "I gotta admit, I thought . . . I thought the girl was . . ."

"Marnie Hoagland?" The judge's daughter.

The kid chuckled, looking down. "Wouldn't put it past her, the way she holds a candle for me. I reckon it wasn't her, though."

"Since you're still here, it doesn't look like it." Like Johnny, Stillman wouldn't have put it past the judge's daughter to try springing the father of the child she was carrying. He'd never seen a girl tumble so hard and desperately for a boy. Two girls had fallen for the boy who called himself Johnny Nevada in the short time—less than a year—since he'd wandered into the country. A father of one of those girls was dead.

Stillman turned, holstered his pistol, and started back up the steps.

"Hey, Sheriff," the kid called behind him. "What the heck's goin' on, anyways? I thought I heard a bunch of shootin' outside not five minutes after that girl left your office."

"You did." Stillman stepped into his office, closed the cell-block door, and locked it.

He returned the keys to the top of the file cabinet and turned to gaze down at Riley Hedges. His guts burned with unbridled anger. A woman had walked in here and shot him. Hedges wouldn't have suspected a woman. She'd taken full advantage of that.

"I'll get her, Riley," Stillman said. "Whoever in hell she was, I'll get her, old friend. In the meantime, we'll get you put to rest. Just hang on, pal."

Stillman squeezed the old deputy's bony shoulder, then walked outside and climbed back into the buggy. He rattled over to First Street and turned right, heading east toward the Boston. More townsfolk were on the street now, talking in anxious tones, discussing the robbery.

A glance to the west told Stillman that word had gotten out and had made its way to the church that all was clear, and the outlaws were gone. Several buggies and leather chaises were making their way into town. Jody and Crystal Harmon were probably giving Fay and Little Ben a ride back to the Stillmans' little farm on a bluff just north of Clantick. Stillman would check on them later.

As Stillman pulled up to the Boston, where several local businessmen were milling on the broad front veranda, smoking cigars, sipping beers, and discussing the robbery, the sheriff paused to glance back in the direction of the church. Whoever had pulled the robbery had likely been aware of Evans's and Katherine Kemmett's wedding, and that Kane's bank transfer would occur at the same time. They'd waited until the church doors were closed and the organ was booming before starting their assault, shooting down Kane's men and Logan Wright and stealing the strongbox.

But first, knowing Stillman had left Hedges in charge, they'd taken care of the old deputy in Stillman's office. They'd sent a woman to do it, knowing old Hedges would never have suspected a woman, and he'd be an easy target. Maybe they'd even known Riley well enough to know what a soft touch he was for the fairer sex . . .

Knowing all that meant they hadn't merely been troublemakers looking for opportunity. The robbers had known what they were doing. They'd probably pulled such stunts before, and they'd probably cased the town and the bank before pulling this one.

Had it been a coincidence that the transfer had happened on the same day as Evans's wedding? The date and time of the wedding had been common knowledge in and around Clantick for over half a year. Anyone could have learned about it. But what about the date and time of the transfer?

Stillman tied the claybank to a hitch rack fronting the Boston, then made his way up the veranda steps. He wanted to check on Carlton Kane, find out what he could about the killers from the man's unpleasant daughter, and then see about organizing a posse he himself would lead, his back be damned.

He'd just gained the top of the steps when the Boston's manager, Bryce Campbell, walked up to Stillman. He'd been smoking and drinking with a group of businessmen clumped on the veranda's east side, where they had a good view of the bank and the blood-splashed street fronting it. The undertaker, Wit Jenkins, and his two beefy sons were loading the bodies into a black-painted buckboard that served as a hearse.

"Ben?" Campbell said, blowing cigar smoke out his nose. He was a nervous little man who always wore a bowler hat and an apron. His long, angular, clean-shaven face and large, pale ears were red from excitement. His right eye twitched anxiously as he glanced at the men behind him, with whom he'd been conversing, and then back at Stillman.

"What is it, Bryce? How's Kane? He hasn't kicked off, has he?"

"Not last I heard."

"Good. If he had, I'd never hear the end of it from his daughter."

Campbell didn't get the joke. He leaned toward Stillman, his eye really twitching now, keeping his voice down. "Ben . . . those robbers. I think I know who they were!"

"You do?" Stillman scowled. "Well, what are you waiting for, Bryce? You have my attention."

Campbell glanced behind him once more, then jerked his chin. Stillman followed him down the veranda a ways to the west, until they were a good ten feet from the nearest clump of men. Stillman scowled at the little manager, whose large dark eyes always seemed to reflect his own inner darkness, his dark inner secrets. But today they did so in spades.

"All right, Bryce. We're alone over here."

Campbell turned from the bank to grimace up at Stillman. "You know those five well-dressed gents and that well-dressed woman, the really pretty brunette, who spent several days in town recently?"

"I believe I do, yeah," Stillman said with a nod. "Seen 'em around a few times."

"They were stayin' here at the Boston. Said they were scopin' out the country up this way, looking to maybe lay a spur railroad line down to Great Falls and Helena. Said they was from Kansas. The girl was the boss's daughter, they said."

"I saw 'em," Stillman said. "I didn't know that's what they were doing, but I figured they were in business, judging by the quality of their duds. They worked for a railroad line, you say?"

"That's what they said. Also said they was seein' about buyin' up land from here to Big Sandy for their rail line. But that ain't what I think they was *really* doin'."

"What do you think they were *really* doin'?" Stillman asked, his own suspicions stirring.

Campbell glanced at the bank. "I think that was them that robbed Kane. At least *part* of the bunch. They was all dressed different, and the men weren't shaved like they were when they were stayin' here last week, so it was hard to tell. There was more of 'em today—must've been eight or nine—and they were movin' fast. But them five was out there, part of it, sure enough. When I seen that woman lead the four horses up to the bank after they'd cut down Kane's men, I was pretty damn sure it was the same bunch."

"A woman," Stillman mused, rubbing his chin. He'd said the

words mostly to himself.

"What's that, Ben?"

"It was a woman, according to the kid, who shot Riley Hedges."

"Oh, no," Campbell said, frowning up at Stillman. "Old Riley's dead?"

"They killed him before they took the payroll. Must've wanted to make sure there were no surprises. They sent the woman to do it, if I can believe what the kid told me."

Campbell shook his head gravely. "Damn. I feel awful bad about this. I hope Mister Kane and Mister Garth don't hold it against me . . . that they was stayin' here while they sized up the situation with the bank and the payroll. I reckon I shoulda known they was trouble when . . ."

Campbell let his voice trail off.

"When what?"

"They had one hell of an argument. The woman and one of the men tore up one of my rooms pretty bad. They paid the damages the next day, but . . ."

"But what, Bryce?" Stillman asked, his voice taut with strained patience.

"I asked a couple of the fellas who farm between here and Big Sandy, between Big Sandy and Box Elder, if they thought they was gonna be rich soon on railroad money. They both told me that no one from no railroad had talked to them about anything like that." Campbell winced as though with a sudden pang of regret, and shook his head. "And they sure spent a lot of time, all five of 'em, sittin' out here on the veranda, talkin' in low tones and starin' at the bank." He winced again. "I reckon I shoulda put it together and talked to you about it."

"Oh, hell, Bryce," Stillman said. "Don't worry about it. I'm the lawman. If anyone should have noticed suspicious folks in—"

A voice cut Stillman off. "Hey, Sheriff—it's McMannigle!"

Stillman looked at Mort Seymour, a gunsmith standing on the far end of the veranda. The sheriff followed Seymour's pointing finger out to where Stillman's deputy was riding into Clantick from the east. Leon trailed four horses tied tail to tail behind him. Dust-powdered, Leon looked grim.

Over each horse, a man was tied belly down across his saddle.

CHAPTER SEVEN

Stillman rushed down the veranda steps.

As he stepped out into the street, it hit him like a clenched fist. A burning pain in his back. Right in the spot the Denver surgeon had cut out the bullet that had been getting way too cozy with his spine for the past ten years, wrapping itself in building layers of scar tissue, pushing against his spinal cord, causing his nerves to gutter like a candle flame, his legs to freeze.

He paused, bunched his lips, placed his fists on his hips, and twisted slightly back and to one side. The burning abated slightly, but he could feel an ominous tingle in his legs.

Shit.

He continued forward, suppressing the eerie, burning numbness in his back that was making his right leg go slightly stiff. Leon McMannigle rode up before him and stopped his steeldust and the four other horses behind him. Stillman stared down the line of the four horses and the dead men tied belly down across their saddles, their tied wrists tied to their tied ankles beneath their mounts' bellies.

"Found all four 'em about two miles straight east, Ben," Leon said, removing his dusty bowler from his head and beating it against his thigh. "Them robbers must've been waiting to take out anyone goin' after 'em. These fellas was layin' in the trail, rifles still in their saddle boots. None of 'em even had their pistols out. Bushwhacked. Dead before they hit the ground, most likely."

"Yeah," Stillman said, pondering the dead men. "Just like Riley Hedges."

"Hedges?"

"They got him, too. Before they hit the bank. Shot him in the office."

"Son of a bitch." Leon turned his head away sharply and barked out another angry curse. He turned to Stillman. "They're cagey, I'll give 'em that. They covered their tracks right after they hit these four Kane riders. Just like they sprouted wings and flew away. I thought I'd head back this way and organize a posse, go back out for a closer look and a hard shadowin'. I'll run 'em down."

"I'll get a posse together," Stillman said, "while you get those fellas over to the undertaker. He's doin' a hell of a business today."

"Maybe you'd best take a load off for a bit, Ben," McMannigle said, looking the sheriff up and down, frowning. "You don't look too good."

"I'm fi—"

"Sheriff!" A woman's voice cut Stillman off.

"Ah, hell," he grumbled, glancing over his shoulder to see Clarissa Kane dropping down the porch steps and striding toward him and McMannigle, chaps buffeting against her slender, denim-clad thighs.

"Sheriff, what is . . . ?" She let her voice trail off and slowed her stride when she saw the four horses standing in the street behind McMannigle, the dead men slumped over their backs.

Stillman turned to her, taking her by the shoulders. "Miss Kane, I'm gonna ask you to go on back into the hotel with your father."

She looked from the dead men to Stillman and flared an angry nostril. "You can ask me all you want, but that doesn't mean I'm going to listen to you."

She jerked free of the sheriff's grip and strode to the four horses. She walked slowly down the line of dead men, only the backs of their heads and their shoulders and backs showing, their cheeks or noses pressed against their stirrup fenders. Their hair slid around in the humid breeze, which was kicking up dust and churning it around.

Miss Kane stayed about seven feet away from the still heads of the dead men, until she came to the last horse. She walked even more slowly to that one, dropped to a knee, and leaned toward the horse's belly so she could get a look at the fourth dead rider. She placed a hand on the back of the dead man's head, then removed it abruptly as though appalled at the feel of death.

She looked back at Stillman, hardening her jaws angrily, then rose and stomped back to him. She stopped in front of him, her face a mask of pinched-up fury. "That's Noah Davis. He was only seventeen years old!"

Quietly, incredulously, McMannigle said, "Ben didn't kill him, Miss Kane. Them robbers did."

"It's all right, Deputy."

"The sheriff allowed those men to ride roughshod in his town. How could you not know such wolves were running off their leashes in Clantick, Sheriff? It is your job to know that!"

"Look, Miss Kane—"

"You know what I think, Sheriff? I think word has gotten around about your ill health. I don't think the bad element sees you as the formidable lawman you once were, so they think they can do what they want here. Why, you were laid up all winter and half the spring! How can we have confidence in your abilities anymore? I have a feeling this is just the start of a return to the lawlessness we all knew before you came!"

"Miss Kane," Stillman said, keeping his cool. "My health is back. If owlhoots had started thinking I was off my feed for

66

good—well, they'll know soon it's not true. Leon and I have this town and this county firmly in hand. If your father had informed me he was picking up a strongbox at the bank, I would have made sure he didn't try to pick it up on the day of one of the biggest weddings this town has ever seen. And I would have made certain there was no 'bad element,' as you call it, wandering the streets."

"You might have let us know, Miss Kane," McMannigle said in fiery exasperation. "Why, Ben and me was both in church!"

She swung around and fired a volley of her own cutting glares at the black deputy still sitting astride his steeldust. "How dare you raise your voice to me, you blue-gummed devil!" she fairly screamed. "Have you no regard for your—?"

Before he knew what he was doing, Stillman whipped his right hand up and slapped her.

There was a sharp *crack* as the hard flesh of his hand met the supple flesh of her left cheek. He hadn't meant to hit her, let alone hit her as hard as he had. He swung her half around. She staggered backward, pressing her hand to her cheek in wide-eyed, open-mouthed shock. She glared at Stillman a whole five seconds, apparently trying to wrap her mind around the fact that he'd had the gall to strike her, before she opened her mouth to speak.

Only a shrill cry issued from her trembling lips.

Her jade eyes filled with tears. She sobbed again, wheeled, and, still covering her cheek with her hand, ran up the veranda steps and into the Boston.

Everyone on the street must have seen the slap. A hush had fallen over this end of First Street. The men on the veranda fronting the Boston stared in wide-eyed surprise at Stillman. McMannigle stared at him, too. Gradually, the fury settled into a low fire in Stillman's chest and then the burn turned into the realization of what he'd done. Shame and embarrassment rose into his cheeks and ears.

The heavy silence was broken when a man on the Boston's veranda chuckled, muttering, "She sure had that comin'!" and then raised his half-empty beer schooner in salute before moving it to his lips.

Several others chuckled as well, and then the hum of conversation resumed.

Stillman turned to McMannigle staring down at him in wide-eyed disbelief. "Like I said, you best get these dead men over to the undertaker's," he said woodenly, numb from the shock of what he'd done. "I'll put a posse together. We'll ride out tonight. There's still plenty of light left. I don't want them to—"

"Ben, you're not riding with any posse."

Stillman turned to see that yet another person had walked up on him from behind. Doc Evans stood there, holding his medical kit down low in his right hand.

"What're you talking about?" Stillman said. "I'm healed."

"No, you're not," the doctor countered. "I can tell by the way you're standing. I could tell by the way you winced when you gave that nasty little filly the sound right backhanded cross she deserved, that you're in pain. You've been on your feet too long today. You've been moving around too much, and the stress of this situation—"

"Doc, I'm the sheriff of this county, and I'll be headin' up that posse," Stillman said.

"No, you won't."

Stillman jerked a shocked look at McMannigle. He knit his salt-and-pepper brows. "What?"

Leon shook his head slowly, resolutely. He turned toward the Boston's veranda and then toward the other side of the street, where another small crowd had gathered in front of a smaller saloon that housed a brothel in its upper story.

Leon raised his voice. "Fellas, we'll be needin' a posse to go after those bank robbers. How many of you will ride in a posse led up by the sheriff here?"

Evans looked around, furrowing his brows with admonishment. He looked like the bare-knuckle fighter he'd once been, giving his opponents the stinkeye.

No one on either side of the street said a word. Several looked away from Stillman's angry gaze, or peered down at their shoes. One man brushed a nervous fist across his nose.

McMannigle raised his voice again to yell, "How many of you will ride in a posse led up by this blue-gummed devil?"

Voices rose from both sides of the street.

"I'll ride with ya, Leon!"

"Count me in!"

"Over here! Let me fetch my rifle and my hoss!"

"Stella's gonna shoot me, but, yeah, I'll ride."

"I don't much care for runnin' down a rich man's stolen stash, but since it just as easily could've been my money stolen out of that bank—yeah, sign me up!"

"When we pullin' out?" another man said . . . until twelve men had thrown themselves into the fray and were splitting away from the crowd to fetch their horses and gear.

"Meet me at Auld's Livery Barn in one hour!" McMannigle shouted.

The deputy turned to Stillman as the crowds on both sides of the street disbursed. He gave a sheepish smile and a half shrug, then said, "I'll send the undertaker over to the office for Riley." He bunched his lips in anger. "We'll run those dogs to ground, Ben." Touching spurs to his steeldust's flanks, he started on down the street toward the undertaker's parlor, the four cadaver-packing horses tagging along close behind.

Stillman's gaze followed him until he saw Jody and Crystal Harmon sitting in the driver's box of their buckboard wagon a few feet away. Little Bill sat between them. All three pairs of eyes were on Stillman, touched with concern. Chagrin swept through the sheriff.

How much of the last several minutes had they seen and heard?

Jody glanced at Crystal and then shook the reins over the back of the dun in the traces, pulling up beside Stillman. "I sure hope you didn't see all of that," Stillman said, removing his hat and running a hand through his hair.

"You've had a long day, Ben," Crystal said. "Fay and Little Ben are waiting for you at home."

"Thanks."

"Katherine?" Evans asked.

"Last we saw her, she was getting into a buggy with Mrs. Bentley," Jody said. "Sure am sorry the wedding got interrupted, Doc."

"Men have died here today," Evans said, glancing around the bloody street. "In the scheme of things, my wedding is a small thing. We'll do it again . . . finish it." He gave a resolute smile. "I'd best go take another gander at Mister Kane, see how my sutures are holding."

Stillman knew the one he was probably really intending to check on was Kane's daughter.

When Evans was gone, Jody gave the reins to Crystal, kissed her and his son on their cheeks, and rose from the wooden seat. "I'll be joining that posse, Ben. Things are quiet out at the ranch just now, before the gather."

Jody leaped from the wagon and into the street. He was a wholesome, handsome young man—clean-shaven, even-featured, and long-limbed. He resembled his old man, Milk River Bill, but he also resembled his mother, a full-blood Gros Ventre Indian, with his dark-tan skin and straight, coarse black hair, which he wore cropped above his ears. "We'll run down those hardcases in no time. I heard they killed Mister Hedges."

"If you can spare the time, I'd appreciate it," Stillman said. "No one knows the Two-Bears like you, and I'm betting they're heading into them right now on their way to the Missouri River breaks."

"No doubt." Jody swung around and began walking in the direction of the livery barn to join the rest of the posse.

"You be careful, Jody Harmon!" Crystal admonished her husband.

She turned to Ben and studied him as though reading his mind.

The young woman wrinkled her nose and said, "You know the kind of man I was raised by, Ben," she said tautly, a flush rising in her cheeks. "I don't cotton to no man hitting a woman, but if you hadn't smacked Miss Kane, I would have climbed down off this wagon and done it for you. She deserved that and more."

Crystal placed her hands over Little Bill's ears, and added, "After what she called Leon, I was ready to pull the rifle out from under the floorboards here"—she stomped a shoe against the boards beneath the seat—"and fill her so full of holes there wouldn't have been anything left to bury but lead!"

With that, she raised her chin defiantly and shook the reins over the dun's back. The wagon lurched forward. Little Bill sagged back in the sack. As he and his mother rattled off to the east end of town and the trail that swung south into the mountains, he threw a hand out in a wave to Stillman, smiling.

The sheriff returned the child's wave and chuckled to himself. "Hold on tight, Little Bill. There's a wildcat in the hurricane deck!"

CHAPTER EIGHT

"Would you like a ride home, Doc?" Evelyn asked Clyde Evans as the doctor mounted the Boston Hotel's front veranda.

"Evelyn," Evans said, "I didn't realize you were still here."

Not only was she still here, she was still dressed for his wedding. As was Evans himself—and half the town. He felt a little ridiculous in the unusually fancy garb, under the circumstances, but he supposed Evelyn felt even more ridiculous to be so overly dressed for the bloody occasion.

"Still here, Doc," the girl said. "I figured you might need some more help or possibly a ride home."

"Thanks. That's very thoughtful." Evans stared up at a second-story window behind which he knew Carlton Kane was healing from the bullet wound in his leg. His daughter was probably with him. "I think perhaps I'd best check on Mister Kane again."

"You just sutured his leg not fifteen minutes ago, Doc."

"Yes, I know, but I just want to check to make sure they're holding."

"I'll join you."

"That's all right," Evans said quickly, a little distractedly. "I'll be right back. And, uh, I could use that ride back to the house if you don't mind waiting for me."

Evelyn smiled. The smile was a little wooden, Evans thought, half-consciously wondering why. She seemed reluctant to have him visit Kane's room alone. "Not at all, Doc."

"Is everything all right, Evelyn? If you've a young man waiting for you, you know I can—"

"Not at all, Doc," she said, her smile ironic now as she slowly shook her head.

"I'll be right back."

Evans brushed past her and into the large, airy lobby, nodding at Bryce Campbell manning the front desk. He strode past the desk and climbed the carpeted stairs to the second story. As he did, he opened his kit, removed a leather-covered flask filled with brandy, unscrewed the cap, and took a long, nerve-mending pull. To his unabashed delight, he'd discovered the flask in his medical kit.

He sighed, smacked his lips, dropped the flask back into his coat pocket, and patted it reassuringly. "Need to keep you close, old friend. Hell of a day."

Kane had taken one of the Boston's four suites—third door on the right side of the hall. Evans lifted his right hand to knock on the door, just beneath the numbered brass plate, but stopped when he heard Clarissa Kane's voice rake out angrily, ". . . and you know he hasn't put in a full day's work in months! He looks old and frail and, given that he had the nerve to hit me— *hit me, Father!*—I think he must be drinking again. You know the stories about him . . . his sloth and drunkenness, as well as his whore-mongering after he'd turned in his deputy U.S. marshal's badge."

Evans cursed under his breath and knocked three times, louder than he'd intended, on Kane's door. "It's Evans, Mister Kane."

"Yes, come in, Doc."

Evans opened the door. Kane lay on the bed to the doctor's left. He was under the covers, sitting up, two thick down pillows supporting him against the headboard. His leg was propped on two pillows under the covers, to avoid blood clots. The rancher looked bleak.

His daughter stood on the far side of the bed, her back to a long, velvet-draped window, arms folded across breasts that Evans always had a hard time keeping his eyes off of, whenever he saw her in town. She was nearly half his age, of course, but you didn't see many spectacular beauties in these parts. She and Fay Stillman were the only two women who could really be called spectacular—at least in the discriminating doctor's estimation.

And he'd never considered the lowly, sophomoric preoccupation of estimating women's beauty beneath him—not when he'd been nineteen and studying to be a man of medicine, and not as the forty-year-old man of medicine he was now. Of course, he should be ashamed of himself, and maybe he was in a vague, general way.

Mostly, however, he indulged himself. Why not? Life was short, and we were dead a long time.

Yes, Clarissa Kane was a ravishing, freckled, green-eyed beauty, all right. But she was also a bitch on high, red wheels. The stories Evans had heard about her were obviously true. He hadn't realized it until now.

Her right cheek was still red from Ben's backhand.

"Did you bring me up some special painkiller, Doc?" Kane asked. "I think I might be needing something a little stronger than the brandy you prescribed"—he glanced at the bottle Evans had ordered from the Boston's saloon and which was standing on the table beside the bed—"after learning that every single one of the men who came to town with me today will be going back to the ranch in wooden overcoats. Including my foreman and a seventeen-year-old boy."

"No," Evans said. "I'm sorry about your men, but that's about as strong as I can do. I rarely recommend laudanum, since brandy or whiskey is nearly as effective and not nearly as habit-forming, though I hasten to add that I'm not exactly a prime example of a man unencumbered by the whiskey habit."

He looked at the girl staring across her father's bed at him. "I can tell you, however, Miss Kane, that Stillman is not such a man."

"What are you talking about, Doctor? Speak plainly."

"Ben's not a drunk. He might have wrestled those demons in the past, but he wrestles them no longer. He's a damned good lawman, the best Montana has ever known."

Clarissa smiled. "Ah, so you were eavesdropping on my conversation with my father."

"I overheard what you said. It was slander, plain and simple. I actually came up here to make sure you were all right. Ben gave you a pretty good whack. Turns out I'm having to battle the urge to give you another good one. You might be beautiful, Miss Kane, and your father might be wealthy, but when you bandy about slurs like *blue-gum* in front of Stillman regarding his deputy and friend, you'll get your hat handed to you. Stillman is many things, most of them good. One of those good things is loyal to his friends. You'd be fortunate to be counted as Ben's friend. Believe me, you don't want to be his enemy. The human condition being as precarious as it is, our bodies vulnerable to injury and disease, you don't want to be mine, either."

"How dare you!" the girl snarled, clenching her hands into tight fists at her sides.

Kane laughed. "Clarissa, I recollect you did bid the man speak plainly!"

"I've had my say." Evans set his hat on his head and turned to Kane. "I'll be back in the morning to check that leg."

Kane pooched his lips and dipped his chin.

Evans did not look at Clarissa again before he left, drawing the door closed behind him and taking another deep pull from the flask before heading downstairs.

Evelyn was waiting for him in the lobby, sitting in a brocade armchair near the front doors. She wore a funny expression. Evans again noticed an oddness in her demeanor. It was probably just due to the recent killings, the ranch hands lying dead in the street. Evans had to remember that not everyone was as inured to such carnage as he was.

"How is Miss Kane, Doc?" Evelyn asked, rising from her chair.

Bryce Campbell cleared his throat meaningfully as he scribbled in his register book. The Boston's manager looked at Evans over the tops of his reading spectacles.

"If you're suffering from a peritonsillar abscess, Bryce," Evans remarked in a menacing tone, "I have a snare right here in my kit."

Campbell winced and returned his attention to his work.

"She's fine," the doctor told Evelyn.

He walked past her onto the veranda. She followed him out. Most of the crowd from earlier had dispersed. In the wake of the killing the street was nearly deserted. It was nearly six-thirty in the evening, with purple shadows deepening as they stretched out from First Street's high false facades. Pigeons flitted in the rays of the westering sun and warbled from the Boston's eaves.

Evans looked around, then glanced at Evelyn standing beside him. "Have you seen Katherine?"

"I saw her earlier. When I rode up to the Boston with your medical kit, I saw her and Mrs. Bentley pull up behind me in Mrs. Bentley's buggy. I haven't seen her since."

"Hmm. Funny she didn't check with me. She must've seen there wasn't much to be done, and gone on home."

"Would you like me to drive you over there, Doc? I'm sure you two have much to talk about."

Evans considered that. He stared off in the direction of Katherine's little house—the one in which she'd lived for many years with her husband, the reverend.

"No," he said. "No, I think I'll go on home. I'd like to get changed out of this monkey suit. With that posse heading out after those fork-tailed demons, I, as well as Katherine, might be needed later this evening. I want to be ready. I'll hitch up Faustus and pay her a visit a little later."

As he and Evelyn clattered east out of Clantick, toward his old, weather-battered house standing on its barren bluff, looking forlorn and abandoned, Evelyn glanced at the doctor and said, "Heckuva day, huh, Doc?"

"I'll say," Evans said with a sigh, loosening his tie. "I really need a nerve tonic. Forgive me." He pulled the flask out of his pocket and took another deep drink. He chuckled and leaned conspiratorially toward Evelyn. "Please don't tell my betrothed."

"Better not, Doc. Like you said, with that posse out, you'd best be ready."

Evans took another drink. "Dear girl," he said, ironically, "have I taught you so little? Whiskey steadies the nerves." He held the flask out to her.

She shook her head and said, "She's pretty, isn't she?"

Evans returned the flask to his pocket. "What's that?"

Evelyn glanced at him sidelong. "Miss Kane."

"Clarissa? Yes, she is. Headstrong, defiant, wrongheaded, foolish, and spoiled. And alluring as all get-out."

"I hear men talking about her in the café all the time when they think I don't hear. They don't realize I'm a snoop and I listen to everything." As she turned the wagon onto the trail that climbed the hill toward Evans's house, Evelyn tossed the sawbones another sidelong glance. "And I can read men's minds, too. That's what happens when you have a boring job you can do in your sleep."

Evans frowned. "And what were you reading in my mind that sparked this line of examination, pray tell?"

Evelyn hiked a shoulder. "Lust."

"Oh, well, hell." Evans laughed. "That doesn't make you clairvoyant. Just a young woman who knows me too well."

Evelyn turned her head sharply to him now, and her cheeks were red with fury, pale blue eyes shooting flame-tipped arrows. "Do you want to sleep with Miss Kane, Doc? And if you did sleep with her, would it be any different than when you slept with me? Or would she, like me, be just another conquest for you?"

"Oh, hell," Evans said as they approached the brow of the hill. Suddenly, he felt as though he'd been slapped. "Oh, Jesus, Evelyn—where did that come from? I didn't think we were talking about that any longer. I thought that was old history, not to mention taboo. If not for some curly wolves confiscating Kane's loot, I'd be a married man!"

They crested the hill. Evelyn pulled the wagon to a halt in front of Evans's front porch, and she turned to him again, her cheeks still aflame. "Answer the question, Doc."

Evans shook his head. "Look, Evelyn, dear . . ."

"Don't Evelyn dear me!"

"All right. All right." Evans threw up his hands. "What do you want me to tell you? Your estimation of me is spot-on. I am a deeply flawed human being. I am a cynical, soulless son of a bitch. I slept with you because you're young and pretty. I'd do it again right now if you were willing. Every man yearns to sleep with a younger woman. Don't let any man tell you different. Deep down, we're all lechers! I knew that by sleeping with you I'd probably be damaging our friendship irreparably—and possibly destroying my relationship with Katherine, as well. But I did it, anyway. My body hungered for yours. Pure and simple! And yes, it hungers for Clarissa Kane despite the demon-eyed, copper-riveted bitch she is. Despite what she said to Ben, despite what she called Leon. There you have it—the man I really am!"

Evans clamored down off the wagon, medical kit in hand. When his feet hit the ground, he stumbled and nearly fell before regaining his balance.

Evelyn stared at him, fury's rose flush rising into her forehead and the tips of her ears. Her lips trembled as she said in a near-whisper, "You're a bastard."

Evans laughed raucously. "Trite but true!"

"A *bastard*!"

Evans laughed harder. "So tell me—why did you want to sleep with *me* when there are many more, younger, handsomer men in town? Surely, you know I'm not wealthy." He threw an arm out toward his humble abode, the last rays of the dying sun reflecting off the windows so that he couldn't see the lamp burning inside. "You couldn't have been gold-digging. If you were, you're even sillier than I thought!"

"Is that what you think I am, Doc? Just a silly girl?" Evelyn stared at him in shock, her gaze probing his. Slowly she shook her head, and a thin sheen of tears shone in her eyes. "I thought I saw the good in you that others didn't. I thought I saw the good in you that you yourself didn't. I thought I saw a man who only needed love to fix him." She nodded. "That's right. I slept with you because I loved you, Doc. But the only reason you slept with me . . . this silly girl . . ."

A tear rolled down her cheek, and she quickly, angrily brushed it away. "The only reason you slept with this silly girl was for the same reason all the other *boys* I've ever known wanted to lay down with me."

Evans slapped the top of the wagon's near wheel. "There you have it!"

"Would you tell me one thing, Doc—straight up?"

"I thought that's what we've been doing here—having a straight-up conversation."

"Tell me that you love Katherine."

Evans scowled, blindsided by the question. "What?"

"Tell me the reason you're going to marry Katherine is because you love her. That you *really* love her. Tell me it's not just because you told her you would."

Evans laughed. "The reason I'm going to marry Katherine is because we'll make a good practice together, Katherine an' me. And because I promised her I would. You can say many things about Clyde Evans, but what you can't say, by god, is that I don't keep my word!"

He leaned forward, winking. "But just between you an' me, I might still give a run at Clarissa Kane . . . because life's short and we're dead a long time!" He winked again, and pressed two fingers to his lips. *"Shhh!"*

He jerked the flask free of his pocket and took another pull until he'd nearly emptied the vessel.

The screen door squawked behind him.

He pulled the flask back down and wheeled unsteadily to see Katherine Kemmett step out of his house and onto the front porch. A cold, wet stone dropped in Evan's belly.

"Katherine . . ."

She let the screen door slap shut. That was when Evans realized the inside door had been open. Now that the sun had faded further, he also saw the lamp burning in the window. Katherine stepped forward. She still wore the wedding dress and veil. The whiteness of her attire fairly glowed against the darkening house behind her.

Now as she walked down the porch steps, Katherine swept off the veil. The pins that had attached it to her hair fell onto the rotting wooden steps, making little *pinging* sounds in the silence. She approached Evans, her face a pale, stony mask, lips compressed in a taut line across the lower half of her face.

"Katherine," Evans said. "I . . . don't . . ."

Katherine stopped before the doctor and turned to Evelyn

sitting motionless in the wagon, the girl's face frozen in a look of shock and horror. "Evelyn, would you give me a ride to my house?"

The girl sniffed, swallowing. Her voice was thick with emotion. "Of course."

Katherine turned to Evans and blinked once, slowly. "I thought we'd have that quiet, private ceremony you wanted. The reverend and his wife and Irma are on the way here. Irma went to Sam Wa's for chicken and potato salad."

Evans said nothing. His heart beat heavily, slowly, painfully. His feet were stuck to the ground; his knees had turned to cement.

"Thank you for preventing me from making that horrible mistake, Clyde. And for letting me know, in your inept, intoxicated but highly effective way what a monster you really are . . . what I knew you to be all along, but for some reason denied to myself."

She gave a stiff, chilling grin. "I won't deny it any longer. You can go to hell, Clyde." She glanced at the house. "Dying alone here, by yourself . . . drunk in your sour old age . . . will be the same thing."

Katherine climbed onto the wagon and sat stiffly beside Evelyn, smoothing her dress against the backs of her legs. She sat staring straight ahead, the breeze touching her long, brown hair with its silver strands glinting in the waning light of dusk.

Evelyn glanced once more at Evans, then clucked the horse into motion. She swung the wagon around and rattled toward the edge of the yard. Two other buggies approaching from the opposite direction crested the hill just as Evelyn and Katherine did. The reverend and the reverend's wife were in the first rig, Mrs. Bentley in the second one. Covered baskets of food sat in the seat beside Irma Bentley.

The buggies stopped. There was a brief conversation. Evans

couldn't hear what was said. He didn't need to.

Evelyn clucked again, and she and Katherine drifted down the hill.

The other two buggies moved forward, then swung around tightly, the reverend, the reverend's wife, and Mrs. Bentley all casting Evans quick, dismissive glances.

Then they topped the bluff and were gone, leaving Evans staring after them, alone.

Chapter Nine

Stillman lifted his head off the cot with a start.

Outside, a dog barked angrily. As loud as the noise was, it had to be close to the courthouse. The sheriff dropped his feet to the floor. At the same time, a gun cracked. He flinched, heart quickening.

The gun cracked again.

The dog yelped.

Stillman had been about to pull his boots on, but now he rose from the cot and hurried over to the window that looked out on Second Avenue, which was gray now with the dawn. A dog was just then bounding into a gap between a lumberyard and an abandoned blacksmith shop. Four horseback riders milled in the street near the gap, one holding a smoking pistol barrel up in his right hand.

He said something and laughed, and then the others laughed as well.

"Damn," Stillman said, scowling out the window, blinking sleep from his eyes.

The man who'd fired the revolver was none other than Ray Bliss—the late Dave Bliss's brother as well as his ranch foreman. Ray was a thickly built, broad-shouldered man with a head like a giant sledgehammer capped with short, stiff, black hair under a low-crowned black Stetson. His face was also broad and flat, clean-shaven except for long black sideburns. He had a mottled, ruddy complexion, belligerent dark eyes, and thick, sneering lips.

The man was the epitome of a bully. Stillman always steeled himself for trouble when Ray and the other Circle 6 ranch hands came to town. He'd warned Dave Bliss about his brother some time ago, and that had helped rein in Ray. Dave had been a sensible man, the good brother. But now that Dave was dead, Ray was no doubt running things for Dave's wife, Ida Anne. The wolf was off his leash. That wolf would likely be running even wilder now that Stillman had Ray's brother's accused murderer locked in his cellblock.

Stillman returned to the cot. Grumbling and blinking, he sat down heavily and pulled on his boots. He'd spent the last two nights here in the office, but he hadn't slept more than a couple of hours either night. He hadn't had time to hire another night deputy since Riley Hedges's murder, and Leon and the posse were still out after Hedges's killers and the robbers of Kane's mine money. Stillman had had to keep an eye on the town.

Now he grabbed his holstered Colt and cartridge belt off his chair and buckled it around his waist. He plucked his hat off the tree by the door, stepped into the hall, and then pushed through the outside door, striding out onto the courthouse's front veranda just as Ray and the three other Circle 6 men swung down from their saddles.

"What the hell's all the commotion about?" Stillman grumbled, spreading his feet a little wider than shoulder width apart atop the veranda steps and hooking his thumbs behind his cartridge belt. "There's an ordinance against discharging firearms in town, Bliss."

Tossing his reins over one of the hitch racks fronting the veranda, Ray Bliss chuckled. "The dog had it comin', Sheriff. He came after us like he thought we was breakfast. Scared the horses somethin' awful. Too early in the mornin' for a racket like that."

He grinned at Stillman, but there was always something jeering even in Ray's smiles. He poked the brim of his black hat up off his broad forehead, planted one foot on the veranda's second step, and leaned forward. "Don't worry. I didn't hit him. Leastways, I don't think I did. Maybe just taught him a lesson."

"The fine is ten dollars."

A black cloud passed over the smiling sun of Ray's obnoxious face. "What's that?"

"The fine for breaking the city ordinance is ten dollars payable in cash. If you want to take it up with the judge, you're free to do so, but then you'll be payin' twenty. It's either ten to me or twenty to the judge. Take your pick, Ray."

Stillman knew to get the jump on Ray Bliss and others like him. Rock them back on their heels, keep them off-balance. If not, they'd just keep bulling forward, making them harder and harder to press back.

"I was shootin' at that damn dog, Stillman!"

"That's the Andersons' dog. A good watchdog. If you shot that dog, Ray, I'll shoot you. Now, like I said, you can either pay me or—"

"Enough about that!" Ray intoned, his face flushing with fury as he straightened his back and pinned Stillman with his typically bellicose gaze. "I understand you got my brother's killer locked up in your cellblock."

"That's right."

"We're here to let him out, Sheriff. Take him for a little walk." This from one of the other three smirking men flanking Ray. He was the shortest of the bunch—a brown-haired, blue-eyed firebrand named Normandy, Stillman thought. He wore a snake tattoo on the back of each hand and on both sides of his neck. Ben remembered Leon had locked him up for a couple of nights last winter, when he'd broken a gambler's nose in the Drovers.

"Yeah, we thought we'd stretch his legs a bit," said the man standing to Normandy's left, then spitting a tobacco quid to one side before grinning back at Stillman.

"We understand you're short-handed, Stillman," Ray said, winking, his wide mouth stretching into a sneering grin. "Thought you could use the help."

"I appreciate that," Stillman said. "You boys are right helpful. I'm going to decline your offer."

Ray hardened his jaws as well as his eyes again. "Look, Stillman, we know that kid murdered my brother. His wife, Ida Anne, is in a bad, bad way. Dave was a good man. He was a better man than me."

"Don't be so hard on yourself, Ray."

That caused Ray to tighten his jaws even more, and flare his nostrils. "We're offerin' to do you a favor, you stubborn son of a bitch! We'll take that killer off your hands for you. Why keep him locked up in there—eatin' an' shittin' an' whatnot? He shot Dave in the back. Let us take him over to one o' them big trees by the river and hang him."

Ray glanced around the street as he ran a grimy sleeve across his mouth. "Come on—it ain't even full light yet. No one's out and about but Sam Wa. That chink's always the first one up, splittin' wood for his stoves. We'll take Nevada wide around Wa's place and do you a big favor by hangin' him. Then you can go on home and get you some sleep. You don't look well."

"Word's goin' around you ain't gettin' back on your feet so fast, Sheriff," added Normandy with that slit-eyed, sneering, lopsided grin of his. His right hand rested over the top of the revolver in the holster on his right hip.

"Johnny Nevada will stand trial in due time," Stillman said. "What you fellas are talking about is vigilante justice. It's against the law."

"It's only right!" Ray barked. "You know the kid's gonna be convicted. Hell, several of Vince Patten's men seen him!"

"So they say."

Ray chuckled. "Why would Patten's men lie? They got no bone in this fight!"

"That is to be determined," Stillman said.

"What's that supposed to mean?" Normandy scowled. "You ain't makin' no sense!"

"Just as soon as my deputy returns to Clantick, I'm going to ride out to Patten's ranch and talk to the men who said they saw the kid shoot Dave. Then I'm gonna ride over and have a look at the murder scene myself. Nothing can or will happen regarding the fate of Johnny Nevada until I've done a thorough investigation."

The truth was, he'd already sent McMannigle out to look at the murder scene, and Leon had uncovered no clues as to the killer's identity. But neither he nor Stillman had yet talked to Patten's men. The judge had rushed the men out of town pretty quickly after they'd signed their affidavits, almost as though he hadn't wanted Stillman, the highest ranking lawman in the county, to talk to them.

That made Stillman suspicious. Especially given the county judge's obvious prejudice against Nevada. Johnny had impregnated the judge's shy daughter, Marnie, who, pushing into her mid-twenties while remaining single, was treading into that dangerous, much-maligned territory of the old maid.

Stillman wasn't sure how many folks around Clantick knew about Marnie's condition, and/or who the father of her unborn child was. So far, the judge and his wife had done a fairly good job of keeping the indignity under wraps and their daughter behind the closed doors of their large house along a creek one mile south of town. Even out there, it was doubtful they could keep the secret for long, however. Not in a town as small as Clantick. When the news broke, it would spread like wildfire. It would become the juiciest scandal the town had seen since its humble start as the sin-infested hide-hunting camp of Bullhook Bottoms.

Stillman had learned about the building scandal from Doc Evans, who'd only informed the sheriff after the judge had issued the warrant for the kid's arrest. Evans had rightfully thought the sheriff should be aware of a possible ulterior motive on Hoagland's part.

"Come on, Sheriff," Ray Bliss urged now, "forget the damn *investigation*. It's a waste of time. The kid's a no-good killer. He killed Dave because Dave ordered him to stay off the ranch and away from my niece. The kid threatened to kill Dave two weeks ago right here in town! Ain't that evidence enough? Besides, the kid's got it in his history. He killed several men in the same way, with a rifle from a tree, out in Nevada. Everybody knows that about him!"

"That's where he got his name, after all," added Normandy. "Johnny Nevada. Killer for hire." He grinned.

Stillman sighed. "Just the same, I'll be looking into the matter before the kid's trial. And he will have that trial. And I'm gonna make sure it's a fair one. Now, you boys go on back to the Circle 6. After you pay that fine, Ray." The sheriff held out his hand, palm up.

Ray's left eye twitched as he glared at Stillman. "You ain't really gonna hold me to that, now, are ya, Stillman?"

"Ten dollars. Right here. Right now. Or you'll be spending time with Johnny Nevada." Stillman added with a smile. "Don't worry—you'll have cell bars between you."

"I don't think you're in any condition to make a threat like that, Sheriff." Young Normandy stepped forward, sliding his Remington .44 from its holster.

Stillman jerked his Colt up and fired without hesitation.

The pistol's bark shredded the early morning silence for one startling second before the silence sank back down over the street, settling even heavier than before.

The shot had frozen all four Circle 6 men, who stood glaring at Stillman in wide-eyed, hang-jawed shock. Young Normandy's own startled eyes dropped to his boot as a warbling sound began rising from his throat. The kid lowered his hand from his pistol as the reedy wail became a long, drawn-out howl.

He raised his right boot from the ground. It had a quarter-sized hole in the middle of it. Blood oozed up out of the hole.

The kid's cry continued to grow shriller as he raised his boot higher, and then he slid his startled, pain-wracked, horrified gaze to Stillman, and said in a disbelieving tone, "That old bastard shot my foot!"

Ray Bliss turned to Stillman. "You're plum loco!"

Stillman slid the barrel of his smoking Colt toward Bliss. "You want one?"

"Hold up! Hold up, goddamnit!" Bliss backstepped, holding up his hands.

"Ten bucks."

"What?"

Stillman lowered the Colt's barrel, taking aim at Ray's right boot.

"Goddamnit!" Ray dug into his right pants pocket, pulled out a ten-dollar gold piece, and tossed it to Stillman.

Stillman smiled as he slipped the coin into his shirt pocket. "This has been an expensive ride into town for you, Ray. You best take your boys home before it costs you even more."

"You're one man, Stillman. Just one man . . . with a bad back."

"My back feels a lot better. But thanks, Ray."

"Just the same, you're one man. Till your deputy gets back, you're just one man."

"He needs a sawbones," said one of the two others crouching over Normandy, who was writhing on his back, both arms wrapped around his right knee, which he was drawing up to his chest. He rocked from side to side. Blood continued to ooze out of the hole in his boot and dribble in a thick string to the ground where it pooled.

"The doc's busy," Stillman growled. "Get him out of here."

"Damn you, Stillman!" the kid howled.

The other three managed to hoist him into his saddle. The kid held his head low, sucking sharply through gritted teeth. His face was as red as a Montana sunset. "You're gonna pay for that!"

Stillman smiled coldly. "You might heal . . . eventually. As long as infection doesn't set in. Gonna need plenty of rest. I did you a favor, kid. I'm giving you a good, long time now to think about your sins and consider your future. Take a long, hard look at it. You don't want to repeat the mistake you made here today."

"Fuck you!"

"And another thing before you go."

The four were mounted now and reining their horses away from the courthouse. They turned to Stillman, all four flushed with fury, the kid grunting, groaning, cursing, and holding his bloody boot down beside his right stirrup.

"If I see any one of you four in town again before next spring, I'm gonna haul you in on charges of attempted murder. That will get you ten to twenty in Deer Lodge."

The four riders cursed him without much imagination, then galloped down the side street toward the north, the direction in which the Circle 6 lay, about ten miles out, to the east of a jog of snaggle-toothed buttes standing up like mounds of charcoal against the eastern horizon as the early morning light gained intensity. The kid fell behind the others, hunkering low over his horse's pole.

When they'd dwindled into the misty distance, the clomps of their galloping horses gradually fading, Stillman holstered his

Colt and turned to go back into the courthouse. Movement on his right spun him in that direction, unsheathing the Colt once more and clicking the hammer back.

"Please, don't shoot me, Sheriff," a girl's high-pitched voice said from inside the female-shaped silhouette, as it moved out from behind the corner of the courthouse.

She was a slender, gray-eyed brunette in a flowered blouse beneath a denim jacket, a flowered gingham skirt hanging to her ankles. The toes of stubby black boots protruded from beneath the skirt's hem. On her head was a plain white bonnet, sitting slightly askew.

Stillman lowered his revolver. He glanced behind him, toward where the Circle 6 riders had disappeared, then turned to the girl again.

"You shouldn't be here, Sarah."

"I couldn't help myself, Sheriff," said Sarah Bliss, moving forward. "I have to see him."

CHAPTER TEN

"Does your mother know you're here?" Stillman asked Sarah Bliss.

The girl shook her head. She was eighteen or nineteen, but she looked younger, maybe because of her diminutive size and the guilelessness in her wide brown eyes. Stillman had seen her in town only a few times, as Dave and Ida Anne Bliss had kept their daughter, their only child, pretty close to the ranch, but he'd known who she was, though he couldn't remember exactly how. The town and county had a small enough population that most everyone knew everyone else, or knew *of* them.

"No one knows I'm here," Sarah said. "I followed Uncle Ray and the other men. I know what Uncle Ray wants to do. I heard them talking in the bunkhouse last night. I was so worried that I just had to come. As soon as they left the ranch earlier, I saddled my own horse and followed them."

"You know your uncle wants to hang Johnny Nevada, then," Stillman said grimly, casting another dark glance in the direction Bliss and the other riders had disappeared.

Again, Sarah nodded. "I told Uncle Ray he was wrong about Johnny. He would never shoot Pa. But Uncle Ray's got his mind made up. He told me just to go on back to the house and see to Ma."

"How's she doing?"

"Not well. She's taken to bed, mostly. She does a few things, but she's quick to tire. I hear her in their room—hers and Pa's—

and she's always crying. Muffled-like, as though she's crying into her pillow." Sarah grabbed Stillman's forearm and squeezed. "Sheriff, please don't hang him. I know Johnny didn't kill my pa. I just know it!"

"How do you know it?"

"I just know . . . and . . . Johnny was with me Friday night."

Stillman studied her skeptically.

"He was, Sheriff," the girl said. "Honest, it's true."

Stillman sighed. Indicating the courthouse's front door with his hand, he said, "Why don't you step into my office, so we can discuss this in private."

When Sarah had settled into the Windsor visitor's chair angled before Stillman's desk, the sheriff hiked a hip on a desk corner, spread his hands out on his thighs, and studied the girl again skeptically. She couldn't meet his gaze head-on but let her eyes flit from side to side, as if they were mice trying to outrun a dog in close quarters.

"All right, Sarah," Stillman said, "if you and Johnny were together, just *where* were you together last Friday night?"

"We met out by Lost Boy Creek just east of our house. We used to meet there once or twice a week—in secret, since Pa didn't want me seein' Johnny anymore, after Patten claimed Johnny long-looped his cows."

"What time did you meet Johnny out there, Sarah?"

"After I finished washing the supper dishes. Around seven-thirty. I told Ma I was gonna go for a walk and pick mushrooms to scramble with eggs for the men in the morning."

"Not to get too personal, and you don't have to be overly specific, but what did you do out by the creek that Friday night?"

"We just strolled along by the water and talked. That's all we ever did. Johnny's a complete gentleman. He'd hold my hand, but that was all. He said he'd never push a girl into doin' anything she wasn't comfortable with. He wasn't that kind of jake, is what Johnny said."

"And you believe him?" Stillman thought of Marnie Hoagland.

"We girls know when to believe a boy, Sheriff. And when not to. We have a good instinct about such things."

"I see."

"It's true," Sarah added defensively.

"Does anyone else know that you and Johnny met out by Lost Boy Creek that night?"

"No." Sarah frowned, shaking her head. "Pa hated Johnny. He forbade me to see him, so we couldn't let anyone know."

"You realize the reason your father hated Johnny was not only because he thought Johnny was steeling beeves from Patten. Dave did some digging and found out about Johnny's reputation out in Nevada."

"Yes. Johnny didn't do that, neither. The killin', like they said. None of that stuff."

"How do you know?"

Sarah jerked her head back, knitting her brows. "Because he told me. Johnny wouldn't lie to me, Sheriff Stillman."

"Okay." Stillman nodded. There was no point in pushing the issue. Obviously, Johnny could do no wrong in Sarah Bliss's soulful eyes. "Sarah, Johnny's grandfather also has an alibi for Johnny that Friday night."

"What's an alibi?"

"Proof that Johnny wasn't where the killing took place. Hec Fenton says Johnny was with him at his cabin that Friday night. All night long. So, you see, if what Fenton says is true, Johnny couldn't have been with you on Friday night."

Sarah sank back a little in her chair and drew a slow breath, a fatalistic sadness darkening her eyes. "So . . . he thinks Johnny is guilty. His own grandfather."

"Why do you say that?"

"Why else would Mister Fenton be lying?"

"You think Johnny's grandfather is lying?"

"I don't like calling anybody a liar, especially one of my elders, but that's the only explanation, Sheriff Stillman. Johnny was with me that night. We strolled together along Lost Boy Creek. No one else saw us, so all I have is my word. But I assure you, Sheriff, Johnny could not have shot Pa. Johnny was with me."

Stillman tossed his hat on his desk and ran a hand through his hair in genuine befuddlement, not sure who or what to believe. "All right, then."

"Sheriff?"

Stillman looked at her.

"I know about Judge Hoagland's daughter."

That rocked Stillman back a little. He jerked his gaze back to hers, frowning in surprise.

Sarah nodded in acknowledgment of Stillman's incredulity, and looked down at her hands resting palms up, fingers entwined, in her lap. "Johnny told me that Miss Hoagland claimed Johnny was the father of her baby."

"Oh, he did."

Sarah pursed her lips and shook her head resolutely. "That's not true about him, neither."

"Johnny told you the child isn't his."

"That's right."

Stillman didn't know what to make of that. To him, Johnny hadn't denied he'd fathered Marnie Hoagland's baby. Had he lied about that to Sarah? If so, it wouldn't be particularly surprising. It wouldn't mean anything about his involvement or uninvolvement in Dave Bliss's murder, either. It just stamped him a liar, which wasn't a hanging offense.

Sarah said pointedly, her tone briskly accusing, "Marnie says the baby's Johnny's, because she's trying to protect another young man—one she really loves—from her father's wrath."

When Stillman didn't address the issue, because he really had nothing to say about this subtopic that had little bearing on Dave Bliss's murder, Sarah continued, sitting forward in her chair, her visage imploring. "The judge won't give Johnny a fair trial, Sheriff. He'll hang Johnny out of spite, because he thinks Johnny shamed Marnie and their family. Oh, please, Sheriff— you have to set Johnny free. Can't you please set him free . . . based on what I just told you, if for no other reason? If you send him to trial, it'll be the same as killing him yourself for a crime he didn't commit!"

Stillman squatted beside the girl and placed a hand on her right wrist, looking up at her gravely. "Sarah, I can't set Johnny free. Not even after you told me he was with you Friday night. All this has to come out in the trial. I'll send the free attorney, Johnny's lawyer, out to get your statement. He'll probably ask you to testify. Concerning—Judge Hoagland, because of his involvement with Johnny, what with what he believes about Johnny and his daughter, he won't preside over Johnny's trial. If he hasn't already, he'll call in another judge from another county. He has to. It's the law."

"Do you promise?"

"Of course." Stillman took her delicate right hand in both of his and patted it reassuringly.

Sarah drew in a quick breath. She seemed reassured. "Can I see him?"

"Yes, you can see him." Stillman rose and arched an admonishing brow at her. "You don't have anything on you that he could use to try to escape—do you, Sarah? You didn't bring a gun or a file or anything like that, did you?"

Sarah flushed, offended. "Certainly not. I would never do anything like that, Sheriff."

"Any pins in your hair? He could use one to try to pick the lock."

She shook her head, letting her thin brown hair swish across her shoulders. "No pins."

"All right." Stillman grabbed the key ring off the filing cabinet and walked to the cellblock door, Sarah close on his heels. "I can't let you into his cell. You'll have to talk through the bars. You have ten minutes."

Stillman pulled open the door.

Sarah smiled up at him as she slipped eagerly into the cellblock. "Thanks, Sheriff."

"Watch your step, young lady."

Stillman closed the door but did not lock it. He left the key in the lock and slumped against the door, weary.

His heart was heavy for the girl. He didn't know if she was lying or if Hec Fenton was lying. But if Sarah was lying, she must have thought there was at least a chance that Johnny had killed her father. Or maybe she was so certain he was incapable of killing her father that she felt compelled to give him an alibi for the Friday night in question, even if she had to make one up.

She must really love him. Whether or not Johnny killed her father, Stillman had little doubt that Johnny Nevada would eventually break her heart.

"Are you all right?"

Stillman jerked his head up to see his wife standing in the open doorway to the hall. He hadn't closed his office door when he'd led Sarah in, and he'd been so lost in thought he hadn't heard Fay approach.

He smiled at his lovely wife. Fay's long, chocolate-colored hair was down, beautifully disheveled from the buggy ride from the house, her oval-shaped face with lustrous brown eyes deliciously flushed. She wore a dark-brown cloak over a cream housedress, and in both hands she carried an oilcloth-covered basket. From the basket emanated the smell of bacon biscuits and coffee.

"Couldn't be better," Stillman said, walking toward her. "Now."

He wrapped his woman in his arms, and kissed her with a passion that had exploded several years ago down along the Powder River near Milestown. The passion hadn't died, though circumstances had caused him and Fay to be separated for several years . . . until he'd discovered her up here in northern Montana. She'd been married to another man, a corrupt man. Stillman had ended up killing that corrupt man and taking his wife, the beautiful young French-American woman who should have been his in the first place.

Now she was. And he'd never let her go.

"How in the hell do you get more beautiful every day?" Stillman asked her, pushing her back a little so he could get a good, long look at her.

Fay had always been striking in an exotic, foreign way. A mystery. Growing up on the ranch had added a rawness about her, an earthiness, a frankness of character. Motherhood had done nothing to dampen her beguiling, erotic beauty. If anything, having the boy had only enhanced her allure, filling out her body, rounding her hips, swelling her breasts, and adding a shadowy depth to her intoxicating gaze that made her downright ravishing.

"It's just early and you're not seeing well yet," Fay said, smiling up at him as he rested his arms on her shoulders and gazed down at her. "Wait till the sun comes up."

"I don't think I'm gonna be able to stand being away from you another night, once I see you with the sun full on you again."

Fay looked concerned. "I take it the posse hasn't returned?"

Stillman lowered his arms. " 'Fraid not."

"Are you worried?"

"Concerned. But there's not much I can do."

"So what was the distraught look I saw on your face when I first came in?" Fay asked, crossing to the desk and setting the food basket on top of it.

"Sarah Bliss is in the cellblock visiting the kid."

"One Johnny Nevada?"

"That's right."

"I've rarely seen her in town. Her parents bring her in on the Fourth of July and Christmas . . ."

"They keep her on a short leash."

"Do you suppose that's why she was so taken with Johnny? She saw him as a bright light in her otherwise dim world?"

"I hadn't thought of it that way, but, thanks, teacher." Stillman grinned. Fay had taught school up until she'd had Little Ben. She currently tutored slower children now and then, those needing a little extra help and patience, but mainly her world now revolved around her small family and their old house on the hill by the river, as well as their chickens whose eggs Fay sold in town. Like Doc Evans, she also read books all the way through.

"Anything to help." Fay smiled.

Stillman lowered his gaze to his wife's ripe body, the mounds of her breasts pushing against her cloak. "Don't tease me."

"Down, fella. Here—look what I brought you and your prisoner."

She removed the cloth from the basket and set two plates wrapped in waxed paper onto Stillman's desk. She lifted the paper from one of the plates to reveal two steaming, buttery croissants stuffed with bacon and scrambled eggs. She lifted a slender crock jug out of the basket and set it beside the plates.

"Oh, god," Stillman groaned. "I didn't realize how hungry I was till now. Nor how badly I needed some mud."

"If you'll find me a relatively clean mug," Fay said, releasing the wire lock from the jug's mouth, "I'll pour you a fresh cup of mud, as you call it, *monsieur.*"

"I love it when you talk French. Could you—"

A light tap sounded on the cellblock door. Stillman, who'd gone to a shelf for a coffee mug, left the mug where it was and walked to the cellblock door. He opened it. Sarah stood in the doorway, looking down, her hair in her eyes. She didn't say anything.

Stillman drew the door wide, stepping back. "Sarah?"

She sniffed loudly, then lifted her face. It was red and puffy and tears were streaming down from her red-rimmed eyes. "I lied about meeting Johnny at the creek!" the girl fairly screamed.

It was more like the cry of an enraged wildcat.

"Johnny Nevada did kill my father, and I hate him for it! I hope he hangs!"

Sarah brushed past Stillman, sidestepped Fay, and ran out the office door.

Two seconds later, she dashed past the office's two front windows, likely heading for wherever she'd tethered her horse, and was gone.

CHAPTER ELEVEN

"Well, I hope you enjoyed your visit," Stillman said when he took Johnny Nevada the two croissants that Fay had made for him. "Sarah didn't seem to."

The kid sat on the edge of the iron cot in his cell. He was leaning forward, elbows on his knees, head in his hands, his right wrist in the cast Evelyn had made.

The kid didn't respond. He just sat there, the picture of sadness and misery.

Stillman knocked the tin plate against the bars. "Come and get your breakfast. Croissants. My wife made 'em. I usually get breakfast for my prisoners, when I have any, from Sam Wa. But Fay wanted to bring me her own cooking, and it wasn't more trouble to bring yours, too. Better than Wa's. You're in for a treat."

"I ain't hungry," Johnny said, not moving.

"Come on—you'll feel better after you eat, kid."

The kid sighed, lifted his head, and then rose slowly to his feet. He walked to the front of the cell and Stillman slid the plate through the small, rectangular opening just above the lock.

"Sure smells good," the kid said. "Maybe I'll have a few bites."

"Sarah left here pretty sad," Stillman said, probing. "Not just sad. Mad. As an old wet hen."

"I heard."

"Then you probably also heard her say that you killed her

101

father. She hopes you hang. A far different tune from the one she was singing earlier."

The kid nodded. He stared down at the plate in his hands, but what he seemed to be thinking about was the girl. He looked up at Stillman. "She knows I didn't kill her pa. She was just mad. I reckon I broke the poor girl's heart, Sheriff."

Johnny took the plate over to the cot and sat down heavily, like an old man.

"What did you say to her?" Stillman asked.

"I told her that there was no point in her comin' to see me anymore. I told her we'd best break off whatever it was we had goin'. Then I told her we didn't really have anything goin', anyway, so she should just go on home and forget about me."

"Why did you tell her that, Johnny?"

The boy scowled at Stillman. "Because you and I both know I'm going to hang for her father's murder, Sheriff. Look, I know you're a fair man, but the cards are stacked against me. I heard Ray Bliss out there earlier, before Sarah came. He has a lot of pull in this county, Ray does. Even if the judge don't hang me, which he likely will, Ray Bliss'll see that I'm wolf bait. If he doesn't dry-gulch me, he'll have someone else do it."

"You'll have a jury trial, Johnny. Six citizens who have no bone to pick will hear your story. And Judge Hoagland will have nothing to do with it. He can't, given your relationship with his daughter."

"Marnie ain't been here, has she?"

"No." Stillman frowned. "Did you think she'd visit?"

Johnny lowered his head again, staring down at his plate in his lap without seeing it. He hiked a shoulder.

Stillman said, "You told Sarah that Marnie's baby wasn't yours?"

"Earlier, I did, yes. It was a lie."

"And this morning?"

"This morning I told her the truth—that the baby's mine," Johnny said, looking up at Stillman again. "That's what really set her off."

"Don't doubt it a bit." Stillman shook his head. "Kid, you sure have a way with women."

Johnny set the plate with the two croissants on the little wooden table and then lay back on the cot, stretching out his legs and crossing his ankles. "Yeah, well, tell me somethin' I don't know, Sheriff. I've been a rapscallion, through and through. Had two goin' at once. I thought I was real smart. One in the country. One in town. I reckon I outsmarted myself, though. I'm gonna hang for seein' two women at the same time, because there's nothin' else they can hang me for. It's the only thing I'm guilty of!"

He grunted a caustic laugh.

Stillman studied the kid lying on the cot, hands laced behind his head, staring at the ceiling. Johnny was obviously a good liar. Had he been lying to Stillman here this morning, the way he seemed to lie to everyone else constantly?

Impossible to know.

He'd probably killed Dave Bliss and was only trying to pluck Stillman's heartstrings.

But if he hadn't killed Bliss, who had?

Who else had a reason to?

If Leon were back, Stillman could ride out to the Circle 6 and talk with Bliss's widow. He also wanted to talk to Patten's Triple Box X riders.

"Eat up, Johnny," Stillman said as he turned away. "You'll feel better."

The kid did not respond.

Stillman climbed the stone steps to his office. He was placing the keys atop the filing cabinet when there was a knock on his office door, and Judge Hoagland's assistant, Maynard Grimm, poked his bespectacled head into the room.

The dandified, rail-thin little man in a three-piece, checked suit and with a carefully trimmed mustache, in his early thirties, carried the weekly *Bugle* in one hand, his crisp derby in the other hand. His shiny bald head reflected the buttery light of the early-morning sun angling in through the courthouse's front windows.

"Sheriff Stillman?"

"What is it, Maynard?"

"The judge wanted me to tell you to have your prisoner upstairs and ready for trial tomorrow morning at ten a.m."

Stillman's lower jaw dropped nearly to his chest. *"What?"*

"He'll be gaveling in the trial tomorrow. I've already seated six jurors from a previous draw. They're all ready to go. The witnesses have been notified."

Stillman shook his head, scowling. "But the judge can't preside over that trial. He knows he can't. Besides, I haven't had time to investigate Patten's men or even talk to Bliss's widow!"

Grimm hiked a shoulder. "The judge seems to think everything's in place, Sheriff. I'm just relaying the message. Have a good day."

"Hold on!" Stillman caught up to the little man in the hall. Maynard looked up at the obviously angry lawman towering over him, and swallowed.

"Sheriff, please . . ."

"Where's the judge? I need to talk to him."

"He's working at home today. His gout flared up again."

"Gout, huh?" Stillman tightened his fists at his sides and ground his molars until they almost cracked. "I'll give him something to take his mind off his gout!"

"Uh . . . good day, Sheriff Stillman." Grimm backed away cautiously, as though from a rabid wildcat that had just walked into his camp. Then he turned and climbed the stairs to the courtroom and the judge's chambers on the second floor.

Clyde Evans lifted his head from his pillow, yowling, *"Good lord in heaven, what in hell is happening to me?"*

Simultaneously, the doctor was struck by a barrage of sundry discomforts, the primary two being the rough lap of a wet dog on his cheek, and the rusty railroad spike being driven through his head by a mallet-wielding giant as angry as a sack full of diamondbacks. The dog was even more persistent than the giant, licking his cheek and lips and nose, all the while whining and moaning without mercy.

"What is it, Buddy?" the doctor said, trying to push the dog away and grimacing against the mutt's shaggy, dew-wet, burr-infested coat. "What in the hell are you doing inside . . . and what has got your tail in such a twist? You haven't been shot at again, have you?"

The black, white, and brown collie dog sat down between Evan's spread legs but kept his chocolate-brown eyes riveted on the doctor's, opening and closing his mouth, lifting each paw in turn, and moaning. Buddy was a stray whom Evans had found in the tumbledown barn on his property some months ago. He'd been eating right along with the feral cats the doctor fed, the cats apparently having no fear of him and Buddy obviously having no fear of the wildcats. He was a fairly young dog, nimble as a coyote, but deathly afraid of humans—aside from Evans, that was, after Evans started leaving his meat bones on the back porch for the obvious stray.

When it appeared the dog was going to stay—between prolonged hunting trips in the countryside, that was—Evans had started calling him "Buddy," mostly choosing the name at random, but also because he'd become a pretty good pal. Better than most humans, anyway, which wasn't saying much. More and more frequently the dog would sleep on the porch, on the blanket the doctor had placed there for him, and there had been a few times when he'd come into the house when Evans had inadvertently left one of the doors open while he fetched firewood.

The doctor must have left a door open again last night. Raking his hands down his face and gritting his teeth against the relentless pangs of his hangover, he chastised himself for the oversight. Once, last year, he'd left a door open and two raccoons had gotten in. They hadn't been hard to chase out but the cloying, sweet odor of the wild they'd left behind had lingered for days.

Had such visitors come calling again?

As if in response to the doctor's unspoken question, Buddy turned to a window on Evans's left, and gave three sharp, anxious yelps. It was then Evans heard the thudding of horse hooves and the clatter of a wagon. The sounds grew louder. Evans turned to gaze through a cracked, grime-streaked window on his left to see a horse cresting the bluff on which his house sat. A wagon followed. It was Sam Wa's buckboard, rattling like a tinker's wagon. Evans recognized the round-faced blonde in the driver's seat as Evelyn.

"Oh, shit," Evans said. "She's back to berate me some more for my sins."

The dog moaned, leaped off the bed, and ran downstairs, barking furiously. The din seemed to energize the mad, club-wielding giant in the doctor's head.

Evans clamped his hands over his ears. "Oh, please . . . for Christ's sake . . . won't everyone just leave me be?"

Quickly, Buddy's barking dwindled into the distance. Frightened by the visitor, he was likely heading for the tall and uncut. Evans knew how he felt. He lay back and, gritting his teeth, clamped his hands over his ears. But if he didn't answer the door, Evelyn would let herself in. And she'd see what a mess he'd made of the house last night, when he'd been stumbling around drunk, knocking over stacks of books and whatnot while he'd been drinking and sobbing and asking God or the Great Spirit or whomever was in charge why he couldn't have turned out like everyone else.

Normal. At least, not a monster.

Not a drunken recluse whose best friends were dogs and wild cats and books, but a stable man who deserved a good, stable woman.

He had to get downstairs . . .

Cursing and gritting his teeth against his agony, he crawled off the bed and, since he was clad only in white cotton balbriggans, he shrugged into his red-plaid robe, donned his deerskin, wool-lined slippers, and negotiated the narrow, creaky stairway, which he'd turned into a dangerous obstacle course by also using it for storage. Buddy had knocked over a stack of medical magazines, making the descent even more treacherous.

Evans slipped once on his journey to the bottom. A part of him wished he'd fallen and broken his neck. He was not only badly hungover and depressed, but he felt hopeless as well. Hopeless and ashamed. He was a bitter, lonely little man, jilted by a good woman for perfectly reasonable reasons, and now a pretty young woman was here to hammer the nails in deeper.

Why couldn't everyone just go away? He wanted to sleep through this day, drink himself comatose again tonight, and start the process all over again. If only no one in two hundred square miles would get sick for at least a month . . .

On his way through the living room, he smacked his lips. His mouth tasted like a barn filled with moldy hay. He glanced around, saw a half-empty bottle of brandy, and took a couple of deep slugs. He sloshed the last slug around in his mouth before swallowing it, then walked to the front door.

He must have left the back door open. This one was closed. He opened it and, squinting against the sun assaulting his eyes like a million tiny javelins, he stepped out onto the dilapidated porch. Evelyn was just walking up from the wagon, her work apron buffeting in the late-morning breeze against her thighs.

She stopped and looked up at the doctor, tucking a vagrant lock of hair behind her ear. She looked skeptical, vaguely sheepish, concerned.

"All right, let's have it," Evans said. "Say what you want to say, let me have it between the eyes. Just know it's not going to change one damned thing."

"I just stopped to check on you, Doc."

"You did?"

"Yeah. We were out of eggs after breakfast, so Sam sent me over to Mrs. Stillman's for some more. You know how those railroad men like having their breakfast served all day long."

The Stillman farm was perched on a bluff only a few hundred yards to the north and east, on the north side of the Milk. Evans's place wasn't much out of Evelyn's way.

She mounted the porch steps to stand beside him. Her voice was soft, sympathetic, caring. The voice with which you'd talk to an invalid. "You look like hell, Doc."

"It's an appropriate way for me to look," Evans said. "Since that's how I feel."

"Did you just get up?"

"Yes."

"What time did you go to bed?"

"I think the sun was just beginning to lift its wretched head."

She squeezed his arm, pressing her forehead to his shoulder. "Oh, Doc."

Evans looked down at her.

"Is there anything I can do to help?" she asked, crinkling her

eye corners as she looked up at him. "Can I make you breakfast?"

"I'm not hungry."

"Have you had coffee?"

"No."

"Can I make you some?"

"The range isn't lit."

"You should have something."

"I have plenty of brandy."

Evelyn's voice was maternal, admonishing. "You've had
enough brandy." She wrapped her arm around his waist.
"Come—let me help you back into bed."

He let her turn him around and lead him into the house.
They both laughed as they negotiated the near-deadly stairway,
knocking over a couple more stacks of books and a crate of
empty bottles. When they finally gained the second story, Evelyn led him into his room and gently shoved him down on the
bed.

"Let's get you out of your robe." Evelyn untied the velvet
drawstring but Evans pulled it away from her.

"No, I'm all right."

"Oh, Doc, let me hel—" She stopped when, having opened
his robe, she glanced down between his legs to see that at least
one part of his anatomy was fully functioning. Evans glanced
down, as well, and was horrified to see that the anatomy in
question was sticking its swollen head out of his longhandles'
fly. He could feel the cool morning air of the room on it.

"Oh, shit," he groused, pulling the robe closed and squirming
around on the bed, hanging his head in shame. "It's just one
goddamned humiliation after another!"

Evelyn didn't say anything for what seemed a long time.

Finally, Evans looked up at her. At first, he thought she was
going to lay into him. Her face was somewhat pale, her eyes

oblique. Slowly, a flush rose into her heart-shaped face, and her lips parted slightly. She lowered her head to his, and he still wasn't sure what she was going to do until he felt her lips on his.

She opened her mouth. Her tongue flicked against his own.

She moaned, wrapped her arms around his neck, and kissed him even more hungrily.

Finally, she pulled her head away, and stepped back.

"Oh, Christ," Evans said, guilt-ridden, breathless, amorous.

He thought she'd turn and run out of the room, but instead, she said, "lay back on the bed, Doc."

She reached up to her collar and began unbuttoning her flowered print dress.

"What?" Evans said, still breathing hard, only vaguely aware of the hangover now.

"Lay back on the bed."

Evans pushed himself up onto the bed and rested his head on his pillow. Lust throbbed in him as he watched the young woman slip out of her dress and pantalets and stockings. She walked over to the bed clad in only a thin chemise. Her pear-shaped breasts jostled behind the wash-worn cambric. She crawled up onto the bed and straddled him.

She leaned down toward him—closer, closer, closer, her eyes and lips and nose growing larger before him, until they were kissing again and she was rubbing herself against him, down there. He could feel the light prickling of her pubic hair on his hardness. Her pale, bare knees were on the bed to each side of him, snugged up tight against his ribs. He placed a hand on each, enjoying the warmth of her flesh.

Oh, Christ, what a sweet sensation. A lovely, nubile young woman in his arms!

Guilt and all other cares, and even the agony of the hangover, rose away from him like an ugly, ungainly bird taking flight.

She lifted her head from his, reached down between them, took him in hand, and positioned herself. As she did, he lifted his hands to manipulate her breasts through the chemise. They came alive at his touch, the nipples reacting to his playful ministrations.

Evelyn closed her eyes, smiled, and slid up and down on top of him.

Her hair danced across her cheeks, which the flush pinkened, suffusing her entire face.

She quickened her pace until her hair was flying wildly across her face and shoulders, and the bed was jouncing and she was yowling and Evans was grunting through gritted teeth. Finally, feeling them both rising toward the apex of their desires, he sat up, threw the girl onto the bed beside him and, keeping himself inside her, finished them both off at once.

Evelyn squealed as she turned her face to one side and chewed her knuckles, her supple body quivering beneath him as though she'd been struck by lightning.

Evans rolled off of her, sweating and breathless.

Evelyn rolled toward him and, propped on an elbow, smiling down at him. She tucked her mussed hair behind her ear. Her face wore the beautiful, glowing aura of sexual satisfaction. The ends of her long blond hair caressed the mottled orbs of her breasts. The nipples were still distended. She kissed his forehead, pressed her right index finger against his lower lip, and considered him for a long time, her eyes slightly crossed.

In the waning of his desire, befuddlement washed back over the man. An ominous prelude to the return of his hangover and the realization of another huge mistake?

Evelyn rose from the bed and gathered her clothes, bouncing lightly on her little pink feet. She seemed as happy and coquettish as a schoolgirl. She kept glancing at him from behind the tattered curtain of her hair.

"What the hell just happened?" he asked, finally finding his voice as she tied her apron around her waist.

"Fate, Doc." Evelyn walked to the door, winking at him over her shoulder. "Just fate."

With one more wink, she left.

Evans let his head sink back against his pillow and stared at the water-stained ceiling. "Fickle bitch, ain't she—fate?"

CHAPTER TWELVE

Stillman pulled back on the claybank's reins.

"Whoa there, boy," he said quietly.

When the horse and the buggy had stopped on the trail south of Clantick, Stillman turned his head to look over his left shoulder. At the same time, he unsnapped the keeper thong from over the Colt riding on his left hip, butt angled toward his belly.

It was after sunset, the sky sprinkled with guttering stars, only a smudge of rouge-colored light remaining in the west. Staring straight back behind him, Stillman could see nothing but the vague outline of the trail running along the shaggy outline of Beaver Creek on the trail's right side. It was quiet enough out here, a half mile from town and with only a slight, intermittent breeze, that he could hear the soft chuckle of the creek as it rippled over rocks.

He also heard the faint clomps of horses.

Suddenly, the comps died. Now there was only the sound of the creek.

A minute before, Stillman had heard something behind him. A horse's snort or whicker. Now, having heard the hooves, which had eerily fallen silent after he'd stopped the buggy, he was sure that someone was back there, possibly following him out from town.

Stealthily following him out from town. They obviously didn't want him to know they were back there . . .

Stillman lightly flicked the reins over the clay's back and swung the horse off the trail's left side. He held the horse to a slow walk, to make as little noise as possible. The buggy's wheels creaked softly, brush whispering around the felloes. He dropped down a gentle decline and pulled the horse and buggy into some chokecherry brambles, where it wouldn't be seen from the trail.

Stillman set the brake and climbed gingerly down, weeds crunching softly beneath his boots.

"Stay, boy," he ordered the horse, patting the clay's rump reassuringly.

He walked slowly, crouching, toward the trail, staying behind a knoll ahead and on his right. When he could see the light-tan line of the trail twenty feet ahead of him, he stopped near a cedar and dropped to a knee.

He waited, pricking his ears, listening.

For a full two minutes he could hear nothing but the creek's murmur in its twisting bed behind him, and the yammering of a pair of coyotes in the Two-Bear Mountains humping blackly against the starry sky to the south.

A faint *clink* sounded ahead of him, off the trail's opposite side and behind a rise of ground to the north. A bit rattled in a horse's mouth?

Stillman slid the Colt from its holster and held it low in his right hand, thumb caressing the hammer. He rose and strode quickly across the trail and into the brush on the opposite side. Crouching, trying to make as small a figure as possible against the sky to the south, he walked along the shoulder of the rise until he could see the faint line of a wash ahead of him.

He took another step forward. A branch snapped beneath his right boot. He stopped, cursing softly but sharply through gritted teeth.

A gun flashed thirty feet ahead of him. For a split second, the red-blue light rent the darkness and blossomed on his retinas. The rifle's crash split the night's hushed silence.

Stillman threw himself to his left and rolled twice as the shooter sent two more rounds hurtling toward him, thudding into the ground behind him. He turned onto his belly, extended the Colt straight out in front of him, and fired twice at the spot where he'd seen the flash. The thunder of the revolver assaulted his ears and set up a low ringing in his head.

The smell of cordite peppered his nostrils.

He rolled two more times to his left, not wanting his own gun flashes to make him a target. He waited, holding his cocked Colt straight out in front of him, aiming at where he thought the dry-gulcher had fired from. Silence had descended once more.

Even the coyotes had stopped yammering to the south. A faint breeze licked at the branches of a nearby, lone cottonwood.

Suddenly, hoof thuds rose. A horse whickered. A man shouted, *"Hi-yahh!"*

Stillman rose and ran forward. He ascended a slight rise, pushed through thick brush, and dropped into a dry wash. The hoof thuds dwindled down the wash to his left.

Another horse whinnied on his right, loudly, maybe twenty feet away.

Stillman threw himself forward as a gun flashed and barked. He rolled onto his left hip, extended his Colt to his right, and fired three times quickly. A man yelped. Hooves thudded off down the draw to the east. They faded quickly until the night's heavy silence had descended once more.

Stillman started to rise, then winced as what felt like the teeth of angry dog chomped into his right leg. He looked down. He couldn't see anything, but when he lowered his hand, he felt the oily blood oozing up from a tear in his denims.

115

The second dry-gulcher's only bullet had grazed him.

"Shit."

Stillman probed the wound with his hand. It probably hurt worse than it was. He didn't think the bullet had gone very deep, merely nipping the outside of his leg about eight inches up above his knee. He'd live.

Removing his bandanna from his neck, he wrapped it around his leg, knotting it tightly, then heaved himself to his feet. The bullet burn continued to feel like that dog's stubborn bite as he moved out of the draw and began retracing his steps in the direction of his rented buggy.

He limped a little, easing the pressure on the burned leg, trying to hold the bleeding at bay. He'd let Doc Evans take a look at it later, maybe sew it up if he thought it needed suturing. At the moment, Stillman had bigger fish to fry.

He wondered who the ambushers were. They'd obviously followed him out from town. Possibly Ray Bliss and his cohorts from the other morning at the courthouse. Or maybe Bliss had sicced someone else on Stillman. There was a chance that Bliss had a party in town right now, trying to drag Johnny Nevada out of his cell to hang him. If so, Bliss wouldn't have much luck. There was only one way into that cellblock, through Stillman's office, and Stillman had taken one set of keys with him. The other set was in his office safe. No one would get through that heavy, iron-banded cellblock door without using a Napoleon cannon or dynamite. And there was heavy steel mesh over the cellblock's iron-banded windows. No one could shoot through it.

The kid would be all right for the time being.

He wouldn't be all right for long, however, if Stillman didn't make it out to the judge's place tonight and try to convince Hoagland not only to recuse himself from the trial but to postpone the trial until Stillman had time to make a thorough investigation into Dave Bliss's murder.

As it was, Hoagland was jumping the gun.

Stillman knew why, and he didn't like it at all. He and the judge had always been friendly but Stillman didn't feel one bit friendly toward him at the moment.

He was crossing the trail when he heard more hoof thuds to the south. A rider coming fast. Stillman unsheathed the Colt. Horse and rider were an inky, jostling silhouette moving up the grade about fifty yards away and closing, the hooves' rataplan growing louder.

"Name yourself!" Stillman yelled.

The horse whinnied as the rider jerked back on the reins. As the horse curveted, rearing, a girl's voice yelled, "Evelyn Vincent!"

"Evelyn?" Stillman lowered the Colt. "What in the hell are you doing out here?"

"Ben?" The girl gigged her horse ahead. As she approached on the filly Evans had given her, she said, "I was taking a ride. Got caught out after dark. Getting later in the year than I thought. What was all the shooting about, Ben?"

"A couple of fellas were badge-huntin'."

"Who?" Evelyn asked in exasperation.

"Didn't catch their names. I think I might have winged one of the sonso'bitches—pardon my farm talk."

Evelyn's eyes dropped to the bandanna tied around Stillman's leg. "Are you hit?"

"Just a burn."

"Let me see." Evelyn swung down from the saddle. She was clad in denims and a checked blouse, a felt hat on her head. Her blond hair was gathered into a horse's tail that trailed down her left shoulder.

"I'm all right. Just bled a little's all. I have to get over to Judge Hoagland's place before he turns in."

"Is it about Johnny?"

"Don't tell me you're on a first-name basis with that kid now, too?"

Evelyn hiked a shoulder. "I've only seen him a couple of times, but he seems nice enough. He thanked me kindly for setting his wrist."

Stillman gave an ironic chuff and shook his head.

"What is it?" Evelyn asked.

"Nothin'. I just don't know what to make of that kid is all." Stillman started walking toward the buggy but then stopped and turned around. "Tell me somethin', will you, Evelyn?"

"I'll tell you anything you want if you let me ride along with you to the judge's place." The girl gave a sheepish shrug. "I'd kind of like to talk to you about something that's weighing on me, Ben."

Stillman looked around. "That might be a good idea. With those two toughnuts around, you shouldn't be alone out here after dark. Not that I'm the safest place to be, either." He continued walking somewhat stiffly toward the buggy. "Wait here. Don't talk to any strangers while I'm gone," he dryly quipped.

Stillman drove the buggy back onto the trail. As he continued his journey south along the two-track stage road that followed the creek's curving path, Evelyn rode her filly up beside him, keeping pace.

"What is it you wanted to ask me, Ben?"

Stillman held the reins high against his chest but loose in his hands. "Would you trust Johnny Nevada any farther than you could throw him uphill against a Texas tornado?"

"I reckon I've never been to Texas, much less faced any tornado, but no, I wouldn't."

Stillman looked at her. "Really?"

"Really." Evelyn shook her head resolutely. "You know about

my past, Ben. You're the one who got me away from . . . well, away from the bad element, shall we say? I've learned from my mistakes. No girl in her right mind should trust a boy like that."

"But you just said—"

"I said I thought he was nice. I've known a lot of nice young men who didn't turn out so nice once I started trusting them and let them wriggle their way into my life. Johnny Nevada's got a syrupy tongue. I don't trust boys with syrupy tongues, no matter how nice looking they are. Not anymore I don't, anyway."

"What do you suppose Sarah Bliss sees in him?" Stillman would have asked her about Marnie Hoagland, as well, but he didn't know if Evelyn knew about Marnie's condition. Stillman loved Evelyn like a daughter. That's why he'd taken her under his wing and gotten her away from a bank-robbing gang several years ago, not long after he'd come to Hill County.

But the girl was not known for keeping secrets. On the other hand, it was her loquaciousness and affability that had made her the sweetheart of most of Clantick and the most well-liked waitress in the county.

"It's not what she sees *in* him," Evelyn said. "It's what she sees on the *outside*. That's what she likes. I doubt Sarah Bliss has had enough experience with boys to fathom the nastiness that can lurk behind a charming pair of eyes and a dimply grin, or hear the lies behind a man's words." Evelyn looked at Stillman. "The same goes for Miss Hoagland."

"You know about that?"

Evelyn nodded. "Sam's other waitress—that new girl, Candace Tate? She's even snoopier than I am, if you can believe it." Evelyn snickered. "Candace said she saw Marnie and Johnny Nevada walking right out here along Beaver Creek one day early in the summer. Once she saw them holding hands, another time they were swimming together and kissing. Candace rides out here with her beau, she does. Right around then it became known she was in the family way. Marnie, I mean."

As he turned his buggy up the drive toward the Hoagland house, where it sat in a grove of trees inside a sharp bend in Beaver Creek, Stillman glanced at Evelyn sharply.

"It wasn't the doc who spread that juicy bit of news," Evelyn said. "Even drunk, the doc doesn't gossip."

"Who let it slip, then?" Stillman wanted to know.

"Who can say? But I know that the Hoagland's housekeeper has churned the rumor mill a time or two, just for fun."

CHAPTER THIRTEEN

Stillman reined the claybank up in front of the judge's house—a three-story, wood frame affair with a mansard roof and wraparound porch. Only a couple of lower story windows were lit. A buggy shed flanked the house. The judge's wife and housekeeper kept an irrigated garden off to the right.

The several acres here were well tended, and at the moment the cool night air was perfumed with the smell of freshly cut grass. An apple tree stood before the house, branches sagging with ripening fruit. The judge had once given Stillman a tour of his well-tended orchard out back, as the judge fancied himself a part-time agrarian. Hoagland hailed from a Kansas City law family by way of Boston—his father had been governor of Kansas—with political connections in Washington, and he believed in all the refinements of a cultured life, which of course did not include a daughter pregnant out of wedlock.

Stillman climbed down from the buggy, wincing at the pain in his leg.

Evelyn remained on her horse. "You all right, Ben?"

He tightened the bandanna he'd wrapped around the wound. "I'll be all right as long as I don't get any blood on the judge's rugs."

Evelyn swung down from her saddle. "You'd best let me take a look at that for you."

"Later, later." Stillman waved her off and started up the porch steps. "You'd best wait here. Under the circumstances, I don't think the Hoaglands are going to be overjoyed at seeing callers in their yard. The judge is gonna see me—whether he likes it or not."

As Stillman gained the porch, he glanced into a window on his right. Beyond the window lay the Hoagland's dining room. Stillman could see through the gauzy, wine-red curtains the three Hoaglands sitting at their long, polished mahogany dining table. They appeared to be enjoying dessert. A pie plate sat in the middle of the table, as well as a silver coffee server and stone cream crock. Candles guttered. Just then, apparently hearing Stillman's tread on the porch, Mrs. Hoagland turned to her daughter and the two of them rose quickly from their chairs, tossed down their napkins, and practically ran from the room. Before she'd slipped from sight, Stillman had seen the swell of Marnie's belly.

The Hoagland's housekeeper—a stout, middle-aged woman named Betsy McCarthy—left the dining room through a separate door. She was heading for the foyer. Stillman didn't bother to knock. He could feel the reverberations of the housekeeper's tread through the wood beneath his boots.

Presently, the front door opened and Mrs. McCarthy looked out, frowning disagreeably. "I'm sorry, Sheriff Stillman, but the Hoaglands are not—"

"Yes, they are."

Stillman opened the screen door and gave the inside door a gentle push, shoving both it and the stout, red-haired housekeeper back into the foyer.

"Sheriff Stillman!" Mrs. McCarthy warbled.

Stillman brushed past her and, turning through the French doors and walking into the dining room, he doffed his hat. The judge sat at the near end of the long table, his back to Stillman, but he was hipped around in his chair, glaring. Bits of meringue and piecrust clung to his salt-and-pepper, soup-strainer mustache and spade-shaped goatee. A cloth bib hung from the paper collar of his silk shirt, over a black foulard tie.

"Sheriff Stillman, how dare you barge in here unannounced!" The judge's stentorian voice rumbled around the large room.

"I'm sorry, Judge—but you're going to see me whether you want to or not. I would have come sooner, but it's been a busy day and the posse isn't back yet."

Stillman did not wait for an invitation to sit. He turned the chair the judge's daughter had vacated toward the judge and eased stiffly into it, favoring his right leg.

"I'm sorry, Judge," the housekeeper said, standing between the open French doors. "He . . . he . . . why, he just—!"

"It's all right, Mrs. McCarthy. I will deal with Sheriff Stillman. Please, leave us." The judge's tone was taut with anger as he glared at Stillman sitting to his right.

When the housekeeper had left, the judge's brown eyes flashed with fury as he leaned toward Stillman and fairly bellowed, "What in the hell do you think you're doing? You have some gall. You have no right—!"

"I have every right." Stillman tossed his hat onto the table. "What in the hell do you think you're doing—scheduling the trial for tomorrow morning? You know very well the posse isn't back yet, which means I've had damned little time to make a thorough investigation of Dave Bliss's murder."

"As far as I'm concerned, the investigation is over. All of the evidence has been turned over to both the county prosecutor as well as the public defender. They and I met last night. Both agreed that it was time to try the case against this . . . this . . . *Johnny Nevada* person. Their offices have sent out subpoenas and the witness list is in place. Six jurors have been seated. The trial will start tomorrow morning at ten a.m.!"

"Is Hec Fenton on that witness list?"

The judge knitted his shaggy, moth-colored brows. "Why

would Fenton be on the witness list?"

"Because he claims Johnny was home with him, Fenton, the night Bliss was murdered. I told Ed Nobel about him. He should have gotten him onto that list." Noble was the public defender, who, if Stillman remembered correctly, had been in the cellblock to visit Johnny only twice, briefly.

"I do believe Ed mentioned something about Fenton," Hoagland said, rubbing his chin. "I think we decided not to include him on the list, however."

"Why the hell not?"

Hoagland glowered at Stillman, the man's angular, heavy-chinned face flushing with anger. "The man is the kid's grandfather. He can't be trusted to tell the truth where that boy is concerned. If we call him to the witness stand, he'll only perjure himself."

"Isn't that up to the jury to decide?" Stillman paused. "Besides, how can you be trusted to preside over any trial where that kid is concerned, given the . . . the . . . well, let's just call it the *situation* and leave it there."

Nostrils flaring, Hoagland studied Stillman, narrowing his angry, gray-blue eyes. "Ben, I don't recollect you doing any reading for the law."

"*What?*"

"My point is, you're not a lawyer. So why don't you stick to your job of arresting those we tell you to arrest and leave the lawyering up to us lawyers?"

Stillman sat back in his chair, staring at Hoagland aghast. It took him nearly a full minute to find words. "You son of a bitch."

It was the judge's turn to fall back in his chair. "What did you just call me?"

"You have no intention of giving that kid a fair trial, do you? That's why you're rushing this along. You already got the kid greased for the pan. Now you just need a fire. That'll come tomorrow when Patten's men file in and testify against him, one after another. They'll go unchallenged, because I'm sure you've warned Ed Nobel about challenging them, and then all that will be left is the sentencing. My guess is you've already commissioned Wit Jenkins and his two sons to start getting the scaffold ready."

The undertaker also served as the Hill County Executioner.

All the blood appeared to run into Hoagland's craggy, pitted face and then run back out again.

That was verdict enough for Stillman. The trial had been rigged against the kid. Hoagland was going to hang him. Frontier justice had returned to northern Montana.

"You son of a bitch."

Hoagland thrust his arm toward the closed French doors. "Out! And I will be filing a complaint against you with the county commissioners."

"You do that." Stillman donned his hat and headed for the doors.

"I will not rest until I have your badge, Ben. Shouldn't be too hard. I'm sure more than one county taxpayer is tired of paying out his hard-earned money to support a sheriff who spent all winter on his back!"

"Like I said, you do that." Stillman shoved open the oak front door, stepped out, and slammed it closed so hard, the entire front of the house wobbled and the windows sang in their frames.

Stillman stepped to the edge of the porch. He removed his hat, ran his hand back through his sweaty hair brusquely, and stuffed the hat back down on his head.

Evelyn stood holding her horse's reins to the right of Stillman's buggy horse. Gazing up at Stillman, she said, "Didn't go so well, huh?"

Stillman dropped heavily down the porch steps. "What makes

you say that?"

"Well, I could sort of hear you way out here."

"If I cussed, I apologize."

"You did."

"Don't tell Fay." Stillman grabbed his reins off the hitch rack and climbed into the buggy. "She's been trying to refine my language so it don't corrupt the boy."

"Your secret is safe with me, Ben," Evelyn said, swinging up onto her filly's back.

When they were back on the trail and headed north toward Clantick, Stillman glanced at the girl riding along beside him. "You said you had something you wanted to talk to me about."

"Oh, it can wait, Ben. It's really nothing compared to what you have going on."

"No, let's hear it. I'd like to get my mind off the judge for a few minutes. Need something to simmer me down so I don't do what I'm sorely tempted to do and ride back and shoot him. Let's hear it."

Evelyn didn't say anything for a time. Her filly was trotting, and Evelyn's hair was bouncing on her shoulders. She stared straight ahead, then turned to Stillman and said, "I . . . think I'm in love . . . with an older man."

"Are you going to tell me who or do you want me to guess?"

Evelyn paused. The clomps of the two horses' hooves and the clatter of the buggy wheels wrapped her and Stillman in a cocoon of raucousness against the backdrop of the otherwise quiet night. It was a fitting accompaniment to the raucousness, each of a very different variety, inside each other's heads.

"It's Evans," Evelyn said, staring straight ahead.

"Yeah." Stillman gave the girl a sympathetic half-smile. "I sort of figured that."

"Has it been that obvious?"

"Yes."

"Oh, boy."

"Well, I'm sorry, girl."

Evelyn frowned. "About what?"

"About him and Mrs. Kemmett getting hitched. It probably doesn't seem like it now, but it's really the best thing for all three of you."

Evelyn's frown deepened, cutting shadowed lines across her forehead. They were visible in the umber light of the three-quarter moon rising over Stillman's left shoulder. "You've been so busy, I guess you'd haven't gotten word."

"Gotten word about what?"

"The wedding is off."

"Whoa!" Stillman halted the clay as he stared up at Evelyn. When the buggy had rocked to a stop, he said, "Off?"

"Yeah, it's off." Evelyn, who had stopped her own horse beside the buggy, looked around in the darkness, as if the key to her perplexity lay in the night-cloaked brush and weeds in which burrowing creatures occasionally scuttled. "I don't know how to explain it, but he was drunk, and . . . he said some things that Katherine heard . . . about love an' such. Not such nice things. You know the doc."

"Ah, hell." Stillman spat to one side. "That damn fool."

"I'm afraid . . . I'm afraid I might have made things worse."

"How?"

Evelyn turned to Stillman, stared at him for several seconds, her eyes growing round and bright. "I slept with him."

Stillman drew a deep breath, then let it out slowly.

"Ben, I love him."

"You know he's not exactly a well man. You do realize that—don't you, Evelyn?"

"You remember what I said about Johnny Nevada?"

"About his syrupy tongue and dimples?"

"The doc doesn't have any of that phony polish. He wears

who he is on his sleeve. I like that about him. And just about everything else I can think of about him. Even his drinking, for some reason. I don't mind it. And I love his crazy dog and his wild cats and his endless piles of books, and how he doesn't clean his glasses or scrape the blood out from under his fingernails after he's tended a wound, and the way he doesn't keep his house up like most folks would think a doctor should. And I like how he doesn't give a good tinker's dam about what anyone thinks of him."

Tears dribbled down her cheeks now. They were the same color as the rising moon.

Somewhere an owl hooted. A cool breeze whispered in a clump of willows.

Evelyn kept her emotion-bright eyes on Stillman.

"Yeah, it sounds like love, all right," he said after a time, loosing another heavy breath.

"What should I do about it?"

Stillman shrugged. "Hold on tight. That's a wild horse. He'll try to buck you off first chance he gets and run to the country."

Stillman clucked to the clay. The buggy lurched forward and continued along the trail to town.

"Yeah . . . I know," Evelyn said, gigging the filly along beside him.

Chapter Fourteen

Stillman got the sense that something had happened as soon as he and Evelyn entered the outskirts of Clantick. He saw no sign of anything amiss in the cabins and shanties and stock pens around him, darkly framed in the moonlight, but a vague apprehension rolled through him like a fever.

"I'll be seein' you, Evelyn," he told the girl by way of dismissing her as they entered the heart of town and came to the cross street on which her boarding house lay.

She gave him a dubious look as she slowed her horse. "Everything all right, Ben?"

"Not sure yet. You go on home."

"That leg should be looked at!" she called from behind him.

Stillman turned south on Second Avenue. The courthouse pushed up on his right, beyond the U-shaped, rock-lined driveway. The first indication something was awry was the lack of light in his office window on the far right end of the courthouse's first floor. The building humped, eerily dark against the moonlit sky.

He pulled the buggy up in front of the veranda, climbed down, moving even more stiffly now as his leg was swelling up around the bullet burn, and limped over to the steps. Something shiny lay on the veranda floor. If it had been winter, he would have thought it merely snow. But as he gained the veranda and walked to his right, the glass crunched beneath his boots.

He looked at the two front windows of his office, the jagged edges of the broken panes glittering in the moonlight. Taking a closer look, he saw bullet pocks in the frame around the glass, and two bullets were lodged in an awning support post near the windows.

Stillman cursed as he hurried to the front door. He'd locked the door when he'd left, but someone had shot out the lock. Both doors were partway open. He slid his Colt from its holster and clicked the hammer back as he stepped slowly between the open doors and gained the inside hall. He moved to one side so he wouldn't be outlined against the opening, and tightened his index finger on the trigger, chewing the inside of his lower lip as he waited for a gun flash.

It didn't come. The silence was heavy, complete. Moonlight tempered the darkness.

He turned to the door of his office. It also stood open, the glass broken out of the upper panel. The bitter musk of coal oil touched his nostrils as he stepped into the office, glass crunching beneath his boots. His heart thudded as he made his way to the cellblock door. He expected to find it open and heaved a heavy sigh of relief when he found it closed, firmly locked and sound in its frame. In the darkness he could see the ragged holes of a dozen or so bullets.

He turned to the small, barred window at the top of the door, and shouted, "Kid, you down there?"

No response.

Stillman fumbled the key out from behind his cartridge belt, hearing the metallic scrapes as he tried to poke the key in the lock, which was hard to find here where little moonlight penetrated. He gave it up and walked over to the lamp on his desk.

He fished a lucifer from his shirt pocket, quickly removed the lamp's mantle, and lit the wick, turning it up, spreading the pale yellow glow throughout the room, hazing shadows into corners and behind the woodstove and under the map table against the far wall.

It was on the table he'd left a lamp burning. The lamp was on the floor near the cellblock door, its chimney in shards, near a glittering pool of oil. Whoever had broken into the office must have tried to burn the place. Purely by accident, the lamp's flame must have gone out before the lamp had hit the floor and ignited the oil. If not, the whole building would likely be engulfed in flames by now.

Stillman grabbed the key again and poked it into the cellblock door. He opened the door, lifted the lamp by its bale handle, and quickly descended the steps, wincing at the tearing burn of the dog's teeth embedded in his right thigh.

Stillman walked over to the kid's cell, the first one on the corridor's right side. He held the lamp high and adjusted it, sliding the gauzy light across the cell floor and onto the cot. The illumination slid over a pair of casually crossed, sock-clad feet. There was a hole in the right sock; the kid's pale right toe protruded from it. Stillman adjusted the lamp so that the yellow light slid up the kid's crossed, denim-clad legs to his head. The kid lay back against his pillow, his arms crossed behind his head.

Johnny Nevada's pale blue eyes were open. They flashed in the lamplight, blinked, and then the kid said, "Nice of you to make an appearance, Sheriff."

"You all right?"

The kid slowly dropped his feet to the floor and, sitting on the edge of the cot, turned to Stillman, his face bunched with anger. "No thanks to you, I'm not! Those sonso'bitches were here to break me out, only they couldn't bust that door up there. So they fired through the window. Eight times. I counted every last fucking one of them shots while I hid beneath the cot and prayed like hell one of the ricochets wouldn't hit me. One did!"

The kid rose, strode angrily to the cell door, and pressed his right index finger to his right cheek, just beneath a three-inch, diagonal line marked in red by the kid's blood. "That's how I got this here!"

"Ouch."

"Yeah, ouch!" the kid cried. "Is that all you got to say? *Ouch?*"

"I'm sorry, kid."

That seemed to rock Johnny Nevada back a bit. He lowered his right hand from his face and gazed through the bars at Stillman, the anger slowly leaving his eyes.

"Who were they?" Stillman asked him.

"Hell if I know."

"Did they say anything to you?"

"When they fired through the window up there, they said they hoped I was a good dancer!"

"Fortunately, you were."

"That ain't funny. I coulda been killed on your watch, Sheriff!"

"You didn't recognize the voice of the one who taunted you?"

Johnny pondered the question, then shook his head. "It was probably Ray Bliss come callin' again. I couldn't hear him very good above the shootin' and those bullets zooming around in here like hornets in a privy."

Stillman turned and started back up the stairs.

"Hey, where you goin'?" the kid asked, indignant. "You can't leave me down here. They're liable to come back!"

"I won't be far, kid. Try to get some sleep."

"*Sleep?*" the kid cried. He followed that up with something else, but just then Stillman closed and locked the door, drowning the kid's bellowing yell.

Stillman walked outside and climbed into the buggy. He

drove up to First Street and stopped, looking both ways along the trace. There were few folks out this time of the night, around ten-thirty. Only the saloons and the Boston Hotel showed lights and the flickering shadows of men moving around. Stillman could hear the tinny patter of piano music issuing from the Drovers a block away on his right.

A shadow flicked in the corner of his right eye.

Stillman jerked his head toward it, closing his hand around the walnut grips of his Colt.

"No need to be alarmed, Sheriff," said a woman's voice. She stepped out into the light being shed by the oil pots fronting the Boston Hotel a half a block away. "It's Clarissa Kane."

Stillman moved his hand away from his gun as he scowled down at the pretty young woman standing at the edge of a boardwalk, staring up at him. Her face was half-hidden by a wedge-shaped shadow. "I think one of the men you're looking for is at Miss Lee's place."

Stillman's scowl deepened. "How do you . . . ?"

He let his voice trail off when she strode forward and then climbed up into the buggy to sit down beside him. "I'll show you."

Stillman looked at her, vaguely bewildered. She stared back at him as though it was only natural that she would be sitting in the buggy beside him, even after what had happened between them a couple of days ago. The sheriff gave a wry snort, then flicked the reins over the clay's back.

Mrs. Lee's Place sat on a near cross street. It was one of the older, finer pleasure parlors in Clantick, run by Mrs. Lee herself, a no-nonsense madam who did not look the part. In fact, if you saw Mrs. Lee on the street and didn't know her, you'd think she was a church-going merchant's wife, maybe even a widow who ran a boarding house. Her house of ill-repute could have been one of the middle-class, clapboard, shake-roofed family homes in Clantick, sitting in a small, neatly tended yard and surrounded by a white picket fence, with a large box elder standing sentinel in a rear corner. In fact, it *was* a family house, only its family was a gaggle of young doves supervised by their adoptive mother, the inimitable Mrs. Lee.

Three saddled horses were tied to one of the two hitch racks outside Mrs. Lee's picket fence, to the left of the half-open gate. One of the three was Doc Evans's beefy gelding, Faustus. A fourth horse stood a ways off, reins dangling. The black-and-white pinto was cropping the grass growing between the pickets of the fence.

"I believe that's the horse of the man you're looking for," said Clarissa Kane.

Stillman set the buggy's brake. "What makes you think I might be looking for anyone?"

"The men who shot up the courthouse met up with the man who belongs to this horse and another man on First Street. The man who belongs to this horse was wounded. He and his friend rode into town from the south. I saw them when I was out stretching my legs, and I followed them until they met up with the others, who shot up the courthouse. The wounded man's friend said you'd shot him. They took him here and sent one of the girls to fetch Doc Evans. After that, they rode away like donkeys with tin cans tied to their tails."

"Who were they?"

She shook her head. "I didn't recognize them. It's too dark out here." He gaze dropped to his leg. "Are you wounded?"

"No," Stillman said, not wanting to talk about it.

He scrambled down from the buggy, turned to the picket fence, stumbled, and dropped to his right knee, cursing. His leg was getting stiffer.

"Good lord!" Clarissa said. "How bad were you hit?"

"Not bad," Stillman said, adding balefully, "I'm just a

decrepit old lawman, that's all."

"Here, let me . . ."

"Leave me alone. Shouldn't you be with your father?"

"Oh, for chrissakes, let me help you up!" she said with a grunt as she wrapped her left arm around Stillman's waist and draped his right arm over her shoulders, hoisting him to his feet.

When they were standing, Stillman said, "I could have done that without your help."

"You and my father!" the young woman cried, throwing her hands up in defeat.

Stillman pushed through the picket fence and limped, wincing, up to Mrs. Lee's front porch. As he climbed the porch steps, the door opened. Mrs. Lee must have heard Stillman and Clarissa. She stood in the doorway.

"Ben . . ."

"I understand you have a patient."

"Yes, come in." Mrs. Lee drew the door wider. She stood in her customarily prim attire with perfectly coifed hair. She looked as though she could have been heading to choir practice. "He's upstairs. Doc Evans is with him. He wasn't doing very well, last I checked. Second door on the right."

"Thanks."

As Stillman started toward the stairs angling down the parlor wall on his left, Mrs. Lee said behind him, "Ben, you don't look well at all!"

"Couldn't be better!"

Stillman gave a cursory nod to the three young, scantily clad ladies lounging around the well-appointed parlor, looking bored. Mrs. Lee was famous for her cats, and as Stillman climbed the stairs, he saw a good half-dozen felines with just a quick, cursory scan of the parlor—spread out on the backs of sofas and chairs and on a cushioned piano bench.

Somewhere in the second story above him came the female moaning and male grunting of a pair in the throes of love—or the facsimile thereof. The sounds grew louder as Stillman tramped down the second floor hall and stopped at the second door on the right. There were no doors on the second floor, only curtains. Stillman pushed through the curtain before him and found himself in a small room with a brass bed, Evans crouched over a man on the bed.

The doctor had been listening through his stethoscope. Now he removed the earpieces as Stillman entered, turned toward the door, and said, "Gabriel just blew this fella's horn, Ben."

Chapter Fifteen

Stillman gazed at the unmoving man on the bed while the sounds of lovemaking continued in the next room. The man on the bed was balding, maybe in his early thirties, with a two- or three-day growth of beard stubble on his long face with a heavy lower jaw. He was tall, slender, and one long leg dangled to the floor next to Evans.

His brown eyes were half-shut, mouth half-open. He wore a blue wool shirt, suspenders, and denims. Evans had opened the man's shirt, and there was a thick, bloody pad over the man's upper left chest. There were two empty holsters strapped around the dead man's waist. Two revolvers sat atop the dresser to Stillman's right. The sheriff walked farther into the room and stared more intently down at the dead man.

"Lung shot," Evans said. "Yours?"

"Yeah."

"Is that his bullet in your leg?"

"No. I mean, yeah . . . er, no there's no bullet in my leg. It's just a burn." Stillman was leaning down over the dead man now. Not recognizing him, he glanced at Evans. "Did he say his name?"

"By the time I got here, he'd bled out enough that his vocabulary was whittled down to only a 'goddamn' or two. His last words were: 'I'm comin', Momma.' "

"Touching."

Evans had to raise his voice to be heard above the growing

din in the next room, which included the thuds of a headboard against the wall, causing the dead man's head to turn slightly from side to side, as though he were saying no to something. "You'd be surprised how many dying men utter those very words," the doctor said. "Let me have a look at your leg."

"Later." Stillman was patting the man down and going through his pockets, finding nothing save a battered silver pocket watch, a comb, a handful of coins, two crumpled silver certificates, and a seven of diamonds playing card folded once and with the name "Clara" scrawled in pencil on it. Stillman tossed everything onto the dead man's chest and headed for the door. "I'm going to check his horse."

"I'll meet you at your office," Evans said.

Stillman stopped when Mrs. Lee appeared in the doorway, holding a kitten in one hand against her matronly bosom and fingering the string of fake pearls around her neck with the other. "Is he gone?"

Stillman nodded.

Mrs. Lee frowned at the next door along the hall, and yelled, "Megan, for heaven sakes, do you and Melvin have to be so consarned loud? A poor man has gone to his reward over here."

From the next room, Megan yelled, "Sorry, Ma, but I think Roy's on his way!"

Mrs. Lee pursed her lips and sighed, then looked at the dead man in the room behind Stillman. "I will say a prayer for him tonight. The girls will, too. We will light a candle in the parlor window." She smiled. "We always do that when one of our clients has been called."

"One of your . . . do you know this fella, Mrs. Lee?"

"Oh, yes. His name is Bernard."

"Bernard what?"

She frowned. The kitten in her hand yawned and swiped at its nose with its paw. "Come to think of it, I don't know what his last name is. I guess I only knew him as Bernard. The girls called him Bernie."

"Bernie, that's his name," said a girl who'd come up to stand behind Mrs. Lee, canting her head to see into the room.

She was a slender little brunette with a comely round face and freckles on her nose and forehead. Stillman didn't frequent Mrs. Lee's place—in fact, since he'd got married, he'd been laying off of whores altogether—but knew the girl's name was Regina, after the Canadian town she hailed from. The name, rhyming with "vagina," was bandied about quite often and with snickering delight in the less refined of Clantick's saloons.

"Never gave his last name," Regina said. "Is he dead?"

When Stillman told her he was, she said she'd say a pray for him.

Stillman told her that would be a nice gesture and asked her if she knew who he rode for. He was dressed in drovers' garb. Stillman assumed he rode for Dave Bliss and was surprised to hear the girl say, "I'm not sure, but I think he said he rode for Mister Patten."

Stillman scowled. "Vince Patten?"

"If that's Mister Patten's first name." The girl hiked a slender shoulder, then turned and walked away.

Stillman asked Mrs. Lee if she'd send her hired man for the undertaker. After the woman had carried the kitten off down the hall, he turned to the two guns on the dresser. They were both Remington .44s. Well-cared for. Sniffing the barrels of each, he could tell one had been fired not long ago, which he'd already assumed but had wanted to confirm. The bullet the gun had fired had cut the nasty burn across Stillman's leg.

"What would Patten have against you, Ben?"

Stillman turned to where the doctor was snapping his leather kit closed and said with a pensive air, "Nothing I can think of. We've butted heads a time or two. He's tried to weed nesters off public graze, and I've had to turn his horns in for him. But I didn't think it was anything personal."

"Maybe Miss Regina has it wrong."

"Maybe." Stillman turned to the door again. "I'm gonna check his horse."

"I'll meet you at your office," Evans called behind him.

"You already said that," Stillman responded as he limped down the stairs.

He walked outside, cursing against the tightness and burning in his leg. He stopped near the gate when he saw Clarissa Kane standing just beyond the fence, the reins of the black-and-white pinto in her hand. The horse was sniffing her hair.

As though she'd been reading Stillman's mind, she said, "This horse came from the Patten ranch." She glanced at the horse's near wither blazed with the Patten Triple Box X brand.

Stillman limped through the gate and crouched to inspect the brand more closely. Rising, he poked his hat brim back up off his forehead, and said, "I'll be damned."

Clarissa arched a brow at him, half-jeering. "Have you and Mister Patten butted heads, Sheriff?"

Stillman glanced at her skeptically as he limped over to his buggy and tried to climb as nimbly as possible, under the circumstances, into the driver's boot. "Thanks for the help, Miss Kane. You'd best go on back to the Boston now. Gettin' late."

"I'm a night owl," the woman said. "I'll take the horse over to Auld's."

"Not necessary. I'm heading there now." Stillman held his hand out for the reins.

She led the horse over to him, and gave him the ribbons, staring at him obscurely.

"Give my best to your pa." He pinched his hat brim, then

flicked the reins over the clay's back.

Evans held up a small, hide-wrapped flask. "Snort?"

"You know I stopped drinking the hard stuff, Doc." Stillman grabbed the flask before Evans could return it to his kit. "But since this is a medical procedure an' all . . ."

He threw back a healthy swallow, considered, and then threw back one more.

He sat on the cot in his office at the courthouse. Two lamps were lit, shunting shadows about the glass-littered, bullet-pocked room. He'd taken off his bloody denims and lay on the cot now, back propped against a pillow and the wall, legs bare. He wore short, summer-weight, cotton underwear. Many men wore longhandles all year long. Stillman was too hot blooded for that. Even the northern-most reaches of Montana Territory were a hot, muggy swamp in which he felt as though he were drowning every July and August and even for a good part of September.

Evans slid a porcelain washbowl beneath Stillman's slightly raised right leg and poured whiskey into the quarter-inch deep gash that ran slightly diagonally across the outside of the lawman's thigh. Stillman sucked a breath, cursing. The sawbones had deemed the graze a minor injury, but a few stitches would keep it from opening up and bleeding.

The doctor pinched together the ragged edges of torn flesh on either side of the gash, then poked his suture needle through, drawing the catgut out the other side and forming the stitch.

Stillman tensed at the burning pain then said, "Doc?"

"More whiskey?"

"I need to ask you a favor."

"Well, you can ask . . ."

Stillman flinched as the doctor pulled the thread through for the third time. Then he said, "Will you watch over the office for me tomorrow?"

As he pulled another stitch taut, tightening his jaws as he did, Evans glanced at Stillman from over his sagging spectacles. "What're you talking about? Where will you be?"

"My prisoner and I are going to take a little vacation."

Evans looked at him dubiously, then chuckled as he poked the needle through the flaps of torn flesh once more. "Your tolerance for whiskey is low, Ben. Best stick with beer."

"I'm not drunk. I have to get him out of town until I can find out what the hell is happening. Judge Hoagland wants to try him tomorrow at ten a.m."

"That soon, eh?" Evans chuckled again, shook his head. "Well, you know they used to call him Cat's Cradle Hoagland on account of how he fancied playin' cat's cradle with fellas' heads. He used to hold his trials in the Drovers, had a permanent gallows right outside for convenience."

"Yeah, well, those days are over."

"Doesn't sound like it."

"They are."

Evans pulled the last stitch taut with the hemostat, then cut the gut with a scissors. "You think the kid's innocent?"

"No. Maybe. Hell, I got no idea. I haven't had time to draw any conclusions." Stillman narrowed an eye in barely bridled fury. "But I do know Hoagland is jumpin' the gun. Further, he's breakin' the law for not recusing himself. You and I both know why he should."

"I never figured he would, though. I've lived out west too long. And you've lived out here . . . been a lawdog out here . . . long enough to know better than to ride around on a high horse about such things."

"I realize that at my age I should be cynical. I suppose I should just let that boy hang. Hell, he more than likely killed Bliss." Stillman raked a hand through his hair. "But I just can't let it happen. A few years ago, I might have. I can't do it now. I guess my hopes are just too damned high for this town. I don't want it to be that place anymore—a place where a judge can hang a boy because he impregnated his daughter."

"Good on ya, Ben." Evans positioned the bowl beneath Stillman's thigh again and poured whiskey over the freshly sutured wound.

"Jesus Christ!" the lawman rasped, tensing.

"Sorry."

"I think you enjoy inflicting pain."

"It's my long-held belief that all we pill rollers have a little of the sadist in us."

Stillman drew another breath through his clenched teeth as the fire in his thigh was slow to abate.

"Ben, I hope you're not intending to ride. You'll take the buggy, right?"

Stillman looked at the medico, then shook his head. "Enough mollycoddling, Doc. I'm the law here. The back is just going to have to hold up."

Evans opened his mouth to object, but Stillman held up a hand. "That's the end of it, Doc."

Shaking his head and grumbling, Evans wrapped a long strip of white flannel several times around the sutured wound. "I don't know if what you have in mind is particularly wise, Ben—beyond the possible damage to your back, I mean. If you figure on being sheriff here for many more years, you might be making the biggest mistake of your life. But yes, I'll don a badge for a day or two. Just don't expect me to break up any bar fights." He pinched his nose. "This beak here is crooked enough the way it is."

"Fair enough. If you need to get Mrs. Sanderson's cat out of a tree, there's a ladder out behind the courthouse."

They laughed. Evans sterilized his instruments with the

whiskey, then returned them to his kit. Stillman donned a fresh pair of denims he'd stowed in a footlocker beneath the map table.

As Evans snapped his kit closed, he turned to the lawman and said with gravity, "What do you have in mind, Ben?"

"Not sure yet." Stillman was tucking his shirttails into the waistband of his fresh trousers. "I need to get him somewhere safe. Somewhere a posse or whoever shot up this office won't find us. Where Ray Bliss can't find us, if he happens to make a play for the kid again, too."

Evans wagged his head and whistled. "Hoagland's gonna be madder than an old wet hen. He'll send for the marshals."

"No doubt. I'm hoping by the time they arrive, I'll know who killed Bliss, and I can get a court order sent up from the capital in Helena, making sure Hoagland steps aside."

"Tall order. Fay's not gonna like it—you bein' gone. Especially ridin' out on horseback."

"No, she won't." Stillman shook his head. "Speaking of her." Stillman glanced at his leg. The bandage made only a slight bulge under his pants. "Mum's the word about my little scratch here, all right?"

"I hope that scratch is all you get out of this deal."

"Me, too."

"Good night, Ben. I'll be back first thing in the morning."

Evans donned his bowler hat and headed for the door.

"Doc?"

Evans swung back around, eyes wide. "Evelyn told me about you and her."

The sawbones grimaced. "Shakespeare said it best: 'The common curse of mankind, folly and ignorance, be *mine* in great revenue.' "

Stillman wagged a cautionary finger at him. "If you break that girl's heart, I'll hang you from that big box elder behind your privy, frontier-style."

Evans nodded, smiling grimly. "If I break her heart, I'll provide the rope."

His shoes crunched glass as he walked out of the office and then out of the courthouse. Stillman walked around behind his desk, brushed glass from his chair, and slacked into it.

Footsteps sounded on the porch to Stillman's left. He could hear the crunch of the shattered glass clearly through the broken windows.

Quickly, he unsheathed his Colt and clicked the hammer back.

Now what?

CHAPTER SIXTEEN

There was a squawk of hinges as the courthouse's front door was pushed open.

A woman's voice said, "Don't shoot, Sheriff."

Stillman recognized the voice. Her boots continued to crunch broken glass as she walked into Stillman's office and stood just inside the doorway. She removed her brown felt Stetson and shook her long, flaxen hair out across her shoulders, then swept her hand through it, straight back over her head.

"I know a place."

Stillman slid his Colt back into its holster. "Pardon?"

"I know a place where you can take him."

"Didn't your parents teach you it's not nice to eavesdrop, Miss Kane?"

"I'm just so bored, Sheriff!" She scowled angrily, her thin brows knitting above the bridge of her nose. "My father insists on staying here in town until your posse returns. That doesn't look to be very soon. I know a remote cabin you can take your prisoner to."

"Thanks—I have a couple in mind." He did. He knew of several abandoned trappers' shacks in the Two-Bears south of town. The problem was all those shacks were farther than he wanted to go—a good, long day's ride. They were also in the wrong direction from town. He wanted to be closer to where Dave Bliss was killed, so he could use the cabin as a base for his investigation.

"Just out of curiosity," he added, glancing sidelong at the girl, "where is this remote cabin you're talking about, Miss Kane?"

"Northeast. It's on my father's range, far southwestern corner. Near the buffalo jump."

"The Rattlesnake Hills?"

"Correct."

Stillman raked a thumbnail along his unshaven jaw. "East of Patten's land, just north of Bliss's . . ."

"Which would make it rather convenient for you—wouldn't you agree?"

Stillman pondered the idea. The area she was talking about was a chewed-up section of remote prairie he'd only traversed the edges of while looking for curly wolves, between the Milk River and Little Crow Creek. The Rattlesnake Hills was a remote and uninviting place, all rocks, cactus, steep bluffs, and deep gorges carved out by an ancient, fast-flowing river and roughed up further by belches roiling upward from the earth's bowels.

There was little water in those badlands now, making it worthless as cow pasture and pretty much anything else but a refuge for coyotes and wildcats. The sorts of fierce creatures bred and reared in such a place made it even too dangerous for most owlhoots to hole up in. Those who knew about it gave it a wide berth. Those who didn't—those who ventured into those forbidden buttes and canyons, ignorantly believing they'd be safe in that natural dinosaur's mouth of ancient geologic devastation—were more often than not never heard from again.

Some believed that if the wildcats or grizzlies hadn't gotten them, Snake Woman probably had. Snake Woman was the specter from a Gros Ventre legend—an Indian witch who haunted those hills, looking for interlopers into whom she could inject her venom with her rattlesnake fangs. She had a rattlesnake head but a human body, and when you heard the loud rasping of a diamondback, Snake Woman was near.

Miss Kane must have been reading Stillman's mind again. "Oh, come on now, Sheriff—don't tell me you actually believe that old wives' tale." She smiled crookedly, admonishingly, and, Stillman only vaguely and reluctantly admitted to himself, rather beautifully.

"I guess I'm about to find out whether it's true or not." Stillman frowned at her. "Why are you helping me, Miss Kane? Not three days ago, I—"

"Not three days ago, what you did would have gotten any other man shot." She looked down at her hands, which she was steepling together against her belly. "But I was out of line. For that I apologize." She looked up at him now from beneath her brows. "Maybe showing you the way to the cabin is my way of making good on that apology."

She smiled with one half of her mouth. "Besides, I'm bored as hell. I lounged around my room all day and I've always been a bit of a night owl, anyway."

Stillman rose from the desk. "Do you think you can find that cabin in the dark?"

"I think so." She nodded. "If we enter the hills where I normally do. We'll have to ride around to the east side, gain entrance from there."

"All right. Why don't you pack your gear, fetch your horse, and meet me on the other side of the river in a half hour? I have to swing by my house."

"Sounds good."

"Clarissa?"

She stopped and turned back to him. "I'm trusting you against the evidence because I guess I'm a little desperate here. Am I making a mistake?"

"Sheriff, I'm not *all* bad!" She smiled and left.

Stillman walked over to the gun rack. He unlocked the

padlock attaching a stout log chain to the rack and removed his Henry repeater, which was snugged inside its sheepskin-lined leather sheath. Running his hand along the scabbard, he was glad his prized rifle had avoided any of the bullets the curly wolves had sent howling through the office. He set the rifle on his desk, then opened the cellblock door and walked down into the block.

Johnny Nevada stood at the door, squeezing a bar of the door in his left hand. He held his injured wrist down by his side. He scrutinized Stillman, who held a lamp up by its bail.

"What's going on?" the kid asked. He seemed anxious, fidgety.

"You and I are going to take a ride."

"A *ride*?" The kid stepped back, cocking his head back and to one side. "At this hour? Where to?"

"Don't worry, I'm not takin' you out to hang you, though it sure would make things easier."

"How do I know they're not forcing you?"

Stillman had just poked the key in the lock, but now he froze and cast a pointed look at the kid regarding him worriedly through the bars. "Who?"

"What?"

"Who would be forcing me?"

The kid moved his lips, then shrugged. "I don't know. Whoever it was who tried to drill me from up in your office!"

"No one's forcing me, kid. But if I don't get you out of here before sunrise, your goose will more than likely be cooked."

"What're you talking about?"

Stillman had hung the lamp on a wooden post near the kid's cell. Now he unlocked the door and swung it open, leveling his Colt at Johnny Nevada's belly. "The judge has scheduled your trial for tomorrow morning. He didn't recuse himself."

"He can't do that!"

"Step out. Move slow. Kid, I'm only going to warn you

once—if you try to make a play for this Colt, I will kick you out with a cold shovel and piss on your grave. Understand?"

"Jesus Christ," the kid yelped as he started up the stone steps. "You're in a hell of a mood!"

The kid was right. Stillman was in a hell of a mood. He was frustrated as hell, and his leg was hurting. His back hadn't healed enough for him to ride a horse, but that's what he had to do.

By straddling a mount, he could undo everything the surgeon from Denver had done for him, and render his prolonged recovery a waste of time. But he saw no other way. He had to get the kid out of town covertly. And stow him away until he'd gathered more evidence about Dave Bliss's murder.

He couldn't do all that from the confines of the rented buggy.

He'd put the buggy and the claybank up with the hostler at Auld's Livery Barn, just down the street from the courthouse. In the hour since, the night hostler, Mort Benedict, had gone to bed in the little lean-to bedroom addition off the barn's east side.

Waking Benedict now, just shy of midnight, put Benedict in nearly as sour a mood as the one Stillman was in. The hostler cussed and spat and yawned as he saddled two horses—a blood bay for the kid and Stillman's buckskin stallion, Sweets, who had been a gift from Jody Harmon when Stillman had first ridden into the country to search for the killer of Jody's father.

The horse was frisky but gentle and light on its feet, which made him a good match for Stillman's compromised back. Stillman was still going against doctor's orders by mounting him, however. Again, he had no choice. The buggy wouldn't make it a mile into the Rattlesnake Hills.

As Benedict finished pulling Sweet's latigo taut, he glanced at Johnny Nevada standing handcuffed near the front of the barn with Stillman, and said, "Where in the hell are you off to this time of the night, Ben? And with that curly wolf pup there?"

"If I told you I'd have to shoot you, Mort."

The kid chuckled at that.

Benedict scowled at the sheriff. The thin, balding, elderly man wore only his badly faded longhandles, barn boots, and floppy-brimmed canvas hat. A cold briar pipe angled from a corner of his mouth. His belly was an unnatural looking ball hanging down inside his sagging balbriggans, where his bowed, stick-like legs forked away from his hips.

Stillman took the bay's reins and wagged his gun at the kid, ordering him to mount up. He turned to Benedict, who held Sweets's bridle reins as he continued to glower skeptically at the sheriff, whom the hostler must have thought was off his nut. Too much night work and too little sleep since the posse had left town.

Stillman took his reins from Benedict and said, "You're gonna be asked that same question, Mort. Tomorrow morning just after ten, I s'pect."

"And . . . when I am . . . ?"

"Tell 'em everything you know." Stillman winked, then turned out his left stirrup, grabbed the saddle horn, and swung up onto Sweets's back. "Go on back to bed, Mort," Stillman said, as he and the kid rode out of the barn, glancing over his shoulder at the hostler. "You look like hell."

Stillman moved quietly around his dark house, trying hard not to wake Fay and Little Ben. He didn't even light a lamp. That was why, trying to fill three canteens at the kitchen well pump, he stumbled against a corner of the table and knocked a basket of apples to the floor.

"Ah, hell!" he raked out.

The apples rolled around his feet.

Stillman stared at the kitchen ceiling, pricking his ears, listening, hoping Fay didn't wake. He wanted to let her sleep. Her days were busy, tending the house and yard and chickens as well as Little Ben, who was at an age now that she couldn't let him out of her sight. Stillman would leave a note, informing her as succinctly as possible that he needed to be gone a few days and that he couldn't explain where he was going or why.

In the second story, a bed creaked. The floorboards cried faintly as Fay rose.

Stillman cursed again.

The stairs squawked. A light slid down them. Fay turned at the bottom of the staircase in the parlor beyond the kitchen, and held the hurricane lamp high in her left hand. "Who's there?"

"It's me, honey."

Fay moved forward, lowering her right hand. She had her pearl-gripped derringer in it. "Good Lord, Ben—why didn't you light a lamp? I might have shot you!"

Stillman met her halfway to the table. "Didn't want to wake you and the rascal."

She dropped the derringer into a pocket of her powder-blue wrap, which was drawn taut against the full cones of her breasts, then glanced around him, taking in the saddlebags he'd draped over a chair, the bedroll he'd set on the table, and the three canteens. "What in the world . . . ?"

"I'm heading out."

"What? *Where?*"

"Can't tell you." She opened her mouth to respond, but he cut her off with, "I'm taking the kid."

"The kid?"

"Johnny Nevada."

"Your prisoner."

"Right."

"Why?"

"The judge won't recuse himself, wants to try him tomorrow at ten a.m."

"Oh, no!"

Stillman grabbed a handful of her chocolate-colored hair, and brought it to his nose, drawing her smell deep into his lungs. She smelled of sandalwood and ripe cherries and sleep in bedding the summer wind had dried. "That's the long and short of it."

Fay placed a hand over his left ear. "What else?"

"Someone else is tryin' to kill the kid. When I drove out to talk to the judge earlier this evening, someone busted into the courthouse and hurled lead into the cellblock. Johnny's all right, but I don't think I can protect him in the courthouse. The judge would find him guilty tomorrow, probably hang him the next day, and Bliss's brother will make sure the kid dances."

Stillman shook his head, gritting his teeth. "I have to get him out of town. I have to look into Bliss's murder myself, which I haven't been able to do with the posse out of town. The judge is jumping the gun on the kid, and I can't let him do it."

"Ben, what about your back?"

Again, he shook his head. "I have to consider it healed. It hasn't given me trouble now in a couple of days. But I won't sugarcoat it. You deserve the truth. I'm riding Sweets."

Fay looked as though she were the one in pain now. "Oh, Ben."

"I'll be all right. I'm pretty well healed." Stillman hoped she didn't look down at his leg and see the bandage. That part he wasn't going to tell her about. She'd worry for no reason.

Stillman drew her to him, kissing her forehead. "Will you do me a favor?"

"Of course."

"Tomorrow, at the first crack of dawn, hitch up your mare, and you and Little Ben head out to Jody and Crystal Harmon's place. I don't want you anywhere around here when the judge and Ray Bliss find out I've lit out with my prisoner. I don't think the judge would do anything to harm you or Little Ben, but someone else might try to get to me and Johnny Nevada through you."

Stillman squeezed her shoulders to convey the urgency of his plea. "Will you do that?"

Fay nodded. "Of course. All right. We'll head out at first light."

"Don't let anyone know where you're going."

"I won't."

"I'll send for you when all is clear."

Fay looked up at him, her dark eyes glinting worriedly in the lantern light. "Ben, this sounds bad. Is it bad? You know you can tell me." She had both hands on his head now, and she tugged on his ears.

"It's not good, honey. But we'll get through it. Just like we've gotten through everything else."

Fay chewed her lip as she studied him skeptically.

Stillman shrugged, grinning with one side of his mouth. "At least you can't say it's been boring."

She did not respond. Her gaze was gently cajoling. She said, "I have roast beef left over from supper. Let me make you a few sandwiches and send you on your way."

"No time to make enough sandwiches for the three of us. We'll have to make do with jerky and game."

Fay arched a curious brow. *"Three?"*

"Clarissa Kane is showing me out to a cabin she knows about. A remote one, and handy."

Fay arched both brows now with suspicion, and placed a fist on her hip. "Clarissa Kane. Hmmm. A beautiful young woman is showing you to a remote cabin in the middle of the night. You know, if I were the jealous type, Ben Stillman, I might just—"

Stillman grabbed her and kissed her long and deep.

When he pulled his head away from hers, she tugged on his ears once more, scowling up at him from beneath her knitted brows. "You get back to us safely, you understand, Sheriff?"

Stillman pecked her nose. "Cross my heart."

"Now," Fay said, stepping around him and setting the lantern on the table, "let me help you with those canteens before you wake your son and half the county."

"I sure love you, honey."

"What's not to love?" Fay said.

CHAPTER SEVENTEEN

Aside from the slow clomps of the three horses, the faint squawk of saddle leather, and the light rattle of bit chains, the night was as quiet as the inside of a coffin. Not as black, for the moon was high, dusting the rolling prairie north of Clantick with a silvery down. But nearly as quiet.

Stillman saw no need to hurry and strain the horses or his back.

To hell with his pride.

He couldn't do anything by way of investigating Bliss's shooting until morning, anyway. There was no point in hurrying.

After he, Clarissa Kane, and Johnny Nevada had left the main, north-heading stage trail to take the less-traveled two track that led to a series of widely scattered ranches northeast of Clantick, including Kane's spread, the kid broke the peaceful quiet with: "You sure are pretty, Miss Kane. I know I said it before, I'll say it again. You're one pretty creature."

He was right—he'd said it the first time he'd met her, when he and Stillman had met her near the bridge at the north edge of Clantick, on the north side of the Milk, and Stillman had had to smile to himself, thinking of Evelyn's description of his voice as "syrupy."

Clarissa merely sighed tolerantly.

"What's the matter, Miss Kane?" the kid said, his blood bay trailing behind Stillman's buckskin. The girl rode to Stillman's right. "Do my words embarrass you?"

"Why, no," she said, with barely maintained tolerance straining her voice. "I couldn't be more flattered." She glanced at him over her left shoulder. "But you really haven't even seen me, have you? It's too dark."

"In other words, Johnny Nevada," Stillman drawled. "Shut up."

"I'll be doggoned," the kid said in an injured voice. "Most girls take a shine to me right away."

Staring straight ahead, Clarissa said in a low, incredulous tone, "If you think I'm going to help you escape the sheriff and run away with you to Mexico, you're badly mistaken, *Johnny Nevada*. I'm sure you're right attractive to some girls. Some girls who haven't had much experience with full-grown men." She looked over her shoulder again at Johnny Nevada. "There are others, however—me included—who prefer men over boys."

She glanced at Stillman. "Men with most of the green gone, in fact. Men with some experience behind them."

Stillman felt his cheeks warm a little. It annoyed him.

Behind him, the kid laughed. "You mean men like the sheriff?"

"Yeah," the girl said wistfully, keeping her gaze on Stillman. "Men like the sheriff."

"Why, he's married, Miss Kane. And even if he wasn't, he's got one foot in the grave—don't you know that? His back an' all, not to mention he's older'n these hills!" The kid laughed.

Clarissa turned her head forward and hiked a shoulder. "Oh, judging by the right cross he's still packing, I'd say he's got a few rodeos left." She turned to Stillman again. "What do you think, Sheriff?"

"I think I'm bored with the conversation," Stillman said. "What's more, I'd just as soon not everyone in the northern half of this territory know where I'm headed. So how about a little peace and quiet?"

"There's no one out here, Sheriff," the kid said. "No one but us and some coyotes up way past their bedtime. You know what I think? I think you're blushin' from ear to ear up there on account o' Miss Kane settin' store by you."

He snickered.

Clarissa turned to Stillman again. In the corner of his eye, he saw the white of her smile. "Is he right, Sheriff?"

Stillman sighed. "Kid, one more word out of you, I'm takin' you back to jail. Then I'm gonna go home and crawl into bed with my"—he turned Clarissa—"wife."

She turned her head forward, and it annoyed him that she was still showing the whiteness of her teeth.

The kid whistled. "You're in some kinda mood!"

They rode on in merciful silence after that. However, Stillman was aware of the girl casting him quick, furtive gazes from time to time. That, too, annoyed him. He vaguely wondered if it would have annoyed him so much if she wasn't beautiful . . . and if he hadn't been married . . . but neither was true, so he pushed the girl out of his mind while he cast his mind over the problem before him—namely, who killed Dave Bliss.

Secondly, how was he going to get another judge to try Johnny Nevada—if a trial was still warranted at the end of Stillman's investigation, that was?

His mind bumped over that uneven ground as his horse negotiated the rugged terrain of the Rattlesnake Hills. As he and the kid followed Miss Kane through creases between steep bluffs and slab-sided mesas limned in moonlight, avoiding the stygian darkness of deep and perilous washes, he kept harking back to the same question over and over:

Why had Vince Patten's men ambushed Stillman?

What dog did they have in this fight, beyond the fact that three of them had claimed they'd seen the kid kill Bliss? Why would they suddenly now want to kill the kid?

Finding the answer to that question would be Stillman's entrance into the investigation, he decided. Tomorrow, as soon as the sun was up, he'd ride over to the Patten ranch and have a talk with Vince Patten. He didn't have much time, and there was a lot of ground to cover, so he hoped his back, as well as his bullet-burned leg, held up.

A few years ago, a graze like the one on the outside of his right leg would have seemed like little more than a shaving nick. Now it grieved him; it burned down there under the bandage like a hot coal.

Age was a nasty thing. The advancement of his years was pointed out by the fact of his being married to a much younger woman. One of the few downsides to such an arrangement.

He looked at the slender back of Clarissa Kane riding ahead of him, her horse lurching over the shoulder of a bluff on the left side of the ancient Indian hunting trail they were following. Something shiny glinted on her right side.

A gun.

Stillman hadn't remembered her wearing a sidearm in town. She must have picked it up with the rest of her gear at the hotel. He wasn't sure why, but the presence of the gun brushed him with a moment's apprehension before his own horse jogged up and over the bluff's shoulder, and he jerked the kid's horse along behind him by its bridle reins, distracted by the more and more precarious, night-cloaked terrain.

The girl's horse whinnied. It jerked with a start and leaped off the trail.

Sweets whinnied in kind, and reared.

A quarter-second later, as Stillman reached for his Colt, a snarling cry rose from somewhere ahead and to Stillman's left.

The girl gasped.

"Cat," Stillman said. "It's all right. We probably just startled it."

"Damn," Johnny Nevada said. "A wildcat on the lurk, and lookee here—I'm all trussed up like a pig about to get its throat slit."

"Shut up, kid."

"We're almost there," Clarissa said, and, glancing into the gauzy darkness from which the eerie cry had arisen, she gigged her horse forward along the narrow, winding trail.

Behind Stillman, the kid said, "You sure it was a cat?"

"What do you mean?"

"An old salt in Patten's bunkhouse last winter told me as how these hills was haunted by some old squaw with a rattlesnake head!"

"I've ridden through these badlands many times," Clarissa said as she rode, holding her reins high. "And I've never seen an old squaw with a rattlesnake head."

"How come you were riding in here alone, Miss Kane?" Stillman asked her. "I don't know your pa real well, but I do know he keeps a tight rein on his men. I assumed that went for his daughter, as well."

"Rest assured, it did . . . and does, Sheriff." She smiled over her shoulder, eyes flashing in the dawn light, which had been gradually intensifying in the east. The moon was nearly down, and the stars were fading. "You can also rest assured that my father is gone a lot, off to the farthest reaches of the range, keeping that tight rein on his men. Therefore, I often have a lot of time to myself, with only our housekeeper to look after me after my mother died."

"I take it she didn't keep such a tight a rein as your pa."

"No." Again, Clarissa smiled devilishly over her shoulder at Stillman. "Oh, she tried at first. But when she quickly realized I was too wild for her to tame, she let me have my head. She's Indian. Three Doves Flying is a full-blood Sioux. She appreciates a little wildness in a girl. She's never told Father of my exploits, partly because she didn't want to see me checked down like a hard-broke filly and partly, I suspect, because she doesn't want my father to know how ineffective she is at controlling me. Don't worry, I've never gotten her into trouble. I'm quite sneaky."

"I have a feeling you are," Stillman said, giving an ironic chuff as he rode around the shoulder of a rocky knob, birds now starting to herald the arrival of a new day. "You ride through here alone, do you, Miss Kane?"

"Sure. I've had the run of these hills over the years. Oh, a few times I'd meet a boy out here. The stable boys fancied me. One of them and I used to play house out here, in the cabin we're headed for."

"I bet you did," said the kid behind Stillman, snickering. "Could you give us a few details about how that went, Miss Clarissa?"

"Stow it, shaver," Stillman admonished.

"But, as I was saying, Mister Johnny Nevada," Clarissa said in her typically sneering tone, "I've ridden all through these hills and I've never once seen your snake-headed squaw."

"She ain't *my* snake-headed squaw," the kid said, glancing around anxiously.

"There was one time, though, that . . ." Clarissa let her voice trail off, staring straight ahead in the darkness.

"There was one time that what?"

"A couple of my father's men disappeared in these hills. Many years ago. Before I was old enough to ride. They'd been staying in the cabin. They'd been sent out here to keep Indians from sneaking down from Canada and steeling our beef. When the men didn't check in at the ranch at the appointed time, our foreman sent men out looking for them. They found the cabin men—dead—about a half a mile from the shack, without their horses. They were all swollen up. It was as if they'd just wandered away on foot from the cabin . . . and been snake-bit."

Clarissa stopped her horse as she glanced over her shoulder at Stillman.

"Snake-bit?" he said.

Clarissa glanced with faint mockery at the kid staring at her wide-eyed from his saddle. "Have you ever been snake-bit, Johnny Nevada?"

"Who—me? No. I hear it's a lousy way to go."

"Oh, it is," Clarissa said. "Judging by how Father's men looked when they hauled them back to the ranch for burial. All swollen up and black, awful snarls frozen on their faces. Why, they looked as though they were staring into the eyes of the devil himself."

Johnny shuddered. "Damn."

Clarissa smiled as she swung down from her horse. "We're here, Sheriff."

Stillman reined Sweets to a stop behind the girl's horse and looked around.

They were on a gently sloping hillside that dropped more sharply several yards to Stillman's left. A cabin humped on the right, beneath the hill's rocky crest atop which the milky dawn light played, casting eerie shadows. The cabin looked small. It appeared a sod-covered bubble with a timbered front entrance and a stout wooden door.

The front wall was constructed of what looked like fieldstone that fairly glowed in the moonlight. A window shone to each side of the door.

A small lean-to stable stood off to the right, on a relatively flat and worn patch of ground. An unpeeled rail corral abutted it. Several of the corral posts were adorned with deer or elk antlers. One was capped with a sun-bleached bear's head.

"Wait a minute," Johnny said. "How do you suppose both o' them men came to be snake-bit?"

"Why, Snake Woman got them, of course, Johnny Nevada!" The girl gazed over at the boy, laughing with wicked delight.

"That ain't one bit funny," Johnny said, tightening his jaws in anger. "This old bastard aims to truss me up in there while he goes ridin' around the county, lookin' for Bliss's killer."

"Don't worry," Clarissa said. "My father's theory is that some Canadian Indians planted rattlesnakes in the cabin. The men were probably bit during the night while they slept and went wandering off, mad from the venom."

"That's his theory, huh?" Johnny said.

"That's his theory, Johnny Nevada."

"You sure like my name—don't you, Miss Clarissa?"

"It indeed has a ring to it, Johnny Nevada."

"Does that mean you'll consider shootin' this badge-toter and ride off to Mexico with me?" The kid grinned. "We could have us a high old time!"

Clarissa looked at Stillman. He returned the look, glancing down at the pistol on her hip. She rubbed the palm of her right gloved hand on the gun's grips.

She pooched her lips out as though considering the proposition, toeing the dirt, then smiled. "Nah." She dropped her hand to her side. "I don't think I'd be partial to Mexico. Besides, without the sheriff, what would happen to law and order in Hill County?"

"The hell with law and order in Hill County," the kid said.

"Sorry, Johnny Nevada," the girl said.

She and Stillman led their horses over to the corral. Stillman made sure there were no horses in either the corral or the stable, then tied his reins and the reins of the kid's horse to the top rail. There didn't appear to be any fresh tracks inside or around the corral, which meant the cabin likely hadn't been occupied in a while and wasn't now.

Still, just in case there were any surprises inside, he shucked his Henry from its saddle sheath and told the kid to sit tight. "I'm gonna take a gander at your new home."

"Where am I gonna go?" the kid asked. "I'm trussed up here in this saddle—"

"I know," Stillman said, strolling toward the dugout. "Like a pig about to get your throat slit."

"That's the size of it, yeah."

"Shut up and keep your eyes skinned for Snake Woman."

"That ain't funny!" Johnny hissed.

CHAPTER EIGHTEEN

"I sure wish you wouldn't leave me here like this, Sheriff," Johnny Nevada said, looking around again anxiously from atop his horse. "I'm sufferin' from the fantods. I don't like this place. Don't like it one bit."

"It'll grow on you, Johnny," Clarissa said as she fell into step beside Stillman, who was walking toward the cabin.

Stillman winced at the sting in his burned leg. The leg had stiffened up during the ride out here, but his back felt fine, he was pleased to note. "Did your pa build this place, Miss Kane?"

She shook her head. "No one seems to know who built it. It was here when my father came to this country from Texas. In fact, he discovered it when he was riding the range, getting the lay of it."

Stillman stopped near the front door. He looked at what he had first thought were ribbons hanging from beneath the eaves. Upon closer inspection, he saw that they were not ribbons. They were snake skins. Rattlesnake skins.

He fingered one of the papery skins and turned to the girl, one brow arched.

She shrugged. "Pa posts men out here from time to time when rustling becomes a problem. There's plenty of rattlesnakes around for target practice."

"Thus the legend," Stillman said. "Snake Woman."

"I reckon. Pa figures maybe a prospector or a sheepherder built this shack years ago. I prefer to think it was built by some old outlaw hermit in his old age, just wanting to be off by himself." She smiled shrewdly. "Or maybe Snake Woman built it. Maybe it was her bite that killed Pa's men." She let her hands slap down against her thighs. "Who knows?"

"You have a whimsical turn of mind, Miss Kane." She reminded Stillman a little of Evans in that way.

She tossed her pretty head impatiently. "Please, Sheriff Stillman—won't you call me Clarissa?"

Ignoring the invitation, Stillman flipped the steel latch and nudged the door wide. It rocked back on dry hinges. He spread his feet defensively and extended the Henry straight out from his right hip, thumb on the hammer.

"Anyone home?" he said, softly, a note of irony in his voice.

There was a scuttling sound of a mouse or a rat. The pent-up air pushing against Stillman smelled of dirt, stone, wood smoke, and mouse droppings. Enough pearl light washed through the two lone windows that he could make out a small monkey stove, two cots, some shelves, and a square eating table with two chairs.

That was about it for the small hovel's crude furnishings.

The girl brushed past Stillman, and walked over to a shelf. There was the squawk of a mantle being raised, then the strike of a match. The lamp's wick blazed, sending a thin sphere of watery light around the earthen-floored room. Between the peeled poles of the ceiling, bits of sod and dirt dangled. Otherwise, the place looked tight.

The girl hung the lamp's bail on a hook in the beamed ceiling.

Stillman walked over and set his rifle on the eating table. When he turned around, the girl stood before him. She threw herself against him, wrapped her arms around his neck, rose up onto her tiptoes, and closed her mouth over his.

"Whoa, whoa, whoa!" Stillman said, pulling her arms down and shoving her away from him. "What do you think you're doing, Miss Kane?"

"You know exactly what I was doing."

"You know that I'm married."

"So?" She looked up at him snootily, poutily. "I'm not asking for your hand, Sheriff."

"I don't step out, Miss Kane."

"I don't believe in beating around the bush, Sheriff. I'm partial to strong men. When you slapped me the other day, I . . . well, frankly, I've never felt so attracted. The burn of that blow sent a shiver deep into my . . ."

Stillman opened his mouth to speak but she stepped forward and pressed two fingers to his mustached lips.

"Don't be too hasty in your decision. Think about it. That's all I ask. I can make you happy. I can also be discreet."

Stillman frowned, thoroughly befuddled. "What do you see in me, Miss Kane? I'm twice your age. I'm happily married, and I have a boy."

"Maybe that's what I see. A happily married man with a boy. I find that attractive. Also rather safe, I would think. There's little chance you would tumble for me and make a fool out of yourself like some of the others have done." She smiled coquettishly. "Just think about it, Sheriff. We could meet out here if you need a break from your duties in town. Or we could meet at the Boston. There's a back stairs, you know. No one, including your wife, need ever be the wiser."

"I take it you're an old hand at this sort of thing."

"Don't act so surprised. Women can enjoy this 'sort of thing' as much as any man. There are plenty of other men in Clantick who would jump at my offer, Ben."

"Let's stick with 'Sheriff,' shall we, Miss Kane?"

"Not necessary. But all right. For now." She walked to the open door, stopped, and glanced back at him. She was twisting her hat's horsehair thong, which hung down over her impressive cleavage. "You just let me know if you change your mind."

"I won't be changing my mind," Stillman said. "But I do appreciate your showing me out here. I know you can keep a secret."

"Of course I can." She winked as she flounced through the cabin's open doorway, then glanced back at him. "I'll be riding over to the ranch for a fresh horse, then ride back to town to check on my father. Would you like me to bring some supplies later in the week?"

"No, I'll manage with what's here and what game I can find." The cabin's shelves boasted several airtight tins of vegetables and beans. "I don't plan to be here for long."

"All right, then. Cheers, Sheriff." She smiled seductively and walked away.

Stillman strode over to the doorway. He watched, feeling annoyingly tight in his throat as he watched her walk over to the corral, which the orange light of the dawn was just beginning to paint. Johnny Nevada sat in his saddle, staring down at the pretty girl walking up to him.

"What were you two doin' in there?" the kid said, leering, cutting his eyes to Stillman standing in the doorway.

"Just making sure you'll be comfortable, Johnny Nevada." Clarissa swung up onto her horse's back, then pinched her hat brim to the boy. "You take care now, you hear? Don't let Snake Woman get you."

She glanced at Stillman once more, then neck-reined her horse around and trotted off in the direction from which they'd come. The thuds of her horse dwindled to silence.

Clyde Evans woke with a start.

He also woke momentarily surprised to find himself in Stillman's chair in the sheriff's courthouse office. He looked around. Orange-tinged, lemon-yellow sunlight drifted through the broken windows. He glanced at the clock on the wall. There was a bullet in its face, and its hands were stuck on nine-forty-nine.

Evans was about to pluck his gold watch from his pocket, but stayed the movement when he heard something through one of the broken windows. It must have been the same sound that had awakened him.

The crunch of broken glass beneath a shoe.

He looked through the windows. The glass remaining in the frames reflected the early light, making it impossible for the doctor to see out onto the porch. He did, however, see a shadow move beyond the near window and slide off toward the courthouse's front door. There was another soft crunch of a stealthy foot negotiating the broken glass, and then the shadow was gone.

Evans rose and picked up his double-barrel Greener from where it leaned against Stillman's desk. Evans was not a shootist; in fact, he doubted he could hit the broad side of a barn from *inside* the barn with a pistol or even a rifle. That's why the shotgun suited him best. You didn't have to be overly accurate to do some damage with a double-barrel gut-shredder loaded with double-aught buck.

He'd loaded the gun when he'd arrived at the office at five that morning, so he didn't bother to check it now. Holding it across his belly, he caressed one of the hammers with his right thumb as he walked to the door whose top glass panel had been broken out. The hall was still dark, though a little light penetrated from a window at the far end, beyond the stairs that rose to the second story.

Evans walked slowly to the double front doors. They were closed but not locked, for the lock had been shot out last night. When he was three feet from the door, a latching bolt clicked, and the door on Evans's left swung slowly into the hall. The sawbones gave a startled grunt and stepped against the wall to his left. He stood pressing his back to the wall and watching the door open toward him—very slowly, the hinges squeaking softly.

When the door was one foot from Evans's face, a silhouetted figure stepped out from behind it and into the courthouse. Evans sucked a quick, quiet breath, summoning his courage and ramming the shotgun against the door, slamming it and yelling, "Hold it right there!"

A girl gasped, then screamed as the door thundered closed. She fell back against the opposite side of the hall as Evans aimed the shotgun at her from his right shoulder, glaring down the barrels.

"Doc, don't shoot me!" Evelyn cried.

Evans cursed and lowered the shotgun, his heart racing. "Good Christ, girl—what in the hell are you doing here?"

"What am *I* doing here?" Evelyn cried, flushed with fear and exasperation. "What are *you* doing here?" Her eyes dropped to the five-pointed deputy's sheriff's star the doctor had pinned to his wool vest. "And . . . and . . . why are you wearing a badge?" She was breathless from the start Evans had given her.

Taking the shotgun in one hand, Evans sagged back against the wall, catching his own breath. "Whew! You scared pure hell out of me. I thought the savages who'd shot the place up last night had come back to finish the job . . . and me in the process."

"What happened here, Doc?" Evelyn looked at the shot-up front doors and the glass from the sheriff's office door on the hall floor at their feet. "Who shot the place up?"

"Ben doesn't know."

"Where is Ben?"

Evans pushed through the sheriff's door and into the office. "Gone. Don't ask me where. I don't know. He wouldn't tell me. Just said he was lighting out to the tall and uncut with his prisoner."

He laid his shotgun over a corner of Stillman's desk.

Following him into the office, Evelyn said, "So . . . you mean . . . Johnny's not here, either?"

Evans shook his head and drew another long breath, replenishing the breaths he'd lost when he'd thought he'd been about to get his wick trimmed. "No. Not here. Both gone. There'll likely be hell to pay in a few hours, when the kid's supposed to go on trial. But there you have it."

Evans looked at the girl. She wore a fresh, cream dress, buttoned vertically across her ripe bosoms to just above her cleavage, leaving her chest exposed to the first rise of her breasts. A small gold pendant dangled from a gold chain, nuzzling her cleavage. She wore a pink apron and was carrying the small canvas medical kit, a field kit that Evans had given her for emergency use. "What do you have there?"

"I was just going to take a look at Johnny's hand, see how it was healing. And I was going to take a look at Ben's leg."

"Oh, his leg," Evans said, nodding. "Yeah, I sewed it up last night."

"Well, that's good." Evelyn looked around at the glass littering the floor, and at the bullet holes in the walls and some of the furniture. "They sure did a nice job on this place, didn't they?"

Evans was staring at the young woman's ripe bosoms. "Damn, you look awful good this morning, Evelyn."

She snapped her head around to his, eyebrows arched. She saw where he was staring, and flushed. "Doc Evans, I do believe you're . . . staring." Her cheeks dimpled coquettishly.

"Sexual hunger on the heels of fear. It's all quite natural, really. In fact, the physical manifestations of both emotions are similar in many respects."

Evans walked to her.

"It's all quite natural, eh?"

"Yes, the blood rushes to the extremities in both cases—in fear as well as in sexual intercourse. One becomes light-headed for lack of oxygen, tingly in the hands and feet, soft in the knees."

"You sure talk funny, Doc." Evelyn snickered as she tossed her field kit onto the map table on her left and wrapped her arms around the doctor's neck. "But I've been around you long enough now that I'm beginning to savvy your language."

"Do you like it?" Evans asked her, his face only inches from hers. Her lips were plump and pink, her eyes soft and blue as they gazed into his. She smelled like talcum and spring lilacs.

"Mm-hmm," she said, nodding and smiling, her dimples burrowing deeper into her smooth, peach-colored cheeks. "I like it very much."

They kissed. Evans groaned his desire for the supple, yielding flesh of the girl in his arms, the swell of her ripe bosoms against his chest. Her tongue toyed with his, and she raked her teeth against his bottom lip as she pulled her head back.

"You know what?" Evans said. "I like you, Evelyn. I like you very much."

She pressed her groin against his and stretched her lips back in a broad, smoldering smile. "I can tell, Doc." She glanced around. "Are we alone here? The courthouse isn't open yet, is it?"

"What are you suggesting, dear heart?"

She smiled devilishly up at him. "Are you on duty, Deputy Evans?"

"Why, yes . . . yes, I am," he said, his breath growing shallow, his limbs tingling, his knees turning to putty. She was unbuckling his belt.

"Oh, how wonderful!" she said with a naughty laugh.

Chapter Nineteen

Minutes later, his pants down around his ankles, Evans sagged forward against Evelyn's back.

He'd spent himself in a passionate fury. Evelyn was bent belly down across Stillman's desk. Evans had pulled down her pantaloons and raised her dress, and they'd gone at it like back-alley curs, both of them laughing and grunting and wheezing and laughing some more in the ribald thrill of their proscribed revelry.

The doctor had never done anything like this in twenty years . . .

He chuckled now against the girl's sweaty neck, breathing hard.

"Good God, you're gonna be the death of me yet, child."

"Now, Doc," Evelyn said, gently admonishing as she hooked her arm around behind her. She placed her hand on the back of the doctor's neck, drawing his head down to hers, and kissed his mouth brusquely. "No *child* could do what I just done."

"No, no," Evans said, still catching his breath, smiling at her. "My heartfelt apologies. You are a woman in all the best ways." He slid his face up close to hers once more, intending to kiss her.

"Sheriff!" a man's voice shouted from somewhere outside. "Sheriff Stillman! Sheriff Stillman, are you there?"

"Oh, shit!"

Evans pulled away from Evelyn's naked rump. He got his feet

tangled around his trousers and cursed again as he fell, hitting the floor hard on his ass.

"Oh, Doc!" Evelyn swung around, pulling her pantaloons up and shoving her dress down. "Are you all right, Doc?"

"Oh, shit . . . yeah, I think so." Evans pulled a small shard of glass from his right butt cheek.

"Sheriff Stillman!" the man shouted again, his voice louder now as he approached the courthouse. Stillman recognized the voice as that of the Boston's manager, Bryce Campbell.

"Help me up! Help me up!" Evans threw up his arm, and Evelyn grabbed it, setting her feet as she hoisted the sawbones to his feet.

"Are you sure you're all right?" she wheezed.

"Yeah, yeah." Evans pulled up his pants, heart hammering anxiously. "Try to look nonchalant."

Evelyn chuffed an involuntary, nervous laugh as she stepped back and tucked back the stray strands of her hair. "I'll do my best."

Evans wasn't sure how nonchalant they looked, however, when Bryce Campbell stumbled into the office, breathless, sweating in the morning heat and looking around incredulously at not only the broken glass and bullet-pocked walls, but at the doctor and Evelyn Vincent. Evans sat on a corner of Stillman's desk, trying maybe a little too hard to look innocent. Evelyn stood a ways away from him, arms crossed on her breasts, looking down at the floor. She could have been a bored traveler awaiting a train. Only she wasn't in a train station.

Campbell walked farther into the room, scowling behind his spectacles, and said, "Good Lord—what in the name of Jehovah happened here, and . . . where's Stillman?"

"Ben's out of town," the doctor said, a little thickly. "Anything I can help you with, Bryce?"

Campbell glanced at Evelyn once more, obviously confused

as well as anxious about some entirely separate matter, and looked down at the deputy sheriff's star on Evans's vest. Absently, he hooked a thumb over his shoulder, and then, as though awakening from a brief trance, said, "That stock buyer from Chicago is shooting up one of my rooms again . . . over at the hotel. Same one as last time—Ernie Atwell. Don't look like he'd hurt a fly, but when he gets to drinkin' he goes loco as an owl in a lightning storm!"

"This Atwell—he's shooting up one of your rooms?"

"That's right," Campbell said. "You gotta help me, Doc. He's got a doxie in there with him. If he ain't killed her by now, he's bound to!"

"Oh, no," Evelyn said.

"All right, all right." Anxious now himself, Evans grabbed his shotgun from where he'd leaned it against the wall when he and Evelyn had gotten down to business, as it were. "I'm right behind you, Bryce."

"Thanks, Doc!" Campbell ran out the office door, then stopped in the hall and turned back toward Evans. "Uh, Doc . . . I hate to mention it, but the horses are gonna head for the open range if you don't close your barn door."

The manager glanced a little sheepishly, a little wolfishly, at Evelyn, then ran out of the courthouse.

Evans glanced down at his trousers. Sure enough, his fly was wide open. So open in fact, that the tongue of one of his shirt-tails was sticking out of it.

"Ah, Jesus!"

Evelyn closed a hand over her mouth and gave a muffled laugh of half humor, half horror.

Evans grumbled another curse as he quickly buttoned his fly and then ran out of the courthouse. As he followed Campbell onto First Street and east, the muffled cracks of a pistol sounded from the direction of the Boston Hotel.

"Did you hear that, Doc?" Campbell said, glancing over his shoulder at Evans jogging several yards behind him, suppressing the pain in his side. He smoked too many cigars and drank too much. Of course, as a man of medicine, he was aware of these faults but managed to ignore them until he pushed himself physically, which he took care seldom to do.

"Of course I did," Evans grumbled, thumbing his sagging glasses back up his nose. "I'm just fat and lazy, not deaf," he added under his breath.

Folks on the street had stopped what they were doing to stare warily toward the hotel. Several called out to Evans, asking him where Stillman was. The doctor waved them off as he followed Campbell up the Boston's steps, across the broad front veranda, and into the hotel.

By the time he'd gained the second story, he had to pause briefly at the top of the stairs to catch his breath. His heart was chugging like a rusty locomotive on a steep incline.

"Come on, Doc," Campbell said, beckoning as he tramped on down the carpeted hall. "Do you know what kind of reputation the Boston would get if folks knew a whore had been killed in one of our rooms?"

As Evans caught up to him, Campbell lowered his voice and said in a tone of hushed anxiousness, "We are not a whorehouse! We do everything we can to discourage our clients from bringing sporting girls to their rooms!" He added in a whisper behind his hand: "We have a Mormon investor!"

"Don't complain to me about sporting girls, Bryce, you blame fool. I, for one, am of the opinion that sporting girls are one of the scant things that make life one bit tolerable." Evans raised his fist to knock on the door Campbell had stopped in front of, but jerked back with a start when another pistol shot rang out from inside the room.

A girl moaned. The moan was muffled, as though she were in

a closet or maybe hiding in a wardrobe.

Evans hammered his fist on the door. "Atwell? Ernie Atwell—what in the hell is going in there? Put down the gun!"

Evans twisted the knob but the door was locked.

"Go away!" a man shouted from behind the door. "There's snakes in here! They're everywhere!"

There were two more pistol blasts. There would have been a third, but from the metallic click that sounded behind the door, Evans could tell the man had dropped the hammer on an empty chamber.

"Oh, god, they're everywhere!" Atwell cried, sobbing.

"Open the door!" Evans ordered, hammering the upper panel again with his fist.

"Who're you?"

"Doc Evans!"

"The snakes are everywhere in here, Doc. The place is sick with 'em!"

"He's the one whose sick!" a girl cried, her voice no longer muffled. "I was in here all night and I didn't see a single snake. Not even a spider. He's crazy! Help me, Doc!"

Evans recognized the voice of a young whore who called herself Purity Smith. She worked for a Chinese madam down along the railroad tracks. In fact, she'd come with the railroad and stayed. She was from Oskaloosa, Kansas. Evans had spent a night with her now and then—a pretty girl, though she was missing some teeth. She had a little girl's high-pitched squeak of a voice, which was always beguiling, though pity the depraved soul who found it so, of course.

"There are no snakes in our rooms!" Campbell wanted Evans to know.

"Oh, for chrissakes," Evans said. "Do you have a key?"

"Here." Campbell thrust a skeleton key at Evans.

The doctor turned the key in the lock, clicked the latch, and, holding his double-barreled shotgun straight out in front of him in both hands, nudged the door wide.

The first thing he saw was the naked Ernie Atwell sitting on the floor against the gilt-and-purple-velvet-papered wall to the left. Atwell was maybe fifty, with nearly entirely gray hair and a soft, pale, little body, though he cut an impressive figure in his tailored three-piece suits with custom-made, hand-tooled boots, a Boss of the Plains Stetson, and an expensive stogie perpetually jammed in a corner of his mouth.

Now, butt-naked, knees drawn up to his sparrow's chest, he looked like a very old, hairless bird. If birds, hairless or otherwise, could reload a pearl-gripped Smith & Wesson, which was what Atwell was doing now from an open box of cartridges on the floor beside him. As Evans stepped into the room, Atwell snapped his Smith & Wesson's loading gate closed, spun the wheel, extended the revolver toward the base of the far wall, and fired.

The pistol's crash made the whole room, including Evans, jump.

From beneath the bed, the girl screamed.

"Stop him, Doc!" Purity cried. "Stop the crazy bastard!"

"Can't you see 'em, Doc?" Atwell said, straightening and looking, horrified, around the room, moving his gun hand as though tracking snakes scurrying across the floor. "There's one there!"

Boom!

"And there!"

Boom!

Both bullets had splintered the floor at the base of a dresser on the other side of the bed from Evans.

Evans might have been wearing a deputy sheriff's badge, but he was first and foremost a man of medicine. His first thought was that the pistol-wielding Atwell, obviously out of his head, needed some gentle reasoning. But when the man aimed his cocked Smithy at the bed under which Purity Smith was cowering, Evans took a step forward, and throwing the Hippocratic Oath to the wind, yelled, "Atwell, you put down that damned gun before I blow your crazy head off!"

"They're under the bed, Doc. Don't you see 'em? They're hidin' in wait!"

Atwell fired the Smithy into the bed. Evans lunged forward, swung the shotgun's butt up, and slammed it into the underside of the crazy man's chin. Atwell groaned as he dropped the pistol and flew over a chair to pile up at the base of the far wall, out like a smothered flame.

"Damn, Doc!" intoned Bryce Campbell, impressed, standing in the open doorway behind Evans.

Evans turned and thrust his shotgun at Campbell. "Take that."

Campbell took the barn blaster.

Evans turned to the bed, sluggish with fear.

"Purity?" he called.

No answer.

Evans's heart thudded.

"Purity . . . are you all right under there?"

Still no answer.

"Oh, hell," Evans said, worry stiffening his joints as he dropped to his knees beside the bed. He bent low and peered under the steel frame.

The girl lay flat, her head tipped away from Evans. She wasn't wearing a stitch, and she wasn't moving.

"Purity?" he called, softly.

After another still moment, the brunette turned her head toward him. Her dark-brown eyes were large and haunted.

"Is it over, Doc?"

"It's over, girl. Come on out of there."

Purity sobbed as she crawled from under the bed. She rose to her knees and collapsed into Evans's arms, sobbing.

"I thought he was gonna kill me, Doc," she cried. "I thought he was gonna kill me for sure. Why, he's as mad as a hatter!"

Evans looked over the girl's bare shoulder to see Evelyn standing beside Campbell. The doctor jerked his head toward Purity Smith and Evelyn dropped to a knee beside them.

Evans shifted Purity into Evelyn's arms. Looking over the whore's shoulder at Evans now, Evelyn said with an approving smile, "You did all right, Doc. I don't think Ben himself could have done no better."

Evans wasn't so sure. He grabbed a bedpost.

"You all right, Doc?" Campbell asked with concern.

Evans nodded, but he wasn't sure he was all right at all. His heart was still racing, and he felt weak in the knees and dizzy. He thought for a minute he might vomit. His first instinct was to look for a drink. Maybe that's what drew his gaze to a table up near the front of the bed. There were two bottles on it, and two glasses. There was also an ashtray bearing the fat butts of two stogies.

Evans walked over to the table and lifted the one unmarked bottle.

"Laudanum," he said.

Campbell had followed him over to the table and now flanked him. "Laudanum, you say, Doc?"

"Laudanum, all right," Evans said, taking another sniff.

He set down the unmarked bottle and turned the other bottle toward him.

"Thistle Dew," Campbell said, as though he were reading the label for the sawbones. "Atwell goes through a quart of that a night whenever he's in town. One quart, at least. Sometimes more."

Evans turned to where the stock buyer still lay inert against the base of the wall. The man's narrow chest rose and fell shallowly. "If he's mixing the Thistle Dew with laudanum, the base of which is opium, it's no wonder he sees snakes. It's a wonder he doesn't see blue bears and pink elephants dancing."

Evans walked over to the fallen stock buyer and checked his pulse. He was alive, all right. Evans checked his jaw, opening and closing it gently. He didn't think it was broken, but when the man came around and sobered up, it would likely hurt like hell.

And then he'd likely go right back to the laudanum and Thistle Dew.

Evans squatted beside the man, studying him, pondering him, feeling a revulsion growing deep inside him. Not only a revulsion, but a fear.

Could this be what he might someday become?

A naked madman firing at imagined snakes?

"Doc, I'm gonna take Miss Purity back to her crib." Evelyn was helping the whore, now silent in shock, get dressed.

Evans nodded dully as he stared down at Ernie Atwell, the moneyed stock buyer now looking like an old, hairless, crazy, passed-out bird on the floor.

"You all right, Doc?" Evelyn asked.

Evans looked at her and nodded. He rose stiffly. He took his shotgun back from Campbell, then headed for the door. He cleared phlegm from his throat and said in a voice that sounded somehow foreign to him, "I'm gonna check on Kane while I'm here."

He left the room, his knees still shaky. He wanted a drink in the worst way, and yet the thought also repelled him. He walked over to Kane's door and knocked.

No answer.

It seemed odd that no sounds issued from behind the door. Hadn't the rancher heard the shooting? Most of the other hotel boarders certainly had, judging by the jaundiced faces peering out of the half-open doors up and down the hall. Even a few folks from the street were milling at the top of the second-story stairs, murmuring.

Evans glanced around for Kane's persnickety daughter. Not seeing her, he beckoned to Campbell strolling slowly up behind him, looking vaguely incredulous.

"Use your skeleton key here—will you, Bryce?" he said, stepping aside.

"What's wrong, Doc?"

"I don't know. That's why I want you to use your key."

Campbell was reluctant. "This here is . . . this is Mister Kane's room."

"Oh, for chrissakes!" Evans grabbed the skeleton key out of the man's hand. He poked it into the lock and twisted it, hearing the scrape of the locking bolt retreating into the door, then stepped into the room.

"Kane?"

Evans stared at the rancher lying on the bed to his left. Carlton Kane's upper torso and head were concealed in shadow. But right away Evans knew something was wrong. It was the way the rancher was sort of slumped to one side, head half off his pillow, chin angling toward his shoulder, and the inert way that he lay in the bed.

Evans knew death when he saw it, even from a distance.

He knew Kane was dead even before he stepped up to the bed and saw that the man's right temple had been caved in by some heavy, blunt object. Dried blood dribbled down from the grisly wound to cover the left side of the rancher's face.

Evans touched two fingers to the man's neck just to be sure.

Yep. Dead, all right.

CHAPTER TWENTY

Stillman woke with a startled grunt.

It had been one of those falling dreams.

"Damn, you're nervy as hell, Sheriff," said Johnny Nevada. "Are all old duffers as nervy as you? I mean, if that's what I got to look forward to, maybe you oughta just bring me back to town."

Stillman looked over at the kid. Johnny sat Indian-style on the cot on the opposite side of the cabin from the cot Stillman had lain down on to catch twenty winks, after Miss Kane had ridden off to leave him and the kid alone here in the remote cabin in the Rattlesnake Hills. Johnny was grinning.

Stillman looked through the windows to either side of the door.

Obviously, he'd caught more than twenty winks. Judging by the sun's height, he'd slept for a half hour at least, maybe closer to an hour.

"Kid, I like you," Stillman said. "But then I'm partial to cracked teeth."

Stillman dropped his stocking feet to the earthen floor, then leaned his elbows on his knees. Leaning forward, he rubbed his hands through his hair, trying to shake off the slumber tugging at him.

"You sure you're gonna make it, old man? You look awful stove up. You got that bullet in your leg, bullet in your back. You haven't slept for days. I can see it in your eyes. Why, you look like death warmed over."

Stillman reached for his boots and drew the right one on. "I feel great, kid. And I ain't that old. I face each new day with a vengeance. Grab it by the tail."

"How old are you, anyway?"

"Forty-five."

"Shit, that's damn near as old as these hills!"

Stillman chuckled. "Not quite. You'll be here soon. Then you'll see how young it is—forty-five. And the time between now and then will seem like the passing of a fast-moving cloud."

Johnny Nevada sat back against the cabin wall, nibbling a long weed. His hands were cuffed before him, and Stillman had tied his ankles together with rope. "You even talk like an old man."

Stillman pulled on his other boot and sat looking at the kid.

"You gonna ride off and leave me now?" the kid asked.

"That's right."

"You can't lock me in here. I'll be a sittin' duck, all alone out here. What if that snake-headed squaw woman comes lurkin' around, lookin' for someone to pump full of rattlesnake venom?"

Stillman glanced at the door. There were locking brackets on the frame. A locking bar was leaning against the wall, ready to be dropped into the brackets. But Stillman didn't see any way to lock the door from the outside. Besides, the kid could just break out a window and run free.

The sheriff rose from his cot. He drew his Barlow knife from his pocket, opened the blade, and crouched over the kid, cutting through the rope binding his ankles.

"You gonna turn me loose, Sheriff?" the kid asked. "I think that's a wise decision."

"Let's just say I'm gonna leave you to your own devices . . . up to a point."

"What's that mean?"

Stillman tossed the cut rope aside and stepped back. "Take off your boots and socks."

Johnny looked worried. "Why?"

"Take them off, kid, or I'll take you back to town. Your trial's likely starting about now. You'll be a little late, but the county hangman works all hours. I'm more than a little tired of your bullshit, anyway."

"Ah, shit. I don't like the sound of this."

Reluctantly, Johnny kicked out of his boots and then peeled off his socks. Stillman ordered him to stuff the socks inside his boots, and then the sheriff picked up the kid's boots.

"There's a canteen and a bag of jerky on the table. Help yourself, but go sparingly. Not much water around. I hope to be back by nightfall, but you never know."

Johnny scowled as he sat on the edge of the cot, cuffed hands in his lap. The cuff on the right one was above Evelyn's cast. The kid had thin arms. "You're gonna leave me handcuffed and barefoot out here?"

"I'm gonna chase your horse away, too. Lots of prickly pear around, not to mention wildcats and grizzly bears. You'd best not stray too far from the cabin."

Johnny opened his mouth to retort but closed it abruptly when the cabin door was nudged open, squawking on dry hinges. Stillman wheeled, palming his Colt and clicking back the hammer.

He eased the tension in his trigger finger when he saw Hec Fenton standing in the open doorway, holding an old Spencer carbine low in his right hand, down along his leg.

"Don't worry, Ben," Fenton said, his long face dark beneath the brim of his weathered, old hat. "I'll make sure he don't stray."

"Hec, what the hell are you doing here?"

"Granddad!" Johnny exclaimed, leaping to his feet.

"Pipe down, younker!" his grandfather cajoled.

Fenton slid his gaze back to Stillman. He looked a little worn out from the long ride from Clantick. His angular cheeks were carpeted in gray beard stubble, above and around his slightly darker mustache. His ancient trail clothes sagged on his bony, sinewy frame, coated in dust and weed seeds. Long, oval-shaped sweat stains shone beneath his arms, pasting his green wool shirt to his sides. An old-model Remington conversion pistol bristled on his right hip.

He said, "I heard what happened in town. About someone gunnin' for Johnny. A friend rode out to the cabin an' told me. I saddled my horse and was on my way into town when I spied you and that girl and Johnny ridin' north from the bridge. I followed you. I knew you'd be on the scout for a shadow, so I laid low and far behind. Lost your sign a few times, I did, but"—the old man grinned with wily, wolfish pride—"I managed to pick it up again. These old eyes ain't what they used to be, but . . ."

Fenton's expression turned serious again. "I appreciate what you're doin', Ben. I'll watch him. He won't get away."

Stillman considered old Fenton, probing the old man's washed-out gaze with his own. Finally, the sheriff said, "What you said about Johnny bein' home that Friday night . . ."

"A lie."

"Granddad!"

"Shut up, Johnny! Sit down there and hold your tongue!"

The kid started to snarl and pinch his face up at his grandfather like a wild young wolf. Apparently realizing he was both cuffed and barefoot, he sat back down on the cot and sagged against the wall.

Fenton turned to Stillman. "I lied about him bein' home that night. That don't mean I think he shot Bliss. I think someone set him up for it. And I know you'll get to the bottom of it, Ben."

"I'm gonna try." Stillman hesitated, glancing from Johnny to his grandfather.

"You can trust me, Ben," Fenton said.

Stillman nodded. "I know."

He picked up Johnny's boots and socks. He stepped around the old man and walked out the door. He tossed the boots and socks up onto the dugout's roof, where the kid couldn't retrieve them without effort, then strode over to the corral. He'd unsaddled both his and the kid's horses, so they could rest and graze and drink plenty of water. He saddled his buckskin now. He'd leave Johnny's horse here. He trusted Fenton to not let the kid saddle up and ride away.

He led Sweets out of the corral, then swung up into the leather. He glanced toward the cabin. Fenton sat in a chair shoved back against the cabin's front wall, right of the open door. Johnny slouched in the open doorway, barefoot, hands cuffed before him. Fenton dipped his chin and pinched his hat brim to Stillman.

The sheriff nodded and rode away.

The range north of the Milk River and east of the Rattlesnake Hills was dun prairie whose table-like flatness under the enormous, blue Montana sky was deceptive. You didn't notice the canyons carved by ancient creeks and rivers until you were right up on them and finding yourself needing to somehow work around them.

Some of the cuts were steep and deep, making night riding treacherous. Stories abounded of drovers out after dark plunging their horses into such ravines and suffering the often-fatal consequences.

Vince Patten's ranch headquarters sat in a bowed-out part of one such canyon, through which a trickle of a stream ran along the base of chalky buttes most of the year. A well-worn trail wended its way through creases between buttes, dropping sometimes gradually, sometimes sharply, from the tableland into the canyon. Stillman followed the trace down to the canyon floor and crossed the muddy stream now alive with biting horseflies and spotted with white seed from the cottonwoods flanking the headquarters on the stream's far side, a good hundred yards back from the stream itself, which was known to flood during the spring snowmelt.

Stillman had been out here several times before. Like many ranchers, Vince Patten had often found himself at odds with his neighbors, especially those homesteaders he regarded as "nesters," having no legal right to the range despite their having filed bona fide claims in the land office in the courthouse in Clantick. Stillman had had to settle such disputes. He'd done so peacefully, so far. But as more and more settlers moved into northern Montana, there would doubtless be more grievances. Stillman had also ridden out here at least once a year to deliver tax bills, which was one of the more onerous but critical tasks of a county sheriff.

He'd ridden out here enough times, in fact, that Patten's old, half-coyote mutt recognized him and barked only a few times before retreating to the shade beneath the main house's front veranda, panting and snapping at flies.

Stillman rode up to the house and swung down from Sweets's back, glancing around at the open yard. The only trees were the cottonwoods out back. Otherwise, the place was flat and featureless all the way back to the ridge of buttes down which Stillman had ridden.

The bunkhouse and other outbuildings sat nearly a hundred yards away on Stillman's left, down a gentle slope, a tasteful distance from the main house. The outbuildings were log constructions with sod roofs. The brassy sun hammered away at them and glistened in the coats of the horses milling in the two main corrals behind the bunkhouse, near a pole barn filled with hay.

Patten's stocky black cook came from the kitchen end of the bunkhouse just then to hang a washtub on a spike in the kitchen's front wall. The apron-clad cook glanced toward Stillman, with the reticence or downright bashfulness of many remote-dwelling folks, then quickly ducked back into the bunkhouse, closing the door behind him.

The bleached deer skull hanging from a nail in the door flashed in the sunshine.

The main house casting its shade over Stillman was a simple, white frame affair with a porch wrapping around three sides. Stillman knew it had started out as a trapper's cabin to which Patten had simply added on to over the years as his herds and his bank account had grown. Now a stranger wouldn't have an inkling of its humble origins. Now it was the rambling, functional ranch house of a modestly well-to-do stockman, and kept in moderately good repair, its windows clean, its shingles intact, flower baskets hanging from porch posts, its shutters recently painted spruce green.

Stillman unbuckled his horse's latigo straps. As he did, he saw a young girl's round, cherubic face staring out at him through a front window flanking the porch. As he raised an arm to wave, the girl's mouth opened and her eyes widened, and she appeared to burst into embarrassed laughter. Sausage curls jostled against her pale, plump cheeks. She turned and ran away from the window, a red velvet curtain dropping over the sashed pane behind her.

The girl's muffled shrieks from inside the house sounded to Stillman like the screeches of mud swallows.

"Oh, Isabelle—don't be daft!" a woman's laughing voice admonished on the heels of a door latch clicking.

Stillman started up the porch steps as the woman came out

onto the porch. She was Patten's current wife, the former Fanny Grisby, a stout, full-hipped young woman with a doll's face and given to frilly white blouses and brocade gowns that only accentuated the roundness of her figure. The nubs of her fleshy cheeks were as red as sunsets. "Sheriff—oh, what a thrill!" She wrung her hands in genuine delight, smiling, and not with one bit of irony asking, "Is it tax season again?"

Stillman smiled stiffly at first, a little puzzled. But then he realized that Mrs. Patten was, indeed, happy to see him as she would have been happy to see anyone way out here. What usually brought him out to these environs, if not her husband's discord with his neighbors, was a tax bill. The more loquacious and friendly of remote-living folks didn't mind getting a bill for the year's taxes after a long Montana winter as long as it also meant an hour's worth of company and news from town.

"Oh, no, nothing like that, Mrs. Patten. Tax season is still several months off, praise the good lord." Mounting the porch, Stillman chuckled as he doffed his hat and held it politely before him.

"Do come in, Sheriff! Do please come in!"

Young, blushing Mrs. Patton rushed out to Stillman a little breathlessly, and grabbed his hand. She pulled him across the porch and into the house, as though she feared he'd flee as fast as he'd appeared.

CHAPTER TWENTY-ONE

Visitors meant a lot to Fanny Patten, for she'd grown up in Chinook, one of nine children, and Stillman suspected the prairie silence out here wore on her young nerves.

Fanny was Vince Patten's third wife, Patten having buried two wives previously, one after hemorrhaging during childbirth, the other from a heart ailment. The current Mrs. Patten was in her later twenties, a daughter of a freight company manager from Chinook, thirty miles to the east. She was now the stepmother of the three daughters Patten still had at home, an older daughter having married the owner of the newspaper in Great Falls.

That oldest daughter was several years older than Fanny. Vince Patten was a good thirty years his young wife's senior.

"I do apologize for Isabelle, Sheriff," the young woman said, large pale blue eyes flashing behind her small, round spectacles. Pearl earrings dangled from her ears, amid the curls trailing from her carefully coifed, rich brown hair. Despite her heft, she was a pretty woman with a frank, open demeanor and an unbridled, nervous laugh. "I swear, she watches the ridge for visitors most of the hours of the day unless I keep her busy, but wouldn't you know that when someone comes, she screams and runs to her room, afraid to make an appearance. Have you ever heard such a silly thing?"

Mrs. Patten tipped her head back and sent a roaring, warbling laugh toward the ceiling.

"Fanny, who's there?" called a man's stern voice from the other end of the house.

"It's Sheriff Stillman, Vincent!" she bellowed cheerily, then, turning to Stillman, said in a hushed, almost conspiratorial tone, "How 'bout some sweet buns and tea, Sheriff? Surely you'll stay for lunch." She cast a glance at a clock hanging on the parlor's papered wall, above the fireplace hearth. "Look there, it's nearly eleven o'clock!"

"I can't stay," Stillman said as the young woman rushed off, embroidered skirt billowing about her stout legs. "I'm sorry, Mrs. Patten, but my schedule is a little tight today."

When she turned a poignant look of disappointment at him, Stillman felt genuinely sorry he couldn't stay and chin with the obviously lonely young woman.

"Fanny, for godsakes, stop your fool dottering!" Vince Patten's voice thundered again from a hidden room—likely from his office on the house's east end. "Send the sheriff back here and fetch a bottle of sherry!"

Flushing with embarrassment, Fanny chortled more nervous laughter and said, "Vincent gets so impatient with me," then beckoned to Stillman as she turned through a doorway beyond that of the parlor.

The sheriff followed her past the kitchen, which smelled richly of boiling stew, fresh bread dough, and sugary piecrust. Two girls of varying ages toiled at a large food preparation table. The girls, both rather plain-faced and stumpy, glanced briefly, shyly toward the doorway as Stillman strode past. He smiled and tipped his hat, and the smaller of the two looked at her sister and gave a bashful snicker.

"Ben, good to see you!" intoned Vince Patten as Fanny led him into her husband's roomy office appointed with several bookcases and a large oak desk as well as a sheet-iron stove. Patten stood near a large window straight across the window from the doorway, a long, thin cheroot smoldering between his left thumb and index finger. "Come in, come in! Have a seat. Fanny, please don't loiter, darling. You've seen the sheriff before. I'm sure he hasn't changed all that much since tax season. Why don't you flutter on over to the parlor cabinet and fetch us that sherry the fancy Dan horse buyer from England brought me last winter? And we'll need a couple of glasses, too!" he yelled as his flushed young wife rambled breathlessly away.

When she was gone, Patten turned full around toward Stillman and said, "She flutters around here like a bird with a broken wing. Makes me nervous sometimes." The rancher, a tall man dressed in a doeskin vest over a wool shirt and baggy, faded denims, with a large gold belt buckle, laughed and smoothed his wild, thick, gray-brown hair back from his temples with his large hands.

As he did, Patten leaned his silver-capped cane against his right leg, which was the leg he'd broken last summer when a broomtail bronc had thrown him against a corral rail. Evans had had one hell of a time putting the man's leg back together. If Stillman remembered correctly, it had been broken in three places, and the knee had been dislocated. Now it was bent at the knee, as if perpetually so, and the limb was slightly, unnaturally crooked, to boot.

Never one to suffer a slight from man or beast without decisive retaliation, Patten himself had shot the bronc that had thrown him and caused him so much misery. He often bragged about it in the saloons in town, whenever the topic of his broken leg came up.

When Fanny Patten had brought a tray bearing the stout sherry bottle and two thick goblets, as well as two hot sweet rolls steaming on a small plate, and set it on a table near the stove and a leather sofa with a conspiratorial wink at Stillman, her husband ordered her sharply away. Stillman caught himself wincing at the brusqueness of the rancher's words. The lawman had never liked Vince Patten, and the man's treatment of his young wife was just another reminder of why. There were other reasons, not the least of which was that Stillman suspected the man of hanging two full-blood Blackfoot braves in a creek bottom south of his range two years ago, but had never been able to prove it.

The two Indians, brothers, had been known to rustle a few cattle now and then to feed themselves and their families through a rough, northern Montana winter. Men like Patten could afford such small losses, but they didn't see it that way. In their narrow, intransigent views, stock thievery was stock thievery requiring hang-rope justice. Stillman was trying to put a final halt to the especially savage instances of vigilante justice in Hill County. Men like Patten would never come around, however. And they were adept at escaping justice while subtly mocking it.

Stillman wondered if Patten's roguish arrogance had drifted so far afield that he'd sent several of his men to town to kill him and hang his prisoner.

If so, why?

He didn't beat around the bush. After he'd taken a seat on the sofa and his host had sagged stiffly into an upholstered armchair across from him, puffing his cheroot, Stillman said, "Had some trouble in town last night, Vince. That's why I'm here."

Patten chuckled as he leaned forward to pour sherry into the two goblets. He handed one across the table to Stillman, and said, "Get right to the point, Ben."

Stillman set the goblet on the table between them, and, leaning forward, elbows on his knees, laced his hands together. "I was ambushed on my way back from seein' the judge. After dark. Nothin' serious, which I'm sure was a big disappointment to the pair who shot at me. One's dead. I think he's one of your men, Vince."

"Oh? I doubt that, Ben. Who?"

"I don't have his last night. Just his first name. Bernard, Bernie for short."

"Hmm." Patten scowled thoughtfully over the rim of the glass he'd filled nearly to the brim. "I don't believe I have any Bernie on my roll."

"He was riding a horse bearing your brand."

"The horse might have been sold. Was this Bernie fella carrying a bill of sale?"

"No."

Patten scowled again over the rim of his glass, this time skeptically. "Say . . . why aren't you in town, Sheriff? I heard that no-account boy you got in custody for killin' Dave Bliss is goin' on trial at ten. *Was,* I should say," Patten added as he glanced at the pendulum clock encased in lacquered cherry on the wall behind his desk. "You're late, Ben."

"The trial was postponed."

"Oh? Why wasn't I notified? I sent three of my men to town early this morning to testify." Patten's tone was crisp, authoritative. "I have tons of hay to get in before the snow flies, and beef to gather, and here it's nearly September. I can't afford to be without one man this time of the year for an entire day, much less three, especially for no good reason!"

"I lied," Stillman said. "The trial wasn't postponed. I pulled the kid out of the jail, hid him away where he won't be found. The judge jumped the gun on the trial and refused to recuse himself. I need to find out who killed Bliss before I'll bring Johnny Nevada back to Clantick. Once I do, I'm gonna call for a new judge."

"Sounds to me like you're overstepping your authority, Ben."

"The judge wasn't the only reason I pulled the kid out of the jail. Someone—I don't know how many, but I'm assuming it was more than one—broke into my office last night around the same time I was ambushed. They wanted to pull the kid out of his cell, and would have if they'd gotten through the cellblock door. Instead, they fired into the block at him."

Patten sipped his sherry, swallowed, frowning. "Who? Uh . . . why?"

"Those are two questions I came here to get answered, Vince."

"You think it was my men." It wasn't a question.

"Since one of the fellas who ambushed me last night was riding one of your horses—yeah, I think it's a good possibility."

"I assure you, Ben—all of my men were here and accounted for last evening."

"Are you sure?"

"Of course I'm sure. I don't get around like I used to, but I still keep track of my men."

Stillman glanced out a window that looked down the slope toward the bunkhouse, corrals, and hay barn a hundred yards away. "How good a track do you keep of your boys after dark, Vince?"

Patten glowered at that and canted his head to one side, studying Stillman dubiously. "It was my men who told you about the killing, Sheriff. They're the ones who told you it was Johnny Nevada who drilled Bliss with the Winchester. If they'd wanted him dead, they could have killed him out on the range and told you nothing."

"What were they doing out there?"

"Clearing brush along Nasty Jack Creek. I don't want to get any yearlings lost in there this winter."

"Nasty Jack's the boundary between your range and Bliss's range, right?"

"That's right."

"What time did the shooting happen?"

Patten shrugged and drew his bushy gray brows down over his eyes. "I don't know. I think it was . . . I think it was around nine o'clock. Just before sunset. I sent the boys to town to inform you the next morning."

"Stueves, Reese, and Thorn?"

"Yes, that's right. They're the ones who saw that no-good kid bushwhack Bliss."

"What was Bliss doing out there that time of the night? That's quite a ride from his headquarters."

Again, Patten shrugged. "Stueves said he'd seen him and Reese and Thorn out there, clearing brush, and he just rode over to chin for a while. You knew Dave. He was a talkative fellow."

"Yeah, but what was he doing out there in the first place? That far from his base that late at night?"

Patten was growing annoyed, his chest rising and falling sharply. He fidgeted around in his chair, toying with his cane. "I don't have an answer for you, Ben. Haven't you talked to his wife? His brother? Ray would probably know." He reached forward, withdrew his cigarillo from an ashtray on the table between him and Stillman, took a deep drag, and exhaled the smoke out his nostrils.

Stillman studied the obviously uncomfortable rancher. "Had he been over here?"

Patten looked up sharply. "Huh?"

"Had Bliss been over here to see you that night? I'm thinking maybe he was on his way home. That would be his route, wouldn't it?"

Patten sat slowly back in his chair. "What are you suggesting?"

"I was asking, Vince. Had Dave been over here to see you that night?"

"No." The rancher's voice was stony, cold. His nose twitched.

"If he had been, I would have told you. I have nothing to hide."

Stillman studied the man; then, finding himself believing him, though he didn't want to, because it meant he was on a cold trail, he nodded. "All right. I won't take up any more of your time, Vince."

"Any time, Ben. We don't get many visitors out this way."

Stillman picked his hat up off the couch and rose. "I'll likely stop by again soon to talk to Stueves and the other two."

"I bet Ray Bliss is fighting mad over Dave." Patten grinned up at Stillman from his chair. "I bet he's gonna be madder'n a wildcat in a trap when he finds out you busted the kid out of your own jail. Him and Dave were close. Ray's the bad one. Dave kept him on a leash of sorts. Now that Dave's gone, Ben . . ."

Patten didn't finish the sentence. He didn't have to. He just sighed and hiked a shoulder, crooking that challenging half-smile again.

Stillman stared down at the man, his expression stony. "One thing I forgot to ask."

"Yes?"

"Do you know why anyone would want Dave Bliss dead?"

"None." Again, Patten smiled and shook his head. He knew Stillman was fishing. He didn't like lawmen, because, like many large ranchers, he thought he was big enough to enforce the law himself. At least, those laws he thought worth enforcing. Now he was enjoying this lawman's struggles, his frustration, and his own superior power that lay simply in the fact that he had a good number of men riding for him.

Stillman was alone.

"All right, then." Stillman walked to the door.

"You're in a whipsaw, Ben."

Stillman stopped in the office's doorway and half-turned back to the rancher. "How's that?"

"You're caught between that worthless wolf cub, a known killer, and Ray Bliss and the judge. Who knows who else you're up against?"

"I reckon I'll likely find out soon, Vince. Don't you fret." Stillman winked at the man, then walked back through the house.

He stopped near the front door when heavy, quick footsteps sounded behind him. He turned to see Fanny Patten waddling toward him, breathless again, smiling her rosy-cheeked smile. She held up a small burlap sack tied closed at the top. "For you, Sheriff. You're bound to get hungry out there. I made up some sandwiches for you. Fresh venison roasted last night, two buns, and a small tin of my sweet and sour pickles." She glanced behind her, as though toward her husband's office, then whispered behind her hand. "I threw in a couple of hard-boiled eggs, as well."

She winked and smiled, showing her fine, little white teeth between her thin, pink lips.

Stillman accepted the pouch, trying not to salivate. He hadn't eaten more than a few strips of jerky in nearly twenty-four hours. "Mrs. Patten, I don't know how to thank you. My belly's as empty as a dead man's boot." He stepped up to her, gently took her thick arm in his hand, and planted a kiss on her left temple.

As he did, he saw that she closed her eyes and gave a luxurious little shudder, her entire face turning beet red. It was as though such signs of affection were totally unfamiliar to her. Unfamiliar but welcome.

"Oh!" she said with genuine surprise, beaming up at him, pressing a plump hand to her breast. "Why, Sheriff . . ."

"Much obliged, Mrs. Patten."

"Please, call me Fanny, Ben."

"All right." Stillman doffed his hat. "Fanny it is."

"Did you and Vincent have a good talk?"

"Yes, we did," he lied. "Good day, Fanny."

Stillman pinched his hat brim to the lonely woman, and left.

Chapter Twenty-Two

"Give me a brandy, Phil," Doc Evans ordered, slapping his hand down hard on the bar in the Drovers Saloon. "Make it quick, will you? I'm weak in the knees. Need some fortitude."

"What in the hell's goin' on over at the Boston, Doc . . . uh, I mean, Deputy Evans?" said the barman, Phil Thompson, as he pulled a bottle off the back bar shelf and, turning, noticed the five-pointed star on the doctor's vest. "First I hear shootin' and a girl screamin', and then the undertaker and the county coroner are goin' in. They come out later with a coffin."

The barman set a shot glass on the bar before Evans, and popped the cork on the bottle. He filled the shot glass.

"Don't ask," Evans said.

"That bad, huh?"

As Thompson started to turn away with the bottle, Evans said, "Bad enough to leave the bottle."

"All right, all right." Thompson set the bottle on the bar and held out his right hand, palm out. "Three-fifty, Doc. That's the good stuff."

"Put it on my account."

"Your account's done filled up, Doc." Thompson picked up the bottle. "No more credit."

"All right," Evans said, smiling icily over the rim of the shot glass he was holding in front of his chin, "I'll remember that next time you come down with a bout of gout like you did last winter."

Thompson grimaced, then set the bottle back down on the bar before the doctor, and sauntered over to his account book. The sawbones threw back the entire shot and refilled his glass. Then he picked up the shot glass carefully between the thumb and index finger of his right hand, picked up the bottle in his left hand, and pushed away from the bar.

He headed for a table near the front of the room, where he could keep an eye on the street. He supposed he should keep an eye on things, since he'd promised Ben he would, but his heart was no longer in lawdogging.

He'd once thought that between him and Stillman, he had the tougher of the two professions. Now he realized he was wrong. Walking into that second-floor room in the Boston and finding Carlton Kane with his head bashed in had thrown him for a loop. It had been like a stiff left jab to the point of his nose.

Not that he hadn't seen dead men before. He'd seen plenty. But that was usually where his job ended. When he'd walked into Kane's room, however, to find the rancher dead, Evans had felt what Stillman must feel all the time when confronted with a murdered man—the enormous pressure of finding the dead man's killer.

Of finding such a man and bringing him to justice.

What an enormous responsibility—to serve justice as well as to meet the needs of the living and the dead. To fulfill the law.

Evans felt a little breathless under the weight of such responsibility. As he sat in a chair by the window, he looked down at the five-pointed star on his vest. Before he'd walked into that second-story room in the Boston, the star had been just that. A few cents' worth of tin cut into the shape of a star. Now it felt as heavy as a gold ingot, and bright as a target drawn there on his chest for all to either hold in esteem or to take potshots at.

Evans threw back another shot of the brandy. As he set his glass back on the table, he glanced out the window and cursed. Clarissa Kane was just then riding into town from the east, toward the saloons. She rode a handsome black horse with one white sock. As she turned the horse toward the hitch racks fronting the Boston, Evans's heart hiccupped.

He was aware of the badge again. It hung heavy on his chest. It burned, in fact.

He could tell by the young woman's expression that she hadn't yet heard about her father's murder. As deputy sheriff . . . as well as her father's doctor . . . he supposed it was his duty to get over there before she pounded on the locked door or, worse, walked into the room where Kane had been killed. Evans didn't know if Campbell had had enough time to have the room cleaned, the bed stripped of its bloody sheets.

"Ah, bloody hell! Shit in a bucket!"

Evans slid his chair back, heaving himself to his feet. He looked at Thompson scowling at him from over the bar while he dropped a pickled pig's foot into a five-gallon crock. "Don't touch this bottle. I'll be back for it."

Evans pointed an admonishing finger at Thompson as he hustled out of the Drovers.

He was halfway up the Boston's carpeted stairs when he heard Bryce Campbell's and Clarissa Kane's voices mingling on the second floor, Campbell telling the woman she couldn't go into her father's room and Clarissa asking why.

"What on earth is going on here, Mister Campbell?" the young woman intoned. "Why won't you let me into my father's room?"

Campbell had opened his mouth to respond, but when he saw Evans making his way down the dimly lit hall, he closed his mouth and sighed with relief. He gestured toward the young woman, who had turned to follow the hotel manager's gaze to

Evans, and said, "Doc, I need help here."

"I got it," Evans said.

Campbell gave another sigh of relief and rushed off down the hall, meeting Evans's gaze with a dark one of his own as he passed.

Clarissa Kane turned full around toward Evans, deep lines of incredulity cutting across her broad forehead. "Doctor Evans, please tell me what is going on." Her voice had a slight tremor in it. She swung her right fist behind her and rammed it against the door with a dull thump. "Why won't that lackey let me enter this room?"

Evans saw that she had a key in her hand.

"Your father's dead, Miss Kane." Evans had spoken such words before. They never got any easier, but he'd come to understand that it was far better to come right out with them rather than beating around the bush. The latter method only caused more anxiety. Miss Kane already knew something was badly amiss. In fact, she already sensed her father was dead.

The words still hit her like a sledgehammer, however. Just as Evans had expected they would.

She widened her eyes in shock. "He's . . . what . . . ?"

She bent forward slightly at the waist, but let her rump sag backward against the door.

Evans stopped before her, placed his hands on her shoulders, and said, "He's dead, Miss Kane. I'm very sorry to have to tell you this. But your father has passed. Do you understand?"

She studied Evans, scrutinized him, almost as though she was wondering if he'd spoken another tongue. "No." She shook her head slightly. "No, he isn't. That's impossible. When I left . . . when I left him last night . . ."

She let her voice trail off as she swung around abruptly to face the door. She stuck the key in the lock. By the scratching sounds, Evans could tell her hands were shaking. He stepped back. He didn't know if Campbell had cleaned the room, but it no longer mattered. She was going to enter the room no matter what, and there was nothing Evans could do, short of knocking her over the head, to stop her.

She fumbled the door open, stepped into the room, stopped, and gasped, slapping a hand over her mouth. Evans walked into the room as she moved slowly toward the bed. Campbell had not attended to it. The covers were thrown back to reveal the rumpled sheet and the bloody pillow still bearing the impression of Kane's head.

"Poppa," Clarissa whispered as she stopped to stare down at the bed.

Evans stood just inside the door, giving her plenty of room. He expected her to crumple, maybe drop to her knees in tears. But she did not. She just stood there staring down at her father's bed, at the pillow, her hand cupped over her mouth in shock.

After a time, she turned stiffly toward the doctor and lowered her hand from her mouth. Her eyes were filled not with grief but with rage, which seemed to Evans much more in tune with her character, after all.

"Who killed my father, Doctor?"

"I don't know."

"You don't *know?*"

"No one seems to have seen anyone enter or leave your father's room. Whoever it was had a key." Evans glanced at the key she'd left in the lock, then turned to her once more. "Did you give your key to anyone, Miss Kane?"

"Surely not," she said, staring down at the indention of her father's head in the pillow again. She'd whispered the words. Staring at her face from over her right shoulder, the doctor thought he saw her lips tremble slightly. She clenched her fists at her sides as though to hold the emotion in check.

"Come, Miss Kane. I'll buy you a drink. You could use one.

So could I."

"I need to see him," she said, woodenly, still staring down at the bloody pillow.

"Later," Evans said. "First, a drink."

She drew a deep breath, then let it out slowly. "Yes." She turned to Evans and walked slowly toward him, her glassy eyes slightly downcast. "I could use a drink."

Evans started to turn away, intending to lead her out of the room, but she grabbed his left arm and turned him back to face her. Suddenly, she thrust herself against him. She was in his arms, pressing her face to his neck. Awkwardly, stunned, Evans wrapped his arms around her. She made a sound in her throat. He could feel her breasts against his chest. She lifted her head from his neck and he thought she was going to pull away from him but instead she pressed her lips to his, kissing him.

Evans found himself shrinking backward, but then he got his legs solidly beneath him again and placed his hands on her arms. He wouldn't have had time to return the young woman's kiss even if he'd wanted to—and he wasn't sure he'd wanted to; in fact, he wasn't sure of anything just now—because she abruptly pulled away from him.

Her eyes were wide. She looked as startled by what she'd done as he was. She brushed her fingers across her lips as she stumbled away from him, into the doorframe, kicking it with a boot heel.

She chuckled, then said a little breathlessly, "Sorry about that, Doc. I . . . I don't know what came over me."

"No," Evans said, flushed with embarrassment, floundering for words. "I don't . . . either."

He had to admit to himself, however vaguely, that the kiss had felt damned nice, though. In fact, now that it was over, he yearned to feel her lips against his once more.

"Maybe we'd better get that drink now," she said, chuckling

again with chagrin, "before I do something else to humiliate myself."

"Please don't feel humiliated, Miss Kane. In traumatic times, we never know what we'll do. Grief causes strange reactions."

He started off down the hall and she followed him a step or so behind.

"Yes, doesn't it?" she said as though to herself.

Evans and Miss Kane walked down the steps and crossed the lobby. Campbell was nowhere to be seen. Evans hoped the manager was off ordering someone to clean Kane's room in case the girl got the itch to visit it one more time. It wouldn't do her any good to see that mess again.

As Evans and Miss Kane crossed the street toward the Drovers, several townsmen touched their hat brims to her respectfully. A couple muttered sheepish condolences. She thanked them, keeping her head down, following Evans up onto the boardwalk fronting the Drovers, then pushing through the batwings behind him.

Evans was glad to see his bottle was on the table where he'd left it, near the large front window. As before, there were only a couple of old, retired freighters in the place, at a table near the back. They sat together in silence, beer and shot glasses on the table before them. Like an old married couple, they'd long ago run out of words for each other.

Thompson wasn't in view. The back door was open. He must have been out in the privy or gathering firewood to start his range, so he could cook the chili he always made available at noontime. Evans returned to his table. Clarissa stood staring down at it, lost in thought. The doctor indicated the chair across the table from his own.

When Miss Kane had sat, Evans dropped into his own chair and splashed brandy into each glass. He slid one across the table to her.

She sat staring at it, her hands in her lap.

"Do you have any idea who might want to see your father dead, Miss Kane?" the doctor asked. Not that he'd really wanted to broach the topic. When it came to murder, he was a fish out of water. But he was wearing the badge, after all, and he supposed Stillman would expect him to inquire.

She looked up at Evans as though deeply insulted. "No. Of course not. My father was not a hated man. I mean, he was . . . wealthy. He's had to fire some men, of course. But, no . . ." She shook her head, bewildered. "No, there is no one I know of who hated my father enough to kill him."

She'd spoken most of those words to the table, but now she looked abruptly up at Evans again. "Was he robbed? Had anyone ransacked the room? Not that there was anything valuable. My father never carried much cash . . ."

She let her voice trail off as Evans shook his head. "I didn't see evidence of a robbery. Ben would know better than I, and he'll look into it when he returns, I'm sure, but . . . I'm afraid I'm not much of a lawman, Miss Kane. I'm sorry Ben isn't here to run the killer down, which I'm sure he'd be doing right now."

"I don't understand any of this." Clarissa lifted the shot glass slowly to her lips, and sipped.

"No, you wouldn't. It will take some ti—"

Evans let the words die on his lips when low thunder rumbled outside the saloon. Only, it wasn't thunder.

It was a gaggle of scowling townsmen led by Judge Hoagland mounting the boardwalk fronting the Drovers. Hoagland pushed through the batwings, his ruddy cheeks apple red with fury beneath his crisp black bowler hat, and said, "Evans! I suspected I'd find you here!" The judge's anger-quivering voice rose until he fairly bellowed, *Where, for the love of god, is Ben Stillman and that killer, Johnny Nevada!*"

CHAPTER TWENTY-THREE

"Whoa!" Evans said, giving a caustic laugh as the judge and his entourage stormed into the saloon. "I didn't realize you'd already tried and convicted him, Judge."

Evans grinned up at the pompous, elderly gent scowling down at him. Hoagland was clad in a black, three-piece suit and was wielding a varnished willow walking stick. He wore black gloves. Pince-nez reading glasses dangled from a ribbon pinned to the lapel of his claw-hammer coat. The portly mayor, Roy Taylor, flanked him, looking flushed and on the verge of a stroke. Near the batwings, Ray Bliss and a few other Bliss riders stood fidgeting with three other drovers whom Evans recognized as Patten's men.

Raw meat was emblazoned on the drovers' retinas. They were fairly salivating, the doctor could tell. No doubt the others in the milling crowd spilling out onto the boardwalk were the six-man jury who'd been cheated out of a necktie party.

The judge's face reddened even more and his head wobbled as he said to Evans, "Everyone knows the so-called *Johnny Nevada* would have been convicted by now if he'd shown up at his trial. His flight is further guilt of his innocence. Where is Stillman? Where is that kid? I heard the sheriff deputized you. You must know where he is. Come on, Evans—out with it!"

The judge raised the varnished willow club in open threat.

"Jesus, settle down, Judge, or you're gonna have a seizure! I don't know where Ben and the kid went. If you brought your

Bible, I'll gladly place my hand on it and repeat myself."

Evans didn't like Hoagland. Never had. The judge was a plucky old buzzard who only thought of his own comforts and political future. It was no secret he had a hankering to run for territorial governor, so he could get his wife and daughter out of this unwashed backwater and off to a modicum of civilized society in Helena, where his odd, comely daughter wasn't in danger of being impregnated by every young gunslinger who rode into town.

Evans snickered inwardly at the thought. His amusement must have registered on his face, for the judge wielded the club again and shouted, "Now, you're mocking me! So help me, Evans, if you don't—"

"Enough! Enough!" cried Clarissa Kane, bounding to her feet across from the doctor. "Please, stop all of this. My god, you men are *savages*! I'll tell you where the sheriff took that boy if you'll only stop shouting and threatening the doctor! I've had enough. My father is dead, and my nerves are shot!"

Clarissa stumbled back against the window, pressing the heels of her hands to her head as though to quell a pounding headache.

"What?" the judge said, slowly lowering the stick he'd raised at Evans and turning to the young woman in shock. "Your . . . father . . . dead? Miss Kane, I'm so sorry. Please accept my sincere condolences." He glanced around at the other men flanking him, including the mayor, before turning back to Miss Kane. "I know this isn't the right time, but, uh . . . but, uh . . . how would you know where Stillman took the boy?"

"Because I led him there!" the girl screamed, sobbing as she leaned back against the window. "The sheriff wanted a secure place not too far from town and the Patten and Bliss ranches, so he could investigate the murder!"

"For godsakes where, Miss Kane?" asked the mayor before

lowering his voice several octaves and doffing his hat. "And I, too, of course would like to offer my condolences. Your father was a good man."

Clarissa lowered her hands. Tears dribbled down her cheeks. She looked at Hoagland.

Evans said with restrained urgency, "Don't. Don't tell them. They'll only—"

"The Rattlesnake Hills," she said, wooden-voiced, not staring at any of them but gazing past them toward the bar, though Evans doubted she was seeing anything except maybe that bloody pillow on the Boston's second floor.

The two retired freighters were staring Evans's way from the rear shadows, wide-eyed with prurient interest.

"That cabin in the Rattlesnake Hills, you mean, Miss Kane?" asked Ray Bliss, scowling from near the batwings.

Evans stared at the young woman in shock. Dread pooled like hot, sour milk in his belly. What in Christ's name . . . ?

"Yes, yes . . . that's the one," she said.

"I'll be headin' home for fresh horses, Judge!" Ray Bliss shouted, grabbing one of his men by the arm. "We'll have the kid back here to stand trial by nightfall!"

"Hold on! Hold on!" Hoagland bellowed. "We must organize!"

Too late.

Bliss and his three men were already mounting their horses at the hitch rack fronting the saloon.

"We'll be out there, too, Judge!" yelled one of Patten's men whom Evans recognized as Patten's foreman, Cade Stueves, a stocky, burly Canadian. He was one of the three Patten riders who claimed to have seen Johnny Nevada murder Dave Bliss.

In seconds, Patten's three men were mounted and riding headlong out of town, as well, whipping their reins against their horses' withers.

"Goddamnit, Drew—don't just stand there!" the judge shouted at his befuddled-looking bailiff standing near the mayor. "Saddle my horse. Your own, as well. We're all heading for the Rattlesnake Hills!"

The judge, the mayor, and the bailiff pushed through the roaring onlookers toward the batwings. The noisy onlookers followed them out, and in the ensuing silence, Evans turned to Clarissa Kane, who remained slumped back against the window.

Fear was like an animal snapping its teeth in the doctor's consciousness.

"Do you realize what you've just done?" he asked the young woman. "You may very well have just signed Ben Stillman's death warrant."

Stillman drew Sweets to a sharp halt and reached across his belly to close his right hand over the grips of his holstered Colt.

Two quick rifle blasts had just sounded from a jog of buttes on his right.

Sweets whickered uneasily.

Stillman's heart thudded with the same apprehension.

Several more blasts sounded, echoing around the buttes, swallowed quickly by the vaulting sky. They came regularly spaced, maybe two, possibly three seconds apart. There was a burst of five and then silence closed down over the buttes and the rangeland speckled with the black smudges of grazing cattle for as far as Stillman could see to the east.

The sun beat down, heavy with late-August humidity.

Cicadas whined. Grasshoppers arced over bending weed tips.

Another shot rang out. It was followed by the more distant sound of a bullet spanging off a rock. Sweets gave another start.

"Easy, boy," Stillman said. "I don't think we're the target." He gigged the horse ahead, saying, "Let's make sure."

He rode through a gap between two buttes. As the shooting

continued, he began to think this was another case of target practice. As he rode through the buttes, a long spine of eroded sandstone rose ahead of him, spotted with cedars, clumps of brush, and large rocks. A horse stood at the bottom of the rise about thirty yards to Stillman's left.

It was a handsome blue roan standing ground-tied. The horse looked at Stillman and gave a low, wary whicker. Sweets switched his tail.

Stillman peered up the rise. There was a clump of brush and a boulder at the spine's crest. A puff of gray smoke wafted above the rise on the heels of each screeching report.

Stillman shucked his Henry from its sheath and eased down out of the saddle.

"Stay, boy."

He dropped the reins and began making his way up the rise, moving slowly and keeping a wary eye on the gray smoke puffs rising from the rocks and brush. He cursed at the stiffness in his right leg, but thought the good doctor's stitches were holding. He didn't feel the oily moistness of blood.

As he climbed, there was a short pause in the shooting, during which he assumed the shooter was reloading. When Stillman was roughly fifty feet from the top of the crest, the shooting resumed. He could tell by the timbre of the reports that the shooter was wielding a Winchester .44.

As another crashing bark rose from the brush just beyond Stillman now, and to his left, he saw a pair of brown boots extending from a gap between the pocket of brush and a boulder. They were scuffed brown stockmen's boots, the shooter's denim trouser cuffs stuffed inside.

Another shot echoed.

There was the metallic scrape of another round being seated, and then Stillman kicked the shooter's left boot. He stepped forward, swinging to his right, and cocked his Henry. The shooter jerked with a start, turned onto his left elbow, and swung his Winchester toward the sheriff.

But it was not a man wielding the Winchester, Stillman saw now as a pair of angry brown eyes were trained on him, framed by long, thin brown hair folding down both sides of the pug-nosed, heart-shaped face of a girl in her late teens. Her calico blouse rose and fell sharply, sporting the lumps of a small, pert bosom.

"Sarah?"

Shock shone on Sarah Bliss's face, beneath the brim of her ragged, snuff-brown hat. "*Sheriff?* What are you doing out here?" She lowered the rifle she held in both her hands, which were gloved in elk hide.

"I was about to ask you the same thing."

"This is Bliss range. I'm home."

"Oh," Stillman said, remembering that he'd crossed the border between Patten Range and Bliss Range about a half hour ago, after he'd inspected the scene of Dave Bliss's shooting, finding nothing helpful. "Right." He glanced at the Winchester the girl held, generally aimed in his direction but low, around the tops of his boots.

A menacing curl of smoke licked up out of the barrel, like a serpent's tongue.

"What are you shooting at?" he asked.

Sarah hiked a shoulder and she scrunched up her face and eyes against the sun flanking Stillman. "Just shooting. At rocks and such."

"Target shooting?"

The shoulder went up and down again. "I reckon."

Stillman stepped forward and used his right boot to nudge the barrel of her smoking carbine a tad to the right, where it was no longer aimed at his ankles. A dark suspicion germinated inside his lawman's brain. "You're good with a rifle, are you, Sarah?"

"I guess you could say that, Sheriff."

"Girls aren't always."

"Is there a law against it?"

"No, there's no law against it. I just never took you to be one good with a rifle. I'm a little surprised."

"Well, I am," she said in a peeved tone, scowling up at Stillman. "Pa never had a boy. Just me. He taught me how to shoot because you never know when it would come in handy. Lots of wildcats in this country. And rattlesnakes."

Sarah depressed the Winchester's hammer, then rose to her feet and brushed off her butt and the backs of her thighs. "What're you doing out here, Sheriff? I figured you . . ." She glanced away darkly as she hesitated. "I figured you'd be at the trial. It's not over already, is it?"

"There was no trial."

Sarah's eyes widened hopefully. "Why?"

"It's not what you think. I busted Johnny out of jail to give me time to find your father's killer and to summon a different judge."

"Johnny?" The girl's tone grew thin, as though the boy's name alone made her drunk on emotion. "Where is he?"

"I thought you were through with him."

She lowered her eyes as well as her mouth corners. "I could never be through with Johnny. I was just angry because he broke up with me."

"You said he killed your father, Sarah. Do you still believe that?"

"No."

"Who do you believe killed him?"

She looked up at Stillman, her eyes grave, sincere. "I don't know, Sheriff. Honest, I don't."

Stillman glanced at the carbine that the girl held in both hands across her thighs. "Your father was shot with a .44."

She followed Stillman's glance, then scowled up at him in shock. "You don't think I killed my own father—do you, Sheriff?"

"At this point, Sarah, everyone's a suspect. Even you . . . now that I know you can wield a Winchester." Stillman gestured at a rock behind her. "Sit down there, will you? I want to talk to you."

Stillman hitched up his denims and eased down on a rock a few feet away from her, at the edge of the brush. She stared at him skeptically, the humid breeze toying with her hair. "First off, how come you're not in town? I'd expected you to be in town for the trial, never mind the trial didn't pan out."

"I was going to go, but then . . . I don't know . . . I reckon I just couldn't bear it. I knew the judge would hang Johnny no matter what, on account of his daughter." Sarah pursed her lips and brushed away the tears that began to dribble down from her eyes. "I didn't want to listen to it. I didn't want to hear him tell Johnny he was gonna hang. And . . . and after Johnny told me he didn't love me . . . I don't know, Sheriff, I've just been so heartbroken lately I can't eat or sleep or do nothin'. All I can do is ride my horse out here and shoot this old coyote carbine, as Pa used to call it."

She patted the stock of the rifle in her hands, lowered her head, and sobbed.

She looked across at Stillman, tears glistening in her large brown eyes. "I still love him, Sheriff. Honest, I do. I'll never love another man as much as I love Johnny, and I just know he's gonna hang, and I know—I just *know*—he didn't kill Pa. He couldn't have killed my pa. Johnny wouldn't do that, Sheriff Stillman!"

"All right, Sarah—let me ask you this. Do you know where

your father had been the night he was murdered? I saw where he was shot, and I saw the tree he was supposedly shot from, but what I'm wondering is where had he been that night. He was a good ten miles from your headquarters."

Sarah sniffed as she wiped tears from her cheeks with her hands. "He must have been riding back from seeing Mister Patten."

"Patten said he hadn't seen him that night."

"Well, then, I don't know where he was riding in from, then."

"Had your father visited the Patten ranch many times in recent days or weeks?"

Sarah nodded. "A few times."

"Do you know what they were meeting about?"

"Pa said that Mister Patten intended to fence off his range. He was tired of nesters moving in. Him and Pa were trying to come to an agreement about where the fence would go. They were trying to do it without lawyers, since neither of them trusted lawyers."

"What do you mean—'trying'? Were they having trouble coming to an agreement?"

"Yeah." Sarah nodded again, wrinkling the skin above the bridge of her nose as she gazed at Stillman with a cast of concern, maybe of suspicion, entering her gaze. "Pa said Mister Patten was as stiff-necked as a graveyard statue."

"So your pa seemed angry after their meetings, did he?"

"I don't know . . . maybe after one time. That was the only time Pa mentioned it. To me, at least. He was washin' up out on the porch and I happened to come out to play my harmonica. I really didn't think that much about it, Sheriff. Do you think that Mister . . . ?"

Sarah let her voice trail off as her gaze dropped with dark speculation.

"I don't know," Stillman said. "But if your pa visited Patten the night he was murdered, it's mighty peculiar Patten lied about it." Stillman rose. "If I can get Johnny a new trial, will you testify to what you just told me?"

"Yes. Of course. Do you think the judge will set Johnny free after he hears what I told you about Mister Patten?"

"He might have to. If a jury tells him to. But I'm hoping to have a new judge assigned to the trial, which I should be able to do." Stillman just had to keep Johnny Nevada alive long enough to be tried at the new trial.

"What about Mister Patten, Sheriff?"

"I don't have any evidence that Patten killed your pa. I doubt I'll be able to rustle up any, either. Patten's men are loyal, obviously. They so far seem to be the only witnesses to the murder."

"Maybe they killed Pa themselves."

"Maybe." But, if so, why did they assault the courthouse ostensibly to kill Johnny the night before the trial? Why not just let him stand trial? They must have known there was a better than good chance a jury would have convicted him, especially after Hoagland weighed the proceedings heavily against the boy.

Stillman rose and shouldered his Henry. He stared seriously down at the girl.

"Sarah, tell me the truth, now. Were you really with Johnny the night your father was killed?"

Sarah drew a deep, raspy breath and let it out slowly. She looked up guiltily at Stillman and voiced a bitter, "No."

"All right," Stillman said with a reassuring half-smile. "Thank you, Sarah."

"But that doesn't mean Johnny killed Pa."

"No, it doesn't. I have to go."

"I'll walk down with you. I'd better be getting back to the ranch."

As the girl walked with Stillman down the rise toward where their horses grazed a few feet away from each other, she said,

"Where is Johnny, Sheriff?"

"I've got him somewhere safe."

"Are you going back to him now?"

"I reckon I am. I think I've done about all I can for him now except to send a telegram down to Helena and ask for a new judge."

He'd probably send the telegram from Chinook tomorrow. He'd request an order be sent immediately to Judge Hoagland from the Territorial Judiciary Committee, ordering Hoagland to recuse himself. The territorial marshal's office would likely send a deputy U.S. marshal to enforce the order.

Then Clantick would likely be safe for Stillman to lock Johnny up again in the courthouse jail, and Stillman could go home.

He wondered how Evans was handling things in town.

The thought had no sooner brushed through his consciousness than the rataplan of several sets of hooves rose in the southeast. Stillman and Sarah had just reached their horses, and Stillman was plucking his reins off the ground. He looked toward where the trail curved along the far end of the rise on which Sarah had been shooting. A group of at least a half-dozen riders was galloping along the trail, heading north.

One of the riders turned his head toward Stillman then pointed, shouting, "Hey—look there, Ray!"

The lead rider, who appeared to be Ray Bliss, reined up sharply, as did the others behind him, their dust catching up to them. They all turned toward Stillman, then swung their horses off the trail and galloped hell for leather in Stillman's direction. It was Ray Bliss at the head of the pack, all right.

And he didn't look happy.

Stillman swung up into his saddle, pumped a round into his Henry's action, and said, "Sarah, you'd best get on home."

CHAPTER TWENTY-FOUR

Stillman counted seven riders. They were coming hard and fast, reins held high. When Ray Bliss jerked back on his reins roughly forty feet from Stillman and Sarah Bliss, the others followed suit behind him, one sliding his revolver from its holster.

"Leather that hogleg!" Stillman shouted, raising the Henry to his shoulder.

The Bliss rider raised the pistol.

Stillman aimed at the dead center of the man's chest and fired, punching the man back in his saddle.

The man riding to the dead man's right bellowed a raucous curse and started to unsheathe his own pistol.

Stillman shot him, too, drilling him a little higher than the first one, who was now rolling in the dust behind his shrieking, pitching horse. The second man screamed and dropped to the left side of his own mount, a foxy Arab that reared sharply, swung around, and pounded off to the east. The rider had gotten his foot caught in his stirrup, and he went bouncing along the ground beside the Arab, bellowing, voice quavering with the violence of his hard ride and quickly dwindling with distance.

"Christ!" Ray Bliss yelled, holding his hand over the grips of his own pistol, but wisely leaving the gun in its holster.

They all watched as the Arab dragged its rider about sixty yards to the east and swerved sharply to avoid a boulder. In doing so, it slammed its rider with a sharp smacking, crunching sound against the boulder's broad side. The man dropped to the ground at the base of the rock, unmoving, while the horse gave another terrified whinny, shook its head, and continued galloping off to the east.

Stillman's gaze had left the five surviving Bliss Box B riders for only a moment. He stared at them now down the smoking barrel of his rifle as they jerked their shocked looks back to him from the dead man near the boulder. All five had their hands on their guns, but all five guns were still seated in leather.

"Any sonofabitch who points a gun in my direction gets blown out of his saddle!" Stillman barked furiously. He loudly racked another round into the Henry's action, flinging the spent cartridge out behind him, and narrowed his eyes with challenge. "Who's next?"

Ray Bliss glared at Stillman, hard-jawed, eyes like dung-brown stones. "You crazy son of a bitch! You had no cause to do that!"

"I told them to keep their irons in the leather. They didn't. Now they're dancing with *el diablo,* and you fellas will be, too, unless you remove your hands from those sidearms by the time I count to two!"

"Shit!" one of the Box B men yelped and jerked his hand away from his hogleg, as though it were a hot potato.

The others, including Bliss, also removed their hands from their guns. Bliss slid his hand to his thigh, scowling, nostrils flaring at Stillman. Sarah sat her own mount to Stillman's left, trying to keep her jittery roan under a tight rein. She looked at the dead man lying back a ways in the short blond grass. He lay spread eagle, belly up, facing the sky. Blood painted the ground around him.

"Oh, god," the girl said, jerking her head at the man by the rock. "Are . . . are they dead?"

"Go on home, Sarah," Stillman said.

"Yeah, go on home, Sarah," Bliss said, keeping his glare

riveted on the sheriff. "This here's a wanted man. Wanted for busting a proven criminal out of his own jail."

"Johnny didn't kill Pa, Uncle Ray. I know he didn't!"

"You hush!" Bliss held up a gloved finger in stern admonishment. "When it comes to that boy, you don't think straight. He's got a reputation as a killer. He acts one way around you, entirely different around everyone else . . . includin' your pa."

"I know him, Uncle Ray," Sarah said, stubbornly shaking her head. "I know him. He wouldn't shoot Pa."

"He threatened Dave in town, fool girl!" Bliss waved angrily. "Get on home!"

"He's right, Sarah," Stillman said. "Best if you ride on home now."

"I want to see Johnny. Won't you please take me to him, Sheriff?"

"No."

"I want to see Johnny, too," Bliss said, puffing up his chest but keeping his rage on a leash. "Now, you gonna take us to him, Sheriff, or are we gonna have to ride *through* you? We know where he is. The judge does, too."

Stillman frowned. "How do . . . ?"

"Kane's daughter told us."

It was Stillman's turn to feel the hot wash of fury. He'd known he shouldn't have trusted her. She'd double-crossed him. Why? He'd thought there was something off about her wanting to help him, but he'd bought her story that she'd wanted to make recompense for how she'd spouted off to him on the street, and that she was bored, holing up in the Boston while her father healed.

Just because Stillman had nearly twenty years of lawdogging experience behind him didn't mean he couldn't make an ass of himself now and then. Obviously, he'd done just that when he'd trusted Clarissa Kane to lead him into the Rattlesnake Hills and keep the secret.

Why had she set the trap for him?

Like Bliss, Stillman kept his rage on a leash. The need he felt to get back to the cabin before the judge got there was a wild horse inside him. He narrowed his angry eyes at Bliss and the four other riders. "I'm riding back to that cabin. Any of you follows me, I'll kill you. You understand, Ray?"

Bliss stared at Stillman. He glanced at the Henry repeater Stillman had aimed at Bliss's belly. Ray glanced at the other men around him. They were hot about the two saddles Stillman had emptied. They wanted satisfaction for those two men, and they wanted Johnny Nevada.

But they were up against a determined lawman who'd already killed two of their own and was obviously a trigger jerk away from kicking another one or two of them out with hot lead. That was the frustrated sentiment conveyed by their wary, angry gazes beneath the brims of their dusty, sweat-stained hats.

"All right, Stillman," Bliss said, holding his gloved hands up, palms out. "Okay. You got it. We have two dead men to bury. You beat us, Sheriff. I understand that."

Sarah cast several dark, anxious looks between Stillman and her uncle. Then she held her gaze on Stillman, and said, "He doesn't mean it!"

"Goddamnit, girl, you shut your mouth!" Bliss kicked his horse toward her, lifting his arm to backhand her.

Stillman shot his hat off.

Bliss jerked his mount down and turned his startled gaze at the sheriff. He looked at his hat lying on the ground beside a rock. The bullet had clipped the crown, making a round, ragged-edged hole. Bliss turned to Stillman again. He smiled. There was no warmth at all in the smile. There was only a hard, challenging rage. It shone in the firm clasp of his off-white teeth, the flintiness of his eyes.

"There I go again, losin' my temper," Bliss said with phony chagrin. He grinned briefly. "You'd best get back to that cabin, Sheriff. If the judge and the Patten riders beat you there, that boy will likely swing. The judge has got his drawers in a real big twist"—he turned to deliver the last words of the sentence to his niece—"on account o' how Johnny spewed his demon seed into his daughter."

Sarah leaned forward over her saddle horn and screamed maniacally, "You go to hell, Ray! You go to *hell!*"

Bliss closed his lips over his teeth and said with slow, quiet menace, "I'm gonna strip you naked and tan your ass raw for that." One of the men behind him chuckled lasciviously, then quickly composed himself, raking a hand down his face, looking sheepish.

Sarah turned to Stillman. "I'm going with you. You can't stop me. You'll shoot them, but I know you won't shoot me."

"All right," Stillman said, not wanting to waste precious minutes by arguing further and in vain. "Ride out. Straight north. I'll be behind you."

Sarah reined her mount around and put the spurs to it.

As she galloped off into the distance, angling away from the rise, Stillman held his rifle on Bliss. "If I see you . . . even just catch a brief glimpse of you on our back trail," he said with the same quiet menace with which Bliss had threatened his niece, "I'll kill you. No questions asked. You'll die, and I'll leave your body to the birds."

"I hear you, Sheriff," Bliss said, raising his hands again, nodding. There was a faint flicker of mockery in his eyes.

Stillman backed Sweets away from Bliss and the other four. They sat watching him stiffly from their saddles. Gradually, as Stillman put more and more ground between them, the dark dots of their eyes faded into the general tan of their faces. Still, he could see Bliss's lower jaw moving as the man turned his head slightly to one side. He was giving orders even as he sat staring toward Stillman.

When Stillman was fifty yards away, he swung the buckskin around and booted him into an instant, ground-devouring gallop. Sarah was a gray-brown speck ahead of him. He angled toward her, kicking Sweets into more speed. The horse put its head down, drew its ears back, and stretched its stride.

Stillman caught up to the girl after about ten minutes of hard riding. Seeing him behind her, Sarah slowed her mount. She stopped when Stillman turned to gaze behind him.

"Are they following?" she asked.

Stillman studied their back trail. He could see nothing behind him now but the chalky bluffs and open prairie, grass ruffling in the breeze and combed by the shade of passing clouds. The riders had disappeared.

"They'll follow," Stillman said, turning Sweets around and continuing north.

"What happens then?" the girl asked, riding along beside him.

Stillman turned to her. He saw no reason to soft-coat it for. It was her choice to be here, after all. Against his own advice. "Your uncle is going to learn I'm a man who keeps his word."

He turned his head forward, and said, *"Hi-yah!"*

Sweets lurched into another lunging lope.

CHAPTER TWENTY-FIVE

"Have you ever been silly in love, Sheriff?" Sarah asked Stillman much later, when the growing darkness had forced them to camp for the night in the Rattlesnake Hills.

"Silly in love?" Stillman said, taking a sip of his smoking coffee. "Sure, I was young once. I may not look like it, but I was. Every kid's been silly in love, I reckon. If they're lucky. If they're lucky, the silliness will go away, but the love will remain."

He took another sip of his coffee and looked at the girl curled on her side, resting her chin on the heel of her hand, gazing at him in the darkness. Her saddle blanket was draped over her shoulders.

Stillman raked a sleeve across his mustache and added, "I reckon knowin' when it's silly and not silly anymore comes with age. I love my wife with all my heart, plum crazy for the gal, but it's not silly anymore. It's honest and real."

"You don't think my love for Johnny is honest and real?"

"I'm not gonna make any judgments about your love for Johnny, Sarah. I reckon what you're going through is what you have to go through, and time will tell if your feelings last."

She sat up with a sigh and grabbed her Winchester carbine, which was leaning against a tree beside her. She picked up an oily cloth, as well, and, for the sixth or seventh time since they'd holed up here in a hollow between buttes, in a scattering of spring-fed willows and stunted box elders and cottonwoods, she ran the cloth across the gun's worn but shiny-clean walnut stock and glistening barrel.

She'd obviously been taught to care for a weapon. And she knew how to use the carbine. Stillman had witnessed that on the ridge.

He studied the girl now. She'd removed her hat and boots. She sat Indian-style, each stocking-clad foot resting atop the opposite knee. She cradled the rifle in her lap the way some girls cradled a favorite doll. Her straight, dark-brown hair fell to her shoulders. She stared at the rifle in her hands as she cleaned it, pressing the tip of her tongue against the underside of her bottom lip. She was in fond reverie. Caressing the gun and thinking of what?

Or who?

The kid who called himself Johnny Nevada, of course.

She was mesmerized by that boy. Infatuated.

Stillman looked at the rifle in her loving hands. Was she infatuated enough to kill her own father to make it possible for her to continue seeing the kid? Was Stillman looking at the killer of Dave Bliss—the man's own, pretty, waifish, lonely, love-haunted daughter sitting only a few feet away from him in the darkness?

That nagging question was one reason he hadn't objected too strongly to Sarah's riding along with him to the cabin. He'd wanted to get to know her better, to feel her out, as it were, about just how much in love she really was with Johnny Nevada. Just how capable she was of murdering the man who'd helped create her.

Now Stillman knew she was probably as deeply in love with Johnny as any girl had ever been with any boy, and that she certainly had the skill to make a killing rifle shot. She also had the motive to make it. Something else strumming the lawman's suspicions was the fact that he hadn't heard Sarah utter one word of sorrow regarding her father's passing. All he'd heard from her was how much she loved Johnny and how deeply she believed the kid hadn't killed her father.

Stillman studied the fire flickering fifty feet away from him in the darkness, in a slight clearing in the trees. That was where he and the girl had originally made camp. After the sun had gone down and while the last light was trailing from the sky, they'd moved over here, leaving their saddles and most of their gear over there.

Stillman intended to keep the fire burning low all night, a good distance away. He'd erected a man-shaped frame from tree branches, and draped a blanket over the frame's "shoulders." He placed his cream Stetson atop a stick poking up from the man's "back," if it had been a man over there—if it had been him over there—leaning against a tree to the left of the fire. A rough imitation of Sarah was over there, as well—just her hat and a blanket draped over saddlebags near her saddle, on the far side of the fire from "Stillman." Over there, "Sarah" lay curled in sleep against the underside of her saddle. Her side of the fire was dark enough to compensate for any crudities in her design.

Or so Stillman hoped. He wanted anyone who might come stalking tonight to believe their quarry was over there by the fire.

Meanwhile, he and the girl should be relatively safe here in the dense darkness with a stone wall behind them, and trees and a dry, rocky riverbed to either side. He'd picketed the horses between their actual bivouac and the fire beyond, to Stillman's right. He could occasionally see the mounts' shadows moving as they cropped the dry prairie grass growing sparsely amongst the rocks. The horses' eyes occasionally caught the light of the fire and glowed a dull umber.

"Do you believe the old legend, Sheriff?"

Stillman glanced at Sarah. She was still caressing her rifle with the cloth. She wasn't looking at him, but staring down at the carbine. He could see her lips spread with a beguiling little smile.

"Snake Woman?"

Now she looked at him, her eyes bright with a young person's eager pleasure in dark tales. "You've heard of her, then."

Stillman took a swallow of his now-cold coffee. "You can't live in this country long without hearing about Snake Woman— some old trader or ranch hand telling about his encounter with her, about how he barely made it out of these hills alive. Or about how his partner rode in here after a herd-quit steer." Stillman smiled across at the girl, then snapped a lucifer to life on his thumbnail. "The partner and steer never to be heard from again, of course."

"Do you believe?"

"No," Stillman said with a sigh. "I don't believe in those things anymore. Too damned old and jaded, I reckon."

"I do. I believe in her. I've known hands who've seen her, roaming these hills. They always hear the rattling, sort of a laughing sound or like the wind in dry fall leaves, they say . . . just before they see her. They say if she looks at you, you'll die of snakebite within seven days."

Stillman grunted.

"One of Pa's old hands saw her during a fall gather. He died three days later in the bunkhouse. From snakebite. But no one could ever find the snake."

"One had gotten in," Stillman said. "And then slipped out again. There's always an explanation for such things, Sarah."

"I don't know," the girl said with a note of shrewd warning in her voice, glancing around in the darkness. She drew the saddle blanket tighter about her shoulders, and shivered. "I've always steered clear of these hills on account of her."

"Oh? Why so brave all of a sudden?"

"Johnny."

Stillman had anticipated the response. He nodded. He had to admit he envied her a little for her innocence. There was something to be said for being young and silly in love and believing in legends like the one about Snake Woman. The world was probably much larger and far more magical for her than it was for him. On the other hand, that same innocence might have compelled her to kill her father in the name of love for a boy who couldn't be trusted.

He didn't want to believe it about her. But he had to admit it was possible.

"Will the judge and Patten's men get to Johnny before we do, Sheriff?" Sarah asked.

"There's a chance. They're likely holed up now on the other side of these hills, to the west, since they're coming from town. But depending on when they got started, they might be closer to the cabin than we are. We'll get started as soon as there's enough light to ride by. Won't do us any good to risk the health of our horses."

She looked at Stillman. Even in the darkness he could see the worried cast to her gaze. "What will the judge do if he gets to Johnny first?"

"I wish I could say. I've always known him to be a tough man, but fair. This whole thing with Johnny and his daughter— well, it's turned him into something else entirely. Someone I don't like a bit, whose actions I can't predict."

"You don't think he'd just hang Johnny, do you, Sheriff?"

"No." Stillman shook his head. It was an honest answer. He didn't think Hoagland would go that far. "But there's no tellin' what Patten's men might do." Again, he saw no reason to sweeten the cream for her. She was tough enough to know what he really thought. She should be prepared for the worst.

She looked down at the rifle in her hands, squeezing it. "They can't kill him. They just can't. Being apart from Johnny is almost too much for my heart to bear." She looked at Stillman again sharply, eyes bright with tears reflecting the light of the distant fire. "If they kill him, I'll just die!"

"You believe in him that much—do you, Sarah?"

"Yes." Sobbing quietly, she lay on her side. She laid the rifle beside her, and placed her hand on it as though for comfort. She drew her knees toward her belly.

She sobbed for a time. Then Stillman could tell by her soft, even breaths that she'd fallen asleep, her head on one open hand, the other hand still resting on the carbine.

Stillman looked around, listening. When he was relatively sure they were still alone out here, he walked over and built up the fire. He walked into the darkness to relieve himself and to check the horses and have a careful look around before returning to his and Sarah's bivouac, where the girl remained asleep.

He sat down and leaned back against a tree, propping his rifle against the tree to his right. He dropped his chin and let himself drift into a shallow slumber.

He heard himself grunt with a start when something woke him.

He looked over at the fire. It had burned down to about half the size it had been when he'd built it up.

He frowned. What had awakened him?

Sweets whickered softly, giving the horse's customary warning to its rider. A cold hand of ominous revelation pressed against the back of Stillman's neck.

They were no longer alone.

Stillman reached slowly for his Henry and set it butt down on the ground beside him, snugged up against his right hip. Even more slowly, he worked the cocking lever, ever-so-quietly sliding a fresh cartridge into the chamber.

He rested his thumb on the cocked hammer and stared

straight out over his crossed boots toward the fire. The flickering, umber light lit only about a ten-square-yard circle around it, jostling shadows against the trees, shunting soft light against the wall of darkness. Stillman could barely see "himself" resting against the tree over there. He could see nothing of the "Sarah" except a smudge of darkness against the slightly paler ground.

In the fire, a branch popped softly. A puff of gray smoke and sparks wafted toward the starry sky.

A dark figure stepped out of the trees to stand on the far side of the fire. It could have been the shadow of a breeze-jostled branch, but there was no breeze. The shadow stood frozen. As Stillman stared at it, he thought he could start to make out the outline of a man's figure standing with his back to the darkness. A wavering ray of firelight flicked across the man's nose, beneath the brim of his hat.

Another man stepped out of the darkness to stand six feet from the first one, to his left. There was no doubt that this figure was a man. The fire cast a finger of dark copper light out that way, and it shone in the man's eyes, glinting off the barrel of the rifle he held in his hands. The two stood there for a time.

And then another man walked out of the darkness to Stillman's far right.

The first two had walked into the camp from the west. This one had come in from the north. He was roughly the same height as the first two, but he was wider, thicker. There was a raw, imposing heaviness about him. That's what marked him as Ray Bliss. He didn't stop at the edge of the camp but walked up along the side of the fire.

He was a silhouette against it now, from Stillman's vantage, carrying a rifle low in his right hand, barrel aimed casually at the ground.

The stocky Bliss walked up to where "Stillman" rested against the tree. Bliss stopped and pumped three rounds into "Stillman's" slack form, each crashing report of the rifle smashing the night wide open, flames lapping from the barrel.

Sarah sat bolt upright with a gasp.

Stillman held up a hand to her for quiet, hoping she could see it in the darkness.

Ray Bliss's anger-pinched voice came to Stillman's ears clearly on the still night air as he stared down at the strewn, broken branches and the blanket he'd just shot all to hell. "I'll be a goddamned son of a bitch!"

"What the hell?" the nearest one of the other two said, starting toward Bliss.

Stillman had quietly gained his feet. He raised his voice to say, "You better not have put a hole in my hat, Bliss."

As the three men jerked their gazes toward him, Stillman raised the Henry and calmly but quickly sent six rounds hurtling through the darkness to rend flesh, perforate organs, and pulverize bone. Amid the Henry's crashing reports, the dying men screamed and groaned as they danced bizarre two-steps around the fire, being punched back from it where they hit the ground and rolled, thrashing briefly before falling silent.

Two fell silent, that was.

"Stay here, Sarah."

Stillman crossed over to the fire, and looked around. In the distance rose the drumming of two horses galloping off into the darkness. That would be Bliss's other two riders. Likely bolting, heading back to the ranch.

One man lay grunting and thrashing just beyond Stillman, in the darkness on the other side of the fire.

Stillman walked around the fire and into the darkness. He stood gazing down at Bliss. He recognized the man's broad, fleshy face in the vagrant rays of dancing flames. Bliss stared up at Stillman, eyes glassy with fast-approaching death.

"You bastard," he said, breathing hard, his lumpy chest rising and falling heavily. He clamped both hands over his belly. He'd taken another round to his upper right thigh. "I just . . . I just wanted to avenge my brother."

"Not on my watch, Ray."

"You go to hell, Stillman! You're a broken-down old lawman!"

"I used to think so." Stillman grinned coldly. He didn't normally feel this much satisfaction, killing men who deserved killing. There was usually a speck of regret that it had come to killing. "But I'm feeling better with every hour that passes. Stronger. My back hasn't felt so good in years. All I needed was to get on my horse again, and get after it. I'm going to live to find your brother's killer, and you're going to die never knowing for sure who really did it."

Bliss gritted his teeth as he glared up at the lawman. He ground his jaws until his teeth cracked. "Go to hell!"

"You want to die for a while, or do you want me to end it right here?"

Bliss almost chuckled at that. It came out as a feeble grunt. He jerked his head a little, blinked, and said, "End it."

Stillman did.

Chapter Twenty-Six

A soft wind blew at dawn, as though somehow the blood-red sun just now lifting its molten ahead above the rolling bluffs to the east of the Rattlesnake Hills were stirring it, sucking the air toward it.

The breeze died. Another one rose. This one had a little more vigor. It rattled the heavy, summer's-end leaves of the gnarled cottonwood crouching over the dugout cabin in front of which Hec Fenton sat, his Spencer carbine resting across his skinny thighs. As the breeze continued to rise, skittering old leaves along the ground fronting the cabin, a rattling sounded.

Fenton's heart thumped.

The old frontiersman pricked his ears, lifting his chin from where it had started to sag as he'd begun to doze with his eyes open. He'd slept sporadically the night before, on the ground beside the small cook fire he'd built fronting the cabin. He widened his eyes now and stared down into the old riverbed that twisted along the base of the long slope the earthen cabin had been dug into. Brush trembled and more dew-dappled cottonwood and willow leaves fluttered there, on both sides of the serpentine cut.

Again, the rattling sounded. Faintly at first, but as the breeze grew, the rattling grew. It became shriller, rising above the raspy sound of the breeze itself.

Again, Fenton's heart thumped. His pulse quickened until he could feel the throbbing in his wrists, his temples.

"No," he heard himself say as he felt himself shrinking back in his chair.

He'd heard the legend. Everyone around here had. Fenton was old enough, had lived long enough, to see enough, to give credence enough to such a tale as Snake Woman . . . to know *it could be true.*

He himself had heard the legend from a Blackfoot brave he'd met long ago, when he'd been hunting game in the Sweetgrass Hills, before so much of this northern country had been cluttered up by ranches and their endless herds of beef that had replaced the buffalo. The brave had told the tale so matter-of-factly, as though he were reporting uncontested fact, and in such a tone of stern warning, that how could Fenton not take it to heart?

After hearing the tale, he'd given a wide berth to these hills. He was only here now because of his grandson.

Fenton hadn't realized, however, just how much stock he'd placed in the story until this minute. Fear grew like a living, fledgling thing inside him as another breeze lifted, and with it, so too did the rattling. He shivered, imagining being pumped full of venom. Imagining the raw poisonous burn, the unbounded agony, vomiting bile, the slow death, bit by bit, limb by limb until the heart swelled, turned black, and ground to a halt.

A shadow moved along the canyon floor, behind the fluttering trees.

She was coming. She was coming for him, Hec Fenton, and soon he wouldn't be merely imagining such a death.

Snake Woman . . .

He never should have come here. Stillman never should have brought his grandson to such a haunted place.

The low rumble of distant hoof thuds rose with the breeze and the rattling sound accompanying it. Fenton stared down the cut, at the shadow flicking through the trees. *Oh, god—she was coming!*

Fenton sat frozen in his chair, hands sweating around the ancient stock of his Spencer, his heart tattooing a war rhythm against his breastbone.

The rattling died all at once. Fenton watched the shadow until it became a flock of crows rising up from the cut, from behind the trees, to go barking off over the buttes to the south, dwindling into the distance, the individual black specks becoming one small, shrinking mass.

The breeze died.

In its place rose the hooves of many galloping riders.

Fenton lifted his gaze toward a tall butte beyond the cut and slightly to the west, on his right. The rising sun just now cast its lemon light on a group of men galloping around the shoulder of the butte, coming hard and fast, dropping gradually toward the cut at the bottom.

The lead rider pointed toward the dugout and shouted, "There it is!"

"Granddad, what the hell's goin' on out there?" Fenton's grandson called from inside the cabin.

Fenton knew a moment's confusion. His relief that Snake Woman's plans for him had been interrupted by the oncoming riders was tempered and then pummeled into oblivion by the fact that he was likely in nearly as much danger as he'd been a moment ago. Just a different kind of danger.

"Granddad!" the kid shouted, hammering on the cabin door.

Fenton rose to his feet, holding the Spencer tightly up high across his chest. "Stay in there, Johnny. Don't come out here. Be quiet and keep your head down."

"What's going on?" Johnny's face was in the window over his grandfather's left shoulder. "Who's coming, Granddad?"

"Stay in there, Johnny. Keep your head down."

The old man moved away from the cabin, his weak old heart again thudding. Fear once again grew in him, making his legs feel spongy. He stared toward the butte on which he'd spied the riders, but they were no longer there. He couldn't see them now, but he could hear the clatter of their horses' hooves on the rocky bed of the ancient river.

"Granddad, you gotta get rid of 'em!" his grandson shouted behind the door. "Granddad, they're gonna hang me!"

"Stay down, Johnny. Keep quiet. You leave this to me."

"Granddad!"

Fenton walked a little ways farther down the slope. He stared into the cut.

The clatter of the galloping horses grew louder. Men were shouting, conversing. Tack squawked and bridle bits rattled in horses' mouths.

The group galloped around a bend and into Fenton's field of vision. Fenton recognized three of Vince Patten's men riding out front. They wore stockmen's traditional chaps and hide vests over work shirts, six-shooters bristling on their hips, rifles poking out of saddle scabbards.

Behind them rode several toughnuts from town—ex-railroaders and saloon swampers. A couple of game hunters and the known brawler, Riley Parkins. For the most part, the posse was comprised of mean, simple-minded men usually found at the center of any trouble in or around Clantick.

Riding at the end of the pack and looking awkward in the saddle was Judge Hoagland. Beside him rode the town's fat mayor, Roy Taylor. Both the judge and Taylor stood out in their fancy-Dan attire complete with gold watch chains, frock coats, and bowler hats. The judge, slender and bony, wore a red silk neckerchief, which ribboned out behind him in the wind. The mayor, short and round as a rain barrel, wore cream slacks shoved down into high-topped riding boots.

Fenton swallowed his fear as the Patten riders swung out of the wash and charged up the rise. When they were fifty yards away and coming fast, Fenton cocked the Spencer and raised it to his shoulder, sliding it somewhat uncertainly across the gang growing before him.

"Put down that goddamn rifle, old man!" barked Cade Stueves, whose long, angular, sunburned face and a drooping mustache were nearly the same color as the roan gelding he was riding. Hair of the same shade curled over his ears. "The kid in the cabin?"

"None of your business where the kid is," Fenton said, snapping the words through gritted teeth. "Ben Stillman left me here to guard over him. He is not to leave that cabin!"

"So he is in the cabin," said Judge Hoagland, putting his gray up through the riders now milling in front of Fenton.

The mayor flanked the judge and then rode up beside him and stopped to the left of Cade Stueves. To the right of Stueves were the two other Patten riders—Reese and Thorn, who also claimed to have seen Johnny ambush Dave Bliss. Both were known to be hard-driving, quick-to-rile, only partially reformed outlaws. Which meant they fit in well with the rest of the men in the Patten bunkhouse, including Stueves.

Stueves drew one of his two pistols from its holster and clicked the hammer back.

"I wouldn't to that, Stueves," warned Fenton, shifting his rifle to the Patten foreman.

To Stueves, Judge Hoagland said, "Holster it, Stueves. I'm in charge here."

"Can't you see he's holding a rifle on us?" Stueves said. "The damn thing is cocked!"

Hoagland turned to Fenton. "My power trumps Stillman's, Fenton. Your grandson should be in jail. In fact, he was to be tried yesterday. Stillman breaking him out of that cellblock was an illegal act. I am here to bring Johnny Nevada back to Clantick to stand trial for the murder of Dave Bliss."

"The hell you are!" This from Lon Thorn, who shared an incredulous look with Stueves. Thorn chuckled. "We didn't ride all this way just to bring him back to town. We're gonna hang that devil!"

"Absolutely not!" Hoagland yelled.

"Bullshit!" Stueves said. "We've wasted enough time on you, Hoagland. We got work to do and wages to earn back at the ranch. We didn't ride all this way to play nursemaid to that kid. We rode out here to hang him for killin' Bliss!"

"No you ain't!" Fenton barked, swinging his rifle barrel back to Stueves. He lined up the sites on the foreman's chest and had just started to take the slack out of his trigger finger when a gun thundered.

Fenton grunted as a strong, invisible hand shoved him backward and to his left. The rifle grew heavy in his arms, and he lowered it as he also dropped his chin to stare down at his right side. There was a ragged tear in his shirt. As soon as he saw it, dark-red blood began to bubble up and stream down toward his cartridge belt.

He was a little befuddled. If he'd been shot, wouldn't it hurt? All he felt down there where the blood oozed was a sharp chill and a prick like a bee sting. Quickly, however, the sting grew into what felt like the hammering blow of a savage fist.

"Oh!" he grunted, taking another two staggering steps backward. "Oh . . . you son of a bitch!" he snarled, gritting his teeth as he raised the rifle once more, this time taking aim at the man who'd shot him—Lon Thorn.

But Thorn was still aiming his Remington .44 at Fenton, glowering down the smoking barrel as he once again took aim.

The pistol roared, flames lapping from the barrel. The second bullet punched Fenton's upper left chest. He cried out with the searing agony of the second wound, triggered his Spencer skyward, then dropped it as he staggered backward before getting his boots tangled and falling hard on his butt in the brush and gravel before the cabin.

He lay writhing, cursing, staring up angrily, helplessly at the cutthroats milling before him.

"Granddad!" he heard Johnny Nevada shout from inside the cabin behind him.

"Bastards!" Fenton raked out, blood oozing over his lips. He felt as though a rusty spike had been rammed into his left lung. Blood leaked into it. He shoved up onto his elbows, looking around for his rifle.

Judge Hoagland stared aghast at Lon Thorn and said, "What in the hell do you think you're doing?"

"You seen him—he was about to shoot Stueves," Thorn said.

"Come on, fellas!" yelled Stueves, swinging down from his saddle. "Forget the old man. Let's pull that fox out of its hole!"

Fenton stared helplessly as the hardtails flanking Stueves shouted gleefully and dismounted, dropping their horses' reins and running toward the cabin on the heels of Stueves and Thorn. Hoagland and the mayor remained on their mounts, staring in horror at the group converging on the cabin door.

"Stop!" Hoagland shouted, having to use both hands to keep his dancing horse under control. "Stop right there! We are not hanging the prisoner! He is to be brought back to Clantick to stand trial for murder!"

"Bullshit!" Stueves shouted, stopping at the cabin door. He pointed a stiff arm and angry finger at Hoagland. "I ain't havin' nothin' to do with your masquerade, Judge! You don't intend on givin' Johnny Nevada no fair trial! You intend to hang him on account o' how he poked a bun in your daughter's oven!"

The others all laughed, casting their mocking smiles at Hoagland.

"We ain't haulin' his scrawny ass back to town just so's you can hold your kangaroo court!" shouted Bill Reese, laughing. "He'll hang just as good out here as he will in town!"

"The kid's a killer!" shouted one of the toughnuts from town. His name was Wesley Stevens, an ex-tracklayer who resembled nothing so much as a short ape. He always wore two big bowie knives; he'd turned to market hunting for the local cafés and restaurants, but everyone knew he wore the knives mainly for show. "We don't need his kind around. You leave a bad turnip in with the others, the whole basket'll spoil!"

"Dave Bliss was a good man!" shouted one of the others as they all turned toward the cabin now, behind Stueves and Thorn. "He didn't deserve to die that way, with a bullet in his back. Go on, Cade—pull that back-shootin' devil out of there!"

"No," Fenton spat out. He'd spied his rifle but he was too weak, in too much agony, to crawl to it.

Hoagland was shouting his own objections from the back of his prancing horse, but no one was listening.

Gasping, feeling his lung fill with blood, Fenton turned his horrified gaze to the cabin just as Stueves kicked the door in. Fenton heard his grandson scream. He saw the crowd bull into the cabin behind Stueves and Thorn, shouting and cursing and laughing.

Johnny screamed again. He shouted words that Fenton couldn't hear above the roar of the crowd. There was much knocking about inside the cabin, as the kid tried to escape, but soon the posse started scrambling out the door followed by Reese and Thorn, who each had one of Johnny's arms. They were half-dragging him—barefoot, his hands cuffed in front of him—out the door. The kid's lips were bloody and there was a deep gash on his cheek.

"Stop!" Hoagland shouted. He'd dismounted now and he was holding a silver-chased pistol low in his right hand, but he didn't appear to have the stomach for using it. "Put him on a horse! We'll take him back to town!"

Still, no one listened.

"There's a good, stout cottonwood right up yonder!" shouted one of the toughnuts from town, pointing at a lone tree up the slope about a hundred yards north of the cabin.

"We'll put him on a horse, all right!" Stueves yelled, laughing, as he and Thorn half-dragged the screaming Johnny toward a horse. "But we sure as hell ain't gonna waste no time wet-nursin' him back to town!"

As several men hoisted Johnny onto a mount, Fenton threw his left arm toward his rifle. But the rifle was too far away. As hard as the old man tried to crawl to it, his muscles wouldn't work. He was having trouble breathing. With each breath, more blood leaked into his throat, and he started to choke on it, cursing.

He must have faded for a few seconds, because suddenly time skipped ahead and he was aware of the crowd of men accompanying a lone horse up the hill beyond the cabin. Johnny sat atop the horse, turning his head right and left and leaning down as he wailed curses at the men to either side of him.

The men laughed.

One pointed an angry finger at the boy and said, "I'd pull you down from there and beat you silly for that, but I reckon gettin' your neck stretched is punishment enough!"

Several of the others laughed.

Hoagland dropped to a knee beside Fenton. The judge's face looked bleached and bony, his eyes bleak. "I swear, Fenton, I . . . I didn't mean for this to happen."

Fenton hacked up a large wad of blood and phlegm from his lungs, and used the last of his strength to spit it at the judge. The liquid gob smacked Hoagland's nose and mouth, staining his gray goatee. The judge jerked back in horror, brushing his arm across his face.

"What the fuck did you think would happen?" Fenton raked out. "I hope that daughter of yours gives birth to a horned owl!"

He collapsed, hearing his grandson bellow, "You can't hang me out here like this, ya limp-dicked peckerwoods! I'll come back an' haunt every one of you sons o' howlin' bitches!"

CHAPTER TWENTY-SEVEN

Stillman checked Sweets down and hipped around in his saddle.

He'd heard Sarah make a strangling sound behind him. He saw now that she wasn't strangling. She was vomiting. She'd stopped her roan, and she was leaning far down over the horse's right wither, retching.

"You all right, Sarah?"

She made one more deep retching sound, lowering her head again, then straightened in the saddle, running the sleeve of her shirt across her mouth. "I think so," she said, breathily.

"You look pale. Not feelin' so good?"

"Sorry," Sarah said. "I don't mean to hold us up. It's just that . . . I never saw a man shot before yesterday. I keep seein' Uncle Ray layin' there, an' . . . *oh, god!*" She lowered her head and cut loose once more.

When she lifted her head again, Stillman studied her. The morning sunlight shone like honey in her hair. She looked away, sheepish. For a moment, Stillman wondered if she was putting on a show for him. But, no. She was genuinely sick. There was no way this girl could have shot her father. Her being sick over seeing her uncle shot wasn't Stillman's only reason for clearing her of Dave Bliss's murder, at least in his own mind. Sarah Bliss was too fragile and guileless, her heart too large, her soul too deep, to be capable of murder.

As she uncorked her canteen and took a drink, Stillman said, "Sarah, I believe I owe you an apology."

She lowered the canteen, frowning. "For what?"

His apology was forestalled by a gunshot.

Stillman jerked his head to stare through the badlands to the north.

Another shot echoed. Both shots had come from the direction of the cabin.

"No!" Sarah gasped.

"Let's go!" Stillman said, nudging Sweets with his spurs.

He galloped around the base of a butte and dropped into the dry riverbed below. He galloped along the twisting wash, and after about ten minutes of hard riding, Sweets's hooves clattering on the rocks, he began hearing voices ahead and on his right. Men were yelling.

He followed the wash around another butte on his right, and then he could see the cabin up the northern slope ahead of him. Horses were spread out across the slope fronting the cabin. A group of men was milling around beneath a cottonwood farther up the slope and to the dugout's left.

"Oh, Christ . . ."

Stillman swung Sweets out of the wash. The horse took several lunging jumps and then it was galloping up the slope, cutting gradually across it, heading toward the cottonwood. As Stillman rode, hunkered low in the saddle, he unsnapped the keeper thong from over his Colt's hammer, sliding the piece from its holster.

He looked up the slope. To his right, a man was down. Judge Hoagland stood at the dugout's left front corner, staring at the cottonwood. The mayor stood a ways behind the judge, staring in the same direction. There was an incredulous, defeated set to both men's shoulders.

Stillman followed their gazes to the group beneath the tree. One man was mounted. He was skinny and red-faced, and he was bellowing curses at his captors. The posse had tied a noose around Johnny's neck, flung the rope over a heavy branch arcing out from the cottonwood's right side, and tied the end off near the bottom of the trunk.

As Stillman galloped headlong past the judge, Hoagland turned to him with a start, dropping his jaw. "I didn't mean for this to happen, Ben!" the judge yelled. "I didn't mean for it to go this far!"

"Lie down with dogs!" was all Stillman said as he crouched lower, letting Sweets eat up the ground between him and the crowd around the tree. "You sonso'bitches," he muttered as he raised his Colt and clicked the hammer back.

Just then a man slapped the rump of the kid's horse.

The horse bolted forward. A stone dropped in Stillman's gut when he saw the kid slide off the back of the horse to hang suspended by the noose around his neck, his bare feet about five feet above the ground. He kicked and jerked and twisted violently while the men around him cheered and the horse he'd been mounted on galloped down the slope, passing Stillman and veering hard to its left, kicking its rear legs, as though the horse, too, were infected with the crowd's dark frenzy.

"Dance, kid—there you go!" one of the men shouted. "Let's see your best Saturday night two-step!"

"Johnny!" Sarah screamed, galloping a good distance behind Stillman. "Oh, Johnny!"

The crowd, comprised of a good dozen men, turned its collective head, eyes growing wide beneath shading hat brims when they saw Stillman and the girl galloping toward them.

"Ah, shit—it's Stillman!" one man shouted, pointing.

Cade Stueves was the man who'd slapped Johnny's horse out from beneath him. Now Stueves, glaring at Stillman, reached for the two pistols on his hips.

Stillman didn't bother with a warning. He aimed and fired true, blowing a forty-four-caliber hole through Stueve's left cheek. Stueves screamed as he dropped his guns and stumbled backward, grabbing his face. More men reached for their guns, and Stillman emptied his Colt into the crowd, dropping at least three more men and sending the rest running for their lives, cursing.

When the sheriff had fired off his last shot, he holstered the Colt and pulled his folding Barlow knife out of his pocket. He reined Sweets to a halt to the right of Johnny's kicking legs, the kid turning quick, sharp circles beneath the branch, the rope creaking and causing the branch above his head to whine.

"Hold on, kid!" Stillman said.

The sheriff pulled his boots from his stirrups and carefully stepped up onto his saddle. Sweets was well trained, rock-solid. He didn't move a muscle. It was as though he knew exactly what his rider needed to do, and he was on board despite the enraged shouting around him from both the wounded posse riders and those still fleeing, trying to catch up with their horses.

Stillman grabbed Johnny around the waist and then reached up to saw through the rope, slashing at it, cutting through three or four strands at a time. The rope broke. As Johnny plunged, Stillman grabbed him around the waist and then, crouching to steady himself against his saddle horn, eased Johnny down until releasing him to let him fall the last three feet to the ground.

Johnny hit the ground and rolled, raking his neck along the ground as though to dislodge some unseen rope still strangling him.

"Johnny!" Sarah cried, running up from where she'd dismounted her horse.

Stillman swung from Sweets's back.

A gun popped. Stillman looked downslope to see one of the posse riders aiming a smoking pistol at him. It was Lon Thorn from the Patten ranch.

"Goddamnit, Stillman—this ain't none of your affair!"

Thorn was on one knee, clutching his other, wounded knee with his left hand. In his right hand, he aimed a cocked Remington. The gun crashed, lapping smoke and flames. The bullet plunked into the cottonwood over Stillman's left shoulder, near where Sarah crouched beside Johnny.

"You two get down!" Stillman shouted.

Quickly, he shucked his Henry from his saddle boot. He pumped a cartridge into the chamber and aimed just as Thorn fired the Remy again. The bullet sliced a burning line across Stillman's right shoulder. Sarah screamed.

Stillman cursed under his breath as he aimed and fired the Henry once, twice, punching one round into Thorn's belly, the other into his chest, sending him rolling backward down the slope, toward where the townsmen were scrambling onto their horses and galloping away.

"Toss me the handcuff keys—will ya, Sheriff?"

Sheriff looked at Johnny Nevada sitting on the ground behind him. Sarah knelt beside Johnny, one arm around his waist. She was sobbing. The kid's neck bled where the rope had raked him.

Stillman dug the handcuff keys out of his jeans pocket, tossed them to Sarah, and then began walking down the slope toward the judge and the mayor and the other man lying near the front of the cabin.

Hoof thuds rose behind Stillman.

"Johnny, no!" Sarah cried.

Stillman swung around too late.

"Hi-*yahh!*" Johnny bellowed.

He rammed Sweets into Stillman's right shoulder.

The horse whinnied shrilly as Stillman flew off his feet. The lawman gave a hard grunt as the wind was punched from his lungs. He twisted around and hit the ground several yards from where the buckskin had bulled into him, and rolled.

He'd struck the ground with such force that his brains were instantly scrambled and a shrill buzzing rose in his ears. He felt as though he'd been hit by a freight train. His ribs and back ached miserably.

His back . . .

Oh, Christ. Instantly, he felt a tingling in his legs and feet.

The surgery and four months of recovery undone in a second.

Stillman found himself lying belly down, his hat gone, his hair in his eyes. He pushed up slowly, heavily, onto his hands and knees. That was all the farther he was getting. His body was wracked with pain, his vision blurry.

He turned his head. The kid galloped toward where the judge stood near the cabin. The judge shouted, "Hold it right there, you miserable young killer!"

"Fuck you, Judge!" The kid raised a pistol. He must have taken it off one of the dead men near the hang tree. The pistol barked. The judge jerked backward, triggering his own pistol skyward.

The kid shot him again. The judge hit the ground, screaming, and rolled. By the time he was through rolling, he was also done screaming.

Behind the judge, the mayor tossed his own revolver away and threw up his arms. "Don't shoot! Don't shoot!" The jowly Taylor put his head down and squeezed his eyes closed.

Johnny laughed, then turned Sweets around and rode back toward Stillman.

"Johnny!" Sarah screamed, standing several feet behind Stillman, staring in shock. Her weak voice quavering, she said, "What are you doing, Johnny? *Johnny!*"

The sheriff looked at his Henry. It lay a good twenty feet away. He tried to crawl toward it, but his legs were stiff, and his hips felt as though they'd been ground to powder. Vaguely, he was aware of the numbness leaving his feet, however. His vision was clearing.

He rolled onto his left hip and stared at the kid now stopping Sweets before him. The kid aimed his smoking pistol at Stillman, grinning.

"You're a damn fool, Sheriff," Johnny laughed.

"Johnny!" Sarah screamed, staying where she was as though frozen in place.

The kid turned to her, scowling with annoyance. "Stop your caterwauling, you stupid bitch!"

Sarah's eyes widened. Her lower jaw sagged.

"Why am I a fool, Johnny?" Stillman asked. "Because I tried to get you a fair trial?"

"Yeah, that's right," the kid laughed again, still aiming his pistol over Sweets's left wither at Stillman. "I shot Bliss!"

"I know you did, Johnny. I always knew there was a good chance, but I finally came to that conclusion."

"I shot the sonofabitch in the back from that tree, just like the Patten men said!" Johnny crowed. "I told him I would, and one thing you can't say about ole Johnny Nevada—he don't break a promise!"

"You're a black-hearted devil—I'll give you that," Stillman said. "But you still should have had your day in court. Your *fair* day in court."

"Now, ain't that noble?" the kid mocked.

"Why did you kill him? Was it over Sarah?"

Johnny looked at Sarah and gave a wry chuff. "Hell, no! Look at her—she's just another plain-faced girl moon-calfin' my heels!"

"Oh, Johnny," Sarah sobbed, dropping to her knees in the grass, tears rolling down her cheeks.

"Vince Patten?" Stillman said. "Did he pay you to kill Bliss?"

"Nuh-uh," Johnny said, slowly wagging his head and grinning like the cat that ate the canary.

"Mrs. Patten." Stillman smiled grimly and nodded. He hadn't realized until now how much he'd suspected Fanny Patten after seeing how lonely she was, how desperate for affection, and seeing what an old, hard-tailed son of a bitch she'd married.

Johnny widened his eyes in shock. "How'd you know?"

"She and Sarah's father were seeing each other on the side, weren't they? Bliss was riding back from the Patten ranch the night you shot him. She paid you to kill him. She got scared that you'd implicate her during the trial, so she hired a few of her husband's riders to break into the courthouse and kill you."

"Hmm," Johnny said, scratching the back of his. "Maybe you ain't as squishy in the thinker box as I thought."

Apparently, Vince Patten didn't keep as tight a rein on his men as he'd let on. Understandable, in light of his bad leg, Stillman supposed. And the rancher had likely lied about not knowing Bernard, or Bernie—the rider who'd grazed Stillman when the sheriff was riding back from the judge's place—because he wanted to pursue his own investigation before giving anything to Stillman, his natural enemy, since Stillman wore a badge.

"Why did she want him dead?" he asked the kid.

"Mister Bliss promised he'd divorce Sarah's ma and marry her and take her away from here. He went back on the deal." Johnny whistled and shook his head. "Boy, you don't wanna make Mrs. Patten mad. She wanted him *dead!, dead!, dead!,* she said." The kid chuckled. "Them was her words exactly. She paid me five hundred dollars that she took out of her husband's safe. She said all the whiskey Patten drank to kill the pain in his leg would confuse him about the missing money. Imagine me with five hundred dollars. I was almost too scared to pocket that kind of money. Hell, it's still in a hollow in a tree at Granddad's place!"

Johnny had lowered his pistol slightly, but now he raised it again and narrowed one eye as he aimed down the barrel. "Sorry to have to do this, Ben. But I won't get far if I let you live. I'm gonna kill you and then I'm gonna kill Sarah."

He turned to the girl and said, "Sorry, Sarah. Can't leave you alive after you watch me kill the sheriff here."

She just knelt, staring in shock. Her face was expressionless, eyes glassy, as though she'd taken in too much information for her to comprehend.

The kid said, "And then I'm gonna have to shoot the mayor over there, too, though I'd just as soon let him live with his own cowardice. Mister Fat Britches, his ownself! Look at him—don't he look like he done shit his pants?"

Stillman glanced at the mayor kneeling in the grass, his arms still in the air, a look of horror and silent pleading on his fleshy, round, clean-shaven face.

"Johnny!"

The voice had come from behind Stillman. Johnny looked beyond the sheriff, and glowered in disgust. "Granddad! You old fool—put that rifle down!"

CHAPTER TWENTY-EIGHT

Stillman looked over his left shoulder. Hec Fenton stood near some bushes beside the dugout.

He was a bloody, bedraggled mess. Blood stained his shirt, his lower lip, and his chin. He held his carbine in both hands across his chest. He'd lost his hat, and his thin hair wisped around in the morning breeze. His sunken eyes were pink-rimmed. The skin of his face hung like wrinkled paper.

"You're right—I am a damn fool," the old man said, glaring at his grandson. "I gave you too many chances. I wanted to believe that my own blood wouldn't do what you done—killed a man in cold blood. Shot him in the back. I was a fool to believe that. I should have seen who you were, that you were just like your father. But I didn't want to. You're the only grandson I got. I'm gonna make amends. You're a bad dog, boy. You need to be brought to heel. Now, drop that gun or I'll blast you to hell!"

"I don't think you got the strength to aim that old rifle, Granddad." Johnny grinned, shaking his head. "Not before I drill ya!"

The kid whipped up his pistol and fired. At nearly the same time, Hec Fenton fired his old Spencer. The kid yowled as he jerked back in his saddle. Sweets whinnied, reared, and twisted around. The kid was nearly thrown from the saddle but managed to grab the horn just in time, losing his pistol in the process.

Sweets galloped down the slope, the kid crouched low over

the buckskin's buffeting mane.

Stillman scrambled over to his Henry, scooped it up, and turned to Fenton. The old man was on his knees, staring straight ahead, mouth agape.

"Hec!" Stillman said.

The old man opened his mouth to speak, but no words came out. There was a fresh wound in his upper chest, pouring more blood down his already soaked shirt. The old man turned to Stillman, opening his mouth once more.

"Sorry, Ben," he rasped.

His eyes rolled back in their sockets. He fell facedown on the ground and lay still.

"Johnny!" Sarah screamed.

Stillman turned to where Johnny was galloping down the slope toward the riverbed. The sheriff whipped the Henry to his shoulder, then lowered it. Horse and rider had just dropped into the riverbed, and were now obscured by the trees lining it.

"Shit," Stillman bit out, heaving himself to his feet, absently relieved that his legs still worked. In fact, they felt fine. The rest of him, including his back, felt fine, as well. Stiff and sore, but that was to be expected at his age, having been run over by a twelve hundred pound horse. The bullet burn in his leg grieved him, but that was to be expected, as well.

Sarah stood a little ahead and to his right, staring after Johnny, her hands to her face.

"You stay here, girl," Stillman said, looking around for a mount. "I'll get him."

He started walking toward the judge's horse standing nearby.

Down in the ancient riverbed, Sweets whinnied shrilly.

Two seconds later, Johnny screamed.

Sarah screamed the boy's name again, running forward half a dozen steps and then stopping again when Sweets reappeared, leaping out of the wash and racing toward Stillman, stirrups slapping against the horse's barrel. The buckskin shook its head so hard, it nearly dislodged its bridle.

From the cut, Johnny yelled again . . . and again.

Stillman and Sarah shared a brief, incredulous look.

As Sweets approached, whickering, eyes large and white-ringed, obviously riled by more than just the shooting, Stillman grabbed the horse's reins and swung into the saddle. He turned the horse toward the wash, then jerked back on the reins.

A sudden breeze had risen.

Along with the scratching of the breeze was a rasping sound. A rattling sound. It was like the hiss of a hundred diamondbacks rising above the breeze's rustling. It appeared to be coming from beyond the trees lining the wash and whose fall-turning leaves flashed in the intensifying sunlight.

The short hairs rose across the back of Stillman's neck.

"Oh, god," Sarah gasped. "Oh, no . . . *Snake Woman!*"

Stillman suppressed his instinctive, irrational dread and spurred the buckskin on down the slope. He could feel the horse's reluctance to return to the river bottom, but Sweets obeyed his rider's commands. Horse and rider dropped into the gravelly cut. Stillman jogged the horse ahead.

As he turned to follow the gravelly bed around the base of a chalky butte rising on the right, Sweets whickered and reared slightly, twitching his ears. Ahead, a diamondback slithered across the gravelly bed, heading from Stillman's left to his right. Seeing the horse and rider, the snake stopped, gathered itself into a tight coil, and raised a ratcheting hiss, flicking its button tail.

Stillman raised the Henry and fired. The bullet cut the serpent into two quivering pieces.

Sweets whinnied, trying to rear again.

"Easy, boy," Stillman said. "Easy, easy!"

"Help!"

The yell had come from just ahead on Stillman's left. He put Sweets ahead a few steps and looked between two boulders. There was a shelving pit on that edge of the riverbed, filled with rocks. A snake had likely spooked the buckskin, and Sweets must have bucked the kid off into the pit. The rocks in the pit appeared to move.

No. The rocks weren't moving.

The snakes lying among the rocks were moving.

A collective, ratcheting hiss rose from the pit in which the kid was down on all fours, trying to make his way up the shelving side, but the snakes were biting him, a few digging their fangs into his legs and arms and clinging, curling their bodies against his.

Johnny lifted his head up above the top of the pit. His eyes and cheeks were so swollen that his head looked massive and round. Already those snakes had filled him with poison.

"Ah, hell," he cried, his voice small and feeble. "H-help me . . . oh, please! Oh, god . . . oh, Jesus—*help me!*"

Stillman swung down from Sweets's back.

Johnny renewed his effort to climb out of the pit, but he was too weak. He sagged backward and rolled down over the rocks to the bottom. He lay writhing atop the rocks and the snakes, flinging his arms up, kicking his legs as though trying to dislodge the stone-colored serpents.

Several of the vipers lay atop him, snapping at him, biting, filling him with poison. One had dug its fangs into his already swollen left brow and clung there, curling its fluttering tail down around his chin.

The ratcheting hiss of the snakes' button tails rose to a low roar.

"Jesus Christ," Stillman said, staring in revulsion at the horror at the bottom of the pit.

He snapped up the Henry, aimed, and triggered three shots

into the boy's head.

Johnny fell slack. Now it was only the snakes moving there at the bottom of the pit.

Running footsteps rose along the wash.

Sarah ran around a bend, saw the pit, heard the hissing of the snakes, and stopped.

"That's far enough, Sarah," Stillman said, backing away from the pit as several of the serpents slithered toward him.

"Oh, Johnny!" Sarah cried, clasping a hand over her wide-open mouth.

"He's gone, girl." Stillman walked over and wrapped his arm around her. "Let's get the hell out of here!"

Stillman grabbed Sweets's reins, then swung up into the saddle. He extended his arm to Sarah. She placed her hand in his, and he pulled her onto the horse behind him.

The breeze rose again. With it, the hissing from the pit rose to a crescendo.

Stillman winced as the sound attacked his ears the way the snakes had attacked the boy in the pit.

"Snake Woman," Sarah muttered behind him, closing her own hands over her ears and stretching her lips back from her teeth.

Stillman looked around, shivering. Suppressing the superstition, not wanting it to get a foothold—he was far too practical for superstitions, for there was enough horror in the world without them—he shook his head and turned back toward the pit.

"That's not Snake Woman. Just a pit full of snakes. Likely many pits just like that one all through these hills. Thus, the legend." Stillman glanced over his shoulder at the girl sitting behind him, looking terrified. He tried a reassuring smile. "The legend's meant to keep men from straying into this treacherous place, that's all. For good reason. I know I won't be back!"

He swung Sweets around and started back the way he'd come.

Behind him, the breeze rose again. It put a chill in the air. It drove the chill deep into Stillman's bones. The hissing of the snakes grew loud once more. With it came the muffled, eerie, almost musical sound of . . . what?

A woman laughing?

Stillman whipped his head around.

Nothing there but the riverbed and the dancing leaves of the breeze-brushed trees.

The laughter . . . if laughter was what it was—*and it couldn't be*—dwindled into the distance. The breeze died.

The chill was still in the sheriff's bones, however. His back was crawling as though with a dozen angry serpents.

Stillman turned his head forward once more and put the buckskin into a lunging gallop away from the horror of the snake pit.

CHAPTER TWENTY-NINE

One week later, Clarissa Kane shuddered as she straddled the long, broad-shouldered, somewhat potbellied body of her partner in crime, Max Reevis.

"Oh, Max," she cooed as the last vestiges of her climax reverberated through her naked body. "Oh . . . oh, Max. That was wonderful!" She leaned down and kissed the outlaw's mustached face.

"Damn," Reevis said, chuckling, gently shoving Clarissa off his legs, then reaching for the bottle on the table on his side of the bed.

They were in Clarissa's bedroom in the Kane ranch house, which belonged solely to Clarissa now that her father was dead, god rest his contrary soul.

Reevis said, "You sure know how to please a man, sweetheart. I ain't forgot that. In fact, I thought about it every day I was stayin' ahead of that Clantick posse, runnin' 'em from one end of the river breaks to the other!"

Clarissa rolled onto her left side, resting her head on the heel of her hand, staring at the naked man as he took a healthy swig of the cheap whiskey he favored. With her other hand, she cupped her right breast, which was slightly chafed from the brigand's brushy mustache.

She blinked, smiling. "You know how to please a woman, Max." She reached over and placed a hand on his crotch, gently fondling. "In more ways than one, I might add."

Reevis looked at her, smiling curiously. "More ways than one?"

"I mean the money, of course. A hundred thousand dollars."

"Oh, that." Reevis was rolling a cigarette from the makings sack resting on his bare, pale belly. "We pulled it off, my darlin'. That money's all ours now. I'm just sorry I didn't kill the old man on the street like we planned. I swear, I sent three or four shots at him and only got him in the leg. It was almost like someone was watchin' over him!"

"Not to worry, darling," Clarissa said, leaning over to nuzzle the outlaw's belly button, below the makings sack. "You made up for it when you swung back to town and finished the job properly."

Reevis twisted the quirley closed, licked it to seal it, then struck a match to life on the table to his left. "You think it looks all right? I mean, you don't think anyone's suspicious of you, do you?"

"Why would they be suspicious?"

"Well, you know—because I used your key to get into the old man's room."

"Anyone could have stolen Mister Campbell's skeleton key from beneath his desk. That makes everyone in the entire town of Clantick a suspect in my father's murder. No one is going to think that I, his grieving daughter, had anything to do with it."

"What about when we head for Mexico?"

"We won't be able to leave for at least six months. I'll put the ranch up for sale in a month. It'll take a while to sell. With all of my father's bad debts and the fact that his lousy operating practices have nearly run the Crosshatch into the ground, no one will suspect my motives. They'll think I simply cannot afford to operate anymore."

She turned a wolfish smile at her co-conspirator. "Especially after the robbery . . . and the one man who managed to outrun the posse and is probably spending my money in Mexico . . . all by himself." She pressed her lips to his belly, making him groan with pleasure. "They'll believe that, heartbroken as well as nearly *broke*, I'm simply taking what little I make from the sale and heading to the West Coast to try to make a new life for myself."

Clarissa gave a devilish grin as she reached up and plucked the quirley from between Reevis's lips. She inhaled deeply.

"What about me?" Reevis said. "I reckon I'd best lay pretty low until we head west together. Don't want no one to get suspicious. Besides, someone might recognize me from town . . . from when me an' the others was sizin' up the bank for the robbery."

He took the cigarette back from Clarissa, who was exhaling its smoke while leaning toward the small table on her side of the bed.

"Oh, you'll be laying low, all right," Clarissa said.

He didn't appear to note the sudden hardness in her voice.

"You think I should go over to Chinook?" Reevis said, taking another deep drag from the quirley. "Maybe get a part-time job just so I don't look suspicious?"

"No, I don't think you need to go that far."

"Don't worry." Reevis grinned at her, winking. "We can meet up just like we're doin' now . . . two, maybe three times a week. Your ranch is only eight miles from Chinook. Hell, I could ride over here every night if you think you'll get lonely."

"No." Clarissa slid her right hand behind her, and opened the night table drawer. "One of the men might see you. We're going to need to take far more severe precautions than that."

"Like what, you sayin'?" Reevis said, reaching over to his table for the whiskey bottle.

He tipped the bottle back and then turned toward Clarissa again just as she cocked the silver-chased, ivory-gripped, over-

and-under derringer she was squeezing in her right fist.

"Like this," Clarissa said, spreading her lips back from her pretty teeth.

Reevis's eyes snapped wide in shock. "Wait, now—*wait!*"

Clarissa sat upright and bunched her lips as she grabbed her pillow, held it in front of her, and triggered the derringer into it. She fired off the second barrel into the pillow.

Feathers flew in all directions.

When Clarissa lowered the remains of the pillow, Reevis's head sagged before her, toward the makings sack still on his belly. Both bullets had carved two round holes in his left temple. Feathers from the pillow stuck to the blood oozing from the holes and painting the entire left side of his face.

Reevis's lips moved beneath his mustache, but no words came out, only a faint gargling sound.

Clarissa took his arm and drew him toward her, laying him flat on the bed. She didn't want him falling to the floor and spilling blood all over the place. She wanted the blood to be contained in the bed for easier cleaning and disposal. She'd get rid of the body just after dark tomorrow night, after the hands had all retired to the bunkhouse. She knew of a handy ravine in which to toss the brigand's body, where no one except turkey buzzards and coyotes would ever find it.

Fortunately, Reevis had no family. And since he himself had killed his longtime gang, including the young woman who'd been riding with them—the sister of one of the other robbers—no one would ever miss him.

A squawk sounded in the hall.

Clarissa jerked her head toward the door. She stared at the door, her heart quickening. "Who's there?"

The only sound came from Reevis. A low gurgling issued from his throat. Clarissa turned to him. He lay unmoving, lips slightly parted, half-open eyes regarding her balefully.

Another squawk sounded from the hall. This one was quieter—a floorboard complaining near the stairs.

Clarissa gasped and threw on her robe. She tied it around her waist and slid Reevis's Colt from the holster hanging by its shell belt from a chair back. Slowly, aiming the pistol half out in front of her, she walked to the door. She opened the door, looking both ways up the short, narrow hall.

Nothing but misty darkness.

Clarissa sniffed. There was the smell of leather in the hall's pent-up air. And the odor of a man. A vaguely familiar and somewhat pleasing odor. Not the odor of Max Reevis. The outlaw had had a mossy smell.

Had a man from the bunkhouse been here, outside her bedroom door? Had he heard the derringer? She'd counted on the pillow to muffle the shots, and she'd been certain it had.

"Hello?" Clarissa called. The frightened, hollow sound of her own voice in the dark house chilled her.

She walked to the top of the stairs, staring down into the first story.

A lamp was lit somewhere near the front of the house. It dully illuminated the blue, figured velvet carpet of the parlor at the bottom of the stairs. As she walked slowly down the stairs, holding the heavy gun steadily in both hands, she could see light coming from the kitchen.

Someone was in there.

She stopped at the bottom of the stairs. "Hello?"

No response.

The light flickered slightly, the flame in the lantern guttering.

Clarissa moved through the parlor and stopped in the doorway between the parlor and the kitchen.

"Oh, Christ!" she gasped, heart thudding against her breastbone. "What're you doing here?"

★ ★ ★ ★ ★

Stillman doffed his hat and tossed it onto the table in the Kane kitchen. He looked at the young woman standing in the open doorway, aiming the pistol at him in both hands. He canted his head to indicate a chair on the other side of the table from him.

"Come in and have a seat, Miss Kane."

She took two steps forward. "I asked you a question," she snarled through gritted teeth. "What're you doing here, Sheri— oh, *ow!*"

Deputy Leon McMannigle had stepped out from the shadows to grab the cocked pistol out of her hands. "I'll take that, Miss Kane. Thank you mighty kindly."

Smiling at Stillman, Leon held the pistol barrel up and depressed the hammer. He shoved the Colt behind his cartridge belt. Stillman didn't return the smile. He wasn't in a smiling mood. When he'd ridden out to the Patten ranch several days ago, intending to arrest Patten's sad wife for hiring Johnny Nevada to murder Dave Bliss, he'd found her hanging from a cottonwood behind Patten's sprawling house. He'd found the rancher inside, staring stoically out his office window at the tree from which his young wife had hanged herself, from which she'd still been dangling.

"How dare you, you son of a bitch!" Clarissa Kane barked at McMannigle before cutting her enraged gaze at Stillman. "Get out—both of you!"

"We'll be getting out soon enough." Stillman reached into the pocket of his buckskin coat—the air had attained a hard autumn chill over the past week—and tossed a pair of nickeled handcuffs onto the table. "All three of us. And you'll be wearing these."

"If you mean that man upstairs—he broke in here and raped me!"

"He brought the strongbox all the way out here, to the home

of the man he stole it from, just to rape his daughter?" Stillman picked up the hurricane lamp that sat on the oilcloth-covered eating table, and tipped it so that the light slid behind him and onto the floor by the front door, revealing the wooden, iron-banded strongbox.

He set the lamp back on the table.

Clarissa opened her mouth, drawing a deep, silent breath. Fear shone in her eyes. Her chest rose and fell heavily. Flanking her, Leon crossed his arms on his chest, over his wool coat.

Stillman said, "Your man—Reevis. That was his name, wasn't it? I apologize for listening through the door. Reevis really took the posse on a wild goose chase. Shot all the rest of his own gang, including the young woman riding with him, just before he headed back north. You see, my deputy here rode for the Tenth Cavalry down in Arizona. Leon's one hell of a tracker. Learned from the Coyotero Apaches."

"The Coyoteros learned from me." McMannigle smiled. "Reevis almost lost me, though. He really wanted me to think he headed south after he killed the others, but I had me a feel-in' he was tryin' to pull the sheep over my eyes. So I looked north and, yep, he was headed north, all right. The mistake he made was ridin' a horse that picked up a hairline crack in its left rear shoe. I saw that crack, and it sealed it for me. He was headin' back north to Clantick for sure."

"Now, why would he do that?" Stillman said aloud. "Maybe he decided to head to Canada, instead. Nah. When I learned of your father's murder, I figured the killer had to be someone in the gang who'd robbed him. Or you. But you were with me when your pa was killed. Smart to give yourself that alibi. But I knew there had to be a reason you double-crossed me with the judge, tellin' him about the cabin. First, by throwin' yourself at me, you intended to confuse me, throw me off your trail, if I should become suspicious. When your charms didn't work, you figured to get me killed. That's why you sicced the vigilantes on me when the chance tumbled into your lap. I figured the reason had to be connected to your father's murder. That connected his murder . . . and you . . . to the robbery. That connected you to the robber who killed the rest of his gang and swung north . . . to kill your father and, finally, to meet up with you. His beautiful co-conspirator. Who made sure your father made the transfer of that money right smack dab on the same day Doc Evans was due to get married."

She only stared at Stillman in shock.

"We've been keepin' an eye on the house, Miss Kane," Leon said, leaning against the wall, head canted slightly to one side. "Me an' Ben figured that one last double-crossin' rider would show up here sooner or later."

"Only a week after your father's funeral might have been a little too soon—don't you think, Miss Kane?" Stillman said. "Sort of unseemly, isn't it? Bringing Reevis and the loot in here so soon after your father passed."

"Shame on you," Leon said.

Clarissa walked forward, placing her hands on a chair back as if to steady herself. She looked as though she might faint. She drew another deep breath as though to steady herself.

"Where did you fall in with Reevis?" Stillman asked, frowning curiously. "You've lived a rather sheltered life out here, I'd assume."

She studied Stillman for a time, then asked, her voice quaking slightly with mind-numbing fear, "If I tell you, will you ask the judge to go easy? I'm young. Maybe young and foolish, but I was desperate. Soon, Father would have lost everything. Where would that have left me?"

"Not in jail," Stillman said. "But, sure—I'll speak to the judge on your behalf."

She told the two lawmen that she'd met Reevis a year ago,

when she'd accompanied her father to Helena on business. The handsome outlaw had made a play for her in a café where she was dining alone, and she'd succumbed to his roguish charms. They'd shared life stories . . . and more . . . while her father had been preoccupied with late-night business meetings with investors and speculators in a desperate attempt to save his ranch.

It was during one such late-night meeting that Clarissa and Max Reevis, who was one of a gang of seasoned train robbers on the dodge from Missouri, had conspired to rob the money she knew would be coming when her father, strapped for cash, sold his half-interest in a Butte gold mine to pay off sundry large debts and to ease the stranglehold of bad investments.

"Don't judge me too harshly, Sheriff," Clarissa said, squeezing the spools of the chair back until her hands were white. "I was desperate. My father was about to lose everything. He would have lost the money for the mine, as well. He was a good cowpuncher but a terrible businessman. What's more, he was dying. Doc Evans had diagnosed consumption last winter."

"Where were you headed? Mexico?"

"Eventually." She smiled. "In spite of what I told Johnny Nevada."

Stillman pursed his lips, nodding. "It's not my job to judge you," he said, rising from his chair.

"No. It's your job to take me back for a fair trial." Clarissa arched an ironic brow. Despite her dire predicament, she'd managed to salvage some of her pluck. "That hasn't worked so well for you recently, though, has it?"

She meant Johnny Nevada. She'd probably heard about Fanny Patten, as well. She was rubbing it in, as was her cold, hard way.

Stillman shrugged, then sighed his agreement. "Well, I don't see any rattlesnakes around, knock on wood. And I don't think you got the stomach to hang yourself." He set his hat on his head. "We have a newly appointed judge, Miss Kane." He tossed the handcuffs to McMannigle. "Come on back to town with me an' Leon. We'll introduce you."

EPILOGUE

Doctor Clyde Evans rolled his buggy up in front of Katherine Kemmett's house on the south edge of Clantick and drew back on the reins.

Faustus halted.

As the buggy rocked to a stop behind the stout horse, Evans looked at the small, neat, white-frame house before him. The house, a former farmhouse with a few unused outbuildings behind it, was surrounded by a neat, white picket fence and flanked by a couple of hearty cottonwoods. The house and the fence fairly glowed in the darkness. The leaves of the cotton-woods shimmered with starlight.

It was nearly ten o'clock in the evening. Evans hadn't meant to stop here. He'd merely been returning to town after a sick call in the country, and he'd simply pulled up the widow's oval, cinder-paved driveway. He'd meant to keep riding on past the widow's house to his own place on the butte west of Clantick.

He looked down at the spray of fall wildflowers in his gloved left hand. The flowers were evidence of his true intentions. Of course, he'd meant to stop here. He'd picked the wildflowers, which he'd found growing alongside the trail a couple of miles back, remembering how much Katherine loved wildflowers, despite how briefly they bloomed. He'd found that particularly endearing about her.

He looked at the house again. A lamp shone in the kitchen window beyond the red curtains. Just now the curtains were shoved aside, and Katherine's silhouette stood there, a couple of lamps burning behind her, staring out. Evans could tell she'd already taken down her hair and brushed it out, and that she was wearing her cream robe. Ready for bed.

Evans ears burned with chagrin. With fear. He should have kept riding. Too late now. She'd seen him. He had to at least walk up to the door. Whether she opened it or not was up to her. He suddenly hoped she wouldn't.

Evans set the buggy's brake, gripped the flowers tighter, climbed down from the carriage, and patted Faustus's rump. The horse whickered softly as though with encouragement. Evans walked past the horse, opened the gate in the picket fence, and stepped through. The brick-paved walk between the gate and the house's small front stoop was only about twenty-five feet, but as Evans traversed it, seeing Katherine's silhouette in the window to the right of the door, it felt a hundred miles long and storm-lashed.

His stomach roiled.

Finally, he came to the three porch steps and climbed them heavily.

As he gained the porch, he was a little startled to see and hear the front door open. Katherine's silhouette appeared behind the white-framed screen. He could smell her feminine odor. She'd bathed a little while ago in water scented with oatmeal soap.

Evans stopped in the middle of the stoop and stared back at the woman staring out at him.

He cleared his throat. "Good evening, Katherine."

"Clyde." Her voice was low. Almost menacingly so. "What are you doing here?"

"I was on my way back from the Rios farm. Tio cut his leg while scything hay. I had to sew him up."

"I see," Katherine said. "I'll ride out tomorrow and change

his bandages. I have to ride that way, anyway. Mrs. Johnson's baby is due any day, and I've been meaning to check on her."

"I see. Let me know if you need any help."

"I will." Katherine stepped back and began to close the inside door.

Evans stepped forward and hurried to say, "Does . . . does that mean we're still working together?"

"Of course. You're the only doctor around. And I'm the only midwife. I guess we really don't have any choice—do we, Clyde?" Katherine gave a caustic, sort of snarling laugh. "Isn't this an unusual situation? Good night, Clyde."

"Katherine, wait."

She drew the door open once more.

Evans looked down at the flowers in his hand. He reached up, opened the screen door, and shoved them inside. "These are for you."

Dark lines cut across her forehead. "What on earth . . . ?"

"I remembered how you loved wildflowers. Especially the autumn ones."

"You stopped here at ten o'clock at night to give me flowers?"

"Yes. I mean . . . no." Evans's heart thudded. His tongue felt swollen to twice its normal size. "I found them alongside the trail and remembered . . ."

He stopped, clearing his throat again. "I really came here because I've been meaning to tell you I'm sorry, Katherine."

Katherine studied him over the flowers he still held in his hand. She crossed her arms on her chest, drawing her robe tighter about her. "Sorry for what, Clyde?"

Evans sighed and looked down at the night-droopy flowers. "For being a monster."

"You're not a monster, Clyde. I was overwrought when I called you that, as you can imagine."

"No? Then how do you explain everything I've done?"

"You're a little boy. A little boy in a man's body. That little boy loves to indulge himself. And he makes excuses for not being able to stop indulging himself by telling himself he's incapable of behaving any other way." Katherine smiled. "You see? It's really quite simple. I've figured you out. You're being far too easy on yourself, Clyde. You don't have the luxury of being a monster. There's really no good excuse for what you've done . . . and continue to do."

He knew she meant Evelyn, his drinking, and the doxies he customarily spent time with.

"Do you think there's any hope . . . for us?"

"For *us*? Oh, god, no!" Katherine laughed that wicked laugh again. She laughed for quite a while, her whole body shaking, then stopped abruptly and shook her finger as though at the little boy she knew him to be. "If you hurt that girl . . . if you hurt young Evelyn . . . you'd better watch your back, Clyde Evans. Because I or someone else in this town might just stick something very sharp in it!"

Evans winced. "So I've been warned . . ."

"Is there anything else?"

"I'm sorry you're alone," Evans blurted out, glancing in at the small, tidy, dimly lit parlor behind her. A teapot was hissing quietly.

Katherine studied him again in silence, her expression grave. "Alone, yes. Well, that makes two of us—doesn't it?"

Evans held up the flowers again. "Take these, will you? I'm tired of holding them. If I take them home, my dog will eat them."

Katherine took the flowers. "Don't tell me you're letting that cur in your house."

"He slept with me last night." Evans snorted.

"Oh, my god, Clyde! You'll wake up with fleas!"

Evans backed away and threw out his arms in hopelessness. "I already have. I've been scratching all day!"

"Throw out that cur and paint your house, Clyde!"

"Right away, Katherine," Evans said, chuckling as he turned and dropped down the porch steps. "Good night, Katherine."

The only reply she offered was the sound of her closing and locking her door.

The doctor climbed into his buggy. He pulled his hide-wrapped flask out of his coat pocket, unscrewed the cap, and stared down at the flask with sudden apprehension.

He thought of Ernie Atwell, the snake-seeing stock buyer from Chicago who'd boarded the eastbound flier with a very sore jaw.

Evans hesitated.

"Ah, hell," he said. "We're dead a long time. Here's to you, Ernie!"

He took a deep pull from the flask. Smacking his lips, he returned the flask to his coat pocket. He shook the reins and rolled off toward home. He still had supper to cook, brandy to drink, books to browse. On the off chance he hadn't caught any rabbits that day, Buddy would be waiting for scraps.

★ ★ ★ ★ ★

Rattlesnake Convention

★ ★ ★ ★ ★

CHAPTER ONE

A bullet ricocheted off a rock with a witch's wail two feet right of Sheriff Ben Stillman's right boot.

It was followed an eyewink later by the crash of the rifle that had chucked it.

Stillman threw himself hard left, leaving his feet just as another bullet ricocheted off the stony ground carpeting this mountain shoulder, lifting another tooth-gnashing scream. As the rifle report reached his ears, the lawman hit the ground with a grunt and rolled behind a stout pine.

Pain blossomed in his shoulder and hip.

There was a time when such a maneuver wouldn't have hurt much more than a firm handshake.

Too damned old . . .

At least his legs weren't going numb. Thank god the prolonged nasty business with his back had finally been taken care of by the sawbones from Denver. Maybe he could find a witch doctor to help him battle age.

He rose to a knee behind the pine and quickly racked a cartridge into the action of his sixteen-shot, .44-caliber rimfire Henry rifle. Before he could snake the rifle around the pine to return fire, more bullets screamed down from the ridge before him, smashing into the pine's bole.

Again and again the bushwhacker's rifle barked, each bark echoing loudly.

One bullet after another hammered the face of the pine.

Stillman could feel the reverberations through his shoulders. The rifle belched angrily over and over, bark from the tree peppering the rocky, needle-littered, uneven stone slope. When the roaring cacophony died abruptly, it was followed almost eerily by the ping of a hammer slapping benignly down against a firing pin.

Quickly, Stillman rose and stepped out from behind the tree. He pressed the stock of the Henry to his right shoulder and aimed toward where he'd just seen the dry-gulcher pull his hatted head and scarf-wrapped neck behind a rock about fifty feet up the jagged, pine-studded escarpment. Smoke from the shooter's rifle still wafted in the still, cold air, nearly invisible against the gray sky pressing low against the top of the scarp.

Stillman flung a good half-dozen rounds into the nest of loosely mounded rocks where the shooter cowered, the rimfire roaring and leaping in his hands. Each roar echoed shrilly, the empty brass cartridges arcing back over the lawman's right shoulder and pinging onto the rocks behind him.

Beneath the cacophony, a man yelled.

The shooter appeared, stumbling out through a gap in the rocks. He tripped, turned a complete circle as though imitating some bizarre dance pirouette, and dropped his rifle. He stumbled again before tumbling out of the rock nest. He fell straight down the face of the escarpment, turning a slow somersault before landing belly down upon the branch of a lightning-split pine rising from the scarp's base.

The branch sagged under the shooter's sudden weight, creaking. It broke with a splintering roar.

The branch and the shooter fell together, separating in midair like two trapeze artists turning away from each other before falling to the base of the scarp, both bouncing once against the unforgiving stone ground, the branch crackling again as it broke against the rocks, dry branches splintering and flying.

The shooter landed with a crunching smack near the branch, likely breaking his back if not every other bone in his body, and then rolled wildly several feet before piling up at the base of another, smaller pine.

A man to Stillman's right said, "I see the other one!"

Stillman turned his head to the see saloon owner, John Stock, run out from behind a boulder and aim his Winchester repeater up the scarp. Still running, he tripped. Tripping, he jerked the rifle's trigger, sending a round into the side of the outcropping, snapping a branch from a stunted cedar.

"Damn!" Stock heaved his ungainly body back to its feet, ran a few steps farther forward, cocking the Winchester, and fired another round sharply upward. The rifle's bark thundered loudly across the shoulder of the slope.

Stock fired four rounds quickly, angrily, before Stillman strode over, wincing at the lingering ache in his shoulder and hip, and pulled the Winchester out of the saloon owner's hands.

Fat and bearded, Stock gave an indignant yelp and said, "Ben, what're you doin'?" He wore a heavy red wool cap from beneath which his curly, tangled, copper-colored hair dangled toward his shoulders, greasy and limp and speckled with sleet. He wore the cap all year long, covering both ears, but he really needed it today, as the temperature was a good five or six degrees below freezing.

Stillman said, "He's gone."

"What?"

"Listen."

Stillman stared at the top of the scarp—a jumble of boulders and stunted cedars and pines. In the silence following the gunfire came the distant tattoo of galloping hooves. They dwindled quickly.

"Goddamnit," Stock complained bitterly. "I had him in my sites, too. Before I fell."

Breathing hard, he dropped to a knee to catch his breath. Stillman could smell whiskey on Stock. He'd been drinking as they rode, off and on all day long. The saloon owner wiped his red knit scarf across his bearded mouth. His copper, gray-streaked beard streaked with chaw hung low against his chest clad in the blue wool of his heavy winter coat.

Stock was a fat man with fat, boyish cheeks that were now rosy from the cold of this late-fall, Montana mountain country fifty miles south of Clantick, the seat of Hill County and Stillman's home, which is where he wished he was right now instead of chasing two petty criminals toward the Missouri River breaks with the drunken saloon owner from Chinook.

"I ain't so good in this rugged country, I guess," Stock added, his breath wheezing in and out of his lungs. "Used to be. No more. Too much chaw an' whiskey." He grinned at Stillman, winking a brow eye. "Too much whorin'."

Stillman handed him back his rifle. "You saloon fellas get all the fun."

Stock spat to one side, and his voice grew hard again. "Till we get robbed. Our best whore shot."

Stillman looked down at the heavy man now leaning forward on his rifle butt. Stock was two years Stillman's junior, but his weight made him older. At least older when it came to trailing curly wolves like the ones who'd robbed Stock's saloon back in Chinook.

Stillman walked to where the man who'd almost outfitted him with angels' wings lay, unmoving. "You'd best light a shuck for Chinook, Jack. Tomorrow mornin', you go on home. We got one of the hardtails who robbed you. I'll track the other one alone."

"Can't do it, Ben. It's my saloon. My whore. We got one more man to hunt."

Staring down at the dead man, his breath frosting in the air before him, Stillman shook his head. "I'll run him down. He won't get far in this rugged country, with a storm bearing down." He glanced at the cold, gray sky and noted the granular flakes of snow stitching the chill breeze around him. The heavy, leaden clouds were hunkering lower. "There'll likely be snow enough soon to make for easy tracking."

Stock spat again. He was still on a knee. His breath sounded like the rumble of a distant train.

Stillman dropped to a knee beside the dead man. He grabbed his shoulder and rolled him onto his back. The sheriff grimaced. The two eyes staring up at him through half-closed lids were light brown and boyishly clear, the whites around the irises as white as porcelain. The face was that of a kid, maybe eighteen or nineteen years old. A chubby, raw-boned, square-headed boy, freckles dotting his red cheeks. A soot-smudge mustache mantled his upper lip, and downy whiskers sprouted from his pale chin mottled with red pimples. His short, dark-red hair was matted to his head and showing the lines of his hat, which was nowhere in sight.

"Shit," Stillman grunted.

"What is it?"

"Just a kid."

Stock heaved himself to his feet with effort, drew a deep, rattling breath, and walked up beside Stillman. He dropped his bearded chin to stare down at the dead boy. Glancing at him, Stillman thought he saw a dark flicker in the saloon owner's eyes.

Stillman frowned. "You recognize him, Jack?"

Stock didn't say anything for a moment. Then he shook his head. "Never seen him before in my life . . . till him an' the other one waltzed into my saloon demanding money." He hardened his jaws and dropped his voice several octaves lower, keeping his angry gaze on the dead boy. "Till he blew Glory to hell when she said she was gonna fetch the constable. Sonso'bitches."

Stillman looked at the back of the kid's right hand. The other hand wore a glove. This hand bore a tattoo in the shape of a heart. Inside the heart was lettered the name "Iris" in gunmetal blue ink.

Blood dribbled from the bullet wound in the side of the kid's head, just above his left ear. One of Stillman's bullets must have ricocheted off the rock wall behind him, and hit its mark. Blood also dribbled from the kid's long, clean nose and across his young, pink lips.

Stillman looked at the kid's faded denim jeans. Something bulged in the right front pocket. The sheriff reached into the pocket and pulled out a wad of greenbacks along with a tarnished silver pocket watch with a dented lid, and some jerky and hardtack crumbs.

"My money," Stock said. "That's it. Right there. Sure as shit."

Stillman gathered up the cash and held it over his shoulder. Stock counted the wad, shuffling the notes like playing cards between his hands, murmuring under his breath.

"A hundred and thirty-seven dollars," he growled, shoving the money into his coat pocket. "Exactly half of what he and the other one stole." He looked up the scarp. "That other devil has the rest." He turned and started striding down the slope toward where they'd tied their horses. "Let's get after him, Ben."

"Hold on, John."

Stillman was going through the rest of the dead kid's pockets, finding nothing to identify him. There was only a comb, a badly faded bill of sale, probably for a horse, and another one for a gun—likely the old Remington residing in the holster on his right hip. The rest was lint, a rattlesnake's button tail, and three strips of deer jerky.

The sheriff sat back on his heels and glanced at the quickly darkening sky. The snow was coming down harder, the cold down brushing his mustached face.

"It'll be dark in less than an hour. Gonna get cold. We'd best hole up here for the night."

Stock had stopped at the edge of the woods to glare back at Stillman. "That bastard has the rest of my money, Ben. And he killed Glory. If we don't run him down now, today, he'll drift deeper into the breaks and we'll never find him."

"We're not going anywhere till first light tomorrow," Stillman said. "Like I said, it'll be dark soon. And we have to tend this younker here."

"What do you mean—*tend* him? You mean, *bury* him? Like hell! He's a thief and a whore-killer!"

"I'm not gonna leave him out here for the wolves."

"Why the hell not? It's better'n what he deserves—the thievin', whore-killin' bastard!"

Again, Stock's gaze drifted to the dead boy and acquired that darkly furtive cast Stillman had seen before. "Go ahead—suit yourself, Ben," he snapped, returning his sharp gaze to the sheriff. "If you want to bury him, bury him. I'm gettin' after that second sonofabitch before he gets across the river."

Stock swung around and strode off through the trees, tripping over a deadfall with a grunt and a sharp, low curse.

"Don't do it, John," Stillman warned.

The only response was the snapping of twigs and brush under the saloon owner's heavy feet.

CHAPTER TWO

An hour later, darkness had descended on the mountain shoulder.

Stillman's fire, built from hastily gathered deadfall branches, pushed inadequately against it. The building wind tore at the flames, for several seconds nearly dousing them so there was only the umber glow of the coals.

After Stock had ridden off after the second whore-killing thief, Stillman had dragged the dead kid into a hollow near where he'd fallen and buried him under rocks. He'd found the kid's horse up the mountain about fifty yards. The calico hadn't been tied, and, apparently frightened by the coming storm, had come running when it had heard Stillman's approach.

The lawman had led the mount back down the mountain and tied him with Sweets, Stillman's fine buckskin, near the hollow ringed with tall trees and boulders in which he'd bivouacked against the storm. When the sheriff had draped a feed sack over its snout and a blanket over its back, the calico had grunted contentedly, glad to have oats, water, and shelter as well as the companionship of another horse and a man he apparently did not fear.

After Stillman had built the fire and erected a tripod on which to boil coffee, he'd gone through the kid's tack, finding nothing in the saddlebags that offered a clue about his identity. There were only the usual trail possibles of a coffee pot, frying pan, and a packet of flour, cornmeal salt, sugar, and coffee, as well as a small pouch of fatback. The kid's single canteen was only about a third full of water. All in all, he'd been carrying enough food and water for only a night or two on the trail, which told Stillman he likely wasn't far from home or a base camp.

The lawman had coiled the kid's shell belt around his holstered Remington .44. It lay near where Stillman's Henry leaned against a tree to Stillman's right, within an easy grab. The gun and holster were snow-dusted, the wind shifting the snow around on it. Sitting by the fire, Stillman considered the old, well-worn revolver, wondering about the identity of its former owner. He took a deep drag off the quirley he'd rolled after pouring himself a cup of piping hot coffee. He blew the smoke into the chill breeze, stitched with snow falling harder than before.

It was getting colder.

The lawman took another drag off the cigarette and considered the smoldering coal. He shouldn't smoke. It wasn't good for him. Fay wanted him to quit. He had a boy to help raise. He'd given up whiskey after a bad bout with the thunder juice some years before, after a bullet to the back had forced him to retire from the U.S. Marshal's Service. He partook of only a beer now and then. For some reason, he needed this last vice, one he'd picked up long ago, when he'd been green behind the ears and fighting for the Army of the Potomac.

The smoke tasted especially good out here in the wind and blowing snow, with the pine tang of the fire and the spicy scent of the brewing coffee lacing the air. He took another drag, blew it out, and once more looked at the tightly rolled quirley pinched between the thumb and index finger of his gloved left hand.

Instead of seeing the half-smoked cigarette, however, he saw the face of the dead kid. The sooty mustache, the freckles, the red pimples stippling the downy whiskers on his chin. The name "Iris" tattooed on his hand. The vaguely pleading, light-brown eyes gazing up at him, glazed with death . . .

"I'm gettin' old . . . too damned old and sentimental," he told himself aloud. *Feeling bad for some firebrand who'd robbed a saloon and killed a whore.*

No. It wasn't the kid he felt sorry for, he realized suddenly. It was the child that lurked behind those eyes he felt sorry for, the child inside the young killer wishing he'd chosen another life. Or that another life had offered itself. One that wouldn't have brought the husky young man here to where he now lay in an unmarked grave of hastily gathered rocks fifty feet from where the man who'd killed him sat, staring off into the storm, but seeing those young eyes staring back at him, stark with the terror of realizing that everything in his life had led him right here.

To this end, lying in a cairn of rocks gathered by the lawman who'd killed him and who didn't even know his name . . .

Had the boy really had such a realization in the moments between the bullet plowing into his skull from behind and his tumbling to his death?

Stillman felt certain he had. He didn't think he was imagining it. He honestly thought the realization . . . or the tearing regret . . . had come to the kid in those last few, sputtering seconds. Of course, he would never know. Maybe his musings really were just old age creeping up on him, and the fact that he had a boy of his own. He would employ all of his earthly power to make sure Little Ben did not end up with a fate similar to that of the husky dead kid in the rocks.

Stillman sipped his coffee and shook his head. He couldn't think about any of this now. He had to focus on the second man, just as guilty as the first one for stealing the money and killing the whore.

He took one last drag off the quirley, then tossed the stub into the breeze. It sparked off a log already accruing a furry mantle of grainy snow, and fizzled out in snow-covered leaves.

Stillman turned toward where the horses stood, tied to the rope he'd strung between two pines. Both appeared content. The wind swirling inside the hollow kept the snow from settling on their blanketed backs. Sweets turned to the sheriff, dark eyes reflecting the fire's deep-red glow. The buckskin twitched his ears curiously, as though somehow sensing his rider's ungainly ponderings and wanting to lend comfort where no comfort was to be found.

Stillman chuckled at the curious flow of his own mind, muttered, "Sleep tight, boy," and was about to take another sip of his coffee when the whipcrack of a distant rifle clove the stormy night.

CHAPTER THREE

Stillman pricked his ears, listening.

Another distant blast. A man's bellowing yell.

The lawman continued to listen, sitting tensely against the woolen underside of his saddle, the collar of his buckskin mackinaw drawn up to keep the snow and wind from slithering down his neck.

Now there was only silence save for the wind's moaning beyond the hollow, the low whickers of the startled horses, the sighing of the snow swirling around the fire, and the crackling of the flames. Stillman's heartbeat had quickened, but it began to slow.

Whatever had happened was over. Likely, one man was dead—either Stock or his quarry.

Either way, Stillman was staying put. It was too dark to ride away from the hollow, too dark to see what had happened. Likely, he'd find out who'd shot whom in the morning. The fresh snow would probably tell the tale, however grim.

He set his cup down, refilled it from the pot hanging from the tripod, then put a kettle of beans on the flames to boil, adding the last of the bacon from his burlap food pouch.

Like the kid he'd shot, he didn't have much in the way of trail supplies. He'd been on his way back to Clantick after a long week hunting illegal whiskey peddlers over near Bad Medicine Creek, when he'd stopped in Chinook, twenty miles from home, and learned from Stock about his saloon being robbed and his best whore being killed.

Stillman had stopped only long enough to have a sandwich and a cup of coffee before he had ridden out after the robbers, Stock in tow. The lawman had wanted to ride alone, and the constable, old Roy Hagen, had put up no quarrel, but Stock had insisted. The saloon owner had seemed so adamant that Stillman had given in, believing the man would have trailed him, anyway. It would be better to have him near, where he could keep an eye on him.

He and Stock had been on the trail for two days, this being the second night, and Stock had been a pain in the ass from the start, taking frequent pulls from one of the two bottles he'd carried in his saddlebags and flapping his gums about nothing.

Well, he was likely dead now. Stillman couldn't work up much grief for the uncouth man's demise, though his saloon had been a good place to stop for a stout ale and a hot bowl of chili when the sheriff was out dogging owlhoots on the county's eastern periphery.

Stillman had just finished scooping the last of his beans and bacon from the bottom of his cast-iron kettle when Sweets gave a warning whicker and turned his head sharply to stare off to the south. Quickly, Stillman set the kettle down and reached for his rifle. He pushed to his feet and stepped out away from the fire's glow.

He'd taken care not to stare into the flames, so his night vision came quickly as he gazed into the darkness pushing in from outside the hollow.

Sweets lifted a shrill whinny.

Stillman jerked with a start, heart pumping.

"Easy, fella," he whispered.

Slowly, quietly, he pumped a cartridge into the Henry's action and then stepped farther away from the fire. He moved off through the trees and boulders encircling the hollow, his boots quietly crunching the new-fallen snow. The wind jostled branches around him, blowing snow against his face. There were the occasional muffled thumps of falling pinecones.

He walked slowly in the direction in which Sweets stared anxiously, hearing both Sweets and the calico whickering nervously about fifty feet to his left. He stopped between two large rocks, a wind-jostled pine just ahead and on his right, and dropped to a knee, waiting.

Shortly, he heard something. Or thought he did. It was hard to tell against the moaning, sighing wind and the constant rake of the snow blowing around him.

But then he heard it again—a thumping sound.

There was another and another, and then he saw a shadow move maybe fifty feet away. A figure was approaching through the trees, the silhouetted shape of the man growing slowly in the darkness and falling snow.

Stillman waited.

Behind and to his left, Sweets gave another shrill whinny. Then the calico whinnied, as well.

Still, the figure kept coming, heavy-footed, stumbling. As he came closer, his outline separating from the darkness around him, Stillman saw he had his arms folded across his broad chest.

When he was about ten feet away from where Stillman waited on one knee between the rocks, he stopped suddenly and threw his head back.

"Ben?" he bellowed, the wind ripping the name from his lips. "Don't shoot! It's Stock! I'm comin' in!"

Stillman rose. Anger hardened his jaws. "What happened to your horse, you stupid son of a bitch?"

Stock jerked his head toward him, gave a startled cry, and stumbled backward. He stared at Stillman for a moment, and then he dropped his arms, his shoulders slumping in defeat, as he said, "Bastard . . . the whore-killin' bastard shot it out from under me!"

CHAPTER FOUR

Stillman cursed and strode back through the pines to the fire.

Stock staggered behind him, dropping to his knees beside the flames as Stillman added wood, building up the blaze.

Stock held his hands out to the fire, closing his eyes and turning his head this way and that, smiling dreamily and groaning as the heat pushed against him, instantly melting the snow covering his coat and red stocking cap, and caking his beard and mustache, lifting an apple glow in his cheeks.

"Oh, lordy . . . oh, Jesus . . . I thought I'd never get warm again. I thought I'd die out there—I really did!"

"No less than what you do deserve, you stupid bastard."

Stillman tossed another log on the fire and leaned his Henry against a nearby pine.

"Had to give it a try," Stock said.

"Giving it a try that late was stupid."

"Ah, hell." Stock removed his red knit cap, tossed it on a rock near the fire to dry out, and looked with wide-eyed beseeching at his reluctant trail partner. "You got any food, Ben? I'm emptier'n a dead man's boot!"

"Fresh out."

"Damn!" Stock dug around in his coat pocket. "I think I still got some jerky . . . somewhere." He pulled a few pieces of deer jerky out of the pocket and set them on his thigh. He stuck one into his mouth and chewed, groaning when the salty meat hit his tongue.

"What happened to your horse?" Stillman asked him.

"I told you," the saloon owner said, chewing. "He shot it out from under me, the sneaky son of a bitch. Must've been waitin' for us to follow him, laid up on a ridge in some rocks an' such. I had no idea he was there till I heard the rifle. My hoss screamed and went down. Would have fallen on my leg, but I sprung off that saddle like a kid. You should have seen me jump!"

Stock gave a dry laugh, pulled a bottle out of his coat pocket, and fumbled the cork from the lip with his gloved hands. He tipped the bottle back. Stillman watched the air bubble bounce as Stock took several deep swallows.

Pulling the bottle back down, Stock said, "Thank god I had this in my coat pocket. Thank god it didn't break! I couldn't get my rifle or my saddlebags out from under my sorrel. Poor bastard." He glanced over his left shoulder toward where Sweets and the calico stood tied to the picket line. "You found the dead one's hoss, I see. I'll ride him tomorrow."

Stock held the bottle out toward Stillman. "You want a pull, Ben? Cold night."

"You're going back tomorrow, John."

Stock frowned as he slowly lowered the bottle and drew it back to his chest. "What's that?"

"You're gonna saddle the dead kid's horse first thing in the morning, and you're going to head back to Chinook." Stillman pinned the stout man across the fire with his gaze. "That's final."

Stock glared at him. Slowly, he sagged against the dead kid's saddle, holding the bottle by its neck in his right hand. He shifted his gaze to the fire and sat staring into the flames, the corners of his fleshy mouth pulled down inside his tangled, wet beard, brooding.

"I lied," he said finally, when Stillman had poured himself a fresh cup of coffee and had set to work running an oily rag over the stock and barrel of the Henry rifle now resting across his thighs.

"About what?" he said.

"I knew that kid."

Stillman stopped moving the rag over the Henry and gave the saloon owner a curious frown.

Glumly, Stock nodded. He took another pull from the bottle, shivered, and said, "He was my son."

Stillman stared at him.

"The other one, too," Stock said, shifting his gaze from the low, leaping flames to the incredulous lawman.

Stillman scowled. "I don't understand."

Stock took another pull from the bottle, stretched his lips back from his small, yellow teeth, and swallowed. "Twins." He ran his coat sleeve across his mouth.

"Twins? Your *sons*?"

"Yep."

"I didn't even know you had a family, John." Not that Stillman knew the man very well. He stopped at Stock's saloon in Chinook maybe three, four times a year, when he was out stalking bad men of one stripe or another in that part of the county.

"I don't. Leastways, I don't consider those two *family*, if you know what I mean."

"No," Stillman said. "I don't know what you mean."

Stock sniffed, shivered again inside his wet coat, and tossed another stout branch on the fire. The flames played across his bearded face as he stared into them.

"I married their ma a long time ago, in Great Falls. Long damn time ago. Hell, I was nineteen years old. May was seventeen. The twins came five months after we exchanged vows." Stock grunted wryly at that. "Her pa ran the Stockmen's Bank down there, hired me as a loan officer after teachin' me how to cypher an' such, balance the books. Well, that didn't last long. After me an' May started havin' trouble, the old man accused me of smudgin' the ink."

"Stealin' from him," Stillman said. "Embezzling."

"Call it what you want. I never done it. But he fired me, just the same. Fired me from the loan desk, I mean. But he kept me on. Gave me a broom."

Stock smiled ironically across the fire at Stillman, who sat staring back at him, saying nothing, his coffee growing cold where the cup rested on his thigh.

"Said all I was good for was sweepin' an' moppin' . . . dustin' the drapes. I told him to go to hell! I threw the broom back at him and went home to find May with another man. *In bed* with another man. A friend of mine—Joe Barden. Joe an' I had growed up together down in Milestown, rode up to Great Falls together lookin' for work. I found a gun an' shot the double-crossin', double-dealin', girl-stealin' sonofabitch! Wounded him. He fired at me, shot May instead. Killed her."

Stock tipped the bottle back once more, taking a long draw. The whiskey sloshed. Stillman could barely hear it beneath the wind and the fire, his own thoughts racing through his brain.

Turning his cold, flat gaze back to Stillman, Stock said, "I got a year in Deer Lodge for shootin' that bastard, which don't make no sense at all, since they hanged him from the gallows in front of the courthouse right there in Great Falls not two days after his trial."

Stock smiled acidly. "That's what you get when you shoot the banker's daughter."

The smile faded. "Anyways, I never went back to Great Falls after I got out of Deer Lodge. I came up here, to Chinook. An old pard of mine wanted me to go into the saloon business with him. So I did. Dave Anderson died two years ago. You knew ole Dave. Good fella. He left his half of the saloon to me. It was right around then them two kids, the twins, Wayne and Blaine"—Stock chuckled at that—"started hangin' around Chinook. Moved up here from Great Falls after their good ole grandpap kicked 'em out an' cut 'em off. The twins came up here lookin' for more handouts. This time they wanted handouts from *me*. I guess they figured it was time I supported 'em . . . now that their granddad was gone."

Stock bunched his lips and snarled, "Like hell!"

"You turned 'em away—your own sons?" Stillman said.

"Pshaw!" Stock said. "They're no sons of mine. They're her kids. His kids—the old man's. They're more like her an' him than me. They spoiled 'em, never taught 'em how to work. I grew up workin' my tail off from sunrise to sunset every day since I was nine years old—herdin' cattle and hawkin' newspapers an' such. You name it, I did it!"

Stillman wondered why he'd never heard about the shooting. Such a scandalous affair would have made the papers. Also, he'd have been a deputy U.S. marshal around that time. But, then, it might have happened a year or two before he'd started wearing the moon and star, based out of Helena.

Stock took another pull on the bottle, emptying it. He threw it angrily into the darkness, where it broke on a rock. Settling back against his saddle and pulling the dead kid's—his dead *son's*—bedroll around his shoulders, hunkering down into it against the growing cold, he said, "They came around askin' for money, sure enough. I told 'em to get jobs. They asked *me* for a job. I told 'em I didn't have nothin' for neither one of 'em.

"I don't know if they found other work or not, but they must've found *somethin'* after that, because they came around heeled, buyin' beer an' whiskey an' enjoyin' my free lunch counter. Even my *whores*—Glory included, even though they knew she was special to me. Maybe *because* they knew she was special to me—that's why they'd take her upstairs, sometimes both at once. I don't allow that kind of thing, but they threatened to shoot up the place, so . . . they took her upstairs and threw the wood to her real loud, knowin' I could hear . . ."

Stock paused, staring into the flames, his expression sour, going through it all again in his head.

Stillman raised his coffee cup to his lips. It was as cold as spring snowmelt. He tossed it into the brush and shoved the cup into his war sack.

"They must work down here somewhere," Stock said after a time. "Maybe rustlin', maybe sellin' whiskey to the Injuns. Maybe robbin' stagecoaches. That's what the owlhoots who haunt the breaks do—ain't it?"

"That's about the size of it," Stillman said.

He picked up a stick and poked at the fire for a time, then added another branch.

"Why didn't you tell me they were your kids, John?" Stillman said, sitting back against his saddle again and drawing his own bedroll up to his chin, crossing his ankles near the fire.

"Hell, I don't know," Stock said after he'd thought about it for a while. "I guess . . . I guess . . . Hell, I don't know. I . . . reckon I was ashamed."

Another pause. Then the saloon owner looked with gravity across the fire at Stillman once more. The flames flickered in his dark eyes.

"You gotta let me ride along with you tomorrow, Ben."

Stillman frowned. "Don't you feel bad about any of this, John? One son is dead. You don't want to ride home and leave the other one to me?"

"Sure as hell I do. But I can't."

"*Why*, for godsakes?"

"Because if we don't kill him, he'll kill me. They want *me* dead, see? They wanted me dead all along . . . after I turned 'em away up in Chinook. I seen it in their eyes. The same wicked

light their mother used to get. A crazy, killin' light! They were
fixin' to shoot me when they robbed me, but I grabbed my
double-barrel from under the bar, and they lit a shuck.
Unfortunately, I'd forgot to load the fuckin' thing!"

He drew a deep, ragged breath. "If you send me back to
Chinook, he might circle around you. He might follow me an'
gun me alone. He's savvy. They both were. That's why he holed
up on that ridge yonder, earlier. He was waitin' for me. To kill
me. To kill both of us, probably, but me *especially*. He'll probably be watchin' from that ridge tomorrow mornin', to see what
we do. If we both go after him, we can run him down. The two
of us can track him easier than just you alone."

"Which one is it?" Stillman said, staring thoughtfully into the
darkness.

"Wayne. Blaine's the dead one. I recognized that name 'Iris'
tattooed on his hand."

"Who's Iris?"

"Hell if I know. Probably some parlor girl from Great Falls."

Stock stared hard at Stillman. "Okay, Ben? You let me ride
along tomorrow. You an' me can take Wayne down. If you turn
me back alone, he'll take me down for his brother an' plenty of
other reasons he's probably been chewin' on since he was two
years old and the whole dustup with Joe and their ma. Knowin'
their old grandpap, he filled their heads full of hateful lies, poi-
sonin' both of 'em against me!"

Stillman thought it through. He considered going ahead and
sending Stock back to Chinook and waiting to see if he was
right about Wayne trailing him. Using the saloon owner as bait,
essentially.

But that seemed problematic. This was big country and even
with the snow, it was easy to lose a man's trail. Wayne might get
around Stillman and kill Stock before Stillman could stop him.

Stock was probably right.

It was probably best to keep tracking the second rider, the surviving twin. It was probably best that he and Stock stay together.

"Okay, John," Stillman said, exhaling a deep, weary breath and pulling his hat brim down over his eyes. "We'll try it your way."

He eased himself into a doze.

Chapter Five

Stillman lifted his head with a start, his heart racing.

He found himself staring into the beady, black eyes of a crow sitting on a pine bough about fifteen feet away from him. The bird looked enormous—a hulking, malevolent figure with its wings semi-spread, glaring at the sheriff.

It was milky dawn. The fire had died to gray, smoldering coals.

The crow lowered its head and cawed loudly, angrily. It cawed again and again, like an angry dog barking. Then it lifted its stygian wings and rose from the branch, flying up, up, up over the crown of the pines and away, its ratcheting cries dwindling gradually, echoing in the dawn's eerie silence.

Gradually, Stillman's heart slowed.

He looked around.

It must have stopped snowing soon after he'd fallen asleep. Only a few powdery inches lay on the ground around the fire ring, swept into small drifts. Pushing up onto his elbows, he glanced to his left, toward where Stock lay on the other side of the fire.

But Stock wasn't there. Only the dead kid's gear was piled over there. His blanket roll lay in front of the saddle, rumpled and empty.

Stillman looked around. "John?"

There was no sign of the man. There was no movement whatever around the camp. The gray light glowed dully, the pines and aspens standing out darkly against it. The branches didn't move. Neither did the few remaining dead leaves clinging to them. There wasn't a breath of breeze.

"John?" Stillman called again. He'd likely only gotten up to relieve himself. Louder, Stillman said, "John? Are you here?"

No response except the heavy silence.

Stillman flung the top blanket of his bedroll aside and pushed himself to his feet. The air was still but cold, like cold steel laid against both cheeks. Shivering inside his mackinaw, he stomped into his boots, then wrapped his Colt and shell belt around his waist, and buckled it. He picked up his Henry and looked around for Stock's tracks in the snow, scowling incredulously at the ground around Stock's bedroll and the fire.

Not a single track anywhere.

"John?" Stillman heard the quavering of a growing dread in his voice. "John, where are you?"

He stepped away from the fire ring, looking around. Still, no tracks. He moved off between two pines and then two more pines, his instincts for some reason directing him south. He'd walked for maybe twenty or thirty yards from the fire, meandering through the forest, stepping over deadfalls humped in their fresh white coats, when he stopped abruptly.

He'd heard something. Maybe smelled something.

He whipped suddenly around to his right, raising the Henry, heart drumming in his ears.

"Christ!"

Stillman's heart hammered away at his breastbone as he stared in shock at John Stock hanging from a stout box elder bough ten feet away from him. A heavy rope was wound around his neck, the other end angling up and over the stout branch, then down to the trunk where it was tied around a knob.

Stock's boots dangled three feet from the ground.

Stock's face was puffed up and blue, twisted into a grimace, lips stretched back from his little, yellow teeth.

Stillman jacked a round into the Henry's breech as he stepped slowly toward the hanged man. He stopped three feet away. Stock's eyes opened suddenly.

"Ben," he raked out through his horror-twisted mouth. "Behind you!"

Stillman wheeled to see the chubby, red-headed kid he'd killed standing behind him, his own mouth twisted in a demonic grin as his light-brown eyes gazed down the barrel of the Winchester aimed at Stillman's head.

The lawman woke with a start, sitting bolt upright so fast that his hat tumbled off his left shoulder.

He gave a loud grunt as he stared into the milky light of a snowy dawn.

"Shit—what is it? What the hell is it, Ben?"

Heart still tattooing his breastbone, Stillman turned to his left. Stock was sitting up now, fumbling his old Colt from its holster but having trouble unsnapping the keeper thong from over the hammer.

"Nothing," Stillman said. "Take it easy. It's nothing."

He looked around just to make sure. There was no one else here except the horses, both of which were whickering softly and shifting their hooves behind him, obviously startled by Stillman's grunt.

Stock left his revolver in its holster and turned to the lawman, scowling curiously.

In his mind's eye, Stillman saw him again as he'd hung from the box elder, face swollen, mouth twisted in silent agony. He saw, too, the fleshy, freckled face of the Stock twin leering down his rifle barrel.

"It's nothing," the lawman said again, chagrin raking through him. He rose, shaking the fresh snow from his blanket. "It's dawn." He gave the blanket another shake. "Time to ride."

"Sure, sure," Stock said. "Time to ride."

Stillman glanced at him. Stock was grinning oddly up at him. Quickly, the man looked away and heaved himself to his feet. "You bet it is—time to ride!"

CHAPTER SIX

An hour later, Stillman stopped his horse at the edge of woods on a mountain slope and looked into a hollow about forty yards downhill, just inside another wooded area. A set of horse tracks, visible beneath the layer of new snow and where the wind had swept snow from the ground, had led him here.

He and Stock had passed Stock's dead horse fifteen minutes earlier. The wolves and coyotes had not found it yet, though Stillman and the saloon owner had scared up an eagle perched on the poor beast's head, dipping its beak into an eye.

Stillman stared into the hollow. The clouds had cleared soon after the sun had risen, and the brassy light glittered blindingly off the new snow. Squinting, he thought he could make out a fire ring inside the hollow.

"Stay with the horses," he told Stock, swinging down from the buckskin's back.

He tossed the man his reins, slid his Henry from its scabbard, racked a round into the chamber, then off-cocked the hammer. He looked around carefully. The stretch of open ground between here and the hollow would be a good place to get bushwhacked. It had become only too obvious that Stock's sons were not above such lowly tactics.

Stillman looked around once more, then walked out into the clearing. He moved quickly through the one-to-two-foot drifts between which lay broad stretches of open ground. He spied two shod hoof prints before he entered the hollow. He stopped just inside the trees and dropped to a knee, looking around again carefully, letting his eyes grow accustomed to the shade of the woods.

An angry squirrel chittered at him from a spruce bough.

Chickadees peeped.

Ten feet away lay a campfire ring. When he was relatively sure he was alone here in the hollow, and his eyes had grown accustomed to the shadows, Stillman moved forward, dropped to a knee, removed his glove, and placed the palm of his left hand on the gray ashes mounded inside the ring of charred rocks.

The ashes weren't exactly warm, but they weren't cold, either. The fire had burned down several hours ago.

The surviving Stock twin had holed up here last night.

When Stillman had tramped around the hollow and discovered the prints of the Stock twin's horse, he decided that Wayne had pulled out about the same time Stillman and John Stock had broken their own camp, two hours ago. He saw where the horse prints led off down the slope beyond the hollow, deeper into the woods.

Stillman stared at the tracks, the kid's scuffed trail foreshortening into the distance bright with snow-reflecting sunlight, toward another purple-green blotch of mountain forest. He squeezed the Henry in his hands, darkly pondering. In his mind's eye, he saw the face of Stock's dead son. Then he saw Stock himself hanging from the tree in his dream.

Then the kid standing behind him, grinning down the barrel of that rifle . . .

The lawman felt oddly unsettled. He wished he hadn't ridden into Chinook when he had, only a few hours after the robbery. He could have done without this bit of nastiness—tracking two sons with chips on their shoulders. They couldn't be blamed for how Stock had treated them. Or not treated them, as the case may be. How Stock had essentially abandoned them when they were very young and turned them away when they were older.

How Stock had likely caused the death of their mother.

You couldn't really blame the twins for turning out bad, having been raised without a mother or a father. They might have been well-provided for by their grandparents, but money didn't replace a real family.

Stillman didn't much care for Stock. He was a drunk and a lout and now here Stillman was, tracking the man's son who'd robbed him and killed his whore. Here Stillman was, having killed the one twin yesterday, leaving him to molder in a stone cairn on that stormy mountain shoulder. He couldn't help resenting Stock for putting him in this position—of having to kill the man's son. The kid had deserved it, of course. He'd fired from ambush.

Still, deep down, Stock was to blame for this—this bit of nastiness Stillman could have done without. He wished he'd skirted Stock's saloon and had continued home to Clantick and his wife and young son. He'd hold them close when he got back. Tighter than he ever had before.

He released a ragged breath, then swung around and started walking to where Stock sat the calico, Sweets standing to his left, curiously switching his tail. Stock regarded the sheriff incredulously, sourly, from beneath his red wool cap.

Just as he started across the clearing, Stillman stopped in his tracks.

His heartbeat quickened.

In the woods behind Stock, a shadow moved. Stillman took the Henry in both hands and started to raise it, when the calico gave a shrill whinny and reared, catching Stock by surprise. The saloon owner screamed as he dropped both the calico's and the buckskin's reins and rolled backward off his mount's left hip.

He hit the snowy ground with a thump. "God*damn!*"

Stillman stared into the woods behind him and at the two startled horses, tightening his right index finger on the Henry's trigger, aiming down the barrel at the jostling shadow in the shape of a man riding lazily toward him. The man was singing loudly and with great conviction, "Me an' my wife live all alone/In a little log hut we're all our own/She loves gin and I love rum/And don't we have a lot of fun!"

The man neared the edge of the woods where Stock lay sprawled on the ground, one leg curled beneath him, cursing and trying to slide his revolver from its holster, but having trouble with the keeper thong again. The newcomer broke off singing and raised both his gloved hands in supplication, saying, "Easy, now, gents. I'm friendly. Friendly if you are, that is."

He stopped his horse, a rangy steeldust with two black rings around its eyes, and glanced down at Stock. "Say there, pard— that hoss of yourn must be a might spooky." He grinned. "Either that or he don't like 'Little Brown Jug,' though how anyone— man or hoss couldn't like such a happy song as 'Jug' is way beyond my ability to fathom!"

He chuckled and turned to Stillman. "Tell him to keep that hogleg in the leather will ya, pard?" he asked, his affable voice trimmed with a dark, menacing chill.

"Leave the pistol," Stillman ordered Stock.

Stock looked up at the newcomer, gritting his teeth. He stopped trying to jerk his Colt free of its holster but kept his hand on the gun's walnut grips. His broad, pasty forehead was cut deep with long gullies as he studied the newcomer, flushing with a slow-building embarrassment based on the realization that he was not confronting his son out to kill him, as he'd feared.

"Say, he's a mite on the nervy side, ain't he?" the newcomer said to Stillman in his slow, casual voice and with his easygoing smile that, for some reason, seemed to the lawman's eyes only skin-deep.

The newcomer was a long-faced man with a broad mouth and close-set eyes. Curly, gray hair shone beneath his black, broad-brimmed Stetson boasting a ragged hawk feather poking up from the band around the crown. His face was so sun-seared that he almost looked black. He had no front teeth, which was obvious when he smiled; the lack of teeth also gave him a definite lisp.

He wore a shaggy coat and scarf, and two pistols showed prominently on his lean hips. Whipcord trousers were shoved into high-topped, mule-eared boots. The faded red of his long-handles showed behind the threadbare patches at his knees.

"Who the fuck are you?" Stock snarled up at him, keeping his hand on his gun handle.

"I got a feelin' I ain't who you thought I was," the stranger said. "But I'm gonna get a mite offended if you don't take your hand off your hogleg there, pard." He leaned forward on his saddle horn, smiling, but also pitching his voice with more menace.

Stock glanced at Stillman. He looked at the newcomer again and then dropped his hand from his Colt. "Ben, I think I broke my leg!"

Ignoring the saloon owner, Stillman set the barrel of his Henry on his right shoulder, keeping his hand around the neck, his finger through the trigger guard. He strode up to where the newcomer sat the steeldust's back. He sized the man up once more, riffling through the endless supply of wanted circulars filed in his brain, and said, "Who're you?"

"Me?" the newcomer said in his easygoing way, dimpling his cheeks with another winning but toothless smile, which gave him a pointedly depraved, even loony, air. "Why, I'm George Williams."

Stillman studied him, again mentally shuffling through those wanted dodgers. Then his own face broke a grin, lifting his gray-brown mustache. "Horace Butterfield."

"Horace Butterfield?" the newcomer said, jerking his head back incredulously. "Who in the hell is . . . ?" He grinned again. "Pshaw. You got you one hell of a good memory, Stillman, you old, law-bringin' devil!"

"When did you get out of Deer Lodge, Horace?"

"Hell, I been outta Deer Lodge for over ten years. The judge only gave me two!"

"Only two for killin' a sheriff's deputy?"

"They couldn't prove that part of the whole mess, so the jury came back from their beer break with a guilty verdict just for the horse thievery. Besides, you an' me both know Wally Slade had been deservin' that bullet from the time he left his rubber pants!" Butterfield leaned backward again, laughing through the large, liver-colored gap in his upper jaw.

"What're you doin' out here?" Stillman asked him.

Butterfield gave him another sly smile and answered the question with a question of his own: "What're *you* doin' out here?"

"Looking for this man's son."

"Stop callin' him that," Stock said, glowering at Stillman as he heaved himself heavily to his feet.

"There, see?" Butterfield said to Stock. "Your leg ain't broke. Why, from here it looks fine!"

"No thanks to you," Stock griped.

Butterfield chuckled.

As Stillman walked to where Sweets stood several feet away and grabbed the buckskin's reins, Butterfield said, probingly, "I see—it's a family matter."

Stillman swung up onto Sweets's back. "You could say that."

He rode to the calico standing some distance away. He grabbed the horse's reins and led the mount back to where

Stock stood, flexing his injured leg and looking owly. "If you're comin', John, mount up."

Stillman tossed the saloon owner his reins.

"I'm comin'," he growled. "You ain't ridin' on without me."

"Which way you fellas headed?" Butterfield asked.

"Whichever way that killer's headed," Stock said, heaving himself into his saddle with another curse.

Butterfield trailed his gaze along the ground. He looked toward where Stillman's boot tracks angled away into the hollow and returned from the same direction.

"South, looks like," the old outlaw said. "Probably headin' for Perdition Bend. That's where most trails out here lead. That's where I'm headed. Good whiskey. A couple nice wimmen-folk."

Butterfield rose up in his saddle slightly, grabbed his crotch, and gave Stillman a lascivious wink.

"Perdition Bend?" Stock said, narrowing an eye at the outlaw. "What the hell is Perdition Bend?"

"Perdition Bend, eh?" Stillman said to Butterfield. "I haven't been there in years. Not since I wore the old moon and star." As a deputy United States Marshal he'd trailed several curly wolves into that den of unwashed miscreants, and dragged them out either dead or screaming. Each time, he'd counted himself lucky to leave the place alive. It wasn't a place he'd ever yearned to return to. No lawman would.

Since he'd left Hill County several miles back, he was out of his jurisdiction as sheriff. That didn't matter. If every lawman abided by jurisdictional boundaries in a territory as large as Montana, they might as well close Deer Lodge pen. He'd square his pursuit with the sheriff in these parts once he got back to Clantick.

"Wonderful place, Ben." Butterfield grinned his bizarre grin, leathery cheeks dimpling, flat eyes touched with their customary menace. "Perdition Bend!"

Stock gave an impatient chuff as he scowled over the calico's ears at Stillman. "What the hell is Perdition Bend, goddamnit?"

"You're about to find out, looks like," Stillman said, absently brushing his right hand across the grips of his .44, making sure the gun was in its holster.

He reined the buckskin south.

Stock and Butterfield booted their own mounts after him, the outlaw singing, "When I go toiling on the farm/I take the little jug under my arm/Place it under a shady tree/Little brown jug, 'tis you and me!"

CHAPTER SEVEN

"Who is this . . . uh . . . *family* you're trailin'?" Butterfield asked Stock when they'd been riding together for a half hour, and Butterfield had sung all the words to "Little Brown Jug" two full times and hummed them a few more.

"Ain't family," Stock said. He spat a stream of chaw down over the calico's left wither and wiped his mouth with the back of his hand. "Oh, I reckon I sewed his seed, but he ain't no son of mine. Not really. Takes after his mother and granddad. I didn't raise him nor his brother lyin' dead now in a pile of rocks, which is a far better restin' place than he deserved. Me—I woulda left him to the wildcats. Stillman's soft-hearted."

Stock and Butterfield were riding behind the sheriff, who rode with an eye skinned on the ground, looking for any sign that the tracks of the twin brother he was following branched off from the trail they were now on—an old army and stagecoach trail, meandering deeper and deeper in to the breaks of the Missouri River.

"Dead, huh?" Butterfield said. "What these two brothers do, anyways?"

"Robbed me," Stock said. "Shot my best whore. A real moneymaker named Glory. Her real name was Betsy but she called herself Glory. Sweet gal. Nice tits. I swear, in the winter she could bring in fifty dollars all by herself in one night!"

"Damn!" Butterfield said.

"Yeah."

"That's a lot of time on her back!"

"Or on her knees. Workhorse is what she was. Now she's dead. I buried her behind the stable, out back of my saloon. Under a tree she used to hang her wash from."

"What saloon is that?"

"Stock's Fine and Dandy in Chinook. I'm sure you heard of it. Glory might've even given you a poke or two."

"Nah. I doubt it," Butterfield said.

"Why's that?"

"I don't, uh . . . I don't get up that way often."

Stillman, who'd been sort of half-following the conversation, cast a wry smile over his shoulder at Stock and said, "What Horace means is, he don't get to town very often. *Any* town. He holes up here in the breaks most of the time, maybe heads to Arizona for the winter. Keeps his head down."

"Why's that?" Stock asked.

Stillman reined Sweets to a halt, curveting the buckskin to sit sideways in the trail. "Yes, why is that, Horace?"

Stock and Butterfield stopped their own mounts behind Stillman. Butterfield reached inside his coat to produce a hide makings sack, and, grinning sheepishly, began building a quirley. "Me?" the outlaw said. "I'm the shy sort. Don't much like the company of people. I like bein' out here by myself. I like wolves and coyotes better than most folks . . . uh, present company excepted, gents."

He laughed.

"Is that so?" Stillman said. "Unless you're one of those rare zebras that can change his stripes, the reason you stay away from towns is because you're likely wanted. I don't remember seein' your toothless mug on any dodgers in my office, Horace, but I'm going to look them over real good when I get back to Clantick."

"Really?" Stock said, arching a brow at Butterfield. "You ride the long coulees—do you, Butterfield?"

Butterfield grinned at the wheat paper troughed between the first two fingers of his right hand. "Don't listen to Stillman. To him, everyone's an outlaw."

"What're you up to these days, Horace?" Stillman prodded. "Rustlin'? Throwin' the long loop seemed to be what you excelled at back when I was wearin' the moon an' star. That an' sellin' whiskey to the reservation Indians . . . when you weren't robbing the occasional stagecoach."

"Hell no, hell no," Butterfield said, sliding the makings sack back into his coat, then holding it over his saddle horn, carefully rolling the quirley closed. "Shit, I cut firewood for old widder ladies." He poked the quirley into his mouth and sealed it with his lips.

"Ain't that nice?" Stillman said. "That's good to hear, Horace. It really is. Warms my heart to hear how a man can change his ways." Suddenly the sheriff scowled up at the sky, noticing that clouds had rolled in once more, and more snow was starting to fall.

Grumbling, he turned Sweets forward and booted the horse along the trail, dropping into another shallow ravine, one of many ravines that scored this rugged country just north of the Missouri. Bluffs and mesas rose around him. Dry creek beds swerved alongside the curving trail to angle away again.

The clouds dropped lower and turned darker. The cold air was rife with the aroma of autumn-cured brush and dead leaves.

Stillman and his two trail partners crossed a creek, traversed a steep-walled, gravel-bottomed gorge peppered with cedars and post oaks, then climbed the opposite bank to stop their horses, resting them, and stare down a gradual grade to the south. The Missouri lay iron-gray beyond—wide and flat and as serpentine as any snake, sheathed on both sides by tall brush and even taller cottonwoods and willows. It was laid out behind a thin, lacy white curtain of falling snow.

A cold wind was rising, whipping the horses' tails up between their hind legs and bending the riders' hat brims.

It was not the river Stillman studied before him. It was the motley little collection of shacks, shanties, and corrals scattered inside a near bend of the Big Muddy.

"There it is, home sweet home," Butterfield said. "Perdition Bend."

"Perdition Bend," Stock said as though testing the name out on his tongue. "What is it? Looks like a little ranch setup."

Stillman raised his mackinaw's collar against the chill breeze slithering down his back like a cold, wet snake. "It's an old buffalo hiders' camp. Woodcutters' camp after that. Steamboats used to stop there for wood. When the woodcutters moved on, the bad element moved in."

"Bad element, huh?" said Stock.

"He means men like myself," Butterfield said, curling one side of his upper lip at Stillman, who was leaning forward on his saddle horn to study the camp below. "Ben's got no forgiveness in him whatsoever."

"I reckon he does, too," Stock said. "He's got sympathy for them whore-killin' thieves   enough to give one a grave."

Stillman was watching a man in buckskin trousers, red shirt, and black hat lead three horses away from a hitch rack fronting the camp's main building toward a weather-beaten barn and corral. The man's long, green neckerchief whipped out in the wind. He turned his head toward Stillman and his two trail partners, and stopped suddenly, staring cautiously.

The horses behind him sidestepped against the building wind and gusting snow, tails blowing toward the southeast.

Finally, the man continued leading the horses toward the corral, casting quick, cautious glances at Stillman and the others.

"Perdition Bend, eh?" Stock grumbled. "I got a feelin' I'm not gonna like this so much. I'm old, cold, and outta shape. I don't got no truck with owlhoots. None but them that killed my whore, I'm sayin'."

Ignoring the saloon owner, Stillman turned to Butterfield. "What am I riding into here, Horace?"

"What you always rode into, most like."

Stillman kept his eyes on the motley buildings below as he said, "Blinky Davis still riding the break country? How 'bout Owen Kilbride? Billy Two Wolves? There's a jasper I never could run to ground, try as I might in my younger days. Slippery as a greased coyote! How 'bout Hector Starr or Rafael Sanchez?"

Butterfield blinked at him in astonishment. "Ben, you've gotten old! Do you know that every last name you just mentioned is chiseled on a gravestone somewhere? All except Two Wolves. I heard Billy killed a rancher in Wyoming and hightailed it to South America. Can you see Billy in South America?"

The outlaw laughed his gap-toothed laugh.

"Outlaw hideout, huh?" Stock sat his saddle heavily, sullenly staring at the weathered gray buildings. "Perdition Bend. Sure, I remember that name."

"There it is," Butterfield said.

Stock turned to him. "You ever hear the names Wayne and Blaine Stock?"

"Wayne and Blaine Stock." Butterfield tapped two gloved fingers against his lips as he pondered the question. "Wayne and Blaine Stock, Wayne and Blaine Stock . . ."

"Forget it," Stillman said with a caustic chuff, nudging Sweets with his spurs and starting on down the grade, following the trail. He glanced at Stock. "You think he'd tell you if he knew? Such talk gets men's throats cut out here."

Stock glowered as he kicked his calico up beside Stillman. "This probably ain't such a good idea, then, is it?"

"What's not such a good idea?"

"Stoppin' here. An outlaw camp, for chrissakes . . ."

"No, it's never a good idea to stop at such a place," Stillman said, "unless you're lookin' for a man . . . or a kid, in this case . . . who might be holed up here."

Suddenly, he drew back on Sweets's reins, again stopping the buckskin. Stock followed suit.

"Listen, John, if you want to head back to Chinook, you better head north now, before this storm gets any worse. You'll reach the Haystack Buttes before dark. You can hole up there overnight."

Stock scowled at the buildings scattered before them. "You mean . . . you'd just head in there . . . alone?"

"I've done it before." Honestly, he didn't think Stock would be much help in a tight spot, anyway. Especially if the booze was flowing, as it always was here.

Stillman unsheathed his revolver, flicked open the loading gate, and turned the wheel one click. Watching Stock, whose face was pale with anxiety, he plucked a fresh cartridge from his shell belt, slid it into the chamber he usually kept empty beneath the hammer, and spun the wheel, making it sing.

He slipped the Colt back into its holster and fastened the keeper thong over the hammer.

"Look, John, Perdition Bend can be a right hot place. You head on back to Chinook, ride out the storm in the Haystack Buttes. I'll find Wayne."

Stock chewed his lower lip as he shifted his gaze between Stillman and the outlaw camp. "Nah," he said. "I rode this far. I'll finish this deal . . . even it finishes me. I reckon I owe Glory that much."

Stock nudged the calico forward.

Butterfield rode up beside Stillman, grinning his grin. "Once more into Perdition's fire—eh, Ben?"

"Once more," Stillman said with a sigh, and nudged Sweets on ahead.

Riding along behind him, Butterfield sang, "Place it under a shady tree/Little brown jug, 'tis you and me/'Tis you that makes me friends and foes/'Tis you that makes me wear old clothes/ But, seeing you're so near my nose/Tip her up and down she goes . . . Tip 'er up an' down she goes . . ."

CHAPTER EIGHT

As Stillman, Stock, and Butterfield approached the yard of the outlaw camp, the man who'd taken the horses to the barn now stepped out from between the barn's two doors and looked once more at the three approaching riders.

He closed the doors, then walked across the yard, his green scarf blowing in the wind. He kept his gaze on the newcomers as he approached the main building and stepped onto the rickety wooden front veranda.

Stillman glanced from the man to the building behind him—a sprawling, hodgepodge affair of weather-beaten logs, adobe bricks, and pine planks. One part of the building was two stories, the second story owning a rusty tin roof. The lower part, which appeared to be a series of rickety whores' cribs, was shingled with sod and brush in some places, shakes in other places.

The entire building looked as though it would fall down in the next stiff breeze. In fact, even as Stillman watched through the thickening pale screen of blowing snow, two shakes sprang up from the lower roof, one after the other, to go tumbling off in the wind to the rear of the place, where cottonwoods bent and shook. The waxed paper windows snapped and popped.

As Stillman and his two compatriots entered the yard, the man on the porch lowered his right hand to the revolver holstered on his right thigh. Quickly and almost imperceptibly, he brushed a finger over the keeper thong, unsnapping it, and loosened the gun in its holster. He kept his dark eyes set beneath the down-canted brim of his black hat on the three approaching riders, the wind batting his light-blue denims against his legs and blowing the long, green neckerchief toward the trailhouse's closed front door.

"Spanish!" Butterfield called above the wind as he, Stock, and Stillman reined their horses to a halt in front of the place. "How you been, *amigo?*"

Spanish just stared cautiously at the two others, his eyes hard and flat. He had a thick handlebar mustache, and both bars were getting a good workout in the wind. Snowflakes danced across the high crown of his hat.

"Who you got with you, Horace?"

"Ben Stillman," the sheriff answered for himself. "Sheriff of Hill County."

Spanish stared at him, lips pursed in a straight line beneath his mustache.

Stillman swung down from his saddle, dropped his reins, and glanced at Stock. "Wait here."

Stillman lifted the hem of his coat above the Colt positioned for the cross-draw on his left hip, and unsnapped the keeper thong from over the hammer. As he strode resolutely toward the rambling trailhouse's front porch, Stock said behind him, "What're you gonna . . . ?" then let his voice trail off as Stillman mounted the porch and stopped beside the man called Spanish.

The sheriff was so close he could see the large pores in the man's weathered cheeks. He could also smell whiskey and tobacco smoke on him.

"Anyone show up here within the last hour or so?"

Spanish stared flatly at Stillman before the corner of his mouth moved in amusement. Stillman returned the look with a similar one of his own, then strode to the door, tripped the latch, opened the door, stepped inside, and closed the door behind him.

Three people sitting at a table in the shadows across the deep, low-ceilinged room stopped talking. On the wall behind them, a large grizzly head snarled. The men turned to look at the newcomer.

One was a young blond woman. She was playing poker with the two men. Both appeared to be in their fifties—grizzled, weathered men. One was tall with a gray beard. The other was swarthy, stocky and broad-faced, with long, chocolate-brown eyes—likely owning some Indian blood. Heavy coats hung from their chair backs.

When Stillman had first entered, the three had been arguing good-naturedly, but now their eyes were on him. Both men had dropped their hands beneath the table.

Stillman kept his own gun in its holster as he said, "Get your hands back up on the table."

They stared at him. The blonde shifted her gaze between them. Finally, they looked at each other, then at the young woman between them, and set their elbows back on the table. With insolent casualness, the half-breed plucked a smoldering quirley from an ashtray and placed it in a corner of his mouth. Squinting one speculative eye at Stillman, he drew on the cigarette, the umber coal glowing in the room's heavy shadows.

The blonde stared at Stillman, quirking her mouth corners as though fighting a grin.

"He's not here."

This had come from the only other person in the room, another young woman, this one with brown hair. A little older than the blonde, she lounged on a burgundy velvet sofa positioned near the potbelly stove ticking in the middle of the room, just ahead of Stillman and on his left. Several other chairs and a couple of tables were haphazardly arranged around the stove. There was a large wood box half-filled with split firewood and kindling.

The brunette was maybe in her twenties, but they'd been a hard twenty-some-odd years. Her brown eyes appeared washed out and cynical. Her frizzy brown hair was pulled up in a hasty bun against which it appeared to be winning the war of rebellion. Half a dozen stray locks dangled across her cheeks.

She wore long, silver earrings studded with red Indian beads. She also wore a shabby, low-cut purple dress, the ragged hem of a cream petticoat showing beneath it. Her shoulders were bare under a black knit shawl.

On her feet were worn, black, side-button shoes with silver tips.

"I haven't told you who I'm looking for," Stillman told her.

"Yes, but I'm a witch, see?" A mocking smile flared in her dark eyes as she poked a long, black, wooden cigarette holder into her mouth and drew on the cornhusk cigarette smoldering at the opposite end of it.

"Just the same, you don't mind if I have a look around, do you?"

She puffed on the cigarette and raised her free hand, palm up. "Help yourself. If you see any rats, please don't shoot them. They've lived with me an' Iris so long, they've become pets."

Stillman had started for a dark, open doorway on the other side of the room, but now he stopped and looked at the brunette lounging on the sofa. "Iris?"

"What can I help you with?" This from the blonde, who was looking at him over the cards she held in her hands. A single purple feather poked up out of her henna-rinsed hair that hadn't been washed in a while. It looked lusterless, oily. The two men at her table were still staring at Stillman, as well, both with vague airs of suspicion and speculation and not a little menace.

Stillman frowned. "You're Iris?"

She gave a shallow sigh. "What can I help you with, love?"

She gave a slow blink and quirked her mouth corners with what she probably thought was an inviting smile.

Stillman turned away from her and stepped into the even deeper shadows of the next room. No, not a room, he saw by smudges of gray light stealing in through curtained windows on his left. A narrow hall. There were a couple of wooden benches at the base of the wall, piled thickly with clothes, some shoes, and a worn pair of men's boots.

Curtained doorways shone on his right. Those were whores' cribs. He remembered dragging an owlhoot out of one of these tiny rooms devoted to the pleasures, if you could call it that, of the flesh. Little larger than broom closets, they smelled faintly of piss, sweat, vomit, wet wool, and sex.

Most of the door curtains hung partway open. Stillman unholstered the Colt, used it to slide a curtain wide, and peered into the first room on his right.

Nothing in there but a small pallet on the floor half-covered by a ragged quilt, an empty slop bucket in a corner. The single sashed window in the outside wall gave a bleary, washed-out, waxed-paper view of the yard with the snow coming down. The wind pressed against it, clawed at it, threatened to tear it free of the frame.

Stillman checked the other five cribs. More of the same. In the last one, a rat peeped loudly as it pushed through a hole in the outside wall. Its tail gave a flick, and then it was gone. Something told him these cribs weren't used much anymore.

Holstering the Colt, the sheriff walked back into the main room and stopped. The blonde stood before him, leaning saucily against a ceiling support post. She wore a chemise over men's longhandles, thick socks, and a tattered red shawl around slender shoulders. Her belly bulged startlingly, as though she were concealing a large ball under the chemise and underwear.

Heavy with child.

Remembering when Fay had carried Little Ben, he figured the blonde was in her eighth month, likely going into her ninth.

"Lana told you he's gone," she said in a voice pitched low with anger. She had a faint southern accent.

"Wayne?" Stillman said.

"He's gone," she repeated, her eyes crossing slightly with rising annoyance, a flush lifting in her pale, smooth cheeks. She was close enough that he could see one of her eyes was healing from a bad bruise. A little blood clot shone where her lilac-colored iris met the white. "Did you kill Blaine?"

"I did."

"Law?"

"Right." Stillman studied her. She gazed up at him with stony defiance, arms crossed on her swollen breasts. "How long was Blaine here?"

"Just long enough for a quick drink and to switch horses."

"Where did he go?"

"He went to talk with Clayton Monk," chimed in the brunette on the burgundy velvet sofa by the woodstove. She'd spoken loudly enough for Stillman to hear above the wind outside, but also casually, sitting half up against the back of the sofa, legs crossed, filing her nails.

The two men had resumed their card game without the blonde. They spoke in hushed voices, tossing pasteboards and coins, glancing occasionally at the lawman, as though they wanted to forget he was here while also wanting to keep track of him.

"Clayton Monk?" Stillman asked.

"You'll know soon enough who Clayton Monk is," said the blonde, one corner of her mouth rising. "They'll likely be riding back this way soon—him an' Wayne. He knows you're shadowin' him, Wayne does. Clayton took Wayne under his wing."

The brunette snickered.

The half-breed hipped around in his chair to glance at Stillman, then gave a coyote grin as he turned forward in his chair, blowing cigarette smoke out his nostrils.

Just then the front door opened.

Stillman jerked with a start, unsheathing the Colt and clicking back the hammer. The blonde gasped and leaped back when she saw the long-barreled revolver come up. Stillman eased the tension in his trigger finger when he saw John Stock enter behind Horace Butterfield and the man called Spanish.

Stock closed the door. The three men batted their hats against their thighs, removing snow.

"Stabled the hosses," Stock told Stillman, as the sheriff lowered the Colt. Stock tossed Stillman his Henry rifle, which Stillman caught in his left hand.

Butterfield looked around, smiling his gap-toothed, narrow-eyed grin before sliding his gaze to Stillman. "Everyone gettin' acquainted?"

Chapter Nine

As Butterfield and Spanish sat down at the table of the two poker players, throwing into the game, Stillman walked to a table near him and the girl, tossed his hat on the table, leaned the Henry against a table leg, and unbuttoned his coat.

"Can I bring you a bottle?" Iris asked him, resting one hand on her very pregnant belly. "Maybe settle your nerves a little." She gave a wry smile as she dropped her gaze to Stillman's .44, which he'd returned to its holster.

Stillman draped his damp coat over the back of a chair and ran a hand brusquely through his thick, salt-and-pepper hair. "Got any coffee?"

"Sure."

"I take it black."

"I could use that bottle," Stock said, walking over to join Stillman. The big man sniffed the air. "Is that chili I smell?"

"Sure is. Got a big kettle on the kitchen range. Lana's even got some bread in the oven. Should be done soon."

"Bring the bottle," Stock said, shrugging out of his wet coat, shivering. "And the chili when the bread's done. I'm so hungry I could eat a horse, tail an' all!"

"There'll be more here soon," Iris said, smiling insinuatingly at Stillman as she walked away.

"Hey, Iris," Butterfield called as she headed for a curtained doorway behind the crude plank bar at the rear of the room, "how 'bout a poke?"

"I ain't in any condition . . . or mood . . . to entertain tonight," Iris said. "I'm sorry, Horace. Ask Lana."

"Not until my bread's out of the oven, hon," Lana said lazily, still filing her nails on the sofa. "Be another ten minutes, fifteen at the most." She held her left hand up close to her face, scrutinizing her nails, and added in the same desultory tone, "Then we can go upstairs and I'll give you the ride of your life."

Butterfield grumbled impatiently. "Bring me a beer while I'm waitin'!"

Lana cursed softly, rolling her eyes with annoyance, then rose from the sofa and followed Iris into the kitchen behind the bar.

As Stillman slacked into his chair, Stock settled into the one across from him. Stillman had his back to the wall. Stock had his back to the room. There was a ceiling support post about five feet away, ahead of Stillman and to his right. It somewhat impeded his view of Butterfield and Spanish and the two other poker players, but he thought he could keep a close watch on the owlhoots, just the same.

Stock saw Stillman eyeing the other men in the room skeptically and said, lowering his head as well as his voice, "Kind of feel like the lone jackrabbit at a rattlesnake convention?" He gave a weak, anxious smile.

"That's one way to put it," Stillman said.

Leaning forward and continuing to lower his voice, the saloon owner said, "I found out from Spanish that Wayne was here. Just for a few minutes. He changed horses and rode out."

"I know." Stillman had produced his makings sack from his shirt pocket, and was slowly, thoughtfully, building a quirley. "Iris told me."

"Iris?"

"You called?" She was walking up to the table, holding a steaming mug of coffee in one hand, an unlabeled bottle with a shot glass turned over the neck in the other.

Outside, the wind was picking up, howling and moaning like savage lovers, blowing snow like sand against the building, snapping the wax paper over the windows. The two or three lamps in the place swung where they hung from wires in the low ceiling, shunting shadows this way and that.

As the pregnant blonde set the coffee on the table before Stillman, he turned the handle to the left and said, "Iris, meet Blaine's old man. John Stock, meet Iris."

Stock glowered up at her, raking his eyes from her face and faintly discolored eye to her swollen belly. He didn't say anything. He fumbled the shot glass off the bottle, popped the cork, and filled the glass with whiskey.

"He had your name tattooed across the back of his hand," Stillman said.

Iris leaned wearily against a chair between Stillman and the saloon owner. "So?"

Stillman shrugged. "I thought maybe it meant that you and he were . . ." He let his voice trail off as he looked at her belly.

"Him an' me were nothin'. Oh, he came around a few times with his brother. Every wolf haunting these breaks finds his way to this den here in Perdition Bend sooner or later. Lana and I run the place alone. The old Injun who ran it last up an' died, so we took over. We had nowhere else to go. I took Blaine upstairs a few times, gave him a poke when he had the jingle." She hiked a shoulder. "So he tattooed my name on the back of his hand. I've had other fellas tattoo my name on their necks. One said he had it tattooed on his pecker. Not that I'm braggin', but . . . I reckon I fulfill their needs all right."

"I bet you do," Stock said, casting her an animal-like, lascivious stare. He looked at her swollen breasts, plump as baby pigs pushing out the corset of her worn, white gown.

She pulled out the chair she'd been leaning against. "I gotta sit down for a minute. My feet hurt."

"Help yourself," Stillman said.

"Sure, help yourself, darlin'," Stock said, raising his glass to her and winking.

Iris regarded him shrewdly. "So, you're their old man. Blaine's and Wayne's?"

Stock lowered the glass and nodded as he ran his hand across his mouth, then quickly combed his fingers through the tangle of his snow-wet beard. He pulled his stocking cap lower on his head and leaned toward the girl and said as though covertly, his voice pitched with impatience, "No, I ain't his pa, hear? I might have sewn the seed that spawned him, but I ain't his pa. Let's be clear on that."

He threw back the rest of the whiskey in his glass, then tipped the bottle once more.

Iris stared at him, brows knit.

Stock continued, "That bastard and his brother robbed my saloon in Chinook. Waved guns at me—both of 'em did. Threatened to kill me if I didn't turn over the cashbox. They killed my best whore, Glory, when she threatened to go for the law."

The saloon owner's eyes grew dark and pensive as he studied the pregnant girl before him once more. Leaning sideways a little, as though to speak to her breasts, he said, "You remind me of her. Sort of. She was special, Glory was. I was of a mind to take her out of the business one day . . . marry up with her . . . take her to the West Coast."

Stock's eyes sparkled with emotion as he raised the shot glass again to his lips and tossed back half the shot.

"Easy, Stock," Stillman said. "Go easy on the stuff or I'll cut you off."

"Why?" Stock snapped. "He's gone. We won't be able to track him till tomorrow."

"He's comin' back," Iris said, her eyes flashing with sneering delight. "And he's bringin' Clayton Monk with him. You know Clayton?"

"No," Stillman answered for Stock.

"Baddest of the bad out here. I mean, I don't rightly know what he's done, or what he's runnin' from, but I know what I've seen. He's killed three men in this very room. Over the summer. He gets drunk and mean, and then he kills you if he don't like the way you look. That's how he is. Everyone around here gives him a wide berth. Only for some reason, he took to your sons, Poppa Stock. Yessir, they rode with Clayton Monk. That's why Wayne rode out of here to fetch Clayton. He knows you're shadowin' him. He don't take it lightly that this badge-toter shot his twin brother. He don't very much like you, neither. So, the sheriff's right. You'd best keep your head clear. Not that it's gonna matter too much once Clayton Monk gets here."

Stock grabbed her arm. "I don't think I like your saucy tone, Little Miss!"

"Ow!" Iris yelped. She tried to pry Stock's big hand from around her forearm. "Let me go!"

"Knock it off, Stock!" Stillman ordered the man.

"Hey, you all right over there, Iris?" Lana called. She was sitting with the poker players but looking at Stillman's table with concern.

Stock released the girl's arm.

"I'm just fine," Iris said, wrinkling her nose distastefully at Stock, her light blue eyes flinty with anger.

"I apologize, Iris," Stillman said tightly, casting an admonishing look at the saloon owner. "It won't happen again. I'll promise you that."

Stock bunched his lips but looked away, sheepish.

Iris looked at the sheriff, a vague curiosity showing in her gaze.

"When are you due?" Stillman asked her.

"How would I know?" she said, leaning back in her chair and placing both hands on her belly.

"Who's the . . . ?"

"The proud poppa?" Iris laughed. "I don't know that, neither. Take your pick." She glanced around the room. "Maybe it's Monk."

She turned again to Stillman, who regarded her with a mixture of empathy and sadness. As she stared back at him, the mocking smile very gradually faded from her lips.

Stock grinned at her with brazen lust. "How 'bout a poke, little girl? Before Monk gets here."

"Forget it," Stillman told him.

"You ain't her pimp!"

Iris looked at Stillman once more, a vague wonder in her eyes. Then she turned to Stock and snarled with disgust, *"No!"*

She rose heavily and walked away.

Stock chuckled. He threw back another shot of the whiskey and set the glass back on the table. Suddenly, he frowned at it, remembering through the building alcohol fog what they were doing here, the danger they were in.

He looked at Stillman, eyes round with trepidation.

"Shit." He cast a quick, anxious glance at the men playing poker behind him, then turned back to Stillman. "If we don't already got enough trouble to contend with—now Clayton Monk is on the way?"

As though the others had overheard, they all laughed and turned toward Stock and Stillman. Lana did, too. They were laughing over some inside joke Stillman and Stock were apparently the butt of.

"How 'bout another round, boys?" Lana said to the men at her table. "Come on—I know you got the jingle!"

Stillman sat back in his chair and raised the coffee to his lips.

Stock took another shot of the whiskey, then rose heavily,

anxiously from his chair, and stomped over to a window to the left of the front door, looking out.

After a while, Iris returned to Stillman's table with the coffee pot. She refilled his cup, casting him dark, worried glances.

"What is it?" Stillman asked her.

"The baby's Blaine's," she said, looking down at her belly.

"How do you know?"

"I know," she said softly, caressing the swollen lump tenderly with her free hand.

"I'm sorry."

Iris looked over at Stock staring out the quickly darkening window. She turned to Stillman again, consternation forming two deep, vertical lines between her eyes, and said in a voice just above a whisper: "It ain't what you think it is."

Before Stillman could respond with anything but a puzzled frown, she turned away with the coffee pot and strode back into the kitchen.

CHAPTER TEN

Outside, the wind moaned like a witch in labor.

A chill draft blew through the crumbled chinking between the logs and through gaps around the window frames. The three hanging coal oil lamps guttered and were occasionally snuffed by especially potent drafts, to be relit by whoever was near.

Stillman was relighting the lamp nearest him when Stock, who'd been sitting at a table by himself in sullen, drunken silence, having finished a bowl of chili, finally got up with a curse and shambled over to where Lana was playing poker with Butterfield, Spanish, and the two other men.

"I need a poke," the saloon owner grumbled, grabbing the brunette's arm.

Lana jerked her arm out of the man's grasp, and glared up at him. "Horace is next in line. Besides, you can't afford me."

"Horace is a little preoccupied," Butterfield said around the braided cheroot in his teeth, studying his cards, a winning flush in his near-black cheeks. His eyes were glazed from a run of good luck and drink. He cast Lana a quick wink and a lusty smile. "Maybe later, sugar."

Stock pulled out the wad of bills Stillman had taken off the man's dead son. "How much?" he said, shuffling through the greenbacks.

"Holy shit," Lana said, brightening. "Honey, you're flush!" To the others, she said, "Hold my place, fellas. I'll be back in a minute."

"I doubt it'll take him that long," said Butterfield, and he and the others laughed.

"Fuck you, you smart-ass son of a bitch!" Stock bellowed, cheeks flushing deeply, eyes slitting. He placed a hand on the grips of the Colt holstered on his right thigh.

The others at the table stared back at him, tense. Slowly, Butterfield slitted his eyes and hardened his jaws. He started to set his pasteboards down on the table, to free his hands, when Lana leaped to her feet, grabbed Stock's arm, and said, "Now, now, boys. None of that. Come on, honey—let's get you upstairs an' bleed off some o' that sap!"

She laughed nervously as she glanced at the poker players and led Stock to a wooden staircase at the back of the room, to the right of the bar. Stock followed her stiffly, heavy on his feet, glaring over his shoulder at Butterfield, who followed him with his own peevish gaze. Lana led Stock up the stairs, yammering at him to distract him from his drunken fury.

The shadows at the top of the stairs consumed them.

Stillman could hear their footsteps in the ceiling. He was glad to have Stock out of the way. In his drunkenness, he wouldn't be much help when Wayne showed up with his friend Monk. He'd only get in the way.

Stock had been upstairs with Lana for ten minutes or so when Iris came out of the kitchen. She must have been cleaning up. She looked tired, stray hairs dangling against her flushed cheeks. Her gaze settled on Stillman, and then she turned back into the kitchen to reappear a moment later with the coffee pot. She brought it over to Stillman's table and filled his cup without saying anything or even looking at him.

Stillman didn't press her about what she'd told him an hour ago. He was curious, of course, but he could tell that prodding her would do no good. Especially with the other men in the room.

Stillman had rolled and smoked another cigarette and nearly finished his current cup of coffee, listening for the sounds of approaching horses beneath the howling wind outside, when Butterfield suddenly looked at him from the poker table. The outlaw smiled, cleared his throat, said, "Time to yellow some snow," and rose from his chair.

Stillman frowned as he lifted his cup to his lips.

The others at the table had fallen suddenly, eerily silent. They sat stiffly in their chairs. The stocky half-breed, whom the others had called simply Crow, sat with his back to Stillman. The lawman could see the heavy muscles expanding and contracting in the man's back beneath his buckskin skirt.

The mustached man called Spanish turned his head to give Stillman a fleeting, edgy, sidelong glance before jerking his gaze back to the table.

Stillman's heart quickened.

Over the rim of his coffee cup, he watched Horace Butterfield walk with a tad too much nonchalance toward the front door. As Butterfield meandered around tables and chairs, he lifted his arms above his head, stretching, brushing his fingers along the ceiling. He lightly knocked his knuckles against the stove's tin chimney pipe as he passed.

When he reached the door, he set his left hand on the knob and left it there a quarter-second too long.

Stillman set his cup down on the table.

A half-second later, Butterfield wheeled toward him, bunching his lips and reaching for the Colt on his right hip. As he did, Stillman bounded out of his chair, clawing his .44 from its holster, instantly clicking the hammer back, quickly aiming, and squeezing the trigger.

The Colt roared.

Butterfield yelped and stumbled back against the closed door as he triggered his own revolver at Stillman, the slug flying wild and plunking into the ceiling over Stillman's head, throwing slivers. Stillman grabbed the Henry off the table before him, and, seeing the three other men bounding to their feet and slapping leather, dove to his right.

Guns thundered and flashed.

Bullets hammered Stillman's chair and table and tracked him across the floor as he rolled. Shoving himself up against a square-hewn ceiling support post, which reverberated against the bullets smashing into it, he snaked his right hand around the post, aimed at the half-breed crouched before him, twelve feet away, and hurled a round through the man's chest, just above his heart.

Crow howled and sent a round into the ceiling above his head as he flew backward onto the table, breaking bottles and glasses and scattering coins.

Stillman aimed down his Colt's smoking barrel at Spanish just as Spanish's big Smith & Wesson thundered. Spanish's bullet burned a hot line across the outside of Stillman's right ear as the sheriff's right index finger took up its slack on the Colt's trigger, and chunked a round into Spanish's forehead, just beneath the brim of his black hat.

The tall, gray-haired man was next.

He screamed just as the hammer of the pistol he'd been triggering wildly, drunkenly, whooping and hollering, pinged down on an empty chamber. Not an eye wink later, Stillman's bullet made a wet crunching sound as it plundered the tall man's chest, then exited his left armpit before clanking off the stove's chimney pipe, splashing it with blood, which sizzled on the hot tin.

The tall man was punched off his feet and thrown onto a table behind him.

"Lord have mercy!" he strangled out just before the table broke beneath him, and the man and table went to the floor

with a thundering crash.

Stillman quickly shoved the near-empty Colt into its holster and grabbed the Henry.

His ear burned. He brushed his fist against it and felt the oiliness of blood.

The room had fallen silent except for the mad screeching of a lamp swaying wildly on its hanging wire, making thick shadows dance to and fro. Outside he could hear the wind and the soft rattling of the blowing snow against the trailhouse walls.

Ahead and to his left, a man groaned.

"Horace?" Stillman called, pumping a cartridge into the Henry's chamber.

"Oh, fuck," Butterfield said. "I'm dyin', you *son of a bitch!*"

"What the hell was that all about?"

Butterfield spat loudly, swallowed audibly, and made a gurgling sound in his chest. "Y–You think we was just gonna sit here and let you *drink coffee*? A damn *lawman* in an *outlaw* lair?" He laughed without mirth. "This is . . . this is . . . our . . . territory . . . you . . . lawbringin' . . . son . . . sonofa . . . sonofabitch. We wasn't gonna depend on . . . on . . . Monk to bring you . . . down . . . !"

There was a strangling sound and then silence.

Stillman rose slowly, looking around. The other three men were down and unmoving. The air that now smelled of burnt gunpowder was also tinged with the coppery stench of blood.

Holding the Henry in two hands before him, Stillman stepped forward. He looked to his left. Butterfield lay flat on his back on the floor to the right of the door. Dark blood pooled beneath him. His head was turned toward Stillman, open eyes reflecting the light of the flickering lanterns.

Iris came out of the shadows near the bar to grab the swaying lantern, silencing the screech, and looked around.

"Holy Christ," she said. "Lana ain't gonna like this." She was shaking her head. "She ain't gonna like this at all." She fixed a hard glare at Stillman. "These men were regulars here, Mister Lawman! Why couldn't you have just stayed—?"

"Shh!"

She frowned at Stillman. Then she must have heard it, too— the fast, crunching clomps of horses' hooves in the fresh snow.

CHAPTER ELEVEN

Iris jerked her head toward the door, and gasped. "Wayne and Monk!"

She gave Stillman an anxious look. "What're you gonna—?"

The young woman's question was clipped by a rifle crack muffled by the storm. The storm didn't muffle the burning punch to Stillman's right arm, however. It had popped through the waxed paper covering the window left of the door. The force of the slug lifted the sheriff a foot off the floor and hammered him straight back to the scarred wooden puncheons, which he hit with a thundering boom and a hard grunt.

His hat tumbled away.

Iris screamed.

Outside, a man shouted.

Stillman lay staring in momentary shock at the ceiling, gritting his teeth against the pain in his upper right arm. The front door exploded inward, and there was a deafening cacophony of gunfire.

Again, Iris screamed.

Stillman reached up with his right hand, grabbed a fistful of the young woman's skirt, and pulled her down to the floor beside him. Then he drew his Colt, remembering he had two bullets left in the wheel, and triggered both over tables and chairs toward the door.

A man yelped. The shooting stopped.

"Clayton?" another man yelled. "Clayton, you *hit*?"

"Back room!" Stillman raked out to Iris, heaving himself to a low crouch, wobbling on his feet.

Iris scrambled to her own two feet, snaked an arm around Stillman, and together they scrambled into the room's deep shadows, tripping over tables and chairs. Behind them, a gun barked. They swerved behind the woodstove. Two bullets clanked shrilly off the stove and two more thudded into a table to Stillman's left.

Another bullet thudded into the wall near Iris just as she and Stillman, concealed by the heavy shadows back here, dashed into the old crib partition off the shack's west side. Darkness consumed them.

"Back," Stillman raked out, clutching his right arm with his left hand, feeling blood soak his coat and the shirt beneath it. "Far . . . far back!"

He needed time to reload the Colt.

Iris stumbled along beside him, her arm around his waist, breathing heavily, anxiously.

"Where'd they go?" a man barked.

"Back there!" said the voice of the younger man—Wayne Stock or whatever last name he was using.

Stillman felt his way into the last crib. Iris stumbled in beside him. They sank together to the floor. Stillman sat back against the wall. Iris turned to him. "How bad is . . . ?"

"Shh."

Quickly, Stillman drew the Colt from its holster. His right hand was heavy and numb. It shook as he flicked open the revolver's loading gate and pinched fresh cartridges from his shell belt. Beside him, Iris shook, holding her hand over her mouth to muffle her uncontrolled sobs.

Slow footsteps sounded in the main part of the building, floorboards squawking under stealthy feet. The footsteps grew louder as the two men approached the crib area.

Stillman thumbed the last cartridge into the Colt's wheel just as one or maybe both of the men ran toward him, down the narrow hall, boots thudding loudly, heavily. A gun banged—once, twice, three times. The bullets tore through the thin walls. One curled the air in front of Stillman's nose to career past Iris and into the wall to their right.

"Sit tight!" Stillman told Iris.

He drew a deep breath and threw himself painfully forward, out the crib's door. He hit the hall floor on his right arm and shoulder. Ignoring the bayonet of hot agony stabbing through his shoulder and chest and into his belly, he raised the Colt and sent three bullets screeching down the dark corridor, toward the glow of the lamplit main drinking hall beyond, into the two man-shaped figures silhouetted against the glow.

A gun flashed redly before him, and then the silhouette who'd fired it staggered backward, twisting around and sending another bullet lapping into the floor at his boots. Stillman shot him again for good measure and slid his smoking Colt toward the man slumped beside the first one, writhing and cursing in the voice of a young man.

Stillman shouted, "Wayne, throw your gun away or I'll give you another blue whistler right now!"

"I'm hit!" the young man cried.

"Throw it away!"

The kid whipped his arm up and sideways. Lamplight glinted off the gun he threw behind him. The gun hit the floor and slid up against the front wall.

"Don't move," Stillman said, heaving himself slowly to his feet, wincing against the misery knifing up and down his wounded arm. "One move, I'll drill you again."

The kid made a choking sound, then raked out, "Shit . . . it hurts!"

Stillman glanced at Iris. She sat back against the crib's rear

341

wall, legs straight out before her, both hands steepled across her mouth and nose. "You all right, girl?" he asked her.

She nodded dully, keeping her hands to her face.

Stillman walked down the hall and out into the main drinking area. The man who must have been Clayton Monk lay twisted on his side to the right of the chubby lad who was Stock's son, Wayne. He was the spitting image of the other young man Stillman had killed. Maybe a little beefier, his dark-red hair a little longer, curling down over his ears. He wore a red kerchief around his neck, beneath the collar of his striped blanket coat.

Like Monk, he wore thick wooly chaps over faded blue denims.

Stillman had hit him high on his right leg, which he kicked out to the side in agony, clutching the wound with both hands.

"Where is he?" the kid said, swinging his head to look around. "Where is that murderin' bastard?"

"If you mean your father, he's upstairs." Stillman turned toward the stairs running up the back of the room, and called, "Stock?"

Wayne gave a caustic chuff. "My father? What the hell you talkin' about, lawman?"

"John Stock," Stillman said. "The man you robbed."

"What about him?" Wayne yelled in frustration.

"Your father!"

Iris stepped out of the shadows to stand beside Stillman. "That man isn't Wayne's father. No more than he was Blaine's father." She looked up at Stillman. "He's the man who killed their parents in Milestown."

"Wait," Stillman said, glowering at the girl staring up at him. "Milestown? I thought . . ."

"We lived in Milestown," Wayne said. "Name's Carpenter. Wayne and Blaine Carpenter. Our pa, Paul Carpenter, was killed by Joe Barden."

"*Joe Barden?*" Stillman said.

"Barden, a young livery hand at the time, broke into our house and savaged our ma," Wayne Carpenter continued. "Pa came home for lunch and walked in on him *raping* Ma! Barden killed 'em both—shot Pa, beat Ma with a stove lid. Our older sister seen the whole thing through the cracks in a broom closet door.

"Me an' Blaine was only two years old and cryin' in our cribs. Our sister, Mary—she was fourteen—ran for the town marshal and described Barden. A posse ran him down, hauled him back to town, tried him, convicted him, and were gonna hang him. He busted out of jail the day before he was to get his neck stretched. The marshal's posse lost his trail. He was never seen again. My brother an' me—we been lookin' for Barden since the day we were able to understand what had happened, after our sister explained the whole thing to us. We took to the owlhoot trail—Blaine an' me—believin' that one day it would lead us to Barden."

Young Carpenter gave a half-laugh, half-sob. Iris was on a knee beside him now, tying the kid's own neckerchief around his bloody wound.

"The long coulees led us to him—it purely did. We were drinkin' in Chinook one day and we saw Barden's ear. See, Ma managed to chew off half the man's ear before he killed her. That's why he always wears that red cap, all year long. We did some pokin' around, asked him some questions about Miles-town, that maybe we knew him from down that way. He got all owly on us, acted right suspicious.

"So the other day we headed over to his saloon to confront him. To kill him. He ran. His whore pulled a gun. I shot her. Didn't want to, but I had to. I'm used to it by now. I've killed a lot of folks. That's how you survive on the owlhoot trail. Well, that coward, Joe Barden, ran. We couldn't hang around because we knew men on the street had heard the shot that killed the whore, so we robbed Barden's cashbox and hightailed it.

"We figured he'd follow his money, and we'd meet up with him again. It wasn't just the money he was followin'. It was *us*. He'd want to shut us up. We didn't figure you would be ridin' along beside him, helpin' that murderin' bastard, take us down!"

Iris looked up at Stillman. "That's what I meant when I said . . ."

" 'It ain't what you think it is,' " Stillman said.

He'd turned away from young Carpenter and Iris now. He was quickly dropping empty cartridges onto the floor and replacing them with fresh rounds from his shell belt as he slowly moved toward the stairs at the back of the room, beyond the body of Clayton Monk and the three gamblers lying dead to the right of the woodstove.

"Barden?" he called.

CHAPTER TWELVE

Stillman gained the top of the stairs and clicked the Colt's hammer back.

He hardened his jaw against the misery in his arm. His knees felt spongy, weak. He was growing light-headed from blood loss.

He stared down a narrow hall between four or five quilts and blankets hanging from ropes. The quilts and blankets formed a wall on each side of the hall. The second story wasn't finished. An open loft area. The ceiling was steeply pitched inward on each side. A single, rusty lamp burned in the middle of the hall, where it hung down from the ceiling by a rope tied to its bail.

One of the quilts to Stillman's left was drawn partly back.

"Barden?" he called again.

He stepped forward, wincing as his boots made a loose floorboard squawk. He tightened his trigger finger slightly as he turned between the parted blankets to stare into a makeshift bedroom. It was a big area, but there wasn't much in it. Only a large bed covered with skins and blankets and a dresser with a candle burning on it.

Stillman peered into the shadows to both sides of the bed.

Nothing.

The room was empty. He swung around sharply, expecting his quarry to steal up behind him. But there was nothing before him now except the blankets strung on the sagging rope forming the wall to the second room.

Stillman frowned. He turned around sharply and moved back into the first room, heading toward the bed. He'd thought the bed was empty, but now he realized that the skins were humped a little, as though someone lay beneath them. Stillman reached down and pulled a bearskin back, and drew a quick, sharp breath.

Lana glared up at him, her eyes wide, her mouth slack. The tip of her tongue poked out of her mouth. Stillman wrinkled his nose against the stench of the blood oozing from the wide gash stretching from ear to ear across her neck. A bloody Barlow folding knife lay to the right of the sodden pillow on which her head lay.

"Barden!" Stillman bellowed, swinging around.

He'd seen a door at the end of the hall area, opposite the stairs. He strode for it now. It stood atop two steps. It wasn't latched. Stillman opened it quickly, poking the cocked Colt out into the cold, dark night at the top of an outside staircase dusted with snow. In the ambient light intensified by the falling snow, he could see the dark shapes of footsteps moving off down the steps to the ground and then angling around the rear of the building toward the stable in the back.

Stillman lunged out the door. Too quickly. He'd been too light-headed to keep his balance through such a maneuver. His right knee buckled. He hit the second step and rolled violently halfway down the steps, losing the Colt, before he managed to fling up his left arm and grab the left rail.

With a yowl of pain, snow brushing his face like cold witches' fingers, he stopped his fall. But the tumble had increased the pain in his arm, and made him weaker. He felt deeply nauseated. Knowing that the longer he sat here, the harder it would be to rise, he cursed sharply and hoisted himself to his feet. He looked around for the Colt. It wasn't on the steps.

He rushed down, saw a dark dimple in the snow several feet

from the bottom step, and scooped up the Colt, brushing snow off the chasing. He wheeled and walked as quickly as he could around the rear of the trailhouse. The stable loomed ahead of him, on the far side of the empty rail corral. Barden's tracks appeared to lead toward the stable's large double doors.

Stillman quickened his pace, holding the Colt now in his left hand. His right arm was useless after his fall on the stairs.

He stopped. A figure ran out from the front of the trailhouse. It was Wayne Carpenter. He was dragging his right foot, throwing his left arm out for balance. He stumbled, fell, heaved himself to his feet, and continued shambling toward the stable.

"Stillman!" he bellowed. "He's in the stable!"

"Hold on!" Stillman yelled into the wind, increasing his pace even more.

But Carpenter made it to the stable well ahead of him. As the young man reached for the handle of one of the doors, both doors burst open with a thundering roar.

A horse whinnied as it and the man on top of it slammed into Carpenter, who screamed as he flew several yards straight back toward the trailhouse and slammed to the ground. Stillman stopped, switched his Colt to his right hand, and forced the hand up despite the protest of the burning, throbbing wound.

He held fire as the horse and rider jostled with young Carpenter, who'd heaved himself up from the ground. There was a red flash. A revolver cracked.

Another red flash. Another crack.

Carpenter screamed, "You murderin' bastard!"

A gun flashed in Carpenter's right hand. Barden sagged backward in the saddle, then raised his own right hand.

"No!" Stillman bellowed as the gun in the killer's hand flashed and cracked.

Carpenter screamed as he flew backward and rolled.

Stillman held his Colt in both hands and loosed two quick

but unsteady rounds toward Barden. The man had just started to rein his horse into the storm, but one of Stillman's two bullets much have hit home. He jerked forward and right.

Stillman fired again . . . again . . . and again as the horse galloped away in the darkness.

As it did, the sheriff watched the killer slump lower and lower in his saddle. Just as the horse disappeared in the darkness, a soft thud sounded beneath the howling wind. The horse whinnied shrilly, the cry dwindling away in the stormy night.

Stillman groaned as he lowered the Colt. He walked over to where young Carpenter lay on his back in the snow, legs spread wide. One was bent back at the knee. The kid wasn't moving. For a moment, Stillman thought he'd passed, but then the kid blinked his eyes and ran his tongue across his upper lip. He moved his mouth. He was trying to say something, but Stillman couldn't hear with the storm howling around them.

He dropped to a knee.

"What is it?" he asked the young man.

"We," Carpenter tried. Tried again: "Did . . . we . . . get him?"

Stillman stared off to where he could barely make out the unmoving form of Joe Barden, alias John Stock, lying in a lump at the edge of the yard.

"Yes," Stillman said. "You can rest now, son. We got him."

The young outlaw gave a weak half-smile that remained on his lips after his chest stopped moving and his eyes grew dark with death.

Stillman rose heavily. The ground pitched around him, the wind roaring. He got his feet set beneath him, then strode over to where Barden lay and made sure the man was dead. Then he walked back to the trailhouse. He pushed through the front door, pulling the door closed on the storm, and glanced at Horace Butterfield lying belly up nearby, staring sightlessly up at the ceiling.

Stillman looked at the other dead men.

His gaze shifted to Iris moving slowly, woodenly down the stairs. She looked like a ghost. She held both her hands on her belly.

When she looked up and saw Stillman, she stopped on the stairs and said in a thin, shocked voice, "Lana . . . she's . . ."

Stillman nodded. "I know. You'll be all right. I'll see to it."

He looked around and found what he wanted when saw the table Barden had been sitting at. The killer had left his bottle there with his empty chili bowl. Stillman sat heavily in Barden's vacated chair. He stared at the man's chili bowl.

Barden.

Why the elaborate story about his dead wife, the lover, Joe Barden, and his vengeance-hungry sons?

An appeal to Stillman's sympathy, probably. To keep the lawman guessing, as well as to amuse his loco self.

Stillman looked at the half-empty whiskey bottle. He grabbed it, splashed whiskey into Barden's empty glass, looked at it, hesitated for only a second, then threw back the entire shot.

He filled the glass again to the brim and rolled a cigarette.

ABOUT THE AUTHOR

Western novelist **Peter Brandvold** was born and raised in North Dakota. He has penned over ninety fast-action westerns under his own name and several pen names, including **Frank Leslie.** He wrote thirty books in the popular, long-running *Longarm* series for Berkley. He is the author of the ever-popular .45-Caliber books featuring Cuno Massey as well as the Lou Prophet and Yakima Henry novels. The Ben Stillman books are a long-running series with previous volumes available as ebooks. Head honcho at "Mean Pete Publishing," publisher of lightning-fast western ebooks, he has lived all over the American west but currently lives in western Minnesota with his dog. Visit his website at www.peterbrandvold.com. Follow his blog at: www.peterbrandvold.blogspot.com.

The employees of Five Star Publishing hope you have enjoyed this book.

Our Five Star novels explore little-known chapters from America's history, stories told from unique perspectives that will entertain a broad range of readers.

Other Five Star books are available at your local library, bookstore, all major book distributors, and directly from Five Star/Gale.

Connect with Five Star Publishing

Visit us on Facebook:
    https://www.facebook.com/FiveStarCengage

Email:
    FiveStar@cengage.com

For information about titles and placing orders:
    (800) 223-1244
    gale.orders@cengage.com

To share your comments, write to us:
    Five Star Publishing
    Attn: Publisher
    10 Water St., Suite 310
    Waterville, ME 04901